Chughta

Tahira Naqvi has been translating Urdu fiction for journals and periodicals in Pakistan and abroad for many years, and has translated many of Urdu's well-known writers, including Manto (*Another Lonely Voice: The Life and Works of Saadat Hasan Manto*); Ismat Chughtai (*The Crooked Line; My Friend, My Enemy*), Ahmed Ali and Premchand. The author of many short stories herself, she is also a published novelist. *Dying in a Strange Country* is her most recent collection of stories.

Syeda S. Hameed has been translating from Urdu to English for some time, and among her translated works are Mohammad Yunus' *Letters from Prison*; S.M.H. Burney's *Iqbal: Poet Patriot of India*; Khan Abdul Wali Khan, *Facts are Facts*; and, most recently, Hali's *Musaddas*. She has also edited the four centenary volumes of Maulana Abdul Kalam Azad, *India's Maulana*.

A CHUGHTAI COLLECTION

The Quilt & Other Stories
The Heart Breaks Free
The Wild One

Ismat Chughtai

Translated by
Tahira Naqvi & Syeda S. Hameed

a Chughtai Collection
was first published in 2004 by
Women Unlimited
an associate of Kali for Women
K-36, Hauz Khas Enclave,
Ground Floor,
New Delhi 110 016

Previously published in 1990 and 1993 by Kali for Women as
The *Quilt & Other Stories*, and *The Heart Breaks Free* &
The Wild One

© Ismat Chughtai
© This anthology, Women Unlimited, 2004

All rights reserved

Cover design: Uzma Mohsin, Visual Vibe

ISBN: 81-86706-77-1

Printed by Pauls Press, E-44/11 Okhla Phase II,
New Delhi 110 020

Contents

1. Veil (*Ghunghat*) — 1
2. The Quilt (*Lihaaf*) — 7
3. Sacred Duty (*Muqaddas Farz*) — 20
4. The Eternal Vine (*Amar Bel*) — 39
5. Kallu (*Kallu*) — 55
6. Chhoti Apa (*Chhoti Apa*) — 65
7. The Rock (*Chatan*) — 73
8. The Wedding Shroud (*Chauthi ka Jora*) — 91
9. The Mole (*Til*) — 110
10. A Morsel (*Niwala*) — 127
11. By the Grace of God (*Allah ka Fazl*) — 142
12. Poison (*Zehr*) — 152
13. A Pair of Hands (*Do Haath*) — 162
14. Aunt Bichu (*Bichu Phupi*) — 176
15. Lingering Fragrance (*Badan ki Khushboo*) — 190

The Heart Breaks Free — 227

The Wild One — 299

Introduction

ONE OF Urdu's boldest and most outspoken women writers, Ismat Chughtai played an important role in the development of the modern Urdu short story as we know it today. Not only did she make strides in the areas of style and technique, she also led her female contemporaries on a remarkable journey of self-awareness and undaunted creative expression. One must not forget that in the India of the Thirties and Forties, writing by and about women was tentative; it was generally held that literature had no place in women's lives. Making a break with tradition, Ismat proved that this was a fallacy.

In 1944 she stepped into the realm of Urdu fiction with her story *Lihaaf* (The Quilt), with such force that she confounded her readers as well as her male counterparts. Since boldness and unconventionality were not characteristics generally associated with women in those days, many of her critics went so far as to suggest that these new stories came from a man's pen, that 'Ismat Chughtai' was a pseudonym for a male writer. In the introduction to *Choten* (Wounds), Krishan Chander says that "as soon as Ismat's name is mentioned, male short-story writers get hysterical, they are embarrassed, they experience mortification."[1] When face to face with the Ismat who blushed at the mention of the mysteriously suggestive ending to her story, *Lihaaf*, Manto, her contemporary and later her friend and harshest critic, was disappointed. "She's a woman after all," he thought in dismay. But when he got to know her better and became familiar with her work, he was compelled to change his opinion. He states in *Ganje Farishte* (Bald Angels), that Ismat was indeed a woman first and foremost, but that in order to fully develop one's art one must remain true to one's basic nature. "If she were not a woman," he continues, "one would never have seen such smooth, sensitive stories like *Bhul Bhulaiyan* (Mazes), *Til* (The Mole), *Lihaaf* and *Gainda* (The Marigold), in her collections.[2]

Ismat Chughtai was born on August 15, 1915, into a middle-class family in Badayun. She was the youngest of six brothers and four sisters. Her father, Mirza Qaseem Beg, was an honest civil servant who rose to the position of deputy collector through his own merit and hard work. Ismat attended the local municipal school, the cantonement school having been disregarded owing to its policy that girls wear frocks, a practice contrary to the Chughtai family tradition.

Since her sisters got married when Ismat was very young, the better part of her childhood was spent in the company of her brothers, a factor she has admitted contributed greatly to the frankness in her nature and subsequently her writing. As she describes it:

> We are all frank, my father, my brothers, all of us. We never used to sit in separate groups ... my father was very progressive and broad-minded. He believed in education and gave me equal chances with my brothers ... I never had the feeling I should be shy and nervous. Be-

cause of that upbringing, I'm this way.[3]

Her brother, Mirza Azim Beg Chughtai, already an established writer while Ismat was still a young girl, was her first teacher and mentor. At his bidding, Thomas Hardy was the first novelist she "consumed"; others followed, as did lessons in translation, both from Urdu to English and vice versa. Later, after she had read her brother's short stories, she began experimenting with fiction herself. The romantic works of Hajab Ismail, Majnun Gorakhpuri and Niaz Fatehpuri filled her head with adventurous ideas and she imagined herself a heroine in a story. Writing in secret, she produced melodramatic stories that would have been regarded as "dirty" and she knew she would be severely reprimanded if they were discovered. She soon realized that what she had written so far was below par and ineffective, so she tore everything up and embarked on a course of serious study. The works of Dostoyevsky and Somerset Maugham had a great impact on her and she also developed a special fondness for Chekhov. And it was O' Henry, she claims, from whom she learned the conventions of storytelling. Of the serious Urdu writers, Prem Chand was her favourite and understandably so. Having been influenced by Dickens, Tolstoy and later Gandhi, Munshi Prem Chand was the first Indian to write cohesive European style Urdu fiction.[4]

With college came the beginning of a new life for Ismat, and writing took a back seat to education. "The world changes after B.A.," she says in the introduction to *Guftagu* (The Conversation), a collection of her short stories. "One grows so much in four years." Beginning with Greek drama, continuing with Shakespeare down to Ibsen and Bernard Shaw, she read voraciously.[5] Finally, when she was twenty-three, Ismat decided she was ready to write seriously; she was certainly old enough, she told herself, and had read the best there was in fiction, Urdu as well as English. Her first story, *Fasadi* (The Troublemaker), was published in *Saqi*, a literary journal of considerable repute. Its readers were perplexed; they wondered why Azim Beg Chughtai had "changed" his name. The man himself was not aware that his little sister, "Munee", had become a writer and had published a short story.

In 1936, while she was completing her B.A., she attended the first meeting of the Progressive Writers Movement in Lucknow, at which Munshi Prem Chand was also present. Here she met Rashid Jahan for the first time. A doctor by profession and "a woman of a particularly strong-willed, liberated sort," Rashid Jahan also wrote stories and radio plays, which appear in the collection titled *Aurat aur Digar Afsane* (Woman and Other Stories), and was the only woman who left a lasting impression on Ismat.[6] Explaining her fascination with Rashid Jahan and the extent to which she was influenced by her, Ismat says: "She spoiled me because she was very bold and used to speak all sorts of things openly and loudly, and I just wanted to copy her. She influenced me a lot; her open-mindedness and free thinking."[7]

After completing her B.A. Ismat went on to obtain a B.T. and became the first Muslim woman to have both B.A. and B.T. degrees. For some time she held the post of principal at the Girls' College in Bareilly and, while she was here, her father passed away. The next few years were spent in Jodhpur from where she went on to Bombay as Inspectress of Schools.

In Aligarh Ismat met Shahid Latif, her future husband. He was completing his Masters degree at the time and the two developed a close friendship. Later he became a film director and it wasn't until Ismat was twenty-nine that she married him. "It was just friendship," she says, "and love or romance didn't have any part in it." Because they were often seen in each other's company, people presumed they were going to be married. "And then we don't know what happened, maybe there was such a scandal, but we found ourselves married".[8] Her brother, Azim Beg Chughtai, vehemently opposed the match, perhaps because he disapproved of Shahid Latif's association with films.

In 1942, two months before she got married, Ismat wrote *Lihaaf,* which proved to be a breakthrough in Urdu short story writing. A frustrated housewife, whose nawab husband has no time for her, finds sexual and emotional solace in the companionship of a female servant. The narrator of the story is a woman remembering a childhood experience. Because of this we get a viewpoint which is utterly refreshing since a child may naively and artlessly say things an adult may not. The lesbian relationship between the begum and her maidservant is vividly drawn, but since we are looking at it from a nine-year-old's eyes, there is none of the awkwardness that would have accompanied an adult's perception of what went on between the two women.

When *Lihaaf* was published two months later, a storm of controversy broke out. Readers and critics alike openly and unequivocally condemned Ismat and her story. Charged with obscenity, she was submitted to a trial in Lahore. Here she had occasion to spend a great deal of time with Manto who was among the few who supported her and who was being similarly charged for his story, *Thanda Gosht* (Cold Meat). The trial lasted for two years; the court could not find any "four-letter words" in the story and finally the case against Ismat was dismissed. According to her own accounts the story is based on fact. As a child she had heard the women in her household giggle and whisper tales about a begum and her female servant. "My brother and I hid under a takht while the women gossiped and as soon as someone caught a glimpse of us, we were told to make ourselves scarce. This led us to believe that the women were talking about forbidden subjects, and although in the beginning what they were saying didn't make sense to us, gradually we began to understand."[9] Ismat's recollection explains the viewpoint in the story and also throws light on the enigmatic last sentence: "What I saw when the corner of the quilt was lifted I will never tell anyone, not even if someone gives me a lakh of rupees." At the time she wrote the story her knowledge regarding the subject of lesbianism was meagre; what she couldn't "tell" was actually what she didn't know.

Although *Lihaaf* set the tone for all of Ismat's later work and established her not only as a mature writer but as someone who was of the same standing as Manto, Krishan Chander, Ahmed Ali, Rajinder Singh Bedi, Ahmed Nadeem Qasmi and others, it also became a focal point of recognition for Ismat's work in popular terms. However, readers of Urdu fiction have a tendency to ignore the fact that Ismat is more than *Lihaaf*, much more. She is also *Kallu*, *Chauthi ka Jora* (The Wedding Shroud), *Hindustan Chor Do* (Leave Hindustan), *Do Haath* (A Pair of Hands), *Terhi Lakir* (The Crooked Line — one of her best novels) and so many others.

Ismat, like her contemporaries, was influenced a great deal by European fiction, especially the works of late-nineteenth century Russian writers. She and others in her class became involved with a new kind of writing which, although it was linked with social themes, was neither didactic nor entirely political in its overtones. A socialist outlook, accompanied by the use of non-traditional techniques to tell a story, gained strength. Having been greatly influenced by Freud's theories of psychosexual development, the new writers also wrote freely and openly about certain aspects of human sexuality, but, as in the case of Ismat, with sincerity and intelligence. In addition to changes in subject matter and tone, a new language evolved, a style that did not waste time mincing words or tip-toeing around the real issues. This was a style that was bold, innovative, rebellious and explicitly realistic in its representation and analysis of character and the human condition.

Ismat began writing at a time when the voices of women writers were still muffled. Tradition and ethical mores held a tight grip on society and any attempt on the part of women to write poetry and fiction was viewed as "intellectual vagrancy".[10] However, despite this taboo, certain women succeeded in making themselves heard; Begum Yaldram, Hajab Ismail and Begum Nazar Sajjad, for example. Although their fiction had gained considerable popularity, these early works by women were largely romances or were instructional and reformist in nature, the characters and subject matter remaining stilted and unbelievable. Ismat herself was affected initially by Hajab Ismail's overly- romanticized themes and larger-than-life characters, but she soon broke free from this influence.

Motivated by the initiative that Ismat's dramatic entry into the world of literature provided, other women writers also came forward valiantly, and many more voices arose to join hers. Qurratulain Hyder, Mumtaz Shireen, Hajira Masroor, Khadija Mastoor, Razia Sajjad Zaheer, Tasneem Salim, Sarla Devi, Sadiqa Begum and Shakila Akhtar were some of the most notable among them.

In her writing Ismat concentrated on what she was most familiar with. Having lived in a family where there was no dearth of mothers-in-law, aunts, uncles, cousins, servants and a whole network of neighbours (*muhalle wale*), she was able to portray these characters vividly and realistically when she used them in her stories. That she frequently drew her fiction from actual events she had been a part of, either directly or indirectly, explains the intense realism we meet with in her work. Many of her stories are clearly autobiographical: *Bichu Phupi* (Aunt Bichu) and *Kunwari* (The Virgin), for instance, but the story loses nothing in terms of fictive value or drama on account of that fact. In her best novel, *Terhi Lakir*, the period spanning the narrator's childhood comes very close to Ismat's own childhood. Several of the characters appearing later in the book are fashioned after people she knew in real life, many of these women being close friends who were not at all happy at finding themselves in Ismat's novel.

Many of Ismat's critics have accused her of being limited in her choice of subject matter. Perhaps that is true. She wrote only of what she knew well. But within these limits she perfected her art. The bulk of her work reflects a deep and abiding preoccupation with themes directly related to women and their cultural status and role in Indian society. Stressing the struggles of women against the oppressive social institutions of her time, she brings to her fiction an understanding and perception of the female psyche that is unique to her alone; no other writer approaches the subject of women in the same sympathetically probing, sharply cognizant and readable way that she does. One cannot discredit anything she offers, whether it be the behaviour of a sexually-frustrated housewife in *Lihaaf*, or the futility and despondency experienced by Madan, the film star in *Kunwari*, who seeks but cannot find respectability.

The world of Ismat's fiction is inhabited by people who come from the middle class, much as she did. Their circles of familiarity include, as hers did, not only relatives, close and distant, but also the entire servant class (*Kallu*), sweepers and sweepresses (*Do Haath*), not forgetting an assortment of neighbours. Perceived as a societal network, this world teems with stories that can be told from diverging viewpoints, offering unlimited variety, colourful and strikingly interesting, to say the least.

Ismat depicts her characters realistically, using language that is so direct, colloquial and down to earth that her characters remain characters no longer, becoming instead people, real people we see every day and know well. Kubra's mother in *Chauthi ka Jora*, struggling to find a suitable husband for her older daughter, is no stranger to us; Bichu Phupi, on the warpath with her brother and his family, but undeniably woman and sister in the end, could be anyone's estranged aunt, and Gori, the dark, sultry temptress in *Do Haath*, and Rani in *Til* we have frequently encountered among the cleaning women in our households when we were children. And the fact of their familiarity doesn't bore us, doesn't render them banal; no, we read on avidly to find out how they fare and what fate awaits them.

In large part it is Ismat's diction, her unique and rich idiom that pulls us along, especially those of us who view Urdu not only as a language, but as an institution. And operating in conjunction with the linguistic patterns characteristic of the Muslim U.P. families, which form the centre of much of her work, there is the colourful, robust and completely unrestrained vernacular employed by the servant class and women who worked at menial jobs and were not beguns. Dialects and idioms explode on every page so that each paragraph becomes more than just a collection of sentences conveying an idea; it shapes itself into a representation of a way of life, traditions, a philosophy.

A thorough study of Ismat's fiction will reveal valuable facts about the social and cultural aspects of life in Muslim U.P. families. Class consciousness, styles in clothing, cooking habits, foods, elements of social exchange, customs regarding such important events as birth, marriage and death are presented to us. For example, in *Bichu Phupi* (Aunt Bichu), we observe the tradition of matchmaking at work. It would be incorrect to say that the tradition is outdated; in India and Pakistan there are still households where the processs of marriage continues to take a somewhat similar, if not the same, route. Kubra, the young woman who is to be married, stays in hiding while her younger sister is sent out by the mother and her old friend to "play jokes" on the cousin who is, without his knowledge, being viewed by all the women in that household as a prospective groom. The idea is to engage his attention indirectly in this manner and prod him into delivering a proposal for the woman he has never seen, and will never see unless he marries her. One may also learn in the same story how the Muslim shroud is prepared, how the cloth is squared and measured and ripped by hand, without the use of scissors. In *Nawala* (The Morsel), we come across more matchmaking, this time of a different nature. We're also offered a rare glimpse of life in a Bombay *chal*. Somewhat like an apartment building, although the comparison can be misleading, the chal is a place where the tenants are more than neighbours; they are members of a large communal family with shared concerns and cares. *Muqaddas Farz* (Sacred Duty), brings us face to face with secularism as a way of life in present day India. The young no longer care whether they are Muslims or Hindus. Representative of a new age, they are content just to be Indians. And in *Ghunghat* (The Veil), we are confronted with a woman whose loyalty to the institution of marriage tragically consumes her entire life, a phenomenon deeply ingrained in the very fibre of our culture.

From the point of view of richness of metaphor and simile, the power of idiom, and the ease with which images fall into place, soundlessly and with absolute clarity, the quality of Ismat's language surpasses that of any of her contemporaries. "Not only does her story appear to be running," Krishan Chander commented in a foreword to *Choten*, "but the sentences, images, metaphors, the sounds and sensibilities of the characters and their feelings—all seem to be moving together and forward with the intensity of a storm."[12]

It is exactly with this impression that one leaves the first paragraph of *Terhi Lakir:*

> She was born at a most inopportune time. Bari Apa, whose friend Salma was to be married soon, was working spiritedly on a saroi-crepe dupatta, stitching gold lace to its borders. Amma, who regarded herself as a youthful maiden despite the fact that she had given birth to so many children, was scrubbing off dead skin from her heels with a pumice stone. Suddenly the clouds rolled in, and in the ensuing commotion the longstanding desire to send for the English midwife came to naught, and "she" was born. The minute she arrived into the world, she let out such a yell...God help us![13]

Of the early writings by Ismat's contemporaries, many reveal shortcomings in the areas of style and subject matter that one generally attributes to professional and literary incipience. In Ismat's earliest stories, however, one observes a forceful viewpoint and a mature handling of subject matter that is surprising when one takes into account the fact that she was a lone voice at the time, a woman severing her ties with tradition, both in literary and social terms. In reviewing Ismat's skill as a writer, Ehtesham Hussain, a leading critic of Urdu literature, has this to say about her art:

> Ismat's undaunted intelligence and her power of expression were so well integrated that from the very beginning her stories caught everyone's attention. It is true that at first she too probed only some of

society's ills, scraped wounds, poured salt over them, and left her readers in a quandary. But it did not take her long to become aware of the truth about her writing and soon she was able to strike an effective balance between her themes and her subject matter.[14]

Kaliyan (Buds), Ismat's first collection of short stories and *Choten*, her second, were published in Azim Beg Chugtai's lifetime. Her other books are: *Aik Bat* (A Word; short story collection), *Terhi Lakir* (Crooked Line; novel), *Chui Mui* (The Sensitive One; short story collection), *Ziddi* (The Stubborn One; novella), *Masooma* (The Innocent; novella), *Dhani Bankpan* (Green Elegance; short stories), Do *Haath* (short stories), *Hamlog* (We People; essays and stories), *Shaitan* (The Devil; plays), *Saudai* (The Madman; novel), *Aik qatra-e-khun* (A Drop of Blood). In addition, Ismat produced scripts of five films in which she collaborated with her husband, Shahid Latif, and made five films independently. She had two daughters by Shahid Latif and after her husband's death continued living in Bombay until her death on 24 October 1991.

A few years ago she was asked why she had not written her autobiography. "I've written it, I've written a lot," she replied. When asked why she had not published it, she had this to say: "Why should I publish it right now? It will be published when I'm dead. Why should I die just yet? At this moment I'm telling you the truth, but it isn't necessary that I speak the truth in my autobiography; you no longer remain objective when you write an autobiography, you begin to think of your own reputation."

A *terhi lakir* to the end, Ismat Chugtai died as she had lived, in the midst of controversy. The news that she had left instructions that she was to be cremated became cause for heated debate in both India and Pakistan, and even those who knew her, who expected her to be unpredictable, were taken by surprise. But the furore over funeral rites could not suppress the facts about her. Ismat's greatness as the Grand Dame of Urdu fiction, as one of the four pillars of Urdu short story writing (the other three being Manto, Krishan Chander, and Bedi), as the indomitable spirit of Urdu afsana, the last chronicler of the U.P. Muslim culture and its associated semantics, was affirmed by fellow writers, journalists and friends.

TAHIRA NAQVI

NOTES

[1] Krishan Chander wrote the Foreword to Ismat's first collection of short stories, *Choten*. In it he explained that what he was writing about her was motivated by the desire on the part of male short story writers to eradicate the feelings of "mortification" they experienced in her literary presence.

[2] This quote is from *Ganje Farishte* (Lahore, Maktaba-e-shero adab, 1984), Saadat Hasan Manto's collection of essays on well-known literary and film personalities. In a similar essay Ismat wrote about Manto after his death, she called him *mera dost, mera dushman* (my friend, my enemy).

[3] *Guftagu* is a short interview with Ismat Chughtai, functioning as a foreword to her collection of short stories titled, *Kharid lo* (Lahore, Raffat Publishers, 1982).

[4] *The Life and Works of Saadat Hasan Manto: Another Lonely Voice* (Lahore, Vanguard Publishers, 1985), pp. 23-27. This book contains a lengthy monograph by Dr. Flemming who teaches at the University of Tucson, Arizona. The stories have been translated by Tahira Naqvi.

[5] *Lady Killer*, a collection of short stories by Ismat Chughtai.

[6] Carlo Coppola, "The All-India Progressive Writers' Association: The European Phase," *Marxist Influences and South Asian Literatures*. Carlo Coppola, (ed.) Vol 1, Occasional Papers No. 23 South Asia Series (East Lansing: Michigan State University, Asian Studies Center), 1.

[7] Tahir Masud, "Ismat Chughtai" from *Ye suratgar kuch khabun ke*, a collection of interviews, p. 344. This interview took place during Ismat's second visit to Pakistan some years ago.

[8] *Guftagu*, p. 1.

[9] *Lady Killer*, p.5.

[10] *Lihaaf, Ismat Chughtai ke behtreen afsane*, (Lahore, Chaudhry Academy, 1979) p.257.

[11] Mahmud Wajid, *Ismat ke afsanon men riwayat aur tajurba* (Tradition and Experience in Ismat's Short Stories), Jamil Akhtar (ed.)*Alfaz*, Ismat Chughtai Issue (Karachi, 1985), 16.

[12] Azhar Qadri, *Ismat Chughtai ka ahang-e-fan* (The Style of Ismat's Art), *Alfaz*, p. 12.

[13] Ismat Chughtai, *Terhi Lakir*.

[14]*Ismat Chughtai ke behtreen* . . : p.12
[15]*Ye suratgar kuch khabun ke*, p. 361

The Veil

SEATED on a divan covered with a white sheet, her hair whiter than the wings of a heron, grandma looked like an awkward mass of marble; it seemed as though there was not a single drop of blood in her body. White had crept up to the edges of her grey eyes which, lustreless, reminded one of casements that were barred, of windows hiding fearfully behind thick curtains. Her presence, shrouded in what could be likened to a stationary cloud of finely-ground silver, was dazzling, and a snowy-white, blinding radiance seemed to emanate from her person. Her face shone with the glow of purity and chastity. This eighty year-old virgin had never known the touch of a man's hand.

She was like a bouquet of flowers at thirteen with hair that fell below her waist and a complexion that shimmered with youthful silkiness and translucence. But her youth had been ravaged by time; only the softness now remained. Her beauty was of such renown in those days that her parents, afraid she might be whisked away by jinns, couldn't sleep at night. Indeed, she didn't appear to be of this world.

At fourteen she became engaged to my mother's uncle. He was as dark as she was fair, although otherwise he was exceedingly well-proportioned and manly in appearance: what a sharply delineated nose he had, just like the blade of a sword, hooded eyes that were ever watchful, his teeth a string of pearls. But he was unusually sensitive about his inky complexion.

During the engagement celebrations everyone began teasing him.

"Dear, oh dear, the bride will be tarnished by the groom's touch!"

"It will be like an eclipse of the moon."

Kale Mian was a stubborn, immature, seventeen-year-old at the time. Terrified by all this talk about his bride-to-be's beauty, he ran away to his maternal granfather's house in Jodhpur. There, hesitatingly, he admitted to his friends that he didn't want to get married. In those days defiance was dealt with severely and a beating or two was not at all uncommon. Under no circumstances could an engagement be terminated; such an act would bring eternal shame upon the family.

And what was wrong with the bride-to-be, anyway? Just that she was exceedingly beautiful? The world idolized beauty and here he was, manifesting extreme bad taste by spurning it.

"She's arrogant," he confessed diffidently.

"How do you know?"

There was no proof, but beauty is known to beget arrogance and it was impossible that Kale Mian should submit to arrogance; he was not accustomed to submitting to the will of others.

A concerted effort was made to explain to him that once she was his wife, Goribi would become his possession and comply with his every wish. She would say 'day' if he wanted her to, 'night' if he wished it thus; she would sit wherever he made her sit, and stand up if he ordered her to do so. Some physical force was also employed to coerce Kale Mian into returning home and finally the wedding took place.

The women singing wedding songs sang of a fair bride and a dark groom. As if that were not enough to incense Kale Mian, someone recited a poem in which a stinging allusion was made to his dark complexion. This proved to be the last straw. However, nobody took his indignation seriously, and, presuming that he was in tune with the spirit of fun that prevailed, continued to jokingly tease him.

When, like a sword out of its sheath ready for attack, he entered the bridal chamber and saw the bride who was enmeshed in glittering red flowers, he broke out in a sweat. Her pale, silken hands made his blood boil, and he was overcome by an overpowering desire to grind in his blackness with her whiteness so that the difference between them would be obliterated forever.

The bride bent over as he extended his hands towards her veil.

"All right then, you lift the veil yourself," he said.

The bride dropped her head lower.

"Lift your veil!" he ordered her sharply.

The bride was all rolled up like a ball now.

"Ohhh! Such arrogance! Hunh!" The bridegroom slipped his shoes under his arm, jumped out of the window which opened on to the garden, made directly for the station and from there, to Jodhpur!

The women in the family knew the bride had not been touched and it was not long before the news reached the men. Kale Mian was interrogated.

"She is defiant," he proclaimed.

"How do you know that?"

"I told her to lift her veil and she ignored my

request."

"You fool! Don't you know a bride does not lift her own veil? Why didn't you do it yourself?"

"Never! I have sworn. If she will not lift her veil, she can go to hell!"

"You are stupid to ask her to lift her veil herself; next thing you know you will be wanting her to take the initiative for everything else. What a damned stupid idea!"

There was no question of divorce in those days. Once married you stayed married. Kale Mian disappeared for seven years, but he continued to send money to his mother. Goribi, his bride, was suspended between her parents' home and that of her in-laws.

Her parents were deeply shocked by the tragedy that had befallen their only daughter. They were hurt; what was wrong with the girl that the bridegroom had not touched her? Who had heard of such injustice?

In order to prove his manhood Kale Mian indulged in all the vices that were available to him; he consorted with prostitutes and homosexuals and, among other things, spent time as a pigeon-fancier; all this while Goribi quietly smouldered away behind her veil.

When his mother fell seriously ill, Kale Mian came home. Considering this to be a stroke of good fortune, the elders made another attempt to bring the bride and groom together. Once again Goribi was clothed in bridal attire. But Kale Mian said, "I've sworn on my mother's life I will not lift her veil."

Everyone reasoned with Goribi: "Now, girl, this is going to affect your whole life. Set your modesty aside, stir up some courage, and raise your veil yourself. There is nothing indecent about this—he is your husband, your earthly God. It's your duty to obey him. Your freedom lies in doing as he says."

Once again the bride was adorned, the nuptial bed was decorated, pulao and sweet rice were cooled, and once more the bridegroom was pushed into the bridal chamber. Goribi was a flowering beauty of twenty-one now; she exuded the warmth of womanhood, her eyelids drooped heavily, her breath came fast. For seven years she had dreamt of this particular night, friends had whispered secrets that made her heart beat wildly. As soon as Kale Mian's eyes fell upon the bride's henna-covered hands and feet he felt emotion take control of him. His bride sat before him, not an unopened bud of fourteen, but a full-blown bouquet. Desire melted him; the night was sure to be filled with delights. Restive, his experienced body yearned for her like a tiger anticipating its prey. Although he had never seen her face, an image of this wondrous bride had tormented him even when he was with other women.

"Lift your veil," he said tremulously.

There was not the slightest movement.

"Lift your veil," he murmured in a pleading, tearful voice.

The silence remained unbroken.

"If you don't do as I say I am never going to show you my face again!"

The bride did not stir.

Kale Mian knocked the bedroom window open with a jab of his fist and jumped out into the garden.

Gone that night, he never returned to her.

Goribi, the untouched bride, waited thirty years for him. Gradually, nearly all the elders in her family died. It was while she was staying with an old aunt of hers in Fatehpur Sikri that she learned about the bridegroom's return.

After leading a life of indiscriminate debauchery, Kale Mian had returned home burdened with disease. On his deathbed he requested that Goribi come to him so that he could die in peace.

When she received Kale Mian's message, Goribi leaned against a pillar for a long time, unmoving and silent. Then she went to her old trunk, took out her tattered wedding suit and put it on, applied bridal oil to some of her grey hair and, her long veil cradled between her hands, she arrived at the side of the dying patient.

"Lift your veil," Kale Mian whispered convulsively.

Goribi's trembling hands reached up toward her veil, and fell.

Kale Mian had taken his last breath.

That very moment Goribi calmly sat down on the floor beside his bed, smashed her glass bangles against the bedpost, and instead of the bridal veil, pulled the white veil of widowhood over her head.

Translated by Tahira Naqvi

The Quilt

In the depth of winter whenever I snuggle into my quilt, its shadow on the wall seems to sway like an elephant. My mind begins a mad race into the dark crevasses of the past; memories come flooding in.

Begging your pardon, I am not about to relate a romantic incident surrounding my own quilt—I do not believe there is much romance associated with it. The blanket, though considerably less comfortable, is preferable because it does not cast such terrifying shadows, quivering on the wall!

This happened when I was a small girl. All day long I fought tooth and nail with my brothers and their friends. Sometimes I wondered why the hell I was so quarrelsome. At my age my older sisters had been busy collecting admirers; all I could think of was fisticuffs with every known and unknown girl or boy I ran into!

For this reason my mother decided to deposit me with an 'adopted' sister of hers when she left for Agra. She was well aware that there was no one in that sister's house, not even a pet animal, with whom I could engage in my favourite occupation! I guess my punishment was well deserved. So Mother left me with Begum Jan, the same Begum Jan whose quilt is imprinted on my memory like a blacksmith's brand.

This was the lady who had been married off to Nawab Sahib for a very good reason, courtesy her poor but loving parents. Although much past his prime, Nawab Sahib was noblesse oblige. No one had ever seen a dancing girl or a prostitute in his home. He had the distinction of not only performing the Haj himself, but of being the patron of several poor people who had undertaken the pilgrimage through his good offices.

Nawab Sahib had a strange hobby. People are known to have irksome interests like breeding pigeons and arranging cockfights. Nawab Sahib kept himself aloof from these disgusting sports; all he liked to do was keep an open house for students; young, fair and slim-waisted boys, whose expenses were borne entirely by him. After marrying Begum Jan, he deposited her in the house with all his other possessions and promptly forgot about her! The young, delicate Begum began to wilt with loneliness.

Who knows when Begum Jan started living? Did her life begin when she made the mistake of being born, or when she entered the house as the Nawab's new bride, climbed the elaborate four-poster bed and started counting her days? Or did it begin from the time she realised that the household revolved around the boy-students, and that all the delicacies produced in the kitchen were meant solely for their palates? From the chinks in the drawing-room doors, Begum Jan glimpsed their slim waists, fair ankles and gossamer shirts and felt she had been raked over the coals!

Perhaps it all started when she gave up on magic, necromancy, seances and whatnot. You cannot draw blood from a stone. Not an inch did the Nawab budge.

Broken-hearted, Begum Jan turned towards education. Not much to be gained here either! Romantic novels and sentimental poetry proved even more depressing. Sleepless nights became a daily routine. Begum Jan slowly let go and consequently, became a picture of melancholy and despair.

She felt like stuffing all her fine clothes into the stove. One dresses up to impress people. Now, neither did Nawab Sahib find a spare moment from his preoccupation with the gossamer shirts, nor did he allow her to venture outside the home. Her relatives, however, made it a habit to pay her frequent visits which often lasted for months, while she remained a prisoner of the house.

Seeing these relatives on a roman holiday made her blood boil. They happily indulged themselves with the goodies produced in the kitchen and licked the clarified butter off their greedy fingers. In her household they equipped themselves for their winter needs. But, despite renewing the cotton filling in her quilt each year, Begum Jan continued to shiver, night after night. Each time she turned over, the quilt assumed ferocious shapes which appeared like shadowy monsters on the wall. She lay in terror; not one of the shadows carried any promise of life. What the hell was life worth anyway? Why live? But Begum Jan was destined to live, and once she started living, did she ever!

Rabbo came to her rescue just as she was starting to go under. Suddenly her emaciated body began to fill out. Her cheeks became rosy; beauty, as it were, glowed through every pore! It was a special oil massage that brought about the change in Begum Jan. Begging your pardon, you will not find the recipe for this oil in the most exclusive or expensive magazine!

When I saw Begum Jan she was in her early forties. She sat reclining on the couch, a figure of dignity and grandeur. Rabbo sat against her back, massaging her waist. A purple shawl was thrown over her legs. The very picture of royalty, a real Maharani! How I loved her looks. I wanted to sit by her side for hours, adoring her like a humble devotee. Her complexion was fair, without a trace of ruddiness. Her black hair was always drenched in oil. I had never seen her parting crooked, nor a single hair out of place. Her eyes were black, and carefully plucked eyebrows stretched over them like a couple of perfect bows! Her eyes were slightly taut, eyelids heavy and eyelashes thick. The most amazing and attractive part of her face were her lips. Usually dyed in lipstick, her upper lip had a distinct line of down. He temples were covered with long hair. Sometimes her face became transformed before my adoring gaze, as if it were the face of a young boy. . . .

Her skin was fair and moist, and looked like it had been stretched over her frame and tightly stitched up. Whenever she exposed her ankles for a massage, I stole a glance at their rounded smoothness. She was tall, and appeared taller because of the ample flesh on her person. Her hands were large and moist, her waist smooth. Rabbo used to sit by her side and scratch her back for hours together — it was almost as if getting scratched was for her the fulfillment of life's essential need. In a way, more important than the basic necessities required for staying alive.

Rabbo had no other household duties. Perched on the four-poster bed, she was always massaging Begum Jan's head, feet or some other part of her anatomy.

Someone other than Begum Jan receiving such a quantity of human touching, what would the consequences be? Speaking for myself, I can say that if someone touched me continuously like this, I would certainly rot.

As if this daily massage were not enough, on the days she bathed this ritual extended to two hours! Scented oils and unguents were massaged into her shining skin; imagining the friction caused by this prolonged rubbing made me slightly sick. The braziers were lit behind closed doors and then the procedure started. Usually Rabbo was the only one allowed inside the sanctum. Other servants, muttering their disapproval, handed over various necessities at the closed door.

The fact of the matter was that Begum Jan was afflicted with a perpetual itch. Numerous oils and lotions had been tried, but the itch was there to stay. Hakims and doctors stated: It is nothing, the skin is clear. But if the disease is located beneath the skin, it's a different matter.

These doctors are mad! Rabbo used to say with a meaningful smile while gazing dreamily at Begum Jan. "May your enemies be afflicted with skin disease! It is your hot blood that causes all the trouble!"

Rabbo! She was as black as Begum Jan was white, like burnt iron ore! Her face was lightly marked with smallpox, her body solidly packed; small, dextrous hands, a tight little paunch and full lips, slightly swollen, which were always moist. A strange and bothersome odour emanated from her body. Those puffy hands were as quick as lightning, now at her waist, now her lips, now kneading her thighs and dashing towards her ankles. Whenever I sat down with Begum

Jan, my eyes were rivetted to those roving hands.

Winter or summer, Begum Jan always wore kurtas of Hyderabadi *jaali karga*. I recall her dark skirts and billowing white kurtas. With the fan gently rotating on the ceiling, Begum Jan always covered herself with a soft wrap. She was fond of winter. I too liked the winter season at her house. She moved very little. Reclining on the carpet, she spent her days having her back massaged, chewing on dry fruit. Other household servants were envious of Rabbo. The witch! She ate, sat, and even slept with Begum Jan! Rabbo and Begum Jan — the topic inevitably cropped up in every gathering. Whenever anyone mentioned their names, the group burst into loud guffaws. Who knows what jokes were made at their expense? But one thing was certain — the poor lady never met a single soul. All her time was taken up with the treatment of her unfortunate itch.

I have already said that I was very young at that time and quite enamoured of Begum Jan. She, too, was fond of me. When mother decided to go to Agra she had to leave me with somebody. She knew that, left alone, I would fight continuously with my brothers, or wander around aimlessly. I was happy to be left with Begum Jan for one week, and Begum Jan was equally pleased to have me. After all, she was Ammi's adopted sister!

The question arose of where I was to sleep. The obvious place was Begum Jan's room; accordingly, a small bed was placed alongside the huge four-poster. Until ten or eleven that night we played Chance and talked; then I went to bed. When I fell asleep Rabbo was scratching her back. "Filthy wench," I muttered before turning over. At night I woke up with a start.

It was pitch dark. Begum Jan's quilt was shaking vigorously, as if an elephant was struggling beneath it.

"Begum Jan," my voice was barely audible. The elephant subsided. "What is it? Go to sleep." Begum Jan's voice seemed to come from afar.

"I'm scared." I sounded like a petrified mouse.

"Got to sleep. Nothing to be afraid of. Recite the *Ayat-ul- Kursi.*"

"Okay!" I quickly began the Ayat. But each time I reached *"Yalamu Mabain"* I got stuck. This was strange. I knew the entire Ayat!

"May I come to you, Begum Jan?"

"No child, go to sleep." The voice was curt. Then I heard whispers. Oh God! Who was this other person? Now I was terrified.

"Begum Jan, is there a thief here?"

"Go to sleep, child; there is no thief." This was Rabbo's voice. I sank into my quilt and tried to sleep.

In the morning I could not even remember the sinister scene that had been enacted at night. I have always been the superstitious one in my family. Night fears, sleep-talking, sleep-walking were regular occurrences during my childhood. People often said that I seemed to be haunted by evil spirits. Consequently I blotted out the incident from memory as easily as I dealt with all my imaginary fears. Besides, the quilt seemed such an innocent part of the bed.

The next night when I woke up, a quarrel between Begum Jan and Rabbo was being settled on the bed itself. I could not make out what conclusion was reached, but I heard Rabbo sobbing. Then there were sounds of a cat slobbering in the saucer. To hell with it, I thought and went off to sleep!

Today Rabbo has gone off to visit her son. He was

a quarrelsome lad. Begum Jan had done a lot to help him settle down in life; she had bought him a shop, arranged a job in the village, but to no avail. She even managed to have him stay with Nawab Sahib. Here he was treated well, a new wardrobe was ordered for him, but ungrateful wretch that he was, he ran away for no good reason and never returned, not even to see Rabbo. She therefore had to arrange to meet him at a relative's house. Begum Jan would never have allowed it, but poor Rabbo was helpless and had to go.

All day Begum Jan was restless. Her joints hurt like hell, but she could not bear anyone's touch. Not a morsel did she eat; all day long she moped in bed.

"Shall I scratch you, Begum Jan?" I asked eagerly while dealing out the deck of cards. Begum Jan looked at me carefully.

"Really, shall I?" I put the cards aside and began scratching, while Begum Jan lay quietly, giving in to my ministrations. Rabbo was due back the next day, but she never turned up. Begum Jan became irritable. She drank so much tea that her head started throbbing.

Once again I started on her back. What a smooth slab of a back! I scratched her softly, happy to be of some assistance.

"Scratch harder, open the straps," Begum Jan spoke. "There, below the shoulder. Ooh, wonderful!" She sighed as if with immense relief.

"This way," Begum Jan indicated, although she could very well scratch that part herself. But she prefered my touch. How proud I was!

"Here, oh, oh, how you tickle," she laughed. I was talking and scratching at the same time.

"Tomorrow I will send you to the market. What

do you want? A sleeping-walking doll?"

"Not a doll, Begum Jan! Do you think I am a child? You know I am . . ."

"Yes . . . an old crow. Is that what you are?" She laughed.

"Okay then, buy a *babua*. Dress it up yourself, I'll give you as many bits and pieces as you want. Okay?" She turned over.

"Okay," I answered.

"Here." She was guiding my hand wherever she felt the itch. With my mind on the *babua*, I was scratching mechanically, unthinkingly. She continued talking. "Listen, you don't have enough clothes. Tomorrow I will ask the tailor to make you a new frock. Your mother has left some material with me."

"I don't want that cheap red material. It looks tacky." I was talking nonsense while my hand roved the entire territory. I did not realize it but by now Begum Jan was flat on her back! Oh God! I quickly withdrew my hand.

"Silly girl, don't you see where you're scratching? You have dislocated my ribs." Begum Jan was smiling mischievously. I was red with embarrassment.

"Come, lie down with me." She laid me at her side with my head on her arm. "How thin you are . . . and, let's see, your ribs," she started counting.

"No," I protested weakly.

"I won't eat you up! What a tight sweater," she said. "Not even a warm vest?" I began to get very restless.

"How many ribs"? The topic was changed.

"Nine on one side, ten on the other." I thought of my school hygiene. Very confused thinking.

"Let's see", she moved my hand. "One, two,

three..."

I wanted to run away from her, but she held me closer. I struggled to get away. Begum Jan started laughing.

To this day whenever I think of what she looked like at that moment, I get nervous. Her eyelids became heavy, her upper lip darkened and, despite the cold, her nose and eyes were covered with tiny beads of perspiration. Her hands were stiff and cold, but soft as if the skin had been peeled. She had thrown off her shawl and in the *karga* kurta, her body shone like a ball of dough. Her heavy gold kurta buttons were open, swinging to one side.

The dusk had plunged her room into a claustrophobic blackness, and I felt gripped by an unknown terror. Begum Jan's deep dark eyes focussed on me! I started crying. She was clutching me like a clay doll. I started feeling nauseated against her warm body. She seemed possessed. What could I do? I was neither able to cry nor scream! In a while she became limp. Her face turned pale and frightening, she started taking deep breaths. I figured she was about to die, so I ran outside.

Thank God Rabbo came back at night. I was scared enough to pull the sheet over my head, but sleep evaded me as usual. I lay awake for hours.

How I wished Ammi would return. Begum Jan had become such a terrifying entity that I spent my days in the company of household servants. I was too scared to step into her bedroom. What could I have said to anyone? That I was afraid of Begum Jan? Begum Jan, who loved me so dearly?

Today there was another tiff between Begum Jan and Rabbo. I was dead scared of their quarrels, because they signalled the beginning of my misfortunes! Begum Jan immediately thought about me. What was I doing wandering around in the cold? I would surely die of pneumonia!

"Child, you will have my head shaven in public. If something happens to you, how will I face your mother?" Begum Jan admonished me as she washed up in the water basin. The tea tray was lying on the table.

"Pour some tea and give me a cup." She dried her hands and face. "Let me get out of these clothes."

While she changed, I drank tea. During her body massage, she kept summoning me for small errands. I carried things to her with utmost reluctance, always looking the other way. At the slightest opportunity I ran back to my perch, drinking my tea, my back turned to Begum Jan.

"Ammi!" My heart cried in anguish. "How could you punish me so severely for fighting with my brothers?" Mother disliked my mixing with the boys, as if they were man-eaters who would swallow her beloved daughter in one gulp! After all who were these ferocious males? None other than my own brothers and their puny little friends. Mother believed in a strict prison sentence for females; life behind seven padlocks! Begum Jan's "patronage", however, proved more terrifying than the fear of the world's worst goondas! If I had had the courage I would have run out on to the street. But helpless as I was, I continued to sit in that very spot with my heart in my mouth.

After an elaborate ritual of dressing up and scenting her body with warm attars and perfumes, Begum Jan turned her arduous heat on me.

"I want to go home!" I said in response to all her suggestions. More tears.

"Come to me", she waxed. "I will take you shopping."

But I had only one answer. All the toys and sweets in the world kept piling up against my one and only refrain, "I want to go home!"

"Your brothers will beat you up, you witch!" She smacked me affectionately.

"Sure, let them," I said to myself annoyed and exasperated.

"Raw mangoes are sour, Begum Jan," malicious little Rabbo expressed her views.

Then Begum Jan had her famous fit. The gold necklace she was about to place around my neck, was broken to bits. Gossamer net scarf was shredded mercilessly. Hair, which were never out of place, were tousled with loud exclamations of "Oh! Oh! Oh!" She started shouting and convulsing. I ran outside.

After much ado and ministration, Begum Jan regained consciousness. When I tiptoed into the bedroom Rabbo, propped against her body, was kneading her limbs.

"Take off your shoes," she whispered. Mouse-like I crept into my quilt.

Later that night, Begum Jan's quilt was, once again, swinging like an elephant. "Allah", I was barely able to squeak. The elephant-in-the quilt jumped and then sat down. I did not say a word. Once again, the elephant started convulsing. Now I was really confused. I decided, no matter what, tonight I would flip the switch on the bedside lamp. The elephant started fluttering once again, as if about to squat. Smack, gush, slobber — someone was enjoying a feast. Suddenly I understood what was going on!

Begum Jan had not eaten a thing all day and Rabbo, the witch, was a known glutton. They were polishing off some goodies under the quilt, for sure. Flaring my nostrils, I huffed and puffed hoping for a whiff of the feast. But the air was laden with attar, henna, sandalwood; hot fragrances, no food.

Once again the quilt started billowing. I tried to lie still, but it was now assuming such weird shapes that I could not contain myself. It seemed as if a frog was growing inside it and would suddenly spring on me.

"Ammi!" I spoke with courage, but no one heard me. The quilt, meanwhile, had entered my brain and started growing. Quietly creeping to the other side of the bed I swung my legs over and sat up. In the dark I groped for the switch. The elephant somersaulted beneath the quilt and dug in. During the somersault, its corner was lifted one foot above the bed.

Allah! I dove headlong into my sheets!!

What I saw when the quilt was lifted, I will never tell anyone, not even if they give me a lakh of rupees.

Translated by Syeda Hameed

Sacred Duty

THE tiny fragment of paper fell from Siddiqi Saheb's hands and fluttered to his lap like a dying moth. He brushed it off hastily, as if it had poisonous fangs that might get embedded in his very being.

Outside, seated on a pile of rugs, his wife supervised the hanging of chandeliers and coloured lanterns. She was also reading congratulatory telegrams that had arrived from abroad, and from Delhi and elsewhere in the country. The wedding of their darling daughter, Samina, who had recently passed her B.Sc. with the highest honours, was only a day away.

The young man, the groom-to-be, was employed in Dubai, received a monthly salary of twelve thousand, had free board and lodgings, and was allowed one pre-paid vacation very year. Progress in the Middle East had brought good fortune to so many single women; this shower of wealth had provided relief to any number of families. From a well-to-do family of good standing, the young man had no one to hassle him for a share in his income. The match had been arranged over the phone. He was not all that good looking, also just a trifle short, but does a girl have to put up her husband for rent? One doesn't bother with a man's physical attributes, it's his qualities that count. And in this case qualities numbered twelve thousand,

and total comforts even more.

Their daughter was like a flower. She had wanted to continue her education, but an opportunity like this doesn't come one's way every day, so the girl was silenced with a few words of censure. What was to be gained by going on to get an M.Sc., or becoming a doctor?

At first she was just quiet, but then she became unusually uncommunicative. These girls are such coquettes, the mother reflected, putting aside the letter she had been reading. Well, it was settled: she would visit her daughter in Dubai in the month of Khali and, on her way back, God willing, be blessed with the opportunity of performing Haj.

At that very moment, suspended in a state of semi-consciousness, Siddiqi Saheb observed with glassy vision the minute fragment of paper which had pulled his world from a great height and flung it mercilessly into an abyss.

> Papa, Mummy — I'm terribly sorry, but I can't go through with this marriage. I'm leaving with Tashar Trivedi to go to his parents' home in Allahabad. We've been married in a civil ceremony. I will consider myself privileged if you decide to forgive me.
>
> Your daughter, Samina Trivedi

May God preserve us! It was true that Siddiqi Saheb was a progressive; allowing girls to obtain a higher education and letting them marry whomever they pleased — he certainly believed in all of this. He also attended Eid prayers regularly, had been living a life of quiet respectability as a member of an enlightened social class, and had never been involved in a dispute over religious convictions. But that wasn't going to stop his blood from boiling if his daughter strayed.

When his wife heard the news she almost fainted. *There's only one thing to do: let's go to Allahabad and shoot them both!* But the mention of the word 'gun' caused Begum Siddiqi to become deeply agitated. Ahhh, their beautiful, their only daughter! God's curse upon the rogue! How charming and harmless he had seemed during those Sunday visits to their house, how he appeared always to be having a good time, and how he and Samina bickered! Where did this blasted love come from, anyway? Such wicked children these days, sneaking off behind your back to get married — and no one had the slightest inkling. How he had flattered her, called her Mummy — indeed he had succeeded in making her his 'Mummy' after all, the wretch! Such a good-for-nothing generation! *No, we have nothing against Hindus:* Did one ever bother with who was Christian and who was Hindu at Papu's Sunday get-togethers? Just think of all the silly nicknames those women had. Pami Deshmukh, for example — was she Razak Deshmukh's wife or Chandra Deshmukh's? And what about Lily? Begum Siddiqi had thought Lily was Christian all along, until she discovered that she was really Laila Razdan. And wasn't it confusing with all those Razdans? Tirmila Razdan, for example, who called herself Nikki, always swore in English and liberally sprinkled her conversation with "Shut up!" and "Hell!" (and was sure to get there) was from an upstanding Shia family; as for Razdan Saheb — *Mohammad* Razdan Saheb — he had performed Haj thrice already. As a matter of fact, Nikki had too. What fabulous saris she had brought back from Haj this time, and all those cosmetics! She brought a gift of the holy water of Zamzam in phials along with a little snippet of the Ka'aba covering; with what cunning she must have used her nail scissors to snip off that swatch! The folds were thick and heavy, she had explained, so no one could tell the difference.

Husband and wife sat late into the night, calling people on the phone and sending telegrams, telling all those who had been invited to the wedding that the girl had come down with a severe attack of pneumonia: *She's in intensive care, the wedding has been postponed for the time being. If she lives, we'll see.*

But there wasn't even a well-sharpened knife in the house with which they could kill their daughter and son-in-law. *Forget the gun.* Getting a license would be such a bother, although, who knows, perhaps if they had tried they might have been successful in procuring one quickly; after all, Allah had blessed them with good connections. But by the time a gun was obtained a child would have been born. The thought of a child made their blood curdle.

Well, Allah has given us two hands; at least the girl's neck can be wrung. First a good hiding place behind some bushes will have to be found. But are there any bushes there? Perhaps the villains live in a neighbourhood devoid of decent shrubbery. This was a case of demanding that the river be full before one jumps into it to drown. If fate had been on our side, our daughter would not have run off, would not have blackened our faces thus.

But it would not be fair if Tashar, the ruffian who seduced their innocent daughter, were allowed to go unpunished. *Perhaps it will help to have the screwdriver sharpened. The tool-sharpener used to appear at the front gate every day; what a shame he had been threatened with police action and asked to set up shop elsewhere. What a dreadful grating noise he made when he sharpened a blade! As though a handful of sand had been thrust between your teeth.*

This was not something that could be shared with friends. But Jawad Jaffrey, who had a very successful practice in Allahabad, was like a member of the family. They called him on the phone and asked for advice. He promised to be with them around tea-time the following day.

And then a bomb exploded.

A newspaper sent to the girl's parents from Allahabad was splashed with pictures of Samina and Tashar's wedding. A civil ceremony had not sufficed. Sethji, Tashar's father, had arranged a religious ceremony complete with a *havan* and pandit. And pictures were taken, snapshots of the girl changing her faith, taking a dip in the holy waters of the Ganga in Banaras (she had been flown there), and finally a picture in which she appeared with Tashar, smiling coquettishly at him like a hussy.

Siddiqi Saheb's uncontrolled fury very nearly caused him to have a heart attack. But Jawad Saheb's timely arrival averted such a dreadful catastrophe. Tashar's father had indeed played it dirty. The man was a staunch Mahasabhi, and by printing those photographs with such aplomb he had succeeded in sprinkling salt over Siddqi Saheb's wounds.

Now the entire family would have to be blown up with a bomb: but how? *I, Siddiqi, who finds even the fireworks at Diwali and Shab-barat disturbing, have been shattered by this explosion. This is a nation of Hindus, after all.* Ah, such fine positions were offered to him in Pakistan, but he had been so full of the progressive spirit then — such stupidity!

"I can't leave my country, I will be buried in the earth that gave me life," he had said, using the Hindi word *janam*. Remembering now, he swore angrily. *That's a Hindi word, inappropriate for someone who is the product of a highly-principled, truly Muslim family.*

Jawad Saheb pacified him with great difficulty, calmed him down a little. Then the two friends convened behind closed doors for hours. Later the scheme was spelled out to the girl's mother. She expressed delight: What a crafty man, she said in praise of Jawad Saheb who, although a Jaffrey Shia, had nonetheless shared years and years of friendship with Siddiqi Saheb. History might look askance at a Siddiqi-Jaffrey alliance, but the association between these two men had remained untouched by discord. Faith and friendship do clash sometimes, but love and friendship generally succeed in emerging victorious. However, the contradiction can be tragic; how often do love and friendship serve to destroy principles!

Siddiqi Saheb told the driver to wait and rang the bell.

In a few minutes his beloved daughter Samina clung to him, shedding tears of joy; disobeying her parents deeply distresses a daughter, she can't be at peace with herself until she is forgiven. It was while she was under her parents' roof that Tashar's love had become a part of Samina's life. Would Tashar have been able to woo her in her own home if her parents had not been so liberal?

And Tashar stood nearby, grinning sheepishly. He had not approved of the newspaper stunt his father had pulled. But he was the only brother of four sisters, and one day he would take charge of his father's business. He was reminded of his duty again and again.

His sisters, all of them younger than he, were now well-settled. A long time ago the youngest had fallen in love with a dark-skinned Christian professor. Sethji had the young man cleverly whisked off to England on a government scholarship. Making a hasty retreat from the battlefield of love, the fellow hadn't even bothered to look back.

Sethji, an important man, was reputed to be a successful promoter of politicians. Although he never accepted a position himself, many of his proteges adorned the assembly and various committees. He was viewed as a very successful "king-maker". And despite the fact that he was not affiliated with any particular group, he was always found firmly positioned behind the winning party. He played a role in both the rise and the fall of the masses — his was a multi-faceted personality.

Jawad Saheb's advice to Siddiqi Saheb, whatever it had been, transformed him. His heart beat within his chest with a new rhythm; in very correct and proper Hindi, studded like diamonds with impressive words from Sanskrit, Siddiqui Saheb thanked Sethji for removing a great weight from his shoulders, that of an unwed daughter — for seven generations the debt could not be paid. All faiths are sacred, he said, and the truest faith consists of the love and respect a father-in-law bestows upon his daughter-in-law. Endowing a daughter-in-law with one's faith together with one's son was indeed commendable. And Ganga was the mother of all, regardless of who was Christian, or Hindu, or Muslim; her pure waters didn't question faith — Brahmin and Untouchable, she invited everyone to drink from her cup.

"Sayed Saheb," he said to Sethji, now using honorific titles, "I'm a human being, I've inherited my religion and accumulated knowledge from the written word: your Bhagwan and my Allah are two names for the same power."

Siddiqi Saheb quoted extensively from the Bible and the Gita, as well as the Quran. Sethji was very impressed. His wife requested a neighbour to cook an elaborate non-vegetarian, roast chicken dinner for their guest; the family bustled with excitement. Sethji's son's father-in-law, a man of great means and even greater principles, had come to bless his daughter — how liberally he passed out those fifty-rupee bills to the servants! Siddiqi Saheb attended many dinners thrown in his honour, but he refused to eat meat; meat weakens faith, he proclaimed repeatedly.

People said, "Listen, he's only half a Muslim, how long can he last?"

"You have enjoyed the fulfillment of your wishes," Siddiqi Saheb told Sethji, "now you must allow me to pay my debt to our family and friends. Samina's mother cries incessantly, although the pictures helped lessen her grief somewhat." (Actually his wife had suggested they tear up the pictures and throw them into the kitchen fire.)

Sethji's wife was a little reluctant to hand over the diamond necklace and earrings to her daughter-in-law at the time of her departure. Sethji admonished her: "Don't be of such small heart; our son's father-in-law is a man of wealth and principles. Didn't you see how gracefully he accepted our unfairness? And here you are, worrying about a few pieces of glass."

With great pomp and show Siddiqi Saheb

returned to Delhi with his daughter and son-in-law. Instructions had already been left with friends and relatives who were present at the railway station, laden with bouquets and garlands. Jawad Saheb had accompanied Siddiqi Saheb from Allahabad for good luck.

The girl's mother seethed with fury. She suggested, "Kill the boy and throw his body in the lawn so he can turn into compost."

"Are you out of your mind? Just be patient and see what happens. Tashar is Samina's husband now. Proposal and acceptance, whether it be in our language or any other, has already taken place — they are now husband and wife. And both are dear to us."

That evening the marquee was set up again and invitations went out to all the important people in the city.

Tashar became agitated when he was told to convert. Fearfully he glanced first at Siddiqi Saheb and then at Jawad Saheb, mentally planning an escape route through the window, no doubt.

"Papa, what's this nonsense? First it was Papaji who forced me to become Hindu, telling me to recite all kinds of holy hymns that sounded like gibberish, and now you've started this farce. We refuse to be part of your games. As soon as we return to Allahabad we'll be forced to dip again, have more photographs taken, and . . ." The girl's mother began to cry at this point, and Siddiqi Saheb floundered.

"There's only one way out," he said, clasping his wife's hand, "let's go and drown ourselves in the Jamuna."

"How can you drown, Papa, you know how to swim. You'll probably let Mummy drown and come out of the water yourself, all nice and clean for your girlfriend, Miss Farzana."

"Sami, be quiet!" Tashar scolded Samina. "Papa, I mean Siddiqi Saheb, I'm ready to be a Muslim."

"Shut up, you fool! I'm not ready to be re-converted. Don't you remember how your mother lovingly put the mangal sutra around my neck? These are diamonds, you know. Look, don't you think it's pretty?"

"You can wear the mangal sutra as a Muslim, too!" Tashar retorted angrily.

"Woe is me! Kill them both and bury them." It was the mother. "What an ungrateful daughter. He's ready to be a Muslim, and this miserable creature has decided to be troublesome!"

"Sami, will you be quiet or not?" Tashar admonished Samina again. "When I opposed Papaji you threatened to jump out of the window. Do you know there's a mouse hole under the window? The big mouse in there would have been surprised out of its hole if you had jumped, scaring you out of your wits!"

Someone said, "My word, the maulvi saheb has been waiting a long time to make the conversion. He hasn't even accepted a cup of tea, says he'll have a complete breakfast after he has performed his sacred duty. What a greedy man!"

"I'm ready, and two smacks across her face will bring her to her senses. Darling, did you lose anything by becoming Hindu? There's no need to be so pigheaded."

"Ohh ... and what about the *arti*, and the lovely mangal sutra you gave me? But I must say, you wear such dirtly socks—I could smell your feet when I bent down to touch them."

"What is all this nonsense!" Siddiqi Saheb roared in anger. "Everything is a big joke for you! Tashar, get ready to submit to the honour." (He used the word *musharraf*, which means 'one who receives the honour'.)

"Musharraf? That Musharraf Hamidullah who is a lowdown thief and a crook? Always cheated in every exam. Sami, remember he pulled out a knife once when Sir caught him redhanded?"

"You're the spoilt son of a rich man, and he's the son of a poor orderly — what a crime! Have you ever wondered how he manages to survive, you bloody capitalist!"

"Look, Mummy, she's rude to me again. I'm going to hit her now."

"They have perished, those who would raise their hands to hit. Unh!" Mummy responded bitterly. Then, "How long is this to continue?" she asked. "Oh dear, I forgot the pudding in the oven." She ran towards the kitchen.

"Look here, these kids are driving me out of my mind — Jawad, help me please ..." Siddiqi Saheb turned to Jawad.

"Well, what do you suggest?" Jawad, who had been quietly listening all this time, said smilingly.

"I've followed your advice until now. What should I do next?"

"Look," Tashar interjected, "you had better convert me right away. I've booked seats for the matinee. We have to be there at three."

"The maulvi still hasn't eaten anything, you should skip the matinee. There's an at-home in the evening."

"But that's at eight!"

Every move made by Siddiqi Saheb was being repulsed.

"Listen to me, children," Jawad Saheb said, clearing his throat.

"Yes, Uncle," Tashar answered respectfully.

"Did you have a civil ceremony?"

"Yes, sir. The certificate is in a safe in Allahabad."

"Did you read the forms carefully before signing them?"

"Yes, I read them, but Samina was too upset to bother. I asked her to sign quickly so we could get out of there."

"How could I sign quickly with such a terrible pen? You can buy hundreds of shoes, but you can't get a decent pen."

"Do you see how rude and disrespectful she is? And we've been married twice, first in a civil ceremony, then a Hindu one. I had refused, but she thought it would be very romantic to be led around the sacred fire. She opposed everything I said just so she could win over my parents."

"Yes, it was romantic like a wedding in a fishing village, with the pandit muttering holy words that sounded like 'shutrum, shutrum', and Papaji, your father, pouring all that real ghee over the fire; it reminded me of carrot halwa when it's being fried — sugary sweet!"

"Ugh! Have you ever smelled real ghee over a burning funeral pyre?"

"You stupid fool, shut up!" Samina folded a newspaper and pounded his head with it.

"Oh, God! This is ridiculous." It was Siddiqi Saheb.

"Let me handle this," Jawad Saheb interjected in

a gentle voice.

"What a disaster! Will this *khachar-khachar* go on forever?" the mother asked as she came back into the room.

"Listen to me, children, and don't interrupt with any of your wisecracks this time. I'm going to ask you a very important question: Before the civil ceremony started, did you read the bit in the form which states that neither of you belongs to any particular faith?"

"No, I don't recall that I did, Uncle, but it doesn't matter. From the very beginning I've done whatever Mataji and Papaji have told me to do and, as a matter of fact, I never really thought much about questions of faith. Religion is for the elderly. In the convent we were exposed to Jesus, in Mathura, Krishanji reigned supreme, and once I accompanied Musharraf to a shrine where, imitating him, I lifted my hands together and moved my lips."

"You mean you've never thought seriously about Allah or Bhagwan?"

"Hmm. What about Dilip Kumar, the actor? Have you ever thought about him?" Siddiqi Saheb's tone was sarcastic.

"Well, Mataji was his fan at one time; personally I prefer Amit, Mithun and . . ."

"That's enough! Now listen, this means that no other proceeding has any meaning unless your civil marriage is dissolved first."

"So the Hindu ceremony was no good?" Tashar asked excitedly.

"Nonsense! It's no use your harping on that ceremony, Tushi. You can divorce me if you want, but you're not going to get back the mangal sutra."

"Oh, what a greedy girl! Here we are , discussing

such serious matters, and all she can think of is this mangal sutra! Tell me honestly, if Mataji had not shown you the mangal sutra and the rest of the jewellery first, would you have agreed to the Hindu ceremony?"

"You're mean, Tushi. Do you think I'm so greedy, you villain? Papa, marry me off to anybody, I don't care who. I called this man my protector, touched his smelly feet ... this ... this ... oh my God!" Samina clenched both fists and ran towards Tashar.

Bloodshed would have ensued if Siddiqi Saheb's wife had not threatened them with an attack of hysteria.

"Jawad," Siddiqi Saheb remarked, "I don't agree with this new point you've raised."

"But perhaps the law ..."

"To hell with the law! I want to get even with Sethji, we'll have a nikah even if I have to go to jail for it or be hanged. He made a fool of me for all the world to see, and I'm not going to ignore that."

"Why, what's the problem?" the mother interjected. "What's the hitch if both are Muslim?"

"My wife is right. She's a maulvi's daughter, after all."

"And she beats everyone at rummy, too," Samina piped in.

"Be quiet, you wretch! Stop interfering."

Maulvi saheb arrived. Giggling at first, Samina finally assumed a serious expression and covered her head. Tashar was offered a Karakuli cap the photographer had brought back from a recent visit to Pakistan. And seeing him handsomely decked out, Samina's eyes lit up provocatively.

Both received the honour of accepting Islam, and

both experienced difficulty reciting Arabic verses from the Quran; Tashar was visibly nervous. Maulvi saheb was a good-natured man, the atmosphere was just right, and Jawad Saheb agreed to act as the counsellor from the girl's side. One other person was needed to act as witness.

"Let Ammi be the witness," Samina suggested, speaking for her mother.

"Then we'll require one more woman."

"Why?"

"One man's testimony is equal to that of two women. But we can use the houseboy Shakura instead."

"Ammi is more important than ten Shakuras! This isn't fair," Samina stubbornly asserted.

"Be quiet, girl; don't keep butting in. There's the girl's father."

"Can I be a witness?" a startled Siddiqi Saheb inquired.

"Of course!" Maulvi saheb was a little disappointed. Residents of large and fancy bungalows were so unreliable; here was this man, a professor, and knew nothing about his own religion.

The nikah ceremony took place, sweets were distributed, the photographer was snapping away at every stage of the ceremony. The photographic sesion would have been a complete success if a shot of the couple affixing their signatures had also been included; such a shot would definitely succeed in scraping knives over Sethji's heart.

The photos were splashed across the morning papers along with the news that the couple was leaving for Bombay that morning, from where, it was said, husband and wife were to depart for England. The report indicated further that, God willing, they would perform Haj before they returned home.

Rooms had been reserved at the Ashoka Hotel for the wedding night. Family and guests accompanied the bride and groom to the hotel, and it was nearly two when the bride's family returned home. Everyone immediately fell into exhausted slumber. Siddiqi Saheb realized, for the first time, how difficult it was to marry off a daughter. All their lives parents wrestle with the fear of this one, special day. A sense of victory made him feel lighthearted the next morning — Jawad Saheb had indeed given a delicious twist to the whole matter. The paper must be in Sethji's hands by now; surely he stayed up for prayers after his ritual morning bath.

Siddiqi Saheb's heart danced with joy.

"I say, Sethji's newfound relative, are we going to get any breakfast today?" Jawad Saheb stood in the doorway. "Why, you appear six inches taller—how grand you look!"

"Not just six inches, a foot at least. By God, I've vanquished a pernicious rival — how riled up he must be! What do you think, shall we have breakfast at the Ashoka?"

"What a wonderful idea!"

"What do you say, my dear?"

"You know I never take long to get ready," his wife replied.

The three of them arrived at the hotel.

"Sir, they've checked out," the clerk at the front desk informed them.

"What? Where have they gone? When did they leave?"

"They sent for a taxi immediately after you left. I

told them again and again they could stay here until tomorrow night, but as soon as they had finished the phone conversation..."

"Phone conversation? What phone conversation?"

"It was a call to Allahabad; I connected them myself with Seth..."

"Seth!" The three of them were stunned into momentary silence. "So, they've run out on us, have they?"

"Did they say they were going to Allahabad?"

"No sir, they didn't mention anything like that..."

"He's going to raise a storm again... the rogue! Did Tashar make the call?"

"Yes, sir, I mean both did, sir, they were together in the booth for nearly twenty-five minutes. Oh, and they left a letter for you, sir." The envelope was heavy, or maybe Siddiqi Saheb's grasp was faltering.

The letter was in English, and contained two different kinds of handwriting: Samina and Tashar had taken equal space to express their ideas.

> Dear Papa, Mummy, Uncle Jawad:
> The best thing to do is to go away. No, not to Allahabad, for there, too, a stubborn father and a hysterical mother await us. Like decent people we spent four years getting to know each other well, then opted for a civil marriage after a great deal of serious thought. I'm not very brave, but Samina is a real coward. No, that's not true. I had suggested in the very beginning that we elope, run off somewhere far from here; that's why I called my father in Allahabad. Lovingly he beseeched us to come home: your mother is crying her heart out, come and calm her down, he said. And when we got there he made us go

around the holy fire. We thought, so what? This ceremony isn't going to kill us. But he played other tricks on us as well. We put up with everything. And then, Papa, you arrived on the scene; you're such a good actor — how genially and amicably you convinced Papaji — I was so touched. My father's so broad-minded, I told myself. Papaji had managed to whisk us off to Banaras with the help of his cronies. First it was Papaji who waved the magic wand at us, but when you warmly expressed forgiveness and brought us to Delhi, you too exposed yourself as someone really petty; you also made us dance like a monkey and its mate. And we took everything as a big joke, that comic drama too. Don't worry, we're not going to give away your secret — tomorrow morning when Papaji looks at the newspaper there'll definitely be an explosion. No, we only said goodbye to them. Goodbye to all of you too — no, you don't want to know where we're going. If we've hurt you, please forgive us. No, we haven't hurt you, it's you who have caused us pain, you're the ones who should apologize. You have made us a laughing stock. What kind of parents are you, who make your children dance like monkeys to any tune you like?

I've told Papaji we don't subscribe to any religion, and now I'm telling you the same thing. We have no religion. All religions are gifts from the same Bhagwan, they're for all mankind; He's also called God. You know Him only as Allah, but we know of His thousand other names,

> He who takes many forms:
> Who is within and without,
> Who is above and below,
> Who exists in darkness and in light,
> Who exists and is not visible,
> Who is in negation and in affirmation.

The letter ended with their signatures.

The girl's mother began to cry noisily. Siddiqi Saheb proceeded to make caustic remarks about women's tears.

Jawad Saheb scraped his pipe intently, almost as if he were trying to somehow disappear into it. After all, he was the formulator of this special prescription a la Galen. Who was to say which ingredient had proven ineffective, diminished the prescription's potency, and subsequently reduced the worlds of two sets of parents to desolation?

Translated by Tahira Naqvi

The Eternal Vine

BARI Mumani's shroud was not yet soiled when the whole family began worrying about a new wife for Uncle Shujaat. A bride was now eagerly sought. Whenever the women sat down after a meal and started leisurely work on garments for a dowry or a son's bride-to-be, the talk invariably turned to the question of probable matches for Uncle Shujaat.

"How about our own Kaneez Fatima?"

"Good gracious! Have you gone mad? If Kaneez Fatima's mother-in-law gets wind of this she will cut off your nose and hand it to you. Since her son's demise she has jealously sat guard over her daughter-in-law. The poor girl isn't allowed to leave the house. If there were a death in her family, the unfortunate creature might just be allowed to visit her parents.

"My dear, there's no dearth of virgins for our brother," Asghar Khanum said, adding, "Why should he go running after used goods when people are ready to present their daughters to him? To be sure, he doesn't look forty at all."

"Good God, sister! You're leaving out ten whole years. Why, with God's grace he will be fifty in the month of Khali..."

Poor Aunt Imtiazi! She regretted opening her mouth. On the one side were Uncle Shujaat's five sisters and on the other, the unfortunate woman. With God's grace, all five possessed tongues that were capable of wagging vigorously; the minute a threat was perceived the sisters immediately formed a front and no one — neither Mughlani nor Pathani — could withstand their attack. Even the Sayyedani and the Sheikhani were reduced to helplessness; the boldest among them lost her cool.

But in opposition to these five Pandus, Aunt Imtiazi held the power of a hundred Kurus. Her most dangerous weapon was her screeching voice, thin and sharp like the point of a drill. When she opened her mouth it seemed as if bullets from a machine gun had whizzed into one ear and come out of the other. As soon as she tussled with someone, news of the altercation travelled like wild fire and soon, jumping over balconies and across rooftops, women from the neighbourhood came running towards the arena.

But the five sisters would spring on Aunt Imtiazi with such force that she was reduced to a state of helplessness. Her third daughter, Gori Begum, was still unwed. She was, unhappily, in her thirtieth year, and there were no signs of her luck changing soon. No bachelors were forthcoming and married men didn't become widowers often. In the old days nearly every man laid at least three or four wives to rest. However, since the advent of hospitals and doctors, wives were not dying as frequently. Aunt Imtiazi had made her calculations while Bari Mumani ailed; little did she know that obtaining even a widower's match would be like dipping bamboo rods in a well.

The question of Uncle Shujaat's age developed into a delicate one. As far as Aunt Qamar and Aunt Noor were concerned, he was still a young boy. Again and again they misrepresented his real age because if it were known, then the truth about their own ages would come to light, too. Consequently all five sisters directed their attack from different directions; they brought up the matter of her grand-daughter's husband, whose very name was a sore point with Aunt Imtiazi; he had married a second time while his first wife, namely Aunt Imtiazi's grand-daughter, was still living.

But our aunt was a tough customer, and a Mughlani to boot. She, whose father had been a musketeer in the King's army, was not about to admit defeat. Immediately she turned the tables on them and attacked Shehzadi Begum's grand-daughter, who had brought shame upon the family; every day she got into a sedan-chair and travelled to Dhankot to attend school there. In those days, going to school was considered as unseemly as singing or dancing in films today.

Uncle Shujaat was a handsome man. Of average height and lean build, he had sharply delineated features. Aunt Imtiazi had often broadcast that he dyed his hair, but no one had ever seen a single gray hair on his head so that there was no telling when he started using dye. He looked quite young, no more than forty. When inundated with proposals he became confused and handed the matter over to his sisters. All he said was that the bride should not be young enough to pass as his daughter nor should she be bedraggled or senile.

A frenzied search began. In the end Rukhsana's name was drawn.

"Oh God, what a name!" Unable to think of anything else, Aunt Imtiazi decided to criticize the name.

But the others formed a formidable front that prevented her from being heard.

"If the girl's a day older than sixteen you can hit me a hundred times in the morning, a hundred times in the evening, and give me tobacco water to drink." In vain she struggled to bring Goribi's boat ashore.

Once you laid eyes on Rukhsana Begum you could not tear your gaze away; coy like a new moon, it was a face you could look at forever. She was slender and fragile and her colouring shimmered like crystal. So supple you would think there wasn't a bone in it, her body was like kneaded dough smeared with butter. Her femininity gave the impression that she had been imbued with the essence of a dozen women; a warm glow emanated from her person. As Aunt Imtiazi had said, she was probably no more than sixteen, but she looked older, nineteen or twenty perhaps. The sisters informed Uncle that she was twenty-five, and although at first he expressed some reservations, he soon acquiesced; youth was no crime. She was the burden of a poverty-stricken home, and Uncle Shujaat had to bear the expenses for both parties. When she arrived in his house after the wedding ceremony, Uncle observed her closely and broke out in a cold sweat. "She's only a child," he exclaimed nervously to his sisters.

"Dear God, brother! Watch what you say. A middle-aged man and a young wife in her twenties — two or three children later all the silver coating wears off. When surrounded by wet diapers little will remain of this beauty, this colouring or the tiny waist. The arms won't stay as supple either. If she doesn't begin to look your age soon you can punish me as you see fit. I'm sure in another ten years she'll start looking like

Bari Apa."

"And then we'll get a twelve-and-a-half-year-old for our dear brother," sister Noor squealed in delight.

"Hush!" said Uncle blushing.

"A second wife doesn't live long, that's why we're already thinking about a third," Shama Begum spoke up.

"What nonsense is this?"

"Yes, dear brother. It is said the second wife's function is only to make way for the third. That is why people in the old days used to hold a ceremony with a doll the second time around so that when the next bride came, she would be the third."

The sisters offered explanations, and Uncle finally professed understanding. And soon Rukhsana Begum helped to carry that understanding further. In two or three years, a good diet, pretty clothes and a doting husband produced a magical effect on her; the new moon was transformed into a full moon whose brightness blinded all those who set eyes on her. Uncle Shujaat became drunk with the luminescence that radiated from her. It was fortunate he was going to retire soon, or his frequent absences from work would have caused problems.

He was the five sisters' only brother. He lost interest in Bari Mumani while she was still a new bride, and her star was never in the ascendant again. As long as he was alive she longed in vain for his companionship. God did not bless her with a child, so she had nothing with which to occupy her time and attention. Her husband was his sisters' beloved and only brother; if they didn't see him they couldn't rest. It was to them he went after work, staying at one or the other's house for supper. Still, Bari Mumani prepared his meals regularly and waited up for him every night. If, perchance he ate supper with her, she felt fulfilled. Nearly every day there was something special going on at one of the sisters' houses. In the beginning she was sometimes invited to these events, but the unfortunate woman was a misfit there and soon she was no longer asked to come. If Uncle Shujaat was to have a party for his friends, or qawalis and mujras, his wife never heard anything about them. Instead, all preparations were handled by the sisters and he simply handed them whatever money was needed for expenses.

Someone advised Bari Mumani that she ought to prepare delectable meals for her husband if she wanted him to stay at home. Well, she got hold of a number of exotic cookbooks, started making garlic pudding, almond balls, fattened chicken curries and fish kababs, and after having partaken of all of this Uncle came to the conclusion that she was trying to poison him.

Bari Mumani died spitting blood.

But the new bride's magic was undeniable. Uncle Shujaat no longer stayed out and didn't want any visitors either. Husband and wife were constantly alone with each other. What a wonderful brother he had been and how he was changed, like roughened twine now, cruel and uncaring. The world turned bleak for the sisters. They had brought this upon themselves; if they had chosen Gori Begum to be his wife instead, their brother would not have become a stranger to them.

They said to Rukhsana Begum, "My word, sister-in-law, how long can you tie him to your dupatta? He's a man, not a baby you can keep in your lap forever."

Husband and wife were ridiculed. But Rukhsana Begum giggled and her husband stammered like a fool. Completely overwhelmed by her, he stared at her as though she were someone from the neighbourhood and not his own wife.

Uncle was not the same Uncle anymore. Gone were the qawalis and the mujras; their place was taken by Uncle dancing to his wife's music.

"You'll see, it's just a matter of days now. She'll lose all her charm as soon as she's pregnant. One day brother will tire of her." Thus were hearts solaced.

After a prolonged wait Rukhsana Begum became pregnant. But, oh Lord! She experienced neither nausea nor vomiting; the gleam on her face intensified, and she exhibited greater energy than before. She lost neither her playfulness nor the loving manner characteristic of a new bride, so that uncle yearned to draw her into his eyes and present his heart to her on a platter. Instead of tiring of his wife, he daily grew more enchanted with her.

Her beauty did not wane even when she reached full term. Her body expanded, but the moon continued to shine. There was no swelling on her feet, no shadows appeared under her eyes, and no change could be seen in the way she carried herself.

After delivery she was up and about in no time. Not a hair's breadth had been added to her waist, and her body, still like that of a virgin, lost nothing of its pliancy and sprightliness. The best of women lose hair after delivery, but hers grew longer, so much so that she had difficulty washing it by herself.

Uncle, on the other hand, became slack, as if it were he and not his wife who had borne the child. His paunch slid forward somewhat, the long crevices along his cheeks deepened, and his hair became grayer; when he didn't shave the stubble appeared on his face like tiny white ant eggs.

When, two years later, a daughter was born to him, his paunch broadened and the skin under his eyes hung in loose folds. Then, the pain in one of his molars became unbearable and he was forced to have the tooth removed. The whole foundation became shaky with the shifting of a single brick.

That was the time when Aunt Rukhsana's wisdom tooth appeared.

Uncle Shujaat's dentures were more attractive than his real teeth. The workings of old age were attributed to an attack of flu.

According to Aunt Imtiazi's calculations, Aunt Rukhsana was now twenty-six years old, although when she romped with the children, she looked no more than sixteen. It was as if she had stopped growing older; like a stubborn mule her age seemed to resist moving further. Her sisters-in-law felt their hearts were being sawed. It's true that when you become weary yourself, the energy of young people disturbs you; you feel like you've been kicked by a headstrong horse, and Aunt Rukhsana was not being fair at all. In keeping with the tenets of decency and good behaviour, she should have stood by her husband in good times and bad. It wasn't at all proper that while he was hunched over with fatigue, she should run vigorously after the chickens in the courtyard.

"Now, sister-in-law, God give you sense — have you any idea what you're doing, running crazily after those hens?"

"What can I do, Aunt, the cursed cat ..."

"Dear me! Just listen to her! Since when have I become your aunt? Brother Shajan is, by God's grace, older than me, and an older brother is like a father. So you, being his wife, are an elder too. Don't ever call me 'Aunt' again."

"Yes, of course ..." Before Aunt Rukhsana got married to Uncle Shujaat, her mother and her sister-in-law called each other 'sister'.

The beauty and youth which had once enslaved Uncle Shujaat now began to rankle in his eyes. When a crippled child is unable to keep up with his playmates, he turns on them and accuses them of cheating. Aunt Rukhsana was betraying him; sometimes when he saw her laughing and frolicking in the company of young girls, he felt waves of pain take hold of him and it seemed to him that he was slowly burning to a cinder.

"You're sticking your chest out to attract young men, aren't you?" He started spitting poison. "Why don't you find someone young for yourself?"

At first she laughed off his sarcasm, then she blushed and reddened. This infuriated Uncle more, and he hurled even worse taunts and accusations at her.

She became silent. Tears flowed thickly from her eyes; dragging her dupatta from the line she covered her body with it and quietly withdrew into her room. Uncle felt terrible; the earth under him seemed to heave. He went to her and begged forgiveness, kissed the soles of her feet, rubbed his head on them, cried and apologized. "I'm a low-down person, a bastard, take your sandal and hit me as much as you want, my life, my Rukhi, my queen, my princess."

And draping her silvery arms around his neck,

Aunt Rukhsana wept noisily. He said, "I love you too much, my life. I burn with envy and jealousy. My blood boils even when you take the baby in your lap. I feel like wringing his neck. Please forgive me, my love." And Aunt Rukhsana forgave him right away; indeed she continued to forgive him until the shadows under his eyes darkened, and for a long time afterward he huffed and puffed like an exhausted mule.

Soon a time came when he no longer begged forgiveness, and stayed away from her in anger many days at a stretch. The sisters became hopeful.

"Brother is destroying dear sister-in-law. It won't be long before all this ends in disaster."

Cloistered in her room, Aunt Rukhsana wept for hours. The redness in her tearful eyes only added to her loveliness, her pale skin reminded one of gold which a dishonest goldsmith had adulterated with silver, and her whitened lips, along with the stray strand of hair on her forehead, created a picture that drove onlookers to madness. This vision of melancholy beauty caused Uncle's shoulders to droop further; the desolation in his eyes grew.

There's a vine — *amar bel* — which has green serpentine tendrils. These tendrils entwine themselves around the healthy, broad trees trunk and the vine burgeons by drawing sap from the tree. As it grows and flourishes, the tree beings to shrivel and die.

As Rukhsana Begum's foliage flowered, Uncle became weaker. The sisters whispered among themselves. Their brother's speedily failing health troubled them deeply. He had weakened, and to add to the problems resulting from arthritis, was an oft- recurring cold. Doctors warned about the dangers of hair dye. Perforce he was compelled to begin using henna instead.

Poor Rukhsana! She went from person to person asking for a formula for turning hair gray. Someone suggested she use perfumed oil. When the fragrance of umber wafted into Uncle Shujaat's nostrils, he levelled the most filthy accusations against her. If she didn't have the children to think of, she would have killed herself by jumping into a well. Instead of graying, her hair grew softer and shinier, the tresses threatening Uncle like a snake.

To counteract Aunt Rukhsana's youth, Uncle began using Grecian drugs, aphrodisiacs and oils. For a few days his speeding youth paused and took a rest, his energy returned. Rukhsana, who had never been trained in the ways of the world, was like a flower growing wild; although twenty-eight now, she behaved like an inexperienced and uninhibited sixteen-year-old.

You can burn out the engine if you overwork a car; when the side effects of the drugs he had been taking manifested themselves, Uncle collapsed. Old age fell upon him in one stroke. If he had not taxed his mind and body to such an extent he would not be drowning at sixty-two. He looked much older than his years.

The sisters wept unceasingly. Doctors and hakims no longer offered much hope. There were many remedies for momentarily halting old age, but no one could come up with a drug which poor Rukhsana could take to hasten the process of aging. Without doubt, there was either a jinn or a saint who was in love with her and prevented her from growing older. Charms and amulets failed to work; all hopes were dashed.

The *amar bel* continued to flourish.

The banyan tree continued to dry up.

One can tear a picture into pieces and throw it away, a statue can be smashed to bits, but if it's a clay form shaped by God's hands, beautiful and alive, its every breath heavy with the spirit of youth, it can't be destroyed easily. There's only one way to bring down this rising sun: starve it. No more eggs, butter, meat or milk for her. Ever since Uncle Shujaat's digestive system suffered a breakdown, Rukhsana had cooked meat and the like only for the children, taking a small portion for herself from their food. Not anymore. Everyone was quite sure that the onset of middle age would now be hastened.

"Listen here, sister-in-law, why wear this shalwar-qamis? It's a young girl's dress," her sister-in-law remarked. "Why don't you put on something more in keeping with your age, something more elaborate."

Aunt Rukhsana donned an embroidered dupatta and gharara.

"Are you readying yourself to warm a lover's arms?" Uncle twisted a poisoned dart in her heart, and she became fearful of clothes as well.

"Look here, sister-in-law, why this occasional prayer? You should be saying your prayers five times a day . . ."

Rukhsana started praying five times a day.

"Are you praying for my death?" Uncle asked.

She was already quite slim, but the day-to-day harassment made her thinner. Abstinence from butter and meat improved her colouring, her skin became clearer and transparent like crystal. Her face became radiant as if illuminated by some inner light. At first those who saw her had lusted after her; now they wanted a place at her feet. When, after morning prayers, she sat down to read the Quran, her face appeared to be suffused with the piety of the Virgin Mary and the purity of Fatima Zehra. And at that moment, her youth more marked than ever, she looked truly virginal.

Uncle's grave moved closer to him and he abused her cruelly, accusing her of having liaisons with nephews, of trying to seduce jinns and angels; he swore she was trying to ensnare jinns, and insisted she was receiving magical herbs from them to keep herself young.

He developed an allergy to henna, every application to his hair resulting in violent fits of sneezing followed by a cold. He had already come to dislike henna. When Aunt Rukhsana applied it on his hair, the tips of her fingers were stained with colour despite her attempts to be careful, and Uncle Shujaat felt that her fingers were stained with his blood. The very hands which he had once compared to unopened jasmine buds he now regarded as the claws of a dangerous red falcon threatening to gouge out his eyes. But the more he rubbed her nose in the dirt, the more she gave out a sandalwood-like fragrance.

The sisters, suspicious that their sister-in-law might be trying to poison their brother, brought him special foods which they proceeded to feed him under close personal supervision. But these foods only helped to worsen his condition. Chronic haemorrhoids flared up again and drained him of more blood. Lingering still were the effects of the ill-fated drug he had procured the previous winter from a well-known hakim in Muradabad, and for which he had paid many hundred rupees. It was a formula so potent that it could have breathed life into a corpse. But it only succeeded in causing Uncle's skin to erupt in sores like a tumescent gum tree.

Poor, sad Rukhsana strained butter a hundred times, blended sulphur with medicated powders and regularly applied the mixture to his sores. She boiled neem leaves in large pots of water and used the water to wash the pus day and night. Some of the sores had developed into chronic ulcers and had begun to consume Uncle.

And then one day something awful happened. Uncle had become extremely weak. His sisters were complaining about their sister-in-law as usual when, God knows from where, Najji, the old crone, walked in. First, mistaking Uncle Shujaat for Grandfather, she tried to flirt with him (a long time ago Grandfather had lavished undue attention on her). The old woman was mad. Grandfather had been dead for nearly twenty years, but she wanted to rekindle ancient dreams in her gummy eyes. Then, after much argumentation and when she finally recognized Uncle, she proceeded to lament Bari Mumani's passing away.

"Oh my, oh my! What a time to go, leaving you alone in old age like this." Suddenly she spotted Aunt Rukhsana who was feeding the pigeons in the courtyard. She made a pretty picture as she sat there with her head tilted to one side, as if posing for a photograph. The pigeons pecked at her glistening, crystal palm while she giggled involuntarily.

"O my God!" the old crone beat her flat chest and cracked her fingers over her ears to ward off ill-luck. "May God protect her from the evil eye! Your daughter's like the moon! If I'm not mistaken she has just started her eighteenth year. Listen, dear ..." She edged closer to Uncle and whispered secretively, "The merchant's boy has just returned from England. I swear by God, it will be the perfect match — sun and moon."

At one time the old hag was a successful matchmaker but she had been out of business for a long time now. As the hair on her head turned gray and she became physically infirm, she began to support herself by begging.

For a while no one was able to make much sense of what she was trying to say. Everyone knew about the merchant's boy who had recently returned from England; no one guessed at first that the strumpet was attempting to arrange a match for Aunt Rukhsana.

"I swear by Imam Hussain, I'll take no less than a pair of bracelets. Shall I go ahead with it?"

When the truth came out it was as if a beehive had been disturbed; guns were directed at the old woman from all sides.

"Dear me, how was I to know? May I rot in hell . . ." The old crone grabbed her sandals and made for the door. As she left she cast a dubious eye at Uncle's dilapidated face and remarked, "Virginity is clearly written on her face."

That day Uncle swore on the Quran that the two children were not his and had been fathered by those others in the neighbourhood with whom Rukhsana Begum flirted.

He wept that night, groaned and tossed as if he were lying on a bed on live coals. Again and again he thought of Bari Mumani, whose hair had turned gray before her time, whose sprightliness and youth were washed away by tears. She had been the image of piety and loyalty, had gathered within herself his share of old age and departed to heaven. If she were alive today he could share with her his henna-covered hair, white at the roots, his blistering sores, his loneliness. Old age would not have troubled him then as much as it did now. They would have grown old together, understood each other's troubles, supported each other.

The *amar bel* grew and flourished; the trunk of the banyan tree was hollowed out; its branches became dry and limp, its leaves fell . . . the vine crawled away to a nearby tree which was alive and green.

What a heart-rending scene it was! Uncle Shujaat's adorned bier lay in the courtyard. His sisters wailed and swooned with grief. Uncle had left his entire property to his sisters.

Aunt Rukhsana leaned against a door, alone, apart from the others. Those who saw her that day proclaimed they had not seen a more beautiful or sadder widow. Her eyes were reddened and heavy-lidded from excessive weeping, her pale, drawn face shone like a topaz. People who came to offer condolences forgot everything and gazed upon her instead. They envied the dead man's fortune.

Rukhsana's face was clouded with helplessness and sorrow. An expression of fear and distress made her appear even more vulnerable. The two children huddled close to their mother who looked like their older sister.

She sat quietly, unmoving, as if she were a masterpiece painted with an unparalleled brush by one of nature's most skilled artists.

Translated by Tahira Naqvi

Kallu

ALTHOUGH not quite seven, Kallu did the work of a grown man. He was shaken out of his sleep early in the morning and, dressed only in an old, tattered shirt in winter with Abba's old woollen cap pulled down over his ears, looking like a midget, dripping at the nose, he promptly set to work. Scared off by the cold water, he was always reluctant to wash his face, and just once in a while he would carelessly rub the tips of his fingers over his teeth which remained permanently coated with a thin film of mildew.

The first thing he did in the morning was to get the stove going. Then he put water on for tea, set the table for breakfast and made a hundred rounds to the door and back carrying butter, bread, then milk and, finally, the eggs — flapping his slippers noisily, he travelled to the kitchen innumerable times. And after the cook had prepared breakfast, Kallu made more trips to the table lugging hot toast and parathas. To ensure their good health, the children (nearly all of whom were Kallu's age), were forcibly fed porridge, milk, eggs, toast and jam while Kallu quietly looked on. When breakfast was over he sat alone in the kitchen and ate left-over burnt ends of toast and paratha, hurriedly downing them with some tea.

His next task involved taking care of small errands

around the house: he polished Maliha bi's pumps, scouted for Hamida bi's ribbons, located Akhtar Bhai's socks, recovered Salima bi's book-bag, fetched Mumani Jan's katha from the almirah, and retrieved Abba's cigarette case from beside his pillow. In short, he spun around like a top until everyone had left for either the office or school. Later, he washed Nanhi's dirty diapers, and then settled down to play with Safia bi; in between he made trips to the front door to receive mail from the mailman or to inquire the name of a visitor at the door. Around midday the cook handed him peas to shell or spinach to rinse. At lunch time he repeatedly dashed to the dining table with hot rotis, giving the baby's cradle a little push every now and then on the way. What more can I say? He came to this household at a very young age, did the work of a bearer and a sweeper, and all this for two rupees a month along with some old, ragged cast-offs. His mother lived in the village and had entrusted him to our care; he would at least have enough to eat, she thought. She herself worked as a cook for the village zamindar.

She visited him sometimes, usually at the Teej festival, and brought him molasses and parched wheat or fried corn. She too put him to work.

"Dear boy, come here and scratch my back."

"Son, bring me some water."

"Get some roti from the kitchen, son. And ask the cook for a little dal as well."

"Rub down my back, boy."

"Rub my shoulders."

"Massage my head."

The truth was, his little hands executed a great foot massage, and once he started you didn't want him to stop; often he would have to continue massaging the entire afternoon. Sometimes he dozed off and fell on your legs. A kick was generally enough to awaken him.

Kallu had no time to play. If, for some reason, he had a little respite between errands, he would be found slumped with exhaustion, silently staring into space like an idiot. Seeing him sitting like this, looking so foolish, someone or the other would stick a straw in his ear surreptitiously, and startled, he would bashfully turn to a task that required his attention.

Preparations for Maliha bi's wedding were under way. There was talk of weddings all day long—who's going to marry whom, how did so-and-so marry so-and-so, and who should marry whom. "Who're you going to marry, Nanhi?" Mumani would jokingly ask.

"Apa," lisped Nanhi, sending everyone into fits of laughter.

"Who're you going to marry, Kallu?" Amma asked in jest one day.

Kallu revealed his yellow teeth in a shy grin. When he was pressed for an answer he lowered his eyes and whispered, "Salima bi."

"May you rot in hell! You stupid fool! A curse on your face!" Peeved by the laughter around her, Mumani proceeded to box Kallu's ears.

Then one day, while he and Salima were playing, Kallu asked her, "Salima bi, will you marry me?"

"Ye ... es," Salima nodded vigorously, her little head bobbing up and down.

Mumani, sitting in the sunny part of the courtyard, combing her hair, was privy to this exchange between Kallu and her daughter. Livid with anger, she removed her sandal from her foot and smacked him one with it. A blow landed in the wrong place, Kallu's nose began to bleed and soon blood was streaming down the side of his face. Kallu's mother, who was visiting at the time, saw the blood and screamed that her son had been murdered.

"Get out of my house, you hypocrite!" Mumani yelled and ordered both mother and son out. Kallu's mother wept and begged forgiveness, but her pleas went unheeded.

The years went by swiftly. As with other servants who came after him, Kallu too was forgotten. Maliha was now a mother. Hamida bi never married. Half the family had migrated to Pakistan, the other half remained here in India. Nanhi, Safia and Salima, having completed their education, were now waiting to get married. But husbands were difficult to come by.

Our uncle, Chacha Mian, was constantly on the lookout for eligible young men. He moved in official circles and had arranged a match for Maliha, but he too was helpless now. These were bad times; nice young men were nearly impossible to find, and those who were around demanded that a car and fare to England be included in the dowry. Such demands could be taken into consideration only if there was one girl in the family to be wed. But here there were many. Also, the loss of land had resulted in a lowering of status and income, and there were no parties any more, no fancy get-togethers; how were young girls to meet eligible young bachelors? Nonetheless, if a rare party did come around, Chacha Mian saw to it that the girls attended. And so, when a dinner was held in honour of Mr. Din, the new Deputy Collector, preparations in our house began several days in advance.

Mr. Din was a bachelor, and the eyes of all the mothers of unwed girls in the city were focused on him. We were stunned when we saw him. He was over six feet tall, had a wheatish complexion, very attractive features, and teeth which shone like real pearls. During introductions, he suddenly quietened at the mention of Salima's name and then quickly moved away from our group to chat with the other guests.

Chacha Mian approached us with an expression of bafflement on his face just as we were getting ready to leave.

"Do you know who this Mr. Din is?" he asked.

"The Deputy Collector, who else" Mumani answered gruffly.

"No, no. I mean, did you recognize him? My dear, he's our own Kallu."

"Kallu?" Mumani crinkled her nose.

"Yes, yes, Kallu. Kalimuddin. This is too much!"

"You mean that little midget who was our houseboy?"

"Yes, the very same, the one who suffered a beating at your hands." Chacha Mian guffawed.

"My God! What's wrong with the government? It seems just about anyone can land a job with it these days! But how did this happen?"

"Why not? He's a Qureshi, that's a good caste, and he even submitted to your beating when the need arose," my mother said in a mocking tone.

"Well, in that case why don't you give him your daughter in marriage?" Mumani spoke archly.

"I wish my daughters were so fortunate," Amma said. "I'd be only too happy to have him for a son-in-law. But why would he want to have anything to do with a family at whose hands he suffered such humiliation? Ayesha, his mother, left him with us so he could become somebody. But you turned him into a servant."

Chacha Mian said, "And the poor woman worked hard, sewed clothes, washed people's dirty dishes and finally succeeded in raising him to such heights. People are willing to present him their daughters on a silver platter."

"May they perish who do—I don't need him," said Mumani sullenly.

One day Chacha Mian arrived at our house in his usual state of nervous agitation.

"We were at the club, talking, and before I knew it, Kalimuddin walked out of there with me as I was leaving. Make some tea, anything!"

Amma ran towards the kitchen, but Mumani, a grimace firmly set on her face, didn't budge. The girls became pale; Salima was especially perturbed. We wondered whether 'Kalim Saheb' should be asked to come in or the ladies be sent to the lawn, or Chacha Mian be allowed to handle everything by himself.

"He's here for revenge," Maliha said with mock seriousness, and Mumani shivered. Salima's face was drained of colour.

"I don't care what happens," Amma said, he's here, which means he's a decent person, and we should respond with the same sort of generosity."

"No, I don't want to be humiliated," Mumani growled. "You are welcome to take your own girls — none of mine is going to stir from here. He's just here to show off his superiority."

"I won't go either. I'm already married," Maliha said with a laugh.

Finally it was decided that we would all go and, of Mumani's daughters, only Maliha would accompany us.

"What's he going to think, such uncivilized people!" Upset and bewildered, Chacha Mian started grumbling.

We arrived in the lawn to find 'Kalim Saheb' engaged in a lively conversation about the past with the old gardener, who smiled sheepishly, somewhat embarrassed, a little uncomfortable.

"Midu Chacha, remember how you used to holler, 'Wate .... er!' at the front door and immediately I used to pull a sheet in front of Dulhan bi (that's what he called Mumani) for purdah? Tell me truthfully, did you ever sneak a look through the sheet?" He burst into laughter, and then, seeing us approach, quickly turned to greet us.

While we were having tea he said, "Maliha bi, do you remember how you boxed my ears for not brushing my teeth regularly?"

Maliha blushed.

"No matter how unpleasant one's childhood has been, one always remembers it like a wonderful dream," he said. "All of you probably forgot about me, but I didn't forget you."

We talked for a long time afterwards, shared jokes and laughed. His carefree manner put us at ease in no time.

"Give my regards to Dulhan bi," he said before he left.

"She's not feeling well," Maliha lied.

He laughed, "Forgive me, but I have a very sharp

memory. I remember that when Dulhan bi was angry with someone she took ill. Well, I have to go, I have a dinner engagement tonight. I'll come again another time."

We talked about 'Kalim Saheb' late into the night.

"What if he proposes . . ." Chacha Mian spoke with some hesitation.

"He'd better stay away from my girls," Mumani retorted curtly.

"Why?" Amma was irritated.

"Because I say so!"

This was all artifice on her part; only God knew what was really going on in Mumani's heart.

Salima became tearful. Everyone had been teasing her.

A month passed. We had almost forgotten about 'Kalim Saheb' when suddenly he arrived at our house one day with Chacha Mian. This time Chacha Mian informed only Maliha and myself of his presence in the lawn.

"He wants to see his crochety Dulhan bi," Chacha Mian said.

"And she won't let him come near her."

We decided that since Mumani would never agree to a meeting voluntarily, the best course of action would be to just bring him in and surprise her.

"My dears, she's a witch! There'll be no place to hide my face if she insults him." Chacha Mian spoke fearfully.

"Don't worry," Maliha said, "She's not a child. I'll go and get her and you bring him in."

Our hearts beat uncontrollably. What if Mumani exploded like a bomb? Except for Maliha and me, all the other girls disappeared into the house.

'Kalim Saheb' walked into the room to find Mumani engrossed in cleaning her paan dan; her back was turned to him.

"Maliha, listen girl, get me the bowl of katha from the cupboard in the kitchen, will you," she called out.

He took the bowl of katha from Maliha and handed it to Mumani. She extended her hand towards it and said, "And some water, too."

Just then she lifted her eyes and found him standing by her side. "*Adab*." He whispered the salutation nervously and kept his eyes glued to the floor.

"God bless you," she responded in a deadened tone and started spooning out katha from the bowl. "Are you well?"

"I am fine, with your blessing."

"Why are you standing? Sit down," she ordered dryly.

He sat on the far side of the charpoy, on the *adwan*.

"Oh-ho! Not there, you will break the *adwan*!" she yelled. He jumped up hastily.

When 'Kalim Saheb' sent a message requesting Salima's hand in marriage, she was unrelenting. "Come hell or high water, I won't give him Salima," she said.

"But why?" Chacha Mian and the others pressed for a reason.

"Who're you to ask? I've decided I won't, and that's that!" she said obstinately.

'Kalim Saheb' said he hadn't taken no from life, and he wasn't going to take no from the old lady either. Determined to get his way, he boldly stationed himself on a chair next to Mumani's bed one day. All of us gathered around them with great interest, as if a fight between two wrestlers in a ring was about to commence. "I'm going to make myself very clear," he spoke firmly.

Mumani frowned.

"You're turning the tables on him, Dulhan bi — that's not fair," Chacha Mian interjected.

"Don't say anything, Chacha Mian, I'll take care of this myself."

'Kalim Saheb' brushed Chacha Mian aside and turned to Mumani. "At least tell me what my crime is, Dulhan bi?" he complained."

"Dulhan bi! Hunh! As long as you call me Dulhan bi . . ." Mumani muttered indignantly.

"Amma bi . . ." he began in a tearful voice.

Mumani's eyes also filled with tears. She began scolding us.

"Is this a circus? Why are you standing around watching like idiots? I know these girls won't be any help with the wedding arrangements. I'll have to take care of everything myself, as usual. Useless, these girls are, good-for-nothing!"

Mumani's cantankerous chastisement fell upon our ears like the sound of wedding trumpets.

Translated by Tahira Naqvi

Chhoti Apa

EVERYBODY knows it's wicked, but how delicious it is to sometimes steal a little something when no one's looking. Secret letters, old scraps of paper, notebooks, precious possessions that people stash away in the folds of old clothing. How delectable if one could lay one's hands on these goodies!

The weather was unusually warm and oppressive. Fed up of Chhoti Apa's lectures, I began browsing through her old books. What superb inscriptions. What an impression she had left on her teachers! Enviable. Last month when the Principal wrote an ambiguous remark on my card, Chhoti Apa burst into a lecture- tirade, "Wild, ill-mannered, insensitive. This trash you read has turned your head! Weak-willed fool, tossed around by the tide." I wanted to hit right back: "What the hell? Who are you? I will do exactly . . . " Suddenly my eye was caught by a few musty sheets thrust inside a crevice. Useful discovery. Ha! Chhoti Apa's diary. A few missing pages were not enough to spoil the anticipation of romance. Just a little effort on my part and wham! My wonderful sibling's myth had exploded!

Written on the first page:

1. *Today, why do I long to pour my heart out to someone? There is Apajan. Talks in breathless whispers to*

her friends. I wonder what the hell she talks about? Does she get the same sensations as me in her heart, mind and body? Hell, who will hear my story? Shammo, the bitch, will laugh her head off, and pour the entire tale into Apajan's ear. Next, Amma will find out. Then in a moment of amorousness she will tell Abba. Then I'll be torn to shreds. God forbid. Today I feel compelled to blurt it all out. Vomit it into my pillow. How quickly these pleasant reveries will soak into the old moth-eaten stuffing. Amma ... she has a passion for taking apart old stuffing. My story will scatter into wisps of old cotton ...

So, today I was putting a leash around the neck of the black puppy when he appeared out of nowhere.

"Why strangle this poor wretch?"

My grip slackened, the pup ran off.

"What if anyone strangled you?" A hand at my neck. I ran.

Chhoti Apa's romances were most amusing. I read on.

2. Now what am I to do? Was taking a glass of milk for Bhaiya ... "Now where will you run?" Materialising out of thin air he stood, arms outstretched, blocking my path.

Lathering his face, he put a great quantity of shaving foam on mine!

3. Amma says Shaukat is very shy! Shy my ... ! His eyes. How they rove and pierce, pierce and rove. Scared the daylights out of me in the upstairs gallery.

"Some people are bloody scared. As if I would swallow you whole." Heart pounding, I ran like a thief. Wanted to cry, but no outlet. Sat concealed behind the lamp during dinner. No — I am not bloody scared. Of the mouse, yes, because it suddenly leaps out at me. But seeing him, well ... makes my whole body a playground for leaping mice.

Gave him a glass of water, and yes ... promised to knit him a sweater. Midnight, and I was still knitting to keep my word. Amma complains that I keep the lights on until very very late. Electricity bill has gone up to Rs. 13! If her favourite daughter reads her trashy novels all night, the bill does not add up!

4. Wherever I go he sneaks up behind me. How quietly and expertly he pinches. Amma says that I am shameless. .. Talking back whenever they discuss my marriage. If I am shameless why do I find the stairs leading to his room so insurmountable? No matter how hard I try, I cannot climb up. Once, having made the heroic ascent, I started rummaging through the cupboards. Looking for ... my lost senses! He did not speak one single word. I ran.

"Listen."

"Just coming." Snatching a few useless items I stumbled out, panting.

At the foot of the stairs I caught my breath, "How can I go upstairs again? Eye of the needle. Damn! Hovered around the stair-well. No guts, no guts. Put one foot forward, and the sweeper arrived to mop the stairs. End of effort. Took a deep breath ... the parrot spoke, "Mith-thu!" Almost fell over. Blast the bastard. Cat should swallow him up. Seeing Amma appear, started ripping out the neckline of a perfectly good shirt. "Why is this neckline being ripped open?" Her tone was acid. Heart sank.

"Tight," I mumbled. My fingers clawed at the stitches, as if the shirt was strangling me.

"It was perfectly alright. Now rip it apart so that half your bosom can show. Such plunging necklines are poison." Wrinkling her nose in disapproval she sat down right there at the foot of the stairs. How could Abba ever have endured Amma, I thought? He should have married Aunt Rahat. Oh God! He will be gone for three years. Wonder when *he'll come back?*

6. At the time of his departure, Amma embraced, Apa kissed. Apa really gets away with murder. She finds every excuse to closet herself with Rasheed Bhai. The moment you enter the room they spring apart. What the hell are they up to, these two? No one thinks of asking her, "Sweetheart, are your molars out yet?"

7. Flipping a few blank pages of life. I cannot remember such a long lesson — history, geography and seventeen questions.

8. Went to a movie with Mahmood. Was reminded of the last time. His hat on my lap, for which his fingers searched time and again. Cigarette and petrol, what a strange mixture in my nostrils. God knows what Mahmood smokes. Smells like burnt cowdung cakes.

9. Mahmood, what a strange guy!

10. During dinner, Mahmood's feet dance under the table. Creeping snakes! Looking intently at his plate he devours his food, the picture of innocence. . . . not responsible for the footwork going on under the table! Like nooses, his legs get hooked here and there.

11. Delightful trip to Delhi. A thousand stairs, almost broke my ankles. Why can't they instal a lift? So bloody dark in here.

12. His Eid gift was a stud for my nose! Was this the only thing he could find for me? And that too with my pierce having closed a while back. Mahmood found a god-given excuse to get even with me. All day he went around suggesting that my nose be pierced with a screw-driver, paper-cutter or industrial needle. I wrote, "This is useless." He also wrote, "This is indeed useless because this girl needs a stronger noose. Send her a massive stud!" What a marvellous gift to look forward to!

13. Shaukat's letter is so engrossing, *like a bloody*

confusing crossword puzzle. Makes me sick!

14. Mahmood says, "In one week I will teach you swimming." The waves at night are like fire-spitting dragons rising from the ocean; my body heats up. Mahmood always threatens to drown me. New bathing suit; all torn. Must buy blue knitting wool.

15. Shaukat writes that life is a vehicle. I think of that fat female who covets the winding stair. The vehicle runs on two wheels, Shaukat says. Him and me. What a horrible thought. I am not a beast; how will I pull my share of the cart?

16. Went for a game of cricket. What a stupid game. Why does the bowler always aim at my nose? I had to lump it, thanks to Askari. What rough hands he has. Feels like he'll break all my fingers.

17. Went for a ride behind Askari on his motor-cycle. Mahmood got wildly jealous. Who cares!

18. Askari burnt my arm with his cigarette. Then wanted to heal the burn. I said to him, hands off. He said, "Honestly ... in two seconds. Tell Mahmood he is an expert." I slapped his face. Talks such nonsense. Will come for dinner tomorrow.

19. Riding behind Askari, a long way from home. Sometimes life is so wonderful, I want to ride forever on its cresting wave. The entire universe should stand still. Ears blocked, eyes closed. Sightless, soundless. Each leaf should become motionless. Only one sound should be heard — the beating of our two hearts, all the rest should drown. Where is that blue handkerchief? Askari had it tied around his neck. This hair, always in my face!

20. Again, Askari forgot the handkerchief. I fought twice with Mahmood. If he failed his exam. . . . Hell! did I ask him to teach me Algebra instead of cramming?

21. Shaukat is to be engaged to Razia. Felt slightly

heartbroken. Tauba! Tauba! A real dog in the manger!

22. When he throws the ball, Askari appears ruthless. Teeth clenched, eyebrows knitted, silk shirt plastered to his body with sweat. Mahmood's nose is covered with sweat. Makes me puke.

23. Tara, the bitch! Started drooling over Askari. As if Askari had not heard everything about her. Is there any fellow she has not lusted after?

24. No news of Askari for two days. Heard he's gone to Delhi.

We consider ourselves alive by virtue of living in this world. But one shock and we realise what it's all about! Life begets life. Stone strikes against stone and a flame is born. Flame which first burns, turns to ash, then fertilizes. Along the mountain slopes the rain-forests start swaying in the wind. Askari is the rock. The volcanic rock.

25. Fickle. How fickle these men are! A parrot's roving eye momentarily focuses on one object. But their eyes, blue, black, brown, flecked, are like a spinning top on an endless spin. Directionless, the spinning top. The kibla is in all directions.

26. Why is there nothing visible in the world? The only visible objects are Askari's blue eyes. Gone for six months. What a long tour!

27. Both letters were returned. Askari has probably gone on a tour of Europe. Throws the ball as if he will first grind it between his teeth. Squeeze, bounce and a long throw! Instantly another ball appears between his fingers.

28. Shaukat has had a son. Why do I care? Wasn't snatched from me. Lovely child.

Pae mera lung neest
Mulk-e-Khuda tung neest.
My leg is not maimed
This Kingdom of God is not narrow!

29. Love should not be left to rot in the grave and become a feast for worms. Love is a restless flame. Once it begins its magnificent dance, the entire universe is subsumed in its embrace. A massive river, once its rises, slices gigantic rocks, uproots trees and drowns deserts. People say that true love occurs only once in a life-time. But define this word "once". Man is a spinning top. Kibla is everywhere. Love has eyes at the back of its head.

In my small world of love, how many Shaukats, Mahmoods, Abbases, Askaris, Yunuses and others have been shuffled together in a pack of cards and spread out. Which one is the knave? Shaukat's hungry eyes, filled with tales? Mahmood's snake-like creeping limbs? Askari's ruthless hands? Is it the mole beneath Yunus' lower lip? Or is it Abbas' vague smile? A thousand broad chests, high foreheads, thick hair, smooth ankles, strong arms. All are jumbled together like freshly spun threads. Helplessly, I look at that entangled mess. Which end shall I pull so that it disentangles into a long skein upon which I can ride and reach out to the horizon?

Crumpled scraps of paper adding up to a beautiful life were gathered before me. Amazed, I started feeling its contours. Chhoti Apa . . . !

Chhoti Apa was cleaning the baby's bottles. Ahmed Bhai was calling her into the drawing room to meet his friends.

She sat quietly in one corner of the sofa, the end of her sari drawn modestly over her hair. "Why are you so shy? Modern girls leave the men light years behind." His sarcastic reference to me did not go unnoticed. But I was busy looking at Chhoti Apa. Like the motionless illusion of a madly spinning top, she was staring vacantly into space. Piled up before her still was that mess of entangled threads and she was looking carefully for a secure end upon which she could fasten herself.

To divert attention, I passed a cup of tea to Ahmed Bhai's most debonair friend.

Translated by Syeda Hameed

The Rock

WHEN Bhabhi came to our house as a bride, she was no more than fifteen. She still had some growing-up to do; in Bhaiya's presence she trembled like a cow about to be butchered. But within a year she was transformed from a tight-lipped bud to a flower. Her body filled out, her hair became more lustrous, and the hunted look in her eyes was replaced by a look of confidence and mischief.

Bhabhi came from a liberal family and had been schooled at a convent. The previous year her sister had eloped with a Christian, so her parents, worried that she might do something similar, took her out of school and quickly married her off.

Having been raised in a modern household, she was as playful as a doe. But her parents and her in-laws were keeping a close eye on her now. Bhaiya was anxious to set her up as a housewife without delay because he was afraid that even though she was married, she might still follow in her sister's footsteps. As a result, he earnestly embarked on the task of moulding her into a homemaker.

In four or five years, with everyone's help, she turned into a complete housewife. As the mother of three children she became overweight and ungainly. Amma fed her chicken soup and sweets and Bhaiya furnished tonics; with each child Bhabhi gained ten or fifteen pounds.

Gradually she stopped using make-up. Bhaiya hated lipstick, and the sight of mascara or kohl on a woman's eyes infuriated him. But he liked pink and red. So Bhabhi generally wore pink or red clothes; red sari with a light-pink blouse, or a pink sari with a red blouse.

She had short hair when she got married. But now it was plastered down and tied at the back so that no one could tell that the bride was a short-haired *mem*. Her hair had grown since then but had become thin because of frequent pregnancies. She usually kept it tied in a pony tail with a dirty old rag. Her husband found her pleasing just the way she was, untidy and bedraggled. And her parents and in-laws also praised her simplicity. She was pretty, no doubt. Fine features, a butter-white complexion and small, dainty hands and feet. But she had let herself go and her body slackened like dough left out overnight.

Bhaiya was nine years her senior, but compared to her he looked really young. Still quite slim, with a well-kept figure, he exercised daily, carefully monitored his diet, smoked only on occasion, and once in a while took a sip of whisky or beer. He was still boyish in appearance. Although he was thirty-one, he didn't look a day older than twenty-five.

Oh, how Bhaiya hated jeans and skirts! He was also repelled by the sight of tight shirts hugging the body and particularly despised shalwars that were tight at the ankles. Anyway Bhabhi, poor thing, couldn't get into shalwar and qamis anymore, and generally went around the house dressed in a blouse and petticoat with a dressing-gown thrown over them. If an informal guest arrived, she stayed as she was, and if someone special came to the house unexpectedly, she chose to stay in her room with the children. When forced to make an appearance, she would come out wearing a rumpled, mousy-coloured sari. She was a housewife, a daughter-in-law, and she was everyone's darling; why should she dress up and deck herself out like a prostitute to please people?

And it's quite possible that Bhabhi would have continued in this bedraggled and untidy state until she became middle-aged and then old; she would have brought home daughters-in-law who would come to her every morning, respectfully offer salutations and then deposit her grandson into her lap to hold and play with. But God had other plans.

It was evening. We were all having tea in the lawn. Bhabhi had gone to the kitchen to fry papads. The cook had over-fried them and Bhaiya liked them lightly browned. He glanced lovingly at Bhabhi and she immediately got up to go to the kitchen to fry some more for him. We calmly continued drinking tea. Ah, what was Bhabhi but an angel! I could never be persuaded to go to the kitchen after I returned from college, and my evening clothes were especially unsuited for cooking. In addition, I didn't know how to fry papads. My sisters were also in the same boat as I. Farida was entertaining her fiance who had come for a visit; Razia and Shameem were busy chatting with their friends and certainly they couldn't be expected to fry papads. Anyway, we were all little birds in our parents' home, testing our wings for flight.

"Boom!" The football landed right over Bhaiya's cup. We all jumped. Bhaiya snapped angrily: "Who is this idiot?" He was looking in the direction from where the ball had come.

A round curly-haired head and a pair of large eyes appeared over the hedge. In one leap Bhaiya was over the hedge and the culprit's hair was in his grasp.

"Ohhh!" the sound of a scream filled the air and in the next instant Bhaiya reared as if stung by a scorpion, or as if he had taken hold of a live coal.

"Sorry ... I'm very sorry ..." he was stuttering. All of us ran to see what was going on. Standing on the other side of the hedge was a slight, fair-complexioned girl dressed in white drain-pipes and a lemon-coloured blouse; she was running her slender fingers through short hair cut Marilyn Monroe style, and laughing sheepishly. We started laughing, too.

Bhabhi returned with the plate of papads and, presuming there was something funny going on, joined in our laughter without really knowing what had happened. Her loose stomach bounced as she laughed. And when she discovered Bhaiya had mistaken Shabnam for a boy and had caught her by the hair, she laughed even louder and pieces of papad went flying from the plate in her hand and landed on the grass. Shabnam informed us she had arrived at her Uncle, Shahid Jamil's house that very morning and when she got bored doing nothing, came out to play with a football which, as luck would have it, landed on Bhaiya's cup.

Shabnam was staring at Bhaiya with her sharp, mascara-laden eyes. Stunned into magical silence, Bhaiya was gazing at her. There was a current darting between them. Cut off from this current, Bhabhi seemed to be miles away from them; her bouncing stomach became fearful and was stilled. Laughter stumbled on her lips and died. Her hands became limp, the plate tilted to one side, and the papads slid and fell on the grass. All of a sudden Bhaiya and Shabnam awakened and returned from the world of dreams.

"Come and have some tea," I said, giving the still atmosphere a little nudge.

In one graceful leap Shabnam swung over the hedge to our side. Tiny moccasins began prancing on the green grass like a pair of doves. Her complexion glowed like molten gold. Her hair was jet black, but her eyes reminded one of small black goblets filled with honey. The neckline of her lemon blouse was very low. Her lips were pink, a model for an American ad. Although she appeared to be much taller than Bhabhi, the difference in their heights couldn't have been more than two inches. She had a delicate bone structure, which is why her waist looked like it could fit into a ring.

Bhaiya sat lost in silence. Bhabhi was watching him the way a cat watches a bird getting ready to take off, waiting to pounce as soon as it flaps its wings. Her face was red, her lips were pressed together, her nostrils flared.

Without warning Munna came and jumped on her back just then. He always jumped on his mother's back like this, as if he were a soft little pillow, and she always laughed at his antics. *"Tarakh! Tarakh!"* Today she slapped him hard twice.

Shabnam became agitated.

"Oh, stop her, please," she touched Bhaiya's hand. Then she turned to me. "Your mother's easily angered," she said. Introductions are rare in our society. And it seemed strange to introduce Bhabhi. Her appearance was unmistakably that of the daughter-in-law of the house. We all burst out laughing at

Shabnam's remark. Dragging Munna by the hand, Bhabhi went into the house.

"No, no, she's our sister-in-law," I said, watching Bhabhi trudge away.

"Your sister-in-law?" Shabnam looked astounded.

"Bhaiya's wife."

"Oh." She lowered her eyes. "I see, I ..." she continued in a serious tone and then stopped, mid-sentence.

"Bhabhi is twenty-three," I explained.

"But ... don't be silly!" She laughed. At this point Bhaiya got up and left.

"I swear."

"Oh, lack of education ..."

"No. Bhabhi graduated at fifteen from St. Mary's."

"You mean she's three years younger than me? I'm twenty-six."

"In that case, certainly."

"Oh God! And I thought she was your mother. Actually my eyesight is quite bad and I hate wearing glasses. Do you think she's upset?"

"No. Bhabhi's never upset."

"Oh, poor thing."

"Who? Bhabhi?" I don't know why I said that.

"Bhaiya dotes on his wife," Shameem said, coming to Bhabhi's defence.

"The poor man must've been married when he was really young."

"He was twenty-six."

"But I didn't know people in the twentieth century got married without seeing each other first," Shabnam said derisively.

"All your conjectures are incorrect. Bhaiya saw Bhabhi, liked her immensely, and then they were married. But at that time she was as delicate and beautiful as a lily."

"So what happened to her after she got married?"

"What could have happened? Bhabhi is the mistress of her house, queen among her children, not a film actress. At any rate, Bhaiya despises thin, skinny girls." I deliberately took a jab at her. She wasn't stupid.

"Well, I don't care if somebody loves me or not, I'm not about to turn into a baby elephant . . . excuse me, your sister-in-law must have been beautiful once, but now . . ."

"Your viewpoint is entirely different from Bhaiya's," I said evasively.

And when she walked toward the hedge, taking small steps, her lean body swinging, Bhaiya was standing in the verandah. His face was ashen white and again and again he rubbed the back of his neck with his hands as if someone had placed burning cinders on it. She skipped over the hedge like a bird. Turning for a moment, she gave Bhaiya a honeyed look and then disappeared into the bungalow in a flash.

Bhabhi was bent over in the lawn picking up the tea things, but she was the invisible strand that had sprung up between Bhaiya and Shabnam.

One day I saw Shabnam from the window. Dressed in a fluffy red skirt and a white blouse open at the neck, she was dancing the samba with Pappu, her cousin. Her little Pekinese bounded between her legs. She was laughing loudly. Her well-shaped, voluptuous legs pirouetted on the green grass, and her black, silken hair flew in the air. Five year-old Pappu was kicking around like a monkey, but she swayed like an intoxicated female serpent. Once she made a face at me and I showed her my fist. But soon I realized her gesture was not meant for me. Bhaiya was standing in the verandah, massaging the back of his neck, and she was tormenting him with her teasing. Her waist was gyrating, her hips moved from side to side, her arms fluttered, her mouth was open and her lips quivered. She thrust her tongue out like a snake and licked her lips with it. Bhaiya's eyes were gleaming, he revealed his teeth in a grin. My heart convulsed. Bhabhi was in the pantry doling out the daily portion of grain to the cook.

Shabnam, you wretch! I said to myself. But I was also angry with Bhaiya. Why was he grinning? He hated *chrantis* like Shabnam, he was repelled by English dances. Why then did he stand there staring at her? And why was he so overcome that his body moved to the rhythm of the samba without his knowing it?

About this time the houseboy came out to the lawn with tea. Bhaiya summoned all of us and instructed the houseboy to get Bhabhi. A sense of formality compelled us to ask Shabnam to join us. I wanted to turn my face away from her, but when she climbed over the hedge with Munna perched on her shoulders, for some reason she seemed perfectly innocent to me. Munna hung on to her scarf as if it were reins, and she cantered like a horse across the lawn. Bhaiya tried to get Munna off her back, but he clung to her stubbornly.

"Let the horse run some more, Auntie!"

"No, my dear. Auntie's exhausted!" Shabnam yelled.

With great difficulty Bhaiya got Munna off and

smacked his face. Distressed by his action, Shabnam immediately picked up the child and slapped Bhaiya's hand.

"Aren't you ashamed? You as big as a camel, and striking a small child?" Seeing Bhabhi approach she handed Munna over to her. Bhaiya smiled at the slap he had received from Shabnam.

"Look how hard he hit the poor thing. If someone tried to hit my child, I'd break his hand." The honey in her eyes was shot with poison as she glared at Bhaiya. "And on top of everything he's laughing shamelessly!"

"Hunh! Do you have the strength to break someone's hand?" Bhaiya twisted her wrist. She turned and let out such a scream that Bhaiya was alarmed and quickly let go of her. She fell on the grass, gasping with laughter.

Shabnam's antics continued during tea; she behaved like a young, mischievous girl. Bhabhi sat in stunned silence. You would think that threatened with Shabnam's presence, she would start taking care of herself. Not at all. She became more shabby in appearance and ate with added vigour. We were all busy laughing, but she kept her head down and proceeded to devour the cake with intense concentration; she ravenously swallowed fried potatoes dipped in chutney, and rapidly gulped down pieces of toast laden with butter and jam. Bhaiya and Shabnam had become a source of apprehension for us, and Bhabhi must have been worried too, but she was burying her dread in rich foods. Constantly suffering from gastric distress, she nevertheless managed to successfully digest pulao and qorma with the aid of churan. Her gaze fell restlessly upon Shabnam and Bhaiya as they chuckled and talked.

Bhaiya looked younger than before. Every morning and evening he went with Shabnam to swim in the ocean. Bhabhi could also swim quite well, but Bhaiya hated women in bathing suits. One day we were all swimming. Wearing only two tiny strips, Shabnam was executing serpentine moves in the water. Just then Bhabhi, who had been looking for Munna, made an appearance. Bhaiya was in a playful mood. He caught hold of her and together we all pushed her into the water. Since Shabnam's arrival Bhaiya had become quite roguish. He would lovingly grind his teeth and squeeze Bhabhi in front of us, or sometimes he would try to pick her up in his arms, but she slipped from his hands like a large fish, leaving him feeling a little foolish. Perhaps in his imagination it was Shabnam he was lifting in his arms. And, rueful like a butchered cow, Bhabhi would immediately leave the room to start planning the pudding or some other delectable dessert. When she was pushed into the water that day, she slid from our hands like a heavy bundle. Her wet clothes clung to her body and revealed her unshapely figure, a frightening sight; it seemed as though someone had wrapped a comforter around her waist. She didn't look that horrible when dressed in normal clothes.

"Oh God, how fat you are!" Bhaiya exclaimed, squeezing a lump of fat on her buttock. "Oh my goodness! Look at your tummy! You look just like Gama the wrestler."

"Hunh! After four children my waist . . ."

"But I also have four children and my waist hasn't been transformed into a Dunlop tyre." He patted his lean, solid body with his hands. Bhabhi made a sour face and walked away looking like a wet chicken, pulling Munna with her as she dragged her feet heavily in the sand. Ignoring her, Bhaiya proceeded to plonk Shabnam in the water. But Shabnam wasn't going to let him get the better of her; she gave him such a push that he turned upside down with a splash.

When they returned from their swim, they saw Bhabhi arranging a layer of cream over apricot jam. Her head was lowered, her eyes were red, her lips were white, and her doll-like plump cheeks were puffier than usual.

At lunch Bhabhi looked extremely unhappy. She proceeded to consume the apricot jam and cream with ardour. Shabnam looked at the dish and shuddered as though it contained not apricots, but snakes and scorpions.

"It's poison, just poison," she said, nibbling on a slice of cucumber. Bhaiya glared at Bhabhi, but she continued to gobble up the jam noisily.

"This is enough!" he muttered, his nostrils flaring.

Bhabhi paid no attention to him and emptied nearly the entire dish of apricots into her stomach. Seeing her devour the jam in this manner, you felt as if she were building a dam to halt the storm of envy and jealousy. The cream would be converted to granite and make the castle that was her body invincible. And perhaps then her heart would ache no more, and the flames that darted every time Bhaiya's eyes met Shabnam's would lose the power to melt those granite walls.

"Stop, for God's sake! The doctor said you shouldn't — what kind of toothsomeness is this!" Bhaiya finally said. Bhabhi melted like a wall of wax. Bhaiya's remark cut through the layers of fat and plunged right into her heart. Thick tears trickled down her puffy cheeks; sobs wracked the pile that was her body and caused a tremor like an earthquake. Slim, delicate-looking girls look so attractive when they cry. But seeing Bhabhi cry one was amused rather than saddened. She looked like a heap of cotton-wool that was being thrashed with sticks.

Wiping her nose, she started to get up, but we scolded Bhaiya and cajoled her into staying. The poor thing sniffled and sat down again. But as soon as she had deposited three spoonfuls of sugar in her coffee and extended a hand towards the cream, she became inert. With a fearful expression in her eyes she looked at Bhaiya and Shabnam. Shabnam curbed a twitter with great difficulty, and Bhaiya fumed.

Things just got worse after this. Bhabhi openly declared war.

There was a time when her Pathan blood boiled easily and she would come to blows at the slightest provocation. Instead of sulking, often she would attack Bhaiya like a ferocious cat when she was angry with him, and scratch his face and rip his shirt-front with her teeth. Bhaiya would crush her in his arms. Reduced to helplessness, she placed her head on his chest and sobbed like a frightened, thirsty little bird. Then they would make up. Feeling sheepish, she'd lovingly apply tincture to the scratch marks on his face, mend the rips in his shirt and continue looking at him with gratitude.

This was when Bhabhi was as delicate as a butterfly, and when she quarrelled with Bhaiya she reminded one of a little Persian cat. Instead of showing anger, he would express great affection for her. But the attack of blubber had left her blood cold. She rarely lost her temper anymore, and if she did, she'd quickly occupy herself with something or the other and soon forget all about it.

That day, ignoring her heavy, thick-set body, she attacked Bhaiya with full force. Her weight was enough to crush him against the wall. He was repelled by the bouncing heap of flab. He didn't get angry, nor did he raise a clamour. Embarrassed and sad, he lowered his head and bolted from the room. Bhabhi collapsed right there and started weeping.

Matters deteriorated further and one day Bhaiya's brother-in-law came to fetch Bhabhi. Tufail Bhai was Bhabhi's cousin. No sooner did she set eyes on him than she put her arms around him and began crying. He had seen Bhabhi after five years. The sight of the domed figure startled him momentarily, but then he clasped Bhabhi to his chest as if she were a little girl. Bhaiya was at a cricket match with Shabnam that day. Tufail Bhai waited until it was dark. When Bhaiya didn't show up, he instructed Bhabhi to pack her things and get the children ready.

Bhaiya made an appearance for a few moments just as they were leaving.

"I'm handing over the houses in Delhi to her as *mehr*," he addressed Tufail Bhai gruffly.

"*Mehr*?" Bhabhi trembled.

"Yes. And the divorce papers will be forwarded through the lawyer."

"Divorce — who said anything about divorce?"

"That's best for all concerned."

"But ... the children?"

"If she wants she can have them. Otherwise I'll send them to boarding school. I've made arrangements."

With a loud scream Bhabhi lunged toward Bhaiya. But she didn't have the courage to scratch him. Terrified, she stood transfixed. Then she relinquished the last shred of her womanly dignity. She fell at his feet. She begged.

"You can marry her ... I won't say a word. But for God's sake don't give me a divorce. I'll spend the rest of my life like this, I'll never complain."

But Bhaiya glanced hatefully at Bhabhi's quivering obesity and turned away.

"I've already given the divorce. Nothing can be done now."

But who could mollify Bhabhi? She continued to lament.

"You fool!" Tufail Bhai pulled her up in one jerk. "You idiot, get up!" Dragging her, he took her away.

What a tragic scene it was! The children howled along with Bhabhi. Amma stared vacantly at everyone. After Abba's death she had no authority in the house anymore. Bhaiya was his own master and our guardian too, as a matter of fact. Amma had tried everything in her power to make him reconsider; she had been expecting something like this to happen. But what could she do?

Bhabhi left. The atmosphere in the house was so depressing that Bhaiya and Shabnam also left for the hill-station after their wedding.

Seven or eight years went by. By now we had all set up housekeeping. Amma passed away. Abba's death had left her in a state of torpor. She had wept and wailed at the time of Bhabhi's divorce, but she knew Bhaiya well; he had never paid attention to anything Abba said either. A son who starts earning his living becomes his own master.

The nest was destroyed. The house that lived and breathed once was now desolate. Everyone was scattered. The years seemed to slip away in the twinkling of an eye. Every two years or so we'd get some news of Bhaiya. He travelled a lot, usually outside India, but when a letter arrived from him saying he was coming to Bombay, childhood's forgotten memories were revived. As soon as Bhaiya got off the train, I ran to him and we clung to each other like children. I couln't see Shabnam anywhere. No sooner had I finished asking Bhaiya about her than a heavy hand fell upon my shoulders with a thud, and a mountain of warm flesh engulfed me.

"Bhabhi!" I said, holding on to the train window in order to prevent myself from falling over.

I had never called Shabnam "Bhabhi". She always looked like Shabnam. But today the word "Bhabhi" suddenly escaped from my lips. How could a sprinkle of dew become a dome of flesh? I looked at Bhaiya. He was the same. Lean and slim, not an ounce out of place. Hair still thick like a boy's. Just two or three shiny strands peeped out from his temples, giving him a rather distinguished look. He was as solid as a rock. Waves leap toward the rock, crash at its feet, shatter and disintegrate, and weak and exhausted, return to the sea. Some die at the feet of the rock, while new waves, nourishing a desire for self-sacrifice, find themselves irresistibly drawn to it.

And the rock? Distanced from this worship, it continues to smile cynically. Unmoving, careless and pitiless! When Bhaiya married Shabnam, we all said that because Bhabhi, Shehnaz (I always called her Bhabhi), was too young and naive at the time of her marriage, she was easily suppressed by Bhaiya. But

Shabnam, who was mature and wordly-wise, would poison Bhaiya with her bite like a female serpent and leave him flagging. She would definitely make him suffer.

But only the rock can make the waves suffer.

"The kids are in boarding school. They didn't have any holidays." Shabnam blew her smelly, hyper-acidic breath in my face.

And I was searching in this heap of flesh for the sprinkle of dew, for the Shabnam who had doused the fire of Shehnaz's love and ignited a new flame in Bhaiya's heart. But what was this? Instead of burning to a cinder in the fire of her love, Bhaiya had come out more burnished than ever, like gold. The fire had consumed itself and turned to ashes. Bhabhi was like a mound of butter. But Shabnam was singed, muddy-looking ash; her dark, gleaming complexion had turned yellow like a lizard's stomach; those liquid eyes had become murky and lifeless; the thin, serpentine waist was nowhere in sight — Shabnam looked permanently pregnant; the well-rounded arms that had glowed like the delicate, shiny limbs of a tree were now thick and ungraceful and looked like a pair of dumb-bells. Her face was plastered with make-up, her eyes were smeared with mascara, and she had probably plucked her eyebrows too much so that she had to use a darker pencil on them.

Bhaiya was staying at the Ritz. We arrived there for dinner.

The cabaret was at its climax. The Egyptian beauty was contorting her flat stomach, her hips gyrated in circles, her voluptuous arms fluttered in the air, her golden legs could be seen quivering like pillars of ivory behind a thin veil of chiffon. Bhaiya's hungry eyes crawled over her body like scorpions. Again and again, he rubbed a secret wound at the back of his neck.

Bhabhi, who used to be Shabnam, who, like the Egyptian dancer, was once an electric current that burned Bhaiya, sat immobilized like a hill of sand. Bad diet and anaemia had given her plump cheeks the yellowed-green look of a mummy. Viewed under the neon lights, her complexion made one think of someone bitten by a cobra. The Egyptian dancer's hips were creating a storm and Bhaiya's heart bobbed up and down like a boat in the maelstrom. Shabnam, Bhabhi now, and the mother of five children, fearfully watched them both. She rapidly downed large morsels of roast chicken in order to distract herself.

The orchestra took a deep breath; the instruments groaned; the drum's heartbeat vibrated; the Egyptian dancer's waist spun for the last time and she slid to the marble floor in exhaustion.

The entire hall echoed with the sound of applause. Shabnam's eyes sought Bhaiya. The bearer arrived with fresh raspberries and a jug of cream. Without thinking, Shabnam filled her plate with raspberries. Her hands were trembling. Restless like a pair of wounded deer, her eyes darted in all directions.

Away from the crowds, on a darkened balcony, Bhaiya was lighting the Egyptian dancer's cigarette. His impassioned gaze tangled with the dancer's rapture-filled eyes. Shabnam's face was colourless, and she sat listlessly like a ponderous mass. Finding her glance directed toward them, Bhaiya led the dancer by the elbow to where we were sitting and introduced us.

"This is my sister," he said, pointing to me. The

dancer swayed in acknowledgement of my presence.

"My wife," he said in a dramatic tone, as if he were showing the dancer an injury received on the battlefield. The dancer was stunned. It seemed that it wasn't Bhaiya's wife she was looking at, but his own body drenched in blood. She stared at Shabnam with horror. Then she filled her eyes with every ounce of maternal affection she could muster and gave Bhaiya a special look in which a thousand stories were concealed. "Oh, this Hindustan! Where such beautiful people are sacrificed on the altar of custom and practice. These people, who submit to such punishment, are to be pitied, are worthy of worship."

Shabnam, my Bhabhi, read all this in the dancer's eyes. Her hands shook. To hide her anguish she quickly picked up the jug of cream and emptying it over the raspberries in her plate, she began eating with great fervour.

Poor Bhaiya! Handsome and pitiable! Beautiful like the sun god, romantic, honey-eyed Bhaiya, unmoving like a rock — he sat smiling in the role of an immortalized martyr.

An old wave, tired and broken, lay dying at his feet.

A new wave, bright and undulating, was waiting breathlessly to be clasped in his arms.

Translated by Tahira Naqvi

The Wedding Shroud

ONCE again a freshly-laundered floor-covering was laid at the entrance of the room with the three doors, the *seh-dari*. Sunshine filtered through the chinks in the broken tiling on the roof and fell over the courtyard below in odd geometrical patterns. The women from the neighbourhood sat silently, apprehensively, as if waiting for some major catastrophe to occur. Mothers gathered their babies to their breasts. Occasionally a feeble, cranky infant would let out a yell protesting an impediment in the flow of sustenance.

"No, no, my love," the thin, scrawny mother crooned, shaking the infant on her knees as if she were separating rice husks in a winnowing basket. How many hopeful glances were rivetted on to Kubra's mother's face today. One side each of two narrow pieces of cloth had been placed together, but no one had the nerve to measure and cut at this point. Kubra's mother held an exalted position as far as measuring and cutting were concerned; no one really knew how many dowries had been adorned by her small, shrunken hands, how many suits of clothing for new mothers had been stitched, nor how many shrouds had been measured and torn. Whenever someone in the neighbourhood ran short of fabric and every effort to correctly mark off and snip had failed, the case was brought before Kubra's mother. She would straighten the warp in the fabric, soften the starch in it, sometimes rearranging the cloth in the form of a triangle, sometimes a square. Then, the scissors in her imagination would go to work, she would measure and cut, and break into a smile.

"You will get the front, back and sleeves from this. Take some snippets from my sewing box for the neck." And so the problem would be solved; proper measuring and cutting having been dealt with, she would hand over everything along with a neatly-tied bundle of snippets.

But today the piece of fabric at hand was really insufficient. Everyone was quite sure Kubra's mother would fail to accurately measure and cut this time, which was why all the women were looking apprehensively at her. But on Kubra's mother's face, which bore a resolute look, there was not even a shadow of anxiety. She was surveying and patterning a four-finger length of coarse cotton. The reflection from the red twill lit up her bluish-yellow face like sunrise. The heavy folds on her face rose like darkening clouds, as if a fire had broken out in a dense forest. Smiling, she picked up the scissors.

A heavy sigh of relief rose up from the ranks of the women.

Infants were allowed to whimper, eagle-eyed virgins leapt up to thread their needles, newly-wed brides put on their thimbles. Kubra's mother's scissors had begun their work.

At the far end of the *seh-dari*, Hameeda sat pensively on a couch, her feet dangling, her chin resting on one hand, her mind somewhere else.

Every afternoon after lunch, Amabi settles down on the couch in the *seh-dari*, opens her sewing box and scatters about her a colourful array of snippets. Seated next to the stone mortar, washing dishes, Kubra observes these colourful pieces of cloth and a red band of colour surges across her pale, muddy complexion.

When Amabi lifts tiny gilded flowerets from the sewing box with her small, soft-skinned hands, her drooping face suddenly lights up with a strange, hope-filled luminescence; the glow of the golden flowerets is reflected on the deep, craggy folds of her face, glimmering there like the flames of tiny candles. With every stitch the gold sparkles and the candles flutter.

No one knows when the net of gold flowerets was first made for the fine muslin dupatta, and when the head-covering was lowered into the grave-like depths of the heavy trunk. The edges of the flowerets had faded, the patterned gilt border had become pale, the coils of gold thread wore a forlorn look, but there was no sign of Kubra's wedding procession yet. When a suit of clothing made especially for *chauthi*, the fourth day of the wedding, lost its lustre with the passage of time, it was discarded on one pretext or another and new hope was kindled by starting work on a new suit. After a thorough search a new bride was selected for the first snip, a freshly-laundered floor covering was laid at the entrance to the *seh-dari*, and the women from the neighbourhood, carrying their babies and paan-containers, their anklets tinkling, arrived on the scene.

"You will get the border from the smaller piece without any difficulty, but you won't have enough left for the bodice."

"What do you mean? We're not going to use the twill for the bodice, are we?" And with that everyone's face took on a troubled look. Quietly, like a silent alchemist, Amabi used her eyes to calculate width and length while the women whispered amongst themselves about the sparseness of the fabrics. A few laughed, one of them broke into a wedding song and before long, someone else, impelled by new-found boldness, launched into a song about unpopular in-laws. All this was followed by a spattering of dirty jokes, teasing and giggling. At this point the young unmarried girls were asked to leave; they were told to cover their heads and find a place to sit somewhere near the tiling. On hearing the sound of laughter the young girls sighed: Oh God, when would they be able to laugh like this?

Overcome by shyness, her head hung low, Kubra sat in the mosquito-infested ante-chamber, far from all this hustle and bustle. Without any warning the measuring and cutting process would arrive at a delicate stage; a gusset had been cut against the grain and one would think the women's good sense had also been snipped in the process. Kubra would watch fearfully from a chink in the door. That was the problem: not one suit had been stitched without trouble. If a gusset was cut the wrong way you could be sure the matchmaker's gossip would create a hitch — somewhere a mistress would be discovered, or the groom's mother would cause a problem by making demands for a pair of solid gold bracelets. A warp in the area of the hem meant there would be a falling out on the matter of *mehr*, or over the question of copper logs for the wooden bed. The omen associated with the dress for *chauthi* was indeed a critical one. But all of Amabi's expertise and capability came to nought; who knows why, at the last minute, something as minute as a coriander seed suddenly assumed undue importance.

With God's grace, Amabi had started preparing Kubra's dowry early. The smallest remnant was immediately stitched into a cover for a decorative glass bottle, adorned with fretted lace of gold thread, and stored. There's no telling with a girl: she grows so fast, like a cucumber. If a wedding procession does appear at the door, this very foresight and astuteness will prove invaluable.

However, this special astuteness lost its edge after Abba's death. All at once Hameeda remembered her father. Abba was as slight as a pole; if he lowered his body he had difficulty straightening up again. Early in the morning he would break off a twig from the neem tree and, with Hameeda in his lap, lose himself in thought. Then, as soon as he started brushing, a small fragment from the twig would go down the wrong way and he would begin to cough violently. Upset, Hameeda would slip off his knees; she did not like being shaken like that. Amused at her childish anger he would laugh, thus causing the choking cough to flutter in his throat like the flapping wings of a slaughtered pigeon. Finally Amabi would come along and slap him on the back.

"Good grief! What kind of laughter is this?"

Raising eyes reddened from the coughing fit, Abba would look at her and smile helplessly. The coughing eased, but he sat huffing and puffing in the same place for a long time afterwards.

"Why don't you find a cure for this cough? I've told you so many times you should do something about it."

"The doctor at the big hospital says I will need injections. He also said I should have a quart of milk and one ounce of butter every day."

"Dust upon the doctors' faces! There's a bad cough and then all that fat on top of it — why, if that does not create more phlegm what will? Go to an allopath, I say."

"I will." Abba would gurgle his tobacco-pipe and start coughing again.

"May this hukkah burn! This is the root of your coughing. Have you ever taken the trouble of looking at your grown daughter?"

And Abba glanced at Kubra's youth with a wistful look in his eyes. Kubra a grown woman — who said she was a grown woman? One would think that soon after the *bismillah* ceremony marking the beginning of lessons, she learned of her impending womanhood, staggered, and came to a standstill. What kind of womanhood was this that never put a sparkle in her eyes, nor allowed her tresses to caress her cheeks; no storm ever raged in her breast, nor did she ever sing playfully to the dark, swirling monsoon clouds for a beloved. Her shrinking, timorous womanhood which stole up on her without warning, left as furtively as it had come. The intoxicating drug first became salty, then bitter.

One day Abba stumbled over the threshold and fell on his face. Neither a doctor's prescription nor an allopath's remedy could lift him up again. And that was when Hameeda ceased to make demands for sweet roti.

That was also when proposals intended for Kubra somehow lost their way. It was as if no one knew that behind the sackcloth curtain at the door there was someone whose youth was drawing its last breath, and someone else whose youth was lifting its head like a cobra's hood.

But Amabi's routine remained unchanged; everyday, in the afternoon, as if she were playing with dolls, she scattered about her in the *seh-dari* all the colourful remnants and snippets from her sewing box.

Scrounging and saving from here and there, Amabi finally succeeded in buying a crepe dupatta for seven rupees and eight annas. Circumstances demanded that the dupatta be purchased immediately. A telegram from Hameeda's uncle had arrived: his oldest son, Rahat, was going to be in town for police training. Amabi was beside herself with anxiety. One would think that the wedding party was at the door and she hadn't even chipped up the gold for the bride as yet. Panicking, she lost her cool altogether and sent for her friend, Bundu's mother, who was also her adopted sister. "You'll never see my face again if you do not come this very moment."

Putting their heads together the two women whispered conspiratorially. Every once in a while they would glance at Kubra who was winnowing rice in the verandah. She knew perfectly well what this hushed conversation implied.

Right then Amabi removed her tiny clove-shaped earrings and handed them to Bundu's mother with the request that no matter what, she was to get her one tola of fettered gold lace, six *masas* of gold leaf and stars, and a quarter yard of twill. The room at the outer end of the house was swept and dusted; using a small amount of slaked lime, Kubra whitewashed the interior of the room herself. The walls became white, but the lime flaked the skin on her palms. That evening when she sat down to grind spices she fell back in pain. In bed she tossed and turned all night, first because of her palms, and then because Rahat was arriving by the morning train.

"Oh God, dear God!" Hameeda entreated after morning prayers. "Please let my sister have good luck this time. I promise I will say a hundred *rakats* at prayer."

Kubra was already ensconced in the mosquito-ridden chamber when Rahat arrived the next morning. After he had partaken of a breakfast consisting of parathas and vermicelli cooked in milk he went to the sitting room. Kubra came out stealthily, taking small steps like a new bride, and started picking up the dirty dishes.

"Apa, here, let me wash these," Hameeda teased.

"No," replied Kubra, hunched over shyly.

Hameeda continued to tease her, Amabi continued to smile and stitch gold lace on the crepe dupatta.

The gold flowerets and cockades and the silver anklets went the way of the clove-shaped earrings. In no time they were followed by the four bangles Amabi's brother had given her at the ceremony marking the end of her mourning period after Abba died. Eating humble fare themselves, the women cooked sumptuous parathas, fried meatballs and biriyani for Rahat; while Amabi herself subsisted on bread and water, she fed the best cuts of meat to her son-in-law-to-be.

"These are hard times, my child," she would tell Hameeda when the girl complained. And Hameeda thought: we remain hungry so that we can nourish the son-in-law. Kubra Apa gets up early in the morning, drinks a glass of water and starts working like a machine. She prepares parathas for Rahat and keeps the milk on boil for a long time so that a heavy layer of cream forms on it; if she could, she would take some of the fat from her own body and knead it into the dough she used to make parathas for Rahat. And why shouldn't she do all this? After all, one day he will be hers, and whatever he earns he will entrust to her care. Don't we all water and nourish a fruit-bearing plant? And then, when the flowers bloom and the bough bends with their weight people who now gossip will be silenced forever. It was this very thought that made my Kubra Apa's face glow with bride-like luminescence. The sound of wedding trumpets echoed in her ears and she rushed to sweep up the dirt in Rahat's room with her lashes; lovingly, as if they talked to her, she folded his dirty clothes, washed his soiled, foul-smelling socks, laundered his stinking undershirts and handkerchiefs filled with mucus, and on his pillow-case she carefully embroidered the words, "Sweet dreams." But things were not falling into place. Rahat ate a hearty breakfast consisting of eggs and parathas every morning, returned at night to eat meatballs, and then went to bed. Amabi's adopted sister whispered complaints.

"Yes, but the poor fellow is very shy," Amabi offered excuses.

"That's all very well, but we should get a hint or a clue from his actions or the way he looks at her."

"Heaven forbid that my daughter should exchange looks with anyone! No outsider has even glimpsed her head-covering." Amabi spoke with pride.

"My dear, no one is suggesting that she come

before Rahat."

Observing Kubra's well-developed acne, Bundu's mother secretly lauded Amabi's foresight. "You are so naive, my dear sister. When is this young thing going to be of use?" She looked at me and twittered. "You, good-for-nothing girl, you must jest with your brother-in-law and clown around with him, you silly child."

"But Auntie, what do you want me to do?"

"Why don't you talk to him?"

"I feel embarrassed talking to him."

"Why? He is not going to tear you to pieces, is he?" Amabi spoke angrily.

"No, but ..." I was speechless. Then everyone conferred. After prolonged deliberation special kababs, using dried mustard seeds, were readied; Kubra Apa smiled a lot through all this. Then she whispered to me.

"Now don't start laughing or else you'll ruin the game."

"No, I won't," I promised.

"I've brought your dinner," I said, placing the tray of food on the stool before Rahat. But when he glanced up and down at me while washing his hands, I ran from the room. My heart was beating uncontrollably; what a fierce expression he had in his eyes!

"You fool, go and see how he reacts to the kababs. You're going to spoil the fun."

Kubra Apa looked at me. There was pleading in her eyes, the dust of departing wedding processions, a sadness reminiscent of old wedding clothes. I lowered my head and returned to where Rahat sat eating.

He ate silently without a glance in my direction.

While he was eating I should have joked and laughed with him. I should have said, "Are you enjoying these special kababs, dear brother-in-law?" But I felt as if someone had clutched at my throat.

Angered, Amabi called me back and scolded me under her breath. How could I tell her that the wretch seemed to be enjoying his food.

"Rahat Bhai, do you like the kababs?" I asked, as I had been instructed by Amabi.

There was no answer.

"Do you like the kababs?"

"Go and ask him properly," Amabi nudged me.

"You brought them to me and I ate them. They must be good."

"What an ignoramus!" Amabi was forced to exclaim.

"Why, you ate kababs made with dried mustard seeds, Rahat Bhai, and you couldn't tell the difference?"

"Mustard seeds? But I eat the same thing every day, don't I? I'm used to eating mustard seeds and chaff."

Amabi's face fell. Kubra Apa couldn't lift her eyes. The next day Kubra Apa spent twice the usual amount of time sewing and when I took Rahat his food in the evening, he said:

"And what did you bring me today? It must be sawdust this time."

"Don't you like our food?" I snapped at him.

"That's not what I mean. It's just a little strange. Sometimes you give me kababs made with mustard seeds, sometimes curry made with chaff."

I was infuriated: we eat dry bread so that we can provide him with enormous rations, stuff him with parathas dripping with butter, and my poor sister, who can't afford medicine for herself, lavishes him with milk and cream. Fuming, I came away.

Amabi's adopted sister's advice worked and Rahat began to spend the better part of his day at home. Kubra Apa stayed at the stove most of the time, Amabi was always busy stitching the *jora* for *chauthi*, and Rahat's filthy looks plunged into my heart like arrows. He teased me without any provocation while he was eating or making a request for water or salt, and made insinuating remarks; embarrassed, I would go and sit next to Kubra Apa. I wanted to say to her, "Whose goat is this anyway, and who's giving it fodder? Dear sister, I won't be able to put a ring in your bull's nose." But Kubra Apa's tangled hair was covered with ashes from the stove ... No! My heart sank. Quickly I lifted the gray lock of hair from the side of her face and tucked it into her plait. A curse on this recurring cold! The poor girl's hair is turning gray from it.

Using another excuse this time, Rahat called me again.

"Hunh!" I was furious. But when Kubra Apa turned around with the look of a slaughtered animal, I had to go.

"Are you angry with me?" Rahat took the glass of water from me and grabbed my wrist. My heart leapt into my mouth, and pulling my hand from his grasp, I fled.

"What was he saying?" Kubra Apa asked in a voice stifled by shyness. Silent, I just stared at her.

Then I began hurriedly, "He was saying, 'Who cooked the food? How delicious it is! I can't stop eating ... I want to devour the hand ... oh, no, kiss the hand of the person who cooked all this'." Taking Kubra Apa's roughened hand which smelt of turmeric and coriander, I clasped it in mine, my eyes filled with tears. These "hands", which grind spices from morning to night, draw water, chop onions, make beds, polish shoes — hapless, these hands are at work from morning to night like slaves. When will their subservience end? Will they ever find a buyer? Will no one ever kiss them lovingly, will they never be adorned with henna, will they ever be drenched in bridal attar? I wanted to scream at the top of my voice.

"What else did he say?" Kubra Apa's hands were rough, but her voice was so melodious and sweet-sounding that if Rahat had ears . . . but he had neither ears nor a nose, just an infernal stomach.

"Well, he said tell your sister she shouldn't work so hard and she should take something for her cough."

"Liar!"

"No, I'm not lying. It's he who's a liar, your . . ."

"Hush, you silly girl! Here, I've completed the sweater . . . why don't you take it to him. But promise you won't tell him I knitted it."

I wanted to say, "Apa, don't give him this sweater. This body of yours which is just a handful of bones needs it more than he does." But I couldn't bring myself to say it. "Apa, what will *you* wear?" I asked instead.

"I don't really need it. I feel scorched from sitting next to the stove."

Upon seeing the sweater Rahat raised one eyebrow mischievously and asked: "Did you make this yourself?"

"No."

"In that case I'm not going to wear it."

I felt like scarring his face. You wretch! Mountain of clay! This sweater has been knitted by hands which are living, breathing slaves; caught in its every stitch are the hopes of an ill-fated woman; the hands that made it are meant to rock a cradle. Grasp these hands, you idiot, they will be like life-saving oars when your boat is threatened by overpowering waves in a storm. They may not play a melody on the sitar, they won't twist and turn in the poses of Manipuri or Bharata Natyam, they haven't been taught to dance over the keys of a piano, they haven't had the good fortune to play with flowers, but these are the hands that toil endlessly to provide sustenance to your body, they sew for you day and night, suffer the heat from the stove, wash your filth so that you can maintain your image of unblemished wholesomeness. Wounded by hard work, they have never been adorned with tinkling bangles, and no one has ever clasped them lovingly. But I remained silent. Amabi says my thinking has been poisoned by my new friends who tell me new things, frightening things about hunger and starvation, about hearts suddenly ceasing to beat.

"Why don't you wear this sweater," Rahat said, "your shirt is so flimsy."

I scratched his face, nose, shirt-front and hair like a crazed cat and, running to my room, fell on my bed. Kubra Apa quickly put the last roti on the pan, washed her hands and, wiping them with a corner of her dupatta, came and sat on the edge of my bed. "Did he say anything?" Unable to stop herself, she asked me, her heart beating fast.

"Apa, Rahat is not a nice person." I decided I would tell her everything today.

"Why?" she smiled.

The Wedding Shroud

"I don't like him ... look, he broke all my bangles." I was trembling.

"He's so mischievous," Apa said coyly.

"Apa, listen Apa, he's not a nice person at all," I said angrily. "I'm going to tell Amabi today."

"What happened?" asked Amabi, unrolling the prayer mat.

"Look Amabi, my bangles."

"Did Rahat break them?" she asked gleefully.

"Yes."

"And why shouldn't he? Aren't you always pestering him? Why are you so upset anyway? You're not going to melt with the first touch." Then she spoke in a pacifying tone. "When the time comes you can make up for all this — Rahat will not be able to forget your revenge!" And saying this she began her prayers.

There was another conference with her adopted sister and, satisfied that matters were moving in the desired direction, they both smiled happily. Bundu's mother said to me, "My word, girl, you *are* a good-for-nothing! When we were young we made life miserable for our brothers-in-law."

She then proceeded to describe how brothers-in-law should be harassed, giving her own example to illustrate her point. She explained how just teasing and mischief had resulted in the marriage of her uncle's two daughters for whom there had seemed to be no hope at all.

One of the men was Hakim ji; whenever the young girls played pranks on him or joked with him, he would suffer one attack of bashfulness after another until he became quite distraught. Finally a day came when he informed Uncle that he wanted to be his son-in-law.

The other was a clerk in the Viceroy's office. No sooner did the girls hear he had arrived in the house than the teasing and pranks commenced; sometimes they sent him paan filled with hot chillies, sometimes vermicelli in which they had put salt instead of sugar. What do you know, he started coming every day, regardless of whether it rained or stormed. And one day he requested an acquaintance to arrange a match for him in that family. When asked, "With which girl?" he answered, "It doesn't really matter." And by God, looking at the older girl you would think a banshee was coming your way. And the younger one, well, she too was something else: one eye faced west, the other east. Her father gave her fifteen tolas of gold in her dowry and also arranged a job for her husband in the Barre Saheb's office.

"Well, how can someone with fifteen tolas of gold and the influence to provide a job in Barre Saheb's office have any difficulty finding a boy," said Amabi with a sigh.

"No, my dear, that's not it. These days men's hearts are just like brinjals on a tray — you can make them roll whichever way you like."

But Rahat isn't a brinjal; he's a mountain. I hope I'm not the one who gets crushed while trying to make him roll, I thought.

Then I looked at Kubra Apa. Seated at the threshold of the room, silently kneading dough, she was listening to everything that was being said. If she could, she would have rent the bosom of the earth and vanished within it, taking the curse of her virginity with her.

Was my sister hungry for a man? No, she had shrivelled up before she had even an inkling of that hunger. The idea of a man has come to her mind not as desire, but as a question of food and clothing. She is a widow's burden and the burden has to be removed.

However, no amount of insinuation or innuendo elicited a word from either Rahat or his family. Despondent, Amabi finally pawned her heavy anklets and arranged a *niaz* in the name of Pir Mushkil Kusha. All afternoon young girls from the neighbourhood created a racket in the verandah, Kubra Apa retreated to her mosquito-ridden room so that the last drops of her blood could be sucked, and feeling spent, Amabi sat on her couch putting the last stitches on the wedding suit. Today the expression on her face spoke of destinations; her ordeal would soon be over. Once again the wrinkles on her face lit up like candles.

Apa's friends were teasing her, they were trying to invigorate the few drops of blood that remained. Her fever had not recurred for many days; her face shone brightly for a moment and then languished like a dying candle. She signalled me to come to her, then quietly handed me a plate containing *malida*, a sweet, buttery cake.

"Maulvi saheb said a special incantation over this." Her hot, feverish breath swept across my ear.

Taking the plate from her I thought, Maulvi saheb has said a special incantation, this *malida* will now be dropped into Rahat's furnace, the furnace that has been kept warm for six months with our blood. This special *malida* will make the dream come true. I heard the sound of wedding trumpets: I run to the roof to see the wedding procession approach, there's a long *sehra* over the bridegroom's face, it is touching the horse's mane ...

Wearing the wedding dress, laden with flowers, Kubra Apa advances shyly, taking slow steps ... the dress glimmers, Amabi's face has blossomed like a flower ... Apa's eyes, heavy with modesty, are raised once, a tear of gratitude slips, becomes entangled in the chipped gold and sparkles like a diamond.

"This is all due to your hard work," Apa's silence seems to be saying. Hameeda's eyes filled with tears.

"Go, my dear sister," Apa awoke her from her reverie and startled, Hameeda advanced towards the sitting room wiping her tears with a corner of her dupatta.

"Here's some *malida*," she said nervously, trying to control the pounding of her heart. Her steps wavered; she felt as if she had entered a snake's hole. The mountain shifted and gaped open. She moved back. But somewhere in the distance wedding trumpets screeched as if they had been strangled; with trembling hands she rolled some *malida* between her fingers and moved it towards his mouth.

With a snatch her hand was drawn into the depths of the mountain, into putrescence and darkness, and a large rock stifled her scream. The plate with the sacred *malida* slipped from her hands and fell over the lantern, the lantern tipped, sobbed for a few seconds and was extinguished.

The next day Rahat took the morning train, thanking them for their hospitality as he left. The date for his wedding had been fixed and he was in a hurry.

After this no eggs were ever fried again in this house, no parathas were warmed and no sweaters knitted. Tuberculosis, which had been pursuing Kubra Apa for a long time, seized her with one pounce and she quietly deposited her weary existence into its lap.

The Wedding Shroud 109

Once again a freshly-laundered floor covering was laid in the *seh-dari*. The women from the neighbourhood gathered. The white cotton of the shroud stretched before Amabi like the mantle of death. Her lineaments were quivering from the burden of constraint, her left eyebrow was twitching, the lines on her face appeared frightening, as if there were thousands of serpents hissing in them.

After straightening the warp in the cotton, she folded the fabric to form a square, and innumerable scissors snipped through her heart. Today there was a look of terrifying peace on her countenance; a flowering calm reigned there, as if she were absolutely certain that like the other suits for *chauthi* which had always remained incomplete, this one too, would be discarded.

All at once the young girls in the *seh-dari* began chirping like starlings. Pushing the past aside, Hameeda joined them. The coarse white cotton . . . the red of the floor-covering! Who knows how many innocent brides have mingled their blood with its redness and how many unfortunate virgins have sunk the despair of their lost hopes in its whiteness. Suddenly everyone was silent. Amabi put in the last stitch and broke off the thread. Two thick teardrops slid slowly down her soft, cushiony cheeks, rays of light burst forth from the wrinkles on her face, and she smiled. It seemed that today, at last, she was convinced that her Kubra's dress for *chauthi* was ready and that the trumpets would sound any time now.

Translated by Tahira Naqvi

The Mole

"CHAUDHRY, O Chaudhry..." Garishchand Chaudhry remained silent.

"Shush."

"Why are you making noises like a cricket?"

"I'm tired."

"Sit still or else..."

"I cannot sit still anymore! My back is as stiff as a board. Hey Ram!"

"Hnnk, hnnk..."

"Brrr.... I'm so cold."

Chaudhry was quiet.

"It feels as though there are ants crawling under my thigh."

"Look here, Rani, it's only been ten minutes and already you're tired."

"So? I'm not made of clay. Hunh!" Stretching her thick lips, Rani grunted and slid off the stool she was sitting on.

"Witch! I'm telling you, sit still. Slattern!" Chaudhry flung the palette on the stool and catching hold of her shoulders, shook her hard.

"Well, all right then... here." She slipped to the floor. Chaudhry was livid. He wanted to mark her smooth, dark cheeks with a whip but he knew that would only make her lose control altogether and give her an excuse to start weeping. And the painting for which he was killing himself would remain incomplete.

"Look, just sit quietly for a little while longer, that's all." He spoke in a subdued tone.

"But I'm tired." She rolled over and stretched.

"Tired! And don't you get tired when you're out collecting cow-dung on the roads all day long? You bitch!" Chaudhry's anger returned.

"Who is collecting cow-dung? You? What a mean one you are, taunting me like a quarrelsome mother-in-law!" Annoyed, she sat up and began to sulk. Chaudhry was certain another day was about to go down the drain.

"All right. Keep still for just another half hour. Understand?"

"Not half-an-hour. Six minutes only," she said, climbing back onto the stool.

The truth of the matter was, she could only count up to six or seven. Chaudhry was sure he could keep her sitting for half-an-hour. Rani straightened her waist, adjusted the heavy, flowered pitcher on her shoulder and sat down. But for how long?

"Is this right?"

"Yes." Chaudhry quickly bent over his canvas.

"Look at me . . ."

"Yes, yes, it's all right."

"Look at me . . ."

"Yes, yes, it's all right."

For some time his brush moved with urgent haste and colours rapidly coalesced into one another, but no sooner had a minute or so gone by than Rani breathed a heavy sigh.

"Ahhh . . . That is all, Chaudhry. Your six minutes

are over."

"Hmm . . ." His glance bolted from his incomplete, dappled painting to her and back again.

"I'm cold. Can I wear my shawl?'

"No."

"Ohhh . . . ahh . . ..It is so cold." She started whining like a dog. Chaudhry was quiet.

"My back, oh my back, Chaudhry ji!" Actually she was in a mischievous mood today. "Shawl, my shawl, my shawl. . . ."

Chaudhry said nothing.

"Hunhi! Didn't you hear me say I'm tired? I will throw down the pitcher if you don't listen to me."

Chaudhry quickly turned to look at her. He had borrowed the pitcher from the museum for his painting. He would crack Rani's skull if she broke it.

"Can I help it if I'm tired? I think there are lice crawling in my hair." Resting the pitcher on the floor, she lifted her hand to her head and began untangling a thick, knotted lock of hair with her fingers.

His feet set apart, the muscles in his face quivering with anger, Chaudhry glared at her. His grizzly beard fluttered like a sailboat flapping wildly in the storm, and tiny beads of perspiration appeared on the surface of his bald, smooth head.

"My back hurts from sitting for such a long time." Scared, Rani quickly eased back into position. Then she burst into tears.

"Boohoo . . ." Her lips flapped as she blubbered.

"Boohoo . . . Nobody cares if I live or die," she said between sobs.

Chaudhry widened his eyes and glared at her again. Whenever she started crying, the muscles in Chaudhry's jaws quivered violently, the bridge on his nose went askew, the brushes in his hand danced like fire-crackers, and the colours on his palette flowed into a muddle and lost their glow. Thought was impossible while this condition lasted, reason returning to him only when the thorn in his brain had been dislodged. And at this very moment, Rani's behaviour was not so much a thorn as a spear that threatened to carve through his very soul.

There wasn't a person alive who could ward off the effects of Chaudhry's histrionics, and Rani was no exception. She quickly sucked in her stomach and making whining noises, sat down again.

For a while the world continued to revolve on its axis, Chaudhry's brush moved rapidly, and his palette began to take on an untidy look.

But, "Chaudhry," Rani spoke lovingly this time. Chaudhry felt something jump in his chest. The foundation of the world's axis swayed just a mite. To be sure, something did happen.

"Chaudhry, have you seen this?"

Chaudhry's shoulders convulsed, beads of sweat broke out on his smooth-surfaced skull. Rani spoke again.

"Look, do you see this black mole, just below my neck, see, to the left here?" Holding the pitcher with one hand, her mouth hanging open as she lowered her face to examine the mole, she looked down at her neck.

"Did you see this mole? So, you are looking, Chaudhry." She pretended to be coy. "Oh, I'm so embarrassed."

"Sit still," Chaudhry growled.

"Hunh! What airs you put on! Why would anyone want to sneak a look at somebody's mole, especially when it is in such a bad place?" She chuckled shamelessly.

"I'm not interested in any mole. I didn't see it and I'm not going to either." Chaudhry's irritation grew.

"Hunh! Liar! You saw it, you looked at it from the corner of your eye. And . . ." she continued to snicker immodestly.

"Rani!"

Rani stuck her nose up at him. Defeated, Chaudhry sat down on a wooden box next to his easel. "Do you know how old I am?" he asked her.

"Hey Ram! How old?" Lowering the pitcher, she leaned towards him.

"I'm older than your father, actually even older than your grandfather. And you? Tell me, how old are you? No more than fifteen, I'm sure. And who taught you all this vulgar talk?"

Chaudhry wasn't even as old as her father. He only said that to shut her up.

"You are the one who talks vulgar. Peeping at my mole! And it is in such a bad place too." She slowly groped for the mole. "And who says I'm a little girl? If I had been that young, why . . ."

"Well, what then?"

"Ratan says whoever has a mole on the breast is . . ." she stuttered.

"Ratan? How does Ratan know where your mole is?"

"I showed it to him." She slowly massaged the mole.

"You . . . you . . . you showed Ratan your mole?"

Chaudhry's blood began to boil again; there was a tremor in his armpits, the flesh in his cheeks began to flutter once more, and his brushes danced.

"Uh . . . well, Oh! he saw it, so what could I do?"

"How . . . how did he manage to set eyes on it when you, you . . ." Chaudhry's jaw shook like a door loose on its hinges.

"I was bathing and he . . ." she began. Picking up the pitcher she climbed on the stool again. "Yes, I was bathing. I was scared to go alone so I took him with me to the pond. I had to wash my blouse and what if someone came just then? I took him along because I was scared, yes." She spoke artlessly.

"Rani . . ." Chaudhry edged forward.

"I told him to keep looking the other way, but . . ."

"But?"

"He sat some distance away. Then I said, 'Ratan, I have a mole in a very bad place.' He didn't say anything. Then I said, 'All right, don't look if you don't want to, I don't care.' Right Chaudhry?"

"But you said he saw it."

"Yes, because I started to drown — the water was this deep, you know," she said, placing a finger just below the mole.

"Slut!" Flinging the brush aside, Chaudhry leapt towards a wooden stick lying nearby.

"Hey Ram! But, but . . . listen, Chaudhry. Would you have liked me to drown?"

"Don't you know how to swim, you bitch? You've been in and out of that pond all your life. Why is it you never drowned before?"

"Why, I wasn't really going to drown. I just wanted to show him my mole."

"So you pretended to be drowning just so you could show him your mole, eh?" Chaudhry waved the thin stick in the air. He was smiling now.

"Hey Ram! Let me put on my dhoti first,

Chaudhry ji." Monkey-like, she jumped from the stool and landed on the mat. "I will run out on the road if you hit me. I will be so humiliated I'll have to tell everyone that Chaudhry, Chaudhry ..."

The old man stopped in his tracks. "What will you tell them?"

"I will say, 'Chaudhry says that my mole ... '" she twittered.

"Slattern!" Chaudhry danced like a mad fox. Rani knew the arrow had hit its mark.

"I will tell everybody, Chaudhry. Do you understand? Come on, hit me if you want to. Why are you staring at me like that? I'm so young, just a little girl ... you are really very naughty!" She gradually edged toward the door.

Chaudhry sat down with his head in his hands. For a moment he was overcome with the temptation to burn the painting and beat Rani to a pulp, but in the next instant he remembered the exhibition at which he was to receive an award of five thousand rupees for his painting.

His mind had been in a swirl to beging with. For years he had been painting pictures of roses blooming timorously, of undulating verdure, of leaping, swirling torrents; he had even successfully endowed pain and fragrance with colour. And women from faraway places, both naked and clothed, felt honoured to pose for him. But this sprightly, illiterate chit of a girl he had picked up from the filthy gutters to sit for his masterpiece, was completely unmanageable. His greatest problem was that despite all his experimentation with hundreds of tints, he was unable to duplicate the exact shade of her skin. He mixed gold with black and then added blue, but the gloss on her skin appeared to come from a mixture of gold, black and blue, along with a wave of ochre. It wasn't just one thing either. One day her complexion was inky, the next he could see early-morning vermilion bursting from it, and then suddenly her body would resemble lilac clouds at night, while at other times he could definitely see the blue of a viper's skin shining through. Her eyes, too, appeared to change colour constantly. On the first day he calmly prepared a coal-black tint. But suddenly he saw fine red circles around her pupils, and then in the area around them he thought he caught a glimpse of blue which reminded him of clouds. He became flustered. So much paint had been wasted. But his vexation knew no bounds when, within minutes, the coal-black pupils changed colour, became green and danced like two emeralds. The surface around the pupils was transformed to a milky-white and the red circles grew redder. "Oh God!" He clasped his head with both hands and shuddered. And to make matters worse, this:

"I got bitten by a mosquito," she was saying, whimpering like a child.

Chaudhry had decided today he would remain unruffled and not say a word.

"They are biting me to death, you know."

No word from Chaudhry.

"Ohh . . . they bite so hard, these mosquitoes . . ." Rani blurted out a filthy invective, not something that you heard often. Chaudhry jumped. He didn't know that many obscenities, and the ones he did know were mild compared to what he had just heard. As a matter of fact, his knowledge of vulgar language was extremely limited.

"Where did you learn to swear like this?" he turned around to ask her.

"Which one? You mean this?" She repeated the obscenity without artifice.

"Rani!" he growled.

"Chunan was cursing once. There are lots of mosquitoes in his *kholi*." She tried to be evasive. "In his *kholi*? You were in his kholi?"

"Yes. He told me he had some *gurdhani* there he was going to give me."

"Did you eat the *gurdhani*?"

"Of course not. There was no *gurdhani* there. He was lying. But he brings it for me now."

"Chunan gives you *gurdhani*?"

"And *kheel* too." She traced the pattern on the pitcher with her finger.

"*Kheel* too?" Chaudhry knew that his surprise was unwarranted. Rani was crazy about *gurdhani*. Not only would she go to Chunan's room for the cane sugar sweet, she would snatch some from the jaws of a dog in the gutter and devour it.

"I've been giving you money and you're still going to Chunan for the sweet?"

"I'm not a beggar, why should I go to him for it? He brings it to me and then he says, 'Come with me to my *kholi*.' I don't like him at all. Such a big moustache he has — it makes me sneeze. Achoo!" She sniffled as if someone had pushed a wick up her nose.

"Chaudhry, can I scratch my back? Can I?"

Once again Chaudhry began to feel the effects of the old madness. He thought he could hear clapping noises in his head, his cheeks fluttered, and five thousand jingling rupees took the shape of tiny stars and danced away from him. Brown, black, gray and yellow

— all the shades coalesced and he felt there were mushrooms sprouting from his skull.

The question he was now faced with was: Should he continue painting or go mad? If this went on any longer he would soon be seen rolling in the dust in the streets like a crazed dog, his clothes tattered, his thin body scratched, or he would be found with his burning head submerged in the waters of the small pond.

His steps led him to the pond. It was not far. He went there frequently to sit on the banks and gaze at the swaying and flickering reflections of sunlight on the water's surface. He was a poet. A poet from birth. He lived in the world, but was distanced from it. He was not an old man, but one couldn't think of him as young either. He had let his beard grow because he was too careless to trim it, and now it was also speckled with gray.

"Ohh ..." Something fluttered in his armpits again. Rani's voice fell into his ears. It sounded like the croaking of a frog. Was it a frog? But the rainy season was still to come. Perhaps it was the sound of a cat growling. It had to be something. When his pious eyes glimpsed Rani and Ratan romping in the water, he thought for a moment he had imagined them there. His imagination tormented him harshly and often. And today it had gone too far.

But the torrent of laughter ceased when he advanced, and the two images, transfixed as if in marble, stared wide-eyed at him. How clear the illusion was! How translucent each feature! The bulge of Ratan's thighs, his wet hair, his small eyes set together. And Rani's tousled, wet plait, the colour of her skin a mixture of charcoal-black, pink, brown, camphorwhite and blue. And the mole. That fleshy, protuberant mole. To Chaudhry it seemed that the mole had struck his chest with a thud, like a flying bullet.

Ratan grabbed his dhoti about him and made his escape from the side, but Rani stood undaunted, noisily slapping the water with her hands. Chaudhry felt as if he were on a swing, swaying, swaying rhythmically.

"You are looking at my mole, aren't you? That is so naughty of you." She spoke coquettishly in an attempt to pacify him.

Chaudhry held himself back at the brink of the precipice.

"Come out of there," he said, pushing aside the new Chaudhry who was slowly sinking.

"Unhuh . . . you will hit me." She lifted her torso above the water.

"If I don't skin you alive today I'll change my name!" Chaudhry realized he was talking to a girl who had been raised like a frog in the gutter.

"Won't you feel ashamed, lifting your hand to hit a woman?"

Chaudhry smouldered.

"Do you hit naked women? What a thing to do!" She lifted herself higher.

"You are not ashamed?" She gazed into his eyes and smiled, the water up to her knees now. Her fear had made her bold.

"Go away, you . . ." she said coyly.

The stick fell from Chaudhry's hands and his height increased by inches; the muscles in his arms bulged and grew taut, and he felt ants crawling inside his brain; a strong gust of cool, black wind blew over the pile of embers, the spark was ignited and soon there were flames leaping in all directions. His eyes plunged at the black, fleshy mole like hungry vultures and ... Ohhh ... As if transformed into a black stone by his revulsion, the mole crashed against his forehead. He turned and ran. Ran like a defeated dog. Where? To his bed.

That same day Chaudhry fired Ratan. Ratan pleaded that he had his loincloth on the whole time, but Chaudhry was like a man possessed. All night he battled with his thoughts. He felt as if someone was trying unsuccessfully to drill a hole through his body, hindered, it seemed to him, by a rock that stood in the way. Tonight he had a myriad tints at his disposal: ochre with a little blue was transformed into a shade that was alive and deep like the bottom of the ocean, and for the eyes a little green mixed with black, no just a hint of purple, edged with a pink border. He wanted to get up and examine his own eyes in the mirror. But he hadn't seen his face in the mirror in ages. What need does an artist have to look at his own face? What is there to see in the mirror? His innumerable paintings constituted the mirror in which he could not only see his face, but also view every nook and cranny in his soul. His heart and his mind, both clothed in paint, appeared before him in his paintings.

Nevertheless, he still wanted to see his face in the mirror. Taking a tin box which had once carried the paints that came for him from all over the world, he turned it upside down and shook it. A couple of crickets jumped out and, brushing against his nose, flew off. With his elbow he rubbed off a spider's web from the bottom of the box and proceeded to examine his face. At first he could not see much. Whatever was visible looked like circles of foam on sea water, or something that one views through blurry, watery vision. Then he saw a hideous beard and eyes burning with hunger. Oh! This was his own face. His face? But he was never like this. Was he? He turned the box upside down and looked for his reflection again. A part of his beard was still visible and if he squinted one eye he could see his smudged nose and some of his moustache. The moustache. If he had scissors he would trim the moustache so it looked like . . . Rani had said Chunan's moustache made her sneeze. Achoo! He made sniffling noises with his nose. He knew Ratan was wearing his loincloth. Or maybe he did have the dhoti on, or was about to don it when he appeared on the scene. But what about Chunan and his *gurdhani*? Chaudhry suddenly had a feeling that the walls of his room were made of *gurdhani* and they were caving in on him, squeezing him, making him stick to the sweet like a half-crushed fly barely able to move.

When he got tired of walking and his legs grew heavy, he sat down on the stool, lifted the cover from his painting and gazed at his unfinished endeavour. Within minutes the spots and dabs began to fly around and then became stationary; the shoulders gleamed like polished leather, the eyes shimmered with blue, black and green lights, and the mole! Where did the mole come from? The mole that protruded like a coiled snake? Tick! Tick! Tick! His heart beat like a clock.

Quickly he rose and his feet carried him in the direction of Rani's hut. A dirty, squalid confining hut with a small door! He would have it enlarged tomorrow. No, the unused room where he stored empty boxes would be right. He advanced in the darkness.

His heart still beat like a clock. The darkness in the hut clung to him like wet charcoal. His hands collided with the charpoy, then plunged into the curve of the charpoy's roped bottom. He groped feverishly, but ... Rani wasn't there!

Mosquitoes attacked his entire body. Large, cackling mosquitoes. Soon after that great slabs of *gurdhani* fell over him. The next morning he wanted to ask Rani, "Bitch, where were you last night?" But someone might want to know why he was in her hut, poking around in her bed.

He continued working quietly and Rani was silent too. He wished she would speak so he could find out where she had been the night before. But, angry with him, she remained silent and sulked.

"Are you tired?" he asked gently when he saw her putting the pitcher down. He didn't want to fight with her today.

"What do you think? I'm not made of clay, you know." She started massaging her waist with both hands.

Chaudhry wanted to say something nice to her, but he felt awkward changing his manner.

"All right, that's enough rest for now." He thought she would respond with belligerence, but instead she lifted the pitcher and straightened her waist again.

Today his colours were mutinous; whatever he dabbed on seemed to ridicule him. He had planned to paint on the mole this morning. Just like that. Could one not have moles in pictures? But when he saw how rebellious his colours were, he postponed the idea.

As Rani got up to leave, a piece of *gurdhani* fell from her dhoti. She was unaware of what had happened, but Chaudhry felt as if the roof had collapsed over his head.

"This *gurdhani*!" he roared, foaming at the mouth with anger.

At first she paused with the intention of picking up the sweet, but changed her mind when she saw Chaudhry's expression of anger.

"You eat it," she said, arrogantly throwing back her head as she walked away.

Chaudhry was numbed into a death-like stillness. He watched her leave. Then he ground the *gurdhani* into the dirt with the heel of his shoe.

The next day Rani disappeared. God knows where she went; she didn't even bother to take her clothes with her, leaving as she had come. The miserable creature had gone back to wallow in the dirt again, no doubt.

Chaudhry's painting remained imcomplete. Five thousand rupees congealed in his mind like a black stain. A stain that looked like a fleshy black mole. But what a bad place for a black, singed mark. Right over Chaudhry's heart!

In the days that followed, Chaudhry's anguish grew. Terrified that people might want to know what his interest in her was, he didn't tell anyone that Rani had run away. And so time passed. He tried to continue painting. But no one wanted to pay even six annas for his work. The reason for this was that now he was filling his flowers and sunsets with such grotesque and frightening shades of black and brown that people thought he had lost his mind. All his colours became jumbled and were reduced to nothing.

Some time later several interesting developments took place. People started asking Chaudhry about Rani. He said he didn't know where she had gone. But people are not satisfied with such simple answers.

"Chaudhry sold Rani."

"He sold her to a businessman for several thousand rupees."

"He had illicit relations with her . . . must have got rid of her."

The gossip about him was unending. Chaudhry's life was reduced to a darkened hole. It seemed that the world wanted to roast and devour him. And that's not all. What excitement, when Rani was caught by the police in the act of depositing a bloody bundle by the side of a road. Immediately people rushed to the village and Chaudhry's remaining sanity was threatened with extinction. The riddle of Rani's disappearance was solved in seconds. Chaudhry was thunderstruck. His mouth fell open in shock and surprise. A life of piety and honour trampled upon so easily! But he knew God was not his enemy. He would be saved just as all other innocent individuals are saved. Truth is without fear. But if only he had remained guilty!

Yes, if only he had remained guilty. Imprisonment, grief and pain, vile disgrace at the world's hands. If he had known, he would have willingly and happily taken it all upon himself. If he had known he would be freed in this fashion, he would not have offered evidence of his innocence to God and begged for help. True, there was that mole. But was God not aware of the weaknesses of His creatures? He is the one who has burdened man with all these weaknesses. But how could Chaudhry know that when Rani was questioned and caught in a net of logic by the lawyer, she would use this special strategy to free or, more appropriately, destroy him completely?

"The baby was not Chaudhry's," she swore before a full court.

"Chaudhry's not a man," she added carelessly. "But ask Chunan or Ratan. I can't tell you which one it is, I don't know.

Hunh!" She assumed her usual coquettish manner.

Accompanied by lightning and a quiet peal of thunder, a black mountain shattered over Chaudhry's being, and far away, in the darkness, a circular, protruding dot gyrated like a top.

To this day Chaudhry traces lines with a piece of charcoal on the side of the road. Long, triangular, round lines, like a singed mark.

Translated by Tahira Naqvi

A Morsel

PANDEMONIUM reigned in the *chal*. Either a snake had been spotted in one of the rooms, or someone was in the throes of labour pains. Women dashed wildly from one room to another, and then, lugging jars, boxes and glass phials, they hastened toward Sarlaben's room as if she were about to take her last breath and could only be saved by her neighbours.

Actually, Sarlaben was indeed nearing the end; her train was about to depart.

She would have been exactly thirty-four if her far-sighted parents had not tampered with her birth certificate and deducted five whole years from her age. But what is officially recorded on paper doesn't always prove helpful. Coming from some nameless village in U.P., she had lived in Bombay long enough to pass off as a true native of that city. As a matter of fact, she did not carry the stamp of any particular region; sometimes she was mistaken for a Gujarati, sometimes a Marwari or a Sindhan. But, once Jagat, now she was only Sarlaben.

Sarlaben was a nurse at E.M. Hospital. Her salary, including the inflation allowance, came to two-hundred-and-forty rupees a month and after paying, the rent for her room, which was twelve rupees, she had enough money left over to lead a very comfortable life. She brought First Aid supplies, APC tablets, Mercurochrome, pure glycerine, and samples of other patent medicines from the hospital and distributed them free of charge among the inhabitants of the *chal*. Her room was something of an infirmary for her neighbours.

Sarlaben was a very useful person. Again, her character (in keeping with her appearance), was such that it never posed a threat to any of the families in the *chal*. For this reason she was extremely popular and well-loved. Wherever she went she was waylaid by whimpering, bawling children she had delivered; people welcomed her at every step, and shopkeepers and vendors gave her discounts. During her shopping rounds she stopped regularly to inquire about the welfare of her patients.

"Hey, Tulsi, how is your wife's backache now? I say, Shakir mian, has the swelling on Amina bi's feet subsided yet? Bring her to me in the evening, I'll give her an injection. Hey, Rajni, how is the pain in your knees? Is your man coming home drunk again?"

She enquired after everyone's well-being as she slowly made her way to the corner bus-stop, leaving in her wake patients who praised and blessed her.

There was just one thing that saddened everybody: Sarlaben was still unmarried. It might have been different if she had been widowed, or if, after marriage, her husband had abandoned her, but oh, woe! her train was about to depart and there was no sign of a life-partner yet. This was Bombay, here life races ahead at top speed. The go-between and the matchmaker have become extinct. In Bombay, your eyes meet and you are wed, and although Sarlaben was no film actress, she was not so plain either that a man could never fall in love with her; as a matter of fact, she was not bad-looking at all.

She lost her father when she was a child and was raised by an ailing mother who provided for her by sewing clothes for people on a Singer machine. When Sarlaben grew up and finally got a job, her mother's health failed altogether. Once or twice the thought of finding a husband for her daughter crossed the old woman's mind, but she passed away before the idea could take any real shape. Sarlaben worked diligently after her mother's death, never really giving any thought to marriage, and even if she did dwell on the subject, she certainly never told anyone about it.

It is said that an unmarried woman is a burden for all creation, the ensuing sorrow leaving its mark on each individual, making everyone accountable. At least that's what Sarlaben's friends and well-wishers maintained. Her unblemished character and virtue were indeed admirable, but there is a limit to how virtuous one should be. Of course, her friends did not want her to throw her arms around the first vagabond who came along, but there was no harm in using (properly, of course), those special womanly wiles. Snaring a husband was a job that parents could no longer tackle on their own; even the most genteel girls tried to capture the prize themselves and then, bashful, with their heads bowed, they handed over the catch to their parents. If an indiscretion occurred, no one came to know about it; parents beamed with the pride of accomplishment, the bride and groom were radiant — and that was how weddings happened. But for the likes of poor, unfortunate Sarlaben, all of this was not possible. No one came along to administer a balm on the wounds of those quietly suffering women who were engaged in providing comfort and solace to others, with no time for themselves. They shared the burdens of others, spent sleepless nights, tended new-born infants, and returned to the half-darkness of their rooms to gulp down whatever there was before stretching out on a lonely bed. No one provided comfort or solace to these women, or offered to heal their bruised, lonely selves.

Was there no man alone and hungering for the love of a woman in the enormous, noisy, tumultuous city of Bombay? Did nobody here yearn for a woman's touch? Sarlaben depended on no one, she took care of herself, and owned a room in the *chal* which was a little jewel — the only one of its kind, no less than a flat: there was a sofa here and a chair, also her own private toilet — what more could one ask for in this life?

What helplessness! If you weren't married you were like an open wound; people tormented you with talk about possible cures, and then once you had found a husband there was talk of having children: such a bother, a baby, even just one, and before long there would be another. Anyway, Sarlaben firmly believed she was not going to remain single forever. There had to be a man somewhere in this vast universe whom God had fated to be her partner in life. That she might never find him, was another matter. With all this chit-chat going on around her, she found herself becoming increasingly preoccupied with thoughts of marriage. But no sooner had she eyed a man from the standpoint of marriage than he turned out to be forbidden fruit; he usually ended up asking her for advice about his wife's secret ailments. Many were willing to spend a little time with her, but she hadn't come across one who was anxious to clasp her hand forever, who wanted to bring a wedding party to her house. Even in the hospital she had never been the recipient of darkly-mysterious glances, and no one ever felt the need to treat her with special consideration; always, people brushed past her rudely as she stood awkwardly flattened against a wall, trying to keep out of their way.

She took the eight o'clock bus every morning at the corner of Gam Devi. Most of the people who travelled with her were old acquaintances, and everyone usually sat in the same seat each time. This morning she absently advanced towards her usual place but on coming closer, saw that it was occupied by a stranger. With a fleeting glance about her, she grasped the nearest strap with one hand and remained standing. The stranger looked up and down at her, then got up.

"Please sit down," he said, motioning towards the seat and, taking hold of a strap, commenced reading his paper.

Baffled, she clutched her purse for fear that he might be a pick-pocket. Then it occurred to her that he might be the husband of one of her patients. She waited for him to embark on an account of his wife's backache or the swelling on her feet, but he continued to sway back and forth silently, his hand still around the strap. She was stunned when she realized he was not suffering from some deadly disease. Things like this just did not happen!

When he relinquished his seat for her the moment she boarded the bus the next morning, she felt quite uneasy and didn't know how to react. Her first impulse was to offer him a handful of sulpha pills, to seek a bruise somewhere on his person, apply a balm of mercurochrome on it and tie it up in a foamy-white bandage. The fact that he was so completely healthy dashed her hopes; she couldn't see even a tiny scratch anywhere. Swaying nonchalantly, he continued to peruse his paper.

Sarlaben broke out in a cold sweat when ne offered her his seat again, for the third time.

You bastard, why do you give me your seat every day — don't you have a mother or a sister at home? She cast about for a reason to shout at him angrily, but watching him swaying unconcernedly made her feel exceedingly foolish for having entertained such thoughts.

A week passed and nothing changed. Sarlaben was stupefied. She was accustomed to helping others, not to receiving favours. Her heart felt burdened; again and again, at work and at home, she asked herself what the right thing to do would be. She knew it would be impossible to get to work on time if she took another bus.

Sarlaben was baffled. She turned inward, as if hurting from some sort of mistreatment; she became irritable and cried often, and when she returned from work she lay on her bed with her eyes shut, oblivious of the need to eat or do anything else. Her friends were afraid to approach her.

"Sarlaben's in love," Satu Pickpocket informed Ramwai.

"You idiot, may you rot in hell! Sarlaben is a saint, a saint!" Ramwai blasted Satu with invectives.

"I'm telling you the truth."

"What are you saying? May ashes fill your mouth!"

But Satu Pickpocket explained that his business

took him to the corner of Gam Devi where making assessments about people and relieving them of the burden in their pockets was his daily job, and he had seen a man regularly offer his seat on the bus to Sarlaben. The man remained standing the entire time, added Satu, and this had been going on for some days; it was obvious something extraordinary was going to happen soon.

"O my God!" Ramwai beat her chest and rushed to tell Shabo.

Shabo was dumbfounded. Then the two went to Saadat Bahu's house. She was in the courtyard with her baby straddled across her hands; he was urinating.

"Wonder of wonders!" The boy nearly fell into the drain.

The news spread like fire throughout the entire *chal*.

"So this is how it happens," Lakshmi Ghai said. She sewed buttonholes on ready-made garments and knew the ways of the world. Her husband's whereabouts were unknown, and her only daughter was in a convent. Her friends constantly admonished her for giving up her daughter to Christians, but Lakshmi allowed their talk to go in from one ear and come out of the other. Was it possible to make a decent living by sewing buttonholes? People also knew she went out every night, and that she didn't bring her clients to the *chal* only because she was scared of Lala, the owner. But what did people care? She never ran amok when she was drunk, unlike Entree (whose real name was Edith and who was just Entree now), who openly carried on the business of selling liquor; Lala was well-paid, and the police also received their weekly payoff. The others didn't bother with Entree because she became rowdy and foul-mouthed when drunk, and swore profusely in English — at least that was what the inhabitants of the *chal* thought it was. Pregnant often, she was grateful to Sarlaben for rescuing her each time. Although there were several respectable and decent women in the *chal*, no one dared to scold or criticize Entree; all of them had something to conceal.

"So, will the wedding be here in the *chal*?"

"Of course. We can hitch up a tent in the maidan in front — some of the best weddings in Bombay are held under tents." Shabo expressed her opinion with an air of confidence.

"Oh, it's going to be such fun, our Sarlaben will be a bride!" Ramwai loved weddings. Every year she celebrated a new one for herself, and after a few days had passed, her husband beat her up or stole her things and disappeared. Her last wedding had been quite authentic; tents etc., would have been expensive, so the pandit brought along a *havan* (which looked like a steel brazier) to her room, and she walked around the sacred fire with her groom right there. She adorned herself prettily as a bride, and it wasn't long before the spirit of celebration overtook the entire *chal*. Henna was prepared in large quantities and all the women applied it generously on their palms; tin canisters were used instead of drums to provide accompaniment to the singing of film songs, and when the ceremonies were over, Ramwai hugged all those who came her way and wept noisily: "Ah, my father, my protector, don't let me leave your courtyard," she wailed in imitation of a scene from a film. The paanwala immediately started up the gramophone and raised the volume: "Why are you being given away to a stranger from a strange land?" Although the women sang with screeching voices, completely out of tune, this damn song cast a pall of gloom on everyone's spirits. A daughter's departure from home is always a disquieting experience, and so it was here, even though Ramwai was not leaving home and her new, cross-eyed husband was going to live with her in her room in the *chal*.

For many days Ramwai went about shyly with her anklets jingling noisily. Then her husband began beating her. Every night he came home drunk and pummelled her until her bones rattled, and in less than a month he was gone, making off with her silver bracelets and nose-ring. Ramwai sulked for a few days, cursing him as she walked around with a limp. But, despite her bitter experiences, the thought of a wedding never failed to excite her' What did it matter that the wedding was not hers — the occasion would be a happy one nonetheless.

Cautiously the women started teasing Sarlaben.

At the first sign of bashfulness on her part they assailed her with advice.

"You must get married now . . ."

"Yes, this is just the time to enjoy life . . ."

"Your parents' souls will finally be at peace . . ."

"O Ram! We're going to have so much fun!"

"We'll set up a tent at the crossing . . ."

"The bridegroom will arrive on horseback."

"Sarlaben, will you wear a long veil?"

"Why not? Have you ever seen a bride without a long veil?" Ramwai interjected. She was considered an expert in these matters.

"Ahhh . . . the *chal* will be so lonely without you."

"Who is going to deliver Saadat's daughter-in-law's baby?"

(Saadat's daughter-in-law sought Sarlaben's assistance practically every year.)

"What a hullabaloo about nothing!" Sarlaben sounded upset. "Who told you there is going to be a wedding?"

"Well, why does he give you his seat on the bus every morning?" Shabo asked tartly.

"He's just polite, that's all," Sarlaben said, breaking into a soft smile.

"Good gracious! Haven't you noticed the signs? Today he's offering his seat, tomorrow he will offer his heart," Saadat's daughter-in-law declared as she pushed the baby up on her hip. The women twittered in agreement.

All this pleasing talk made Sarlaben dreamy-eyed; overcome by affection for these ignoble, chatty women, she felt her heart swell with gratitude.

"You're not having any problems with breastfeeding this time, are you?" Anxious to change the subject, she became a nurse again.

"Not yet," Saadat's daughter-in-law murmured.

"And Edith, you had better watch out. If you get into trouble this time I'm going to hand you over to the police. Anyway, why don't you get an IUD?"

"It's not my fault. Every time I go there they want my husband's name." Edith exclaimed in exasperation.

"Entree, why don't you give them Sadik Babu's name?" Ramwai suggested.

"But I am Catholic and that son-of-a-bitch is . . ."

"Well, how about Sarmaji then?"

"Be quiet, you witches!" Sarlaben scolded them all, and taking the boy from Saadat's lap she proceeded to give him a teaspoonful of syrup to quieten him. "Get out of here now."

"First you have to tell us when the wedding is going to be," Shabo said stubbornly.

"Yes, we have to pick a date," declared Lakshmi.

"Whose wedding, what date? No one has said anything yet!" Sarlaben shouted angrily.

"No one has said anything? The groom is mute, is he?" The women giggled in unison.

And then everyone explained to a confused and bewildered Sarlaben that it was because of her own laxity and indecisiveness, that she, despite her many qualities, was not married yet. Men, by their very natures, are slow; until they are fed morsels forcibly, they are capable of nothing. The women were all her friends, they were not her enemies, and if she only gave the word, they would sacrifice their lives for her; the bird should not be allowed to escape.

"I can talk to him if you like," Saadat's daughter-in-law said.

"Hey, I'm ready to talk to him! I'll say, 'If you like the girl, come right out and say so.'" But Ramwai's offer met with resistance; no one trusted her. True she had had great practice in ensnaring men, but the woman had acquired a taste for marriage. What if temptation waylaid her? No, no, may God save us all from Ramwai.

"Perhaps men just don't have the nerve to approach her. She dresses so soberly, looks so prim, and those glasses are no help either — the unfortunate creatures are probably afraid to look at her lovingly because they think she'll scold them." Shabo offered her own analysis of the situation.

"Of course, clothes and appearance do make a

difference."

"It's one thing to be dressed like this when you're on duty, but to look like a doctor all the time, well . . ."

"A woman has to wear some make-up. I tell you, a little colour on her face — the gentleman will lose his cool altogether!"

"And pretty clothes, colourful and bright . . ."

"Also some oil and perfume . . ."

"Bangles on her wrists . . ."

"Earrings too — and then we'll see how the gentleman stays mute."

At the time Sarlaben scolded everyone, but later she began to ponder: This is the way of the world; when women dressed in flashy clothes, with heavy make-up, are milling around Bombay, why would anyone want to pay attention to someone drab and colourless? One's mode of dress must suit the occasion, after all.

But all she had were a few simple bordered saris, and perhaps one or two others that were dull-coloured Khatau. And her only jewellery was the flattened chain around her neck which had belonged to her mother and could not really be called jewellery.

In the still of the night her mind came alive with images of brightly coloured clothes and jewellery.

"Maybe he is already married," Shabo said in a worried tone the next morning.

"No, he's not", replied Satu.

"How do you know?"

"On the bus a friend of his asked him if he had found a room yet, and he said, 'Yes, I have.' And then his friend said, 'You should get married now.'"

"And what did he say to that?" Ramwai edged closer.

"He laughed."

"Well, we don't have to worry about that, then. What about his caste? Is it okay?"

"Yes; the name-tag on his bag said, 'Ram Sarup Bhatnagar.' I checked the very first day."

"Then why is she dilly-dallying ?"

"He hasn't said anything yet."

"But he must have said something with his eyes?"

"No, and even if he did, Sarlaben would never notice. If it were Ramwai or Edith, or even Shabo, she'd get the message in a second and in two days the gentleman would be in her clutches."

"Did he sigh?"

"No."

"God! What is he made of, the wretch!" Saadat s daughter-in-law was losing her temper.

After much debate it was decided that Sarlaben should use some foresight. Properly armed, she should place a morsel in this man's mouth — only then would her boat come ashore.

And that was why all the women had brought out their armour and were rushing to Sarlaben's aid. Shabo had once been an extra in films and had accumulated all kinds of things; Saadat's daughter-in-law found some Hazeline Snow which had been lying around for nearly a year; and Edith was in possession of all the smuggled cosmetics imaginable. Not only did she personally know a hairdresser, she could also fashion a stylish, balloon-like, elevated hairdo herself. In addition, she had special sparse items of clothing which were guaranteed to convert an idol.

Now began a concentrated effort to repair Sarlaben. She resisted, but to no avail. Shabo wrapped her in her pink nylon-georgette sari which had been embroidered with sequins. The selection of the right blouse was preceded by much debate; Shabo insisted that the latest fashion dictated that the petticoat and blouse should be red so that one could see flashes of colour from under the sari. And, only red sandals would do. Poor Sarlaben, what did she know of fashion or the secrets of matching colours? She was like a pliant toy in their hands.

First a lot of cream was applied to her face, including Saadat's daughter-in-law's Hazeline Snow which was now dry but had to be used so as not to hurt her feelings. Next came a plastering of rouge and powder, followed by the creation of a huge dome-like hairdo which necessitated the use of large amounts of black cotton yarn. Finally the jewellery. About this time a battle among the women was averted with some difficulty: each wished her contribution to be the greatest.

When Sarlaben arrived at the bus stop wearing high-heeled gold sandals, swaying and tottering, she found stars dancing before eyes that were now bereft of glasses. Her whole body was drenched in sweat.

Is it not enough to be a woman? Why should one need to stuff in so many condiments and chutney in just one morsel? Tears floated in her eyes. And then, a lifetime of punishment to preserve this one little morsel.

Not too long afterwards people saw a dishevelled Sarlaben scurrying back to the *chal*. They were shocked. Trembling and unsteady on her feet, she was walking home alone, without the groom by her side. Her face was heavily streaked with kajal, and she nearly fell as she stumbled towards her room.

The morsel had been spat out!

How did this happen? Why did it happen? Felled by the onslaught of questions, exhausted and numb, Sarlaben fell on her bed.

He did not rise from his seat when she boarded the bus; he continued reading his paper as always and never once did he look in her direction. She stood nearby, swaying as she gripped the strap. Frequently he lifted his face to glance expectantly at the entrance to the bus, as if he were waiting for someone. She aimed her every glance at him but, face averted, he continued to watch the door.

She allowed her scarf, which was drenched in perfume, to slip down, but he did not look up from his paper even once.

She stretched languidly, but failed to see sensuousness floating in his gaze. He glanced stonily at her, and then, ignoring her splendour, bent over his paper once more.

She dropped into a vacant seat before her. All the carefully aimed strikes made with her arrows had missed their mark and the empty quiver now shook and trembled forlornly.

Cautiously, with trepidation, she turned to look at him again. He was getting off the bus. As he alighted, he asked Satu Pickpocket, engaged in his usual business at the bus-stop, "Hey, you scoundrel, where is Sarlaben today? Why didn't she come?"

Satu Pickpocket could only stand there stammering while the stranger, taking large strides, walked off in the direction of a galli and disappeared from view.

Translated by Tahira Naqvi

By the Grace of God

"O GOD! You tell me, what should I do?" Sakina asked with tears in her eyes.

"I still believe that Farhat should ask for talaq."

"Talaq! O God no!" She was trembling. "No one in our family has ever asked for talaq. What with Razia still a millstone around my neck ... who will marry her? Where are the suitors for my sweet little daughters?"

"Suitors" need not necessarily mean healthy, handsome young men. It means bulging wallets and well-to-do parents. Something to fall back on.

"We had to beat the bushes to find a boy for the older one. (The 'boy' is no more than 60 or 65, one wife, four daughters, but no son.) Married Farhat for a male issue. But let alone a son, she has not even managed to produce a daughter fox six years! Her dried up tree has seen neither flower nor fruit, nor even the light of day. What all didn't I try? Amulets, charms, chants — nothing worked. Even Khwaja Sahib of Ajmer Sharif has turned a deaf ear to poor Sakina."

"Now don't get into this charm-chant rubbish. Take her to a proper doctor."

"The best of doctors have looked inside her womb. They say there's nothing wrong with the girl. It is the will of God. If she produces, well and good; if not, who's to blame?"

"Problem with Imdad Mian?"

"*Tauba! Tauba!* God forbid that menfolk should start having problems. Damn! People are beginning to hint at a third try! No scarcity of girls. The best of families will offer their daughters to him on a silver platter."

One day I met Farhat at the cinema. Buxom, fair, with laughing eyes — seemed ready for the kill. It was the mother whose juices were sapped, worrying continuously about her daughter's blighted kismat.

Farhat herself was not the least bit concerned. She was barely twenty-two or three. My friendship with this family was of recent vintage. They lived in a beautifully furnished four-room flat. Imdad Mian's first wife had been banished to Khar to live with her father. This flat was especially set up for Farhat, but the property deed had not been transferred in her name. To hell with Imdad Mian! Farhat can get thousands of suitors. I thought of Anwar who was staying with me those days. Gets Rs.550 now, and is destined for better things!

That day, at the movie theatre, Farhat was stealing glances at Anwar. Sakina Behan, too, was bestowing kind looks on him. When I spoke to her, she beamed.

"What can be better? They are made for each other. Sun and moon, they'll dazzle the world!"

"You arrange the talaq, I'll take care of the rest," I promised.

Anwar got a bit of a shock. "I don't want to get into this mess," he protested.

"Silly boy! She's such a nice girl."
"After the divorce . . . .?"
"The old lady's a witch."
"For shame! Such a sweet old lady!"

Anwar was outnumbered and outwitted. Trapped between Sakina and me, he found himself entangled in the Farhat web. We found every excuse to throw them together. Eyes brimming with tears, Sakina Begum never tired of telling me how grateful she was.

From a reluctant dragon, Anwar was transformed into an eager beaver! Farhat was now the focus of his attention. Although married, Farhat had never known love. Anwar gave her life a new dimension. At first he was openly hostile towards Sakina, but before long he started adoring her. And she openly doted on him. Her very breathing seemed somehow connected to him! My presence was no longer required. Even before the formal announcement, Anwar had become a part of their family. He often stayed over till two in the morning. Sometimes Farhat would drop by and, behind closed doors, I could hear them romping around. I had to leave for Poona, but when I returned I learnt that Farhat had spent most of her time at her mother's place. Her visits to her own flat were a rare occurrence. Their romance, undoubtedly, had reached its peak.

"So . . . what are your plans?" I asked Sakina.

First she tried to side-step the issue. Then, "Swamiji from Ahmedabad has given us a special herb . . ."

"To hell with Swamis! Damned fakes! I'm asking about the talaq."

"I hate the word, talaq."

"Then what?"

"By the grace of God it will be all right."

"Don't count on God's grace. You will live to regret this — a young boy and girl meeting like this every day..."

"Why? Has Farhat said anything?"

"No. But I have eyes in my head." For a long time I sat down and explained the pros and cons to her. She sat with downcast eyes thinking God alone knows what.

"Swamiji has given seven packets. Every Tuesday, one packet with paan or hot milk."

"For Farhat?"

"No, for Imdad Mian."

"Imdad Mian!" I fumed. "If he were to swallow seven bombshells instead of seven packets, the result would still be zero. Does he visit?"

"Every Tuesday. After a bath and two *rakat* prayers he swallows the stuff with hot milk."

"And then? What the hell are you up to?"

"He is her husband, after all!"

"But Anwar...? Damn Imdad Mian!"

I didn't know how to shake her out of her complacency. Was the idiot blind as well as deaf? I couldn't make myself give her the turn of the screw that she deserved.

"Next Tuesday it will be packet number four."

What was on her mind? "Swamiji says, God willing, packet number five...."

"Sakina, this is no joke. Now smarten up and do something about the talaq. Get her *mehr* out of the old fool."

I had thought that Anwar and Farhat would be able to set up a separate flat and live happily together for the rest of their lives.

"*Mehr*!" She looked at me aghast.

"How much is it?"

"A pittance! Why should I hide anything from you? Of the total 55,000, Sarfaraz Mian borrowed 10,000 for a ticket to England. Now he doesn't talk of returning home. Married a honky and produced a brat."

Farhat's marriage had been arranged through a friend of Sarfaraz's. Although Imdad Mian was quite aged, Sakina did not allow that to come in the way since her son's future was at stake. After all, chances were that Sarfaraz would do well and get them out of a tight spot. As it turned out, despite borrowing another 6,000 for his return fare, Sarfaraz never came back. Every paisa thus advanced was entered by Imdad Mian into the ledger of Farhat's *mehr*.

"So that makes 16,000. What about the rest?"

"Flat at Worli. But that too is in Razia's name. Thought there should be something for her, too. These days all eligible boys have perpetually growling stomachs!"

I felt sorry for Farhat. A sacrificial lamb for her siblings' futures. Striking similarities between Sakina Begum and the *naikas* of the brothels. No wonder she was so petrified of talaq.

"If Imdad Mian remarries we will be ruined. You would be surprised how many *mannats, wazifas* and *chillas* I have promised to prevent him from contemplating another marriage. But you know these busy-bodies, always provoking a childless man."

This really got my goat. What a blockhead this woman was. Didn't she understand? What if something happened between the young couple?

"Look, behan, stop worrying. You will make your home with Anwar and Farhat. Razia will be married off, inshallah, even without a flat. You just arrange the talaq."

As usual, the answer I got was evasive. What happened next was exactly what I had predicted. One day Anwar looked more disoriented than usual. Farhat was equally distraught. I asked, "Have you two fought?" They looked at me, startled.

At night there was a commotion behind closed doors in Anwar's room. I could hear Farhat sobbing. I knocked.

"Come in." He took me by the hand. "Now try to reason with this fool."

"What . . . .?"

"Aunty!" She fell at my feet.

"She was climbing over the window sill . . ." Anwar was trembling from head to toe.

"Have you taken leave of your senses?" I lifted her tear-stained face. "Stop crying. Everything will work out after the talaq . . . ."

"Never! She'll never agree. I could die," she howled.

"You would rather die than stand up for your rights?"

"Can't see her in that state. Yesterday she almost had a stroke. Clenched jaw, cold sweat. All I said was that she should stop him from this business of Tuesday visits. Ugh! I don't even want to look at him — repulsive animal!" She dissolved into more tears.

"Did you say this to your mother?"

"No!"

"When she finds out she will definitely see reason. I will talk to her tomorrow morning. And, within eight days, talaq . . ." My consoling seemed to work. She started to smile through her tears. She looked beautiful. Anwar's blue eyes rained love all over her radiant face.

I returned to my room and tried to sleep. Tossing and turning, I thought that if Imdad Mian found out he would raise hell; and Anwar in the military! The wretch would be court-martialled. Imdad's first wife was already on the warpath and would tear strips off Sakina Begum and Farhat.

With great kindness I spoke to Sakina about Farhat's condition. I swore to her that Anwar would never betray her daughter. Sakina seemed to have gone into a trance. Her reactions were dazed. Then it seemed as if she had been shot through with a machine gun. She started laughing madly, then wept like a baby. Trembling like a leaf, she fell in a heap. Razia was in college. Farhat sat terrified in her room. Sakina neither cursed anyone nor spat in my face for having been the cause of her daughter's betrayal.

"*Now*. Come at once to the lawyer's. I will immediately despatch Farhat to my sister in Bombay. Every type of pressure will be applied to make Imdad pay. Just stop this hysteria."

Completely broken, she sat down with her head bowed. "Lawyer . . . lawyer," she repeated incoherently. "Now, at this time . . . .Go home now, I'll phone you later. May God give you every joy in this world." Closed her eyes.

All day I waited anxiously for the phone to ring. What if the mother and daughter committed a double suicide? I would be stuck with the guilt of it for the rest of my life. How was I to know that things would take this drastic turn?

Anwar was in a frenzy. It is normally believed that men are fickle. After getting women into trouble, they usually take off. But Anwar was on the verge of a breakdown. By the evening I had had enough. The phone rang and rang. Where was everyone? In desperation I sent Anwar. When I saw his face I almost died.

"What's happened?"

"No one was home. I knocked. Lock on the door. The Gurkha said they've gone."

"Gone where?"

"Didn't know."

All night I felt I was being raked over the coals. Anwar dialled every corner of the country but the only answers he got were: "Gone somewhere, no one knows where. Maybe Versova." Anwar dashed to Versova. I tried to stop him but he was like a demon. A servant informed him, "Maybe Khar, maybe Churchgate, possibly Peddar Road." No trace of them in any of these places. A few days later we heard that they had gone overseas. Called the office. The wretch had three or four offices. No one could help us.

On the sixth day we got a soggy, dirty envelope. "Help me, for God's sake. I am under continuous surveillance. Can't breathe. O, God."

It was as if a bombshell had exploded in our faces. With great difficulty we read the seal: Begumpeth. So she was in Hyderabad.

Save her? How the hell? Anwar dashed to Hyderabad but, after knocking around, returned empty-handed.

Acutely depressed, I tried to pull myself together. When I think back, I choke at the memory of those oppressive days. What an uphill task it was to bring Anwar round. I felt like an accomplice in this crime. My hands were stained with the blood of innocents!

That year Anwar was transferred to Delhi, thank God. Several years went by. A beautiful wife and a clutch of kids helped him get over this unfortunate incident. I was stepping out of Marks and Spencers when I almost collided into her. For a few seconds we gaped at each other.

"You!" Wrapped in a sable fur she threw herself into my arms. "It's been such a long time."

"Sakina!" I was barely able to croak.

"Staying a Sarfaraz's. He never returned. So I thought, what the hell! I better swallow my pride. In any case it's a good excuse for travelling.. What a beautiful place these *feringhis* have built for themselves!" And she rambled on about her travels in France, Italy and Switzerland.

She was utterly changed. This youthful looking woman with pleasantly distributed flesh around her formerly emaciated body, seemed to have stepped out of a beauty parlour. The barren heath had become a resplendant garden.

"Farhat — how is she?" I asked, almost dreading the answer.

"Both husband and wife are very well, by the grace of God. Nadir Mian, *mashallah*, goes to school. Nadir is such a beautiful child. Ditto his father."

"Father?" By now I was thoroughly confused.

"The same fair complexion ... the same blue eyes."

"Imdad Mian's blue eyes!"

"Now don't *you* start pretending." Laughing shamelessly, she started piling up her shopping cart.

"Those seven packets?" I was groping my way down memory lane.

"I swear, you don't forget a single detail. Swami,

the old goat, took four thousand rupees!"

"For the packets or the knack?"

"The wretch did mutter some such gibberish."

"Was offering his services, no doubt."

"And asked for another 10,000! But he was sickening."

"Was Imdad Mian suspicious?"

"Suspicious! If all men started becoming suspicious about their children . . . ! If he had any brains he would never have blamed my innocent child, but taken a close look at his own shrivelled self. Oh, let's forget all this, it makes me sick."

"Anwar was inconsolable. And you people . . . you never showed your faces again."

"Don't give me that tragic line! When they litter the streets with their bastard offspring, don't their hearts break with remorse? May he live long and produce a dozen brats." Started on a string of blessings for Anwar.

I took one long look at her expensive furs and China-silk scarf. Then I visualized the sprawling mansion at Nazimabad, glanced at the packets of currency notes at the bottom of her handbag. Started feeling a wave of nausea coming over me. Why had I felt so guilty? My sympathies had played a major role in Farhat's motherhood. And how stupid Anwar was! Living with guilt all these years. What his innocent mind regarded as the greatest sin, turned out to be the greatest blessing, by the grace of God.

Translated by Syeda Hameed

Poison

WHAT a strange death it was! People who had attended her lecture and had tea with her the previous evening simply couldn't believe that Mrs. Nu'maan was dead. Because of her chronic insomnia she had to rely heavily on sleeping pills — surely there could be no suspicion that she had mistaken that little bottle for something else?

As usual, she returned home at midnight. Mr. Nu'maan's door was closed. He was used to going to bed at 10 p.m. When the Ayah asked if she wanted dinner, she refused, but accepted a glass of milk. That glass however, remained untouched. Late to bed and late to rise was Mrs. Nu'maan's usual routine. Her husband faithfully went off to the office at his normal time. When, at 11 a.m., she had still not asked for her tea, the Ayah got worried. No sooner did she touch her feet to wake her up, than she screamed as if she had touched a naked wire. The doctor's report stated that the death had occurred between 2 and 3 a.m., a clear case of an overdose of sleeping pills.

Mrs. Nu'maan's death created pandemonium in the entire city. She had quite a following, a large circle of friends and acquaintances, plus the labouring classes whom she visited as part of her social work routine. A great believer in education for women, a torchbearer of women's rights, her sudden and untimely death led to the closure of many schools. For months afterwards, condolence meetings were held all over the city.

The gods had been overly generous to Mrs. Nu'maan. The only daughter of a wealthy father, she was beautiful and educated. As soon as she graduated from Rohini College, her admirers started lining up at her doorstep. Ever since she was a little girl, Mrs. Nu'maan had been extremely bright. A superb tennis player and an ace rider, she had also won innumerable swimming trophies. Her skill in handling the sitar reminded people of Vilayat Khan. Her excellent repartee and wit made people adore her wherever she went. It was as if she had ensnared their innocent hearts in her magical fingers.

When the Muslim League came into prominence she detached herself from the Congress Party and became a rostrum-thumping supporter of the League. Her days and nights were dedicated to the movement. People were moved to tears by her commitment. Prominent among the women who protested against purdah, Mrs. Nu'maan was one of the first to cast aside the veil and stride into the political arena.

The best thing that could happen to any town was Mr. Nu'maan's posting there as Deputy Commissioner. The moment she stepped into her husband's territory, Mrs. Nu'maan took charge of its various clubs and committees. Heart and soul, she dedicated herself to reforming local conditions. You could safely call her Mr. Nu'maan's right hand. A born hostess, she was at her best while arranging social events. Mr. Nu'maan was meek and mild-mannered; had his better half not been excessively capable, he would never have progressed so rapidly on the social and career ladder. Mr. Nu'maan's plush job was a fringe benefit of his marriage, a gift from his influential father-in-law; were it not for this, he may never have left his childhood fiancee, Ayesha Begum. When Mr. Nu'maan got married Ayesha Begum resolved to stay single. A school-teacher by profession, she moved into the school quarters after her parents passed away. There she started leading the life of a reclusive spinster.

In matters pertaining to the heart, Mrs. Nu'maan was extraordinarily lucky. Within her circle of friends, there existed an inner core of admirers. During her college days she was considered a ravishing beauty. A few young students, smitten by her, had gone to the extent of committing suicide. Inspired by her beauty, progressive writers of the day had written sublime poetry and prose. Several short stories owed their success to the liveliness of Mrs. Nu'maan's personality sparkling through the narrative. An anthology of anonymous love letters addressed to her had become an instant bestseller. Some envious wags had spread the rumour that the letters had been written by none other than Mrs. Nu'maan herself. Still no one could deny that the letters were literary gems. It therefore followed that in addition to all her other talents, Mrs. Nu'maan was a first-rate letter-writer as well!

Mrs. Nu'maan was a staunch believer in birth control. She often said that it was these innumerable children who were responsible for the deplorable condition of our country. They were born of poverty and poverty is born because of them. Only illiterate peasant women have a limitless capacity for littering babies all over the place.

I recall my mother, who was always a little scared

of Mrs. Nu'maan, seeing that she had nine other children in addition to me. The ten of us, robust little urchins, were living proof of Ammi's boorishness. Poor Mrs. Nu'maan used to have a fit whenever she saw the dirt plastered on our knees and the sores on our feet. Our noisy games made her head ache, and our greedy gestures at mealtimes made her throw up. She had a habit of taking us by surprise. And while we stood around her with our mouths open, Ammi felt like drowning herself and all of us in the nearest pond. Some foul mouths had floated the rumour that Mrs. Nu'maan was barren.

Her visits always led to the commencement of a massive hygiene programme that lasted for several days. Ammi became obsessed with cleaning her whole brood. Our snot-filled noses were threatened with a pair of iron tongs; shoes, like the curse of hell, were strapped around our chubby feet. My mother's innate slovenliness, however, came to our rescue, and before long, we were allowed to romp around the backyard like wild animals again.

Mrs. Nu'maan gave Ammi innumerable recipes to keep her womb from succumbing to the onslaughts of pregnancy. But thanks to Abba's sabotage, Mrs. Nu'maan's prescriptions never worked. He was a strange man, our father. If he had had his way he would have ordered us in pairs! It was thanks to him that we had the pleasure of growing up like free-wheeling cave-children!

Great people often have a great number of enemies. Mrs. Nu'maan's popularity led to many raised eyebrows and unkind comments, but no one dared to speak a single word to her face.

"Did you hear the small-minded comments of

these people?" she said, laughing, to Ammi. "You know Nu'maan Sahib. Can you believe such disgusting behaviour being attributed to him?"

"Senseless gossip!" agreed Ammi readily. "He is crazy about you, and why not? Is there a single quality you lack? If there were more ladies like you, I swear our country would not remain as backward as it is today." Ammi repeated a few well-rehearsed lines.

"No, my dear, not me. I am a rough stone, not worth anything at all." This generous display of self-effacement was most touching.

"You're much too modest," protested my mother. "The city has taken on a new personality since you came on the scene. Take the growing literacy among the common people as an example ..." Ammi borrowed sentence after sentence from the local newspaper. "Women's education was in the garbage bin before you arrived." Ammi made desperate attempts to divert her attention so that she would not catch a glimpse of the ten of us running wildly behind the chickens. She mentally cursed and despatched us to hell for causing her severe embarrassment. She knew that if Mrs. Nu'maan's gaze came to rest on us, she would abandon all other reforms and concentrate on the uplift of our snot-filled noses.

"Honestly, sometimes I tire of the love he showers on me! Can you believe that if I am not at the dinner table he goes to bed hungry?" My mother knew this wasn't true, but she wouldn't dream of contradicting Mrs. Nu'maan. Quite inadvertently she said, "Perhaps he eats elsewhere." (She could have swallowed her words or bitten her tongue, but it was too late.) "People spin such stories, you know," she said in a desperate bid to cover up her faux pas.

"Oh, they love splattering dirt on snowhite linen! This is precisely why we are backward and illiterate. Mr. Nu'maan's spotless reputation is an undeniable fact. And on top of that, can anyone hide anything from one's own wife? If something were brewing, would I not know?" Looking quickly at my mother she added, "You are an innocent, my dear," (meaning you are a blockhead, a simpleton and a fool). "But as for me . . . Mr. Nu'maan can't hide anything from me!"

"How can anyone hide anything from you?" said Ammi hastily.

"And who is the subject of their insinuations? Ayesha Begum! Have you seen Ayesha Begum?"

"A shrivelled sourpuss, may God forgive me."

"Oh no, please, she's human too. Who am I to talk? Who can be plainer than me? But Ayesha . . . she looks like . . . like . . ."

"The soul of tragedy."

"Precisely! A cursed barrenness."

"Without a man's love a woman's face becomes the index of her damned desolation."

"Lifelong spinsterhood devastates the countenance."

For a long time Ammi and Mrs. Nu'maan would sit and talk, using medical and social arguments to prove that Ayesha Begum was destined to look like a dried up bean for the rest of her life. *Tauba, tauba*, they kept repeating, while Mrs. Nu'maan's florid prose reached its peak.

Even Ammi became eloquent: "Time hasn't been kind to Ayesha Begum. But to tell you the truth, even at her best, she couldn't have touched the hem of your skirt. Otherwise why would Nu'maan Sahib have left his childhood fiancee and become enamoured of you?

Although some people say that Nu'maan left her because, more than anything else, he wanted the position of Deputy Collector." Ammi could say the oddest, almost cruellest, things with complete ingenuity.

"Bloody lies!" said Mrs. Nu'maan angrily. "Nu'maan would never have taken such a big obligation. All these rumours have been started by her relatives. After all, it isn't easy to bring up half a dozen brothers and sisters. Ayesha was one of them, naturally the family was disappointed. Let's face it, if a woman cannot defend her basic rights, who else can protect her? If she were all that attractive why would Mr. Nu'maan have rejected her?"

"Her looks are what God gave her, poor thing," sighed my mother.

"Of course they are, but what about brains? Nature's deficiencies can be corrected if only one tries. With a little care, the most homely face can look attractive. Poor Ayesha Bi! She cannot conduct even an ordinary conversation. Tell me, is there any liveliness at all in her? The slightest trace of animation?"

"Good heavens, no! I dread her company. She seems to have taken a vow of silence."

"In Europe there are schools that train women to become attractive to their men. And our women ... no wonder we're so backward." Mrs. Nu'maan was off on her hobby horse again.

One day when she had soundly lectured Ammi on women's rights, my mother asked Abba, "Why do you flirt with English women?"

"Come along with me one day. You too can flirt with their men!" said Abba mischievously.

"God help me!" exclaimed Ammi, but from that day on she didn't dare assert her conjugal rights!

Mrs. Nu'maan was given to teasing her husband. "You have ruined her life, poor thing." But he usually laughed off such remarks.

"She must curse me with every sip of water she drinks." Mr. Nu'maan began to look embarrassed.

"Tell me, did you dislike Ayesha Begum from your very childhood?"

"Something like that." He tried to evade the issue.

"Then did your family force the engagement?"

"A helpless man can be forced into doing anything," he sighed, playing with Mrs. Nu'maan's hair.

"Men are such frauds!" said she reeling with the intoxication of Mr. Nu'maan's love. Nu'maan puffed nervously at his cigar and turned away.

Mrs. Nu'maan's heart was a boundless ocean which overflowed with sympathy for the plight of humanity. She felt a surge of pity for Ayesha Begum. Had she been married to the Deputy Collector, a grand life would have been hers! Parties, at-homes ... alas! She shuddered at the thought of Ayesha's mismanagement of it all! More likely, the house would have been full of squealing brats. At least Mrs. Nu'maan had kept her environment free from this epidemic. One of her favourite sayings was that a woman who refrains from producing kids renders a great service to her country. There was just one fallacy with this line of thinking. Had Mr. Nu'maan married Ayesha Begum, he would have remained a school-teacher all his life.

During school inspections Mrs. Nu'maan sometimes ran into Ayesha Begum. Naturally, Ayesha Begum was jealous, although, she reasoned, it was no one's fault, not hers nor Mr. Nu'maan's. How could he have turned from the shimmering moon to a piece of dried tamarind?

People said that after presiding over the school function Mrs. Nu'maan walked across the compound towards Ayesha Begum's quarters.

"Won't you give us a cup of tea?" she said with her usual grace. Ayesha invited everyone, and served tea with her own hands. As usual, Mrs. Nu'maan began to tease her.

"Sorry, I snatched your fiance, but you can hardly blame me."

Ayesha smiled with embarrassment. "Begum, why should it be your fault?"

"How angry you must have been with me!" Mrs. Nu'maan laughed even louder.

Ayesha Begum turned pale but spoke with the utmost dignity.

"Nothing to be angry about, Begum. These are the vagaries of kismat."

"Kismat! Stuff and nonsense! These outdated notions make life a living hell for our women. Man gets up and goes, leaving the woman in an abject state of despair. And the woman, her lips sealed, spends all her life in jahannam." Mrs. Nu'maan's lecture had begun. That day Ayesha Begum was in a surprisingly bad mood. She seemed to have lost her cool. Trembling, she spoke in a clipped voice. "Snatching is a fine concept, Begum. Is a human being no more than a clay toy that anyone can grab? Physically, you can smash and grab, Begum, but who can seize the heart?"

"You are almost a philosopher, Ayesha Begum. But your concept of empty love . . ."

"Love is never empty, Begum. It is life's greatest bargain." Ayesha Begum was beginning to lose control. "Oh, Begum, you poor simpleton."

Mrs. Nu'maan and her coterie went into peals of

laughter. Mrs. Nu'maan a simpleton! What an absurd idea!

"Irfan," Ayesha Begum called out to someone on the other side of the screen. "Son, come here."

A sixteen or seventeen year old boy appeared from the other side, racket in hand. "Come, son, say *adab* to your aunt."

The cup fell from Mrs. Nu'maan's hand. Standing before her was Mr. Nu'maan, as he must have been twenty years earlier. Ayesha Begum, affectionately stroking his thick mane of hair, was heard saying, "This is the only memory I have of my late sister. Greet your aunt, my boy."

People still whisper that Ayesha Begum must have administered poison in Mrs. Nu'maan's tea.

Translated by Syeda Hameed

A Pair of Hands

RAM AUTAR was returning from the war. The old sweepress came to Abba Mian with a letter. Ram Autar had been granted leave — the war was over, was it not? That was why he was finally coming home after three years. Tears glimmered in the old woman's eyes as she ran from person to person, bending to touch everyone's feet in sheer gratitude, as if these were the very people responsible for her only son's safe return from the battlefield.

She could not have been more than fifty, but looked at least seventy years old. Of ten or twelve pregnancies, some full-term, others not, only one had resulted in the birth of a child who survived, and that too after many prayers and offerings. Nearly a year after his wedding, Ram Autar was summoned to the front. The sweepress wailed and lamented, but to no avail. And when Ram Autar donned his military uniform and came to touch her feet, she was vastly impressed, as if he had been promoted to the rank of colonel.

There was sniggering among members of the servant class. All of them eagerly awaited the drama they expected would unfold at Ram Autar's return. Although he had not gone to the front to fight, nevertheless, the three years he spent in the company of soldiers cleaning their excrement must have imbued him with a certain degree of soldierly pride and dignity. Surely he would not be the same Ram Autar now that he wore a military uniform; there could be no doubt that when he heard of Gori's misdeeds, his young blood would boil with the fury of insult.

How meek she had been when she first came here after her wedding, and as long as Ram Autar was around, her veil hung low and no one saw even a glimpse of her glorious face. And how she cried when her husband left, as if the sindhur were about to be permanently removed from her hair. For a few days afterwards she quietly minded her business, the basket of refuse set on her hip, her head cast down, her eyes reddened. Then, gradually, the length of her veil began to diminish.

Some people blamed it all on the season of basant. Others bluntly asserted that Gori was a woman of loose morals to begin with and as soon as Ram Autar disappeared from the scene, she immediately reverted to type and began to exhibit bold and bawdy behaviour. The fool, she giggled constantly, provocatively swung her hips, and whenever she walked by with the basket of refuse on her hip, her brass anklets jangling noisily, men lost their cool. The cake of soap slipped from the hands of the washerman and fell into the fountain, the cook's gaze wandered away from the roti which soon burned on the pan, the water-carrier's bucket descended deeper and deeper into the well, and the turbans of the watchmen came loose and fell about their necks. When this disastrous vision of delight had retreated from view, the entire servant class stood transfixed, as if drained of life. Then, startled, they would begin to taunt each other. In anger the washerman's wife threw down the pot of starch, the watchman's wife, for no apparent reason, began scolding her infant son who had quietly clung to her breast all this time, and the cook's third wife swooned in a fit of hysteria.

Gori was her name, the feckless one, and she was dark, dark like a glistening pan on which a roti had been fried but which a careless cook had neglected to clean. She had a bulbous nose, a wide jaw, and it seemed she came from a family in which brushing one's teeth was a habit long forgotten. The squint in her left eye was noticeable despite the fact that her eyes were always heavily kohled; it was difficult to imagine how, with a squinted eye, she was able to throw darts that never failed to hit their mark. Her waist was not slim; it had thickened, rapidly increasing in diameter from all those handouts she consumed. There was also nothing delicate about her feet which reminded one of a cow's hoofs, and she left a coarse smell of mustard oil in her wake. Her voice, however, was sweet. When she sang folk songs at the festival of Teej, her lyrical voice rose and fell mellifluously above all others'.

The old sweepress, Gori's mother-in-law, became distrustful of her as soon as her son left. To be on the safe side, she verbally abused her every now and then, often for no good reason. Sometimes the old woman followed Gori just to keep an eye on her, but she was getting on in years and her back was bent to one side from forty years of lugging baskets of refuse. She had been our sweepress for a long time and had been present to tie off our umbilical cords. As soon as Amma went into labour, the sweepress stationed herself in the doorway, often giving the lady doctor valuable advice, and occasionally she would tie an amulet to our mother's bedpost to ward off evil spirits. She held a position of considerable respect in our household.

And it was this very sweepress' daughter-in-law who had, quite suddenly, become a thorn in everyone's side. The behaviour of the cook's wife or that of the watchman's wife was understandable, but lamentably, our own proper sisters-in-law had also begun to view Gori's swaying hips with displeasure. If Gori happened to be sweeping the floor in the bedroom while one of our brothers was present, our sister-in-law would immediately snatch her breast from the baby in her lap, and run to the room in alarm in order to prevent Gori from casting a spell on our brother.

What was Gori but a loose-limbed, long-horned animal? People clung to their fragile china if she chanced to be coming their way. When things got completely out of hand, a delegation consisting of the female members of the servant class approached Amma. The danger and its possible repercussions were hotly debated and discussed; a committee for the preservation of husbands was formed, our sisters-in-law voted in its favour, and the honour of being the leader of the committee fell to Amma. The women occupied places according to their status, some squatting on the floor, some sitting on stools, while others settled on charpais. Paan was distributed among them and the old woman was summoned. Infants were calmly given their mother's breasts to maintain quiet in the assembly, and the proceedings began.

"You witch! Why have you given your daughter-in-law absolute freedom to disrupt our lives? What are you thinking of? Are you getting ready to have your face blackened?"

Already quite upset, the sweepress became tearful and exclaimed, "What can I do, Begum saheb? I have beaten her, the good-for-nothing wretch, and starved her, but she is out of control."

"My, why should she want for food?" the cook's wife cried out sarcastically She was from Saharanpur and belonged to a family of cooks of long standing, and to top that, she was the third wife. What airs she put on! Following this, the watchman's wife, the gardener's woman, and the wife of the washerman further qualified the case against Gori. The poor sweepress simply sat on the floor scratching her dirty ankles as she meekly listened to the women's complaints.

"Begum saheb," she finally pleaded, "I'm ready to do whatever you ask — but what can I do? Shall I wring her neck?"

The thought of wringing Gori's neck proved to be a happy one and, pleased, the women immediately expressed sympathy for the old woman.

"Why don't you send her back to her parents?" Amma suggested.

"Oh no, Begum saheb, that is impossible." The old sweepress proceeded to explain that the daughter-in-law had cost money. An entire lifetime's savings, all of two hundred rupees, had been used to obtain this strumpet. With the same money two cows could have been bought instead, and easily there would have been a bucketful of milk every day. But this strumpet knew only how to kick. If she were sent back to her parents, her father would sell her right away to another sweeper. A daughter-in-law not only warms a son's bed, she also does the work of four people. In Ram Autar's absence the old woman could not have managed by herself; in her old age she was being tended by her daughter-in-law's two hands.

The women were not fools. The matter had shifted from a question of morals to a question of economics. There was no doubt in anyone's mind that the daughter-in-law's presence was essential to the old woman's existence; who can throw away two hundred rupees? Besides, what of the money spent on clothes for the wedding, and the amount borrowed from the merchant? Guests were entertained, other family members had been put up during the wedding — how were all these expenses to be met with all over again? Ram Autar's entire salary went into repaying old debts. A well-built, stalwart daughter-in-law like this one could not be had for less than four hundred now. After cleaning one bungalow she was able to tackle four other houses; at least the strumpet was hardworking.

Nevertheless, Amma delivered her ultimatum: "If something is not done about the slattern very soon, she will not be allowed to set foot in this house."

The old woman protested noisily, then went home and, dragging the daughter-in-law by the hair, beat her soundly. The daughter-in-law had been bought. She quietly submitted to the old woman's anger without a single word of reproach. But the next day, as an act of revenge, she openly aired the servants' dirty linen. Exasperated, the cook, the water-carrier, washerman and watchman, all came home and beat their wives. That was not all; my civilized brothers and their repectable wives also began having disagreements, and soon telegrams from my respectable sisters-in- law were dispatched to their parents. In short, Gori was like a spike in a wire chain for this once happy family.

But not too long afterwards, the old sweeper's brother-in-law's son, Ram Rati, came to visit his aunt and stayed on. There was additional work in one or two houses which he took charge of. Back in his village there was nothing for him to do, and his bride, who was a minor, still lived with her parents.

Following Ram Rati's arrival in the village, a sudden change came about. It was as though thick clouds had suddenly been dissipated by gusty winds. The daughter-in-law's laughter became muffled, her copper bracelets were silent, like a deflated balloon slowly coming down to earth, her veil gradually dropped lower, and instead of acting like an unruly bull, she started behaving like a shy, retiring bride. All the women heaved sighs of relief. Now when one of the men teased her, she cast a sidelong glance at Ram Rati with her squinted eye, and coming forward quickly, scratching his arm, he stationed himself before her. The old crone quietly sat on her doorstep, gurgled her tobacco pipe and through half-shut eyes, watched this comedy unfold. A soothing calm settled all around, as though an abscess had been completely drained of purulence.

However, a new front now came into existence, comprised this time of the male members of the servant class. The same cook who used to fry parathas for the daughter-in-law now repeatedly scolded her for not cleaning the pots carefully; the washerman complained that whenever he starched laundry and hung it out to dry, the strumpet came along and swept up dust; the watchman made her sweep the men's sitting room ten times over and still complained that she had done a sloppy job; and the water-carrier, who in the past had always readily given her water to wash her hands with, now avoided sprinkling the courtyard before she swept it, so that the dust rose in the air and descended on the clothes the washerman had hung on the line, thus giving him reason to reprimand her.

But the daughter-in-law mutely submitted to all the abuse and ignored whatever was being said. No one knows what she told her mother-in-law afterwards, but the old woman came out screaming angrily at people; as far as she was concerned, her daughter-in-law was now pure and chaste and beyond all blame.

And then, one day, Daroghaji, who was the head of all the servants and was regarded as Abbaji's special messenger, appeared before Abbaji and embarked on a long tirade about the gross and abhorrent vileness resulting from the illicit relationship between Ram Rati and the daughter-in-law, which threatened to infiltrate and contaminate the entire fabric of the servant class. Abba referred the matter to the sessions court, namely Amma. Once again, the women congregated and the old woman was summoned.

"Listen, you foolish woman, do you know what your daughter-in-law is up to?"

The old woman stared at them dumbfounded, as if she didn't know what they were talking about. When she was told that her daughter-in-law and Ram Rati were guilty of improper behaviour and had been caught, several times, in compromising situations, she didn't thank the women, who had only her best interests at heart. Instead she started to rant and rave, violently protesting that if Ram Autar had been here he would have been greatly disturbed by the unjust accusations levelled at his innocent wife. The daughter-in-law mourns the absence of her husband, works hard so that no one need complain, and does not indulge in any kind of unseemly behaviour; people have become her enemies for nothing. Everyone tried to explain the matter to her, but the old sweepress beat her breast in a frenzy and lamented that the whole world was out to destroy her daughter-in-law. After all, what had they done, the two of them? She herself had nothing to do with anyone's business, she was everyone's confidante, never had she betrayed a secret; what reason could she have for interfering in someone else's affairs? What was there that didn't take place in the outer courtyards of the houses she cleaned? No one's dirt was hidden from the sweepress; her old hands had buried the crimes of many a respectable person. If she wanted to, she could overthrow the thrones of many a queen with these very hands. But she bore no ill will towards anyone. It would be a mistake to threaten her with a knife at her throat. But she was not about to let any secrets slip out of her heart.

The old woman's outspoken remarks caused the hands on the knife to slacken; the women rallied to her viewpoint. Regardless of what the daughter-in-law had done, at least their own castles were secure. So why complain? For some time after this episode, talk about the daughter-in-law's misconduct waned and people ceased to make a fuss about what was going on. However, the discerning guessed that something was terribly amiss. The daughter-in-law's heavy body could no longer conceal her secret and, once again, people made an effort to explain the situation to the old woman. But talk of this new subject seemed to fall on deaf ears; she pretended she couldn't hear properly and ignored what the people were saying. These days she spent most of her time reclining on her sleeping mat from where she issued orders to her daughter-in- law and Ram Rati. Sometimes, coughing and sneezing, she came out of the house and sat in the sun while the two waited on her as if she were a queen.

The respectable wives did their best to make her see the truth. Throw out Ram Rati and find a cure for the daughter-in-law before Ram Autar returns. She was an expert herself, in two days she could have the mess cleaned up. But the old woman was impervious to all talk about the girl. She complained of this and that instead; her knees hurt more than they had ever done before, the inmates of the big houses were eating too much of something they could not properly digest because everyone had diarrhoea all the time, etc. This very obvious attempt by her to turn a deaf ear to the good advice being showered on her angered her well-wishers. It was true the daughter-in-law was a woman, simple-minded and foolish — the best of women in the most respectable of families make mistakes. But mothers-in-law from such families do not assume attitudes of total negligence. Why had this old woman become so senile? The monster she could easily bury under the pile of excrement from one of the houses she cleaned was being allowed to grow unhindered, while she pretended to shut her eyes to it, refusing to accept its existence.

Ram Autar's return was anxiously awaited. The old woman continually threatened: "Wait until Ram Autar comes back, he'll break your bones . . ." And Ram Autar was coming home, returning from the war alive. People waited for a dreadful catastrophe.

But they were disappointed when the daughter-in-law gave birth to a son. Instead of poisoning it, the old woman beamed with joy and displayed no surprise at the fact that her daughter-in-law had borne a child two years after Ram Autar's departure from the village. Going from house to house, she collected old baby clothes and money, and when her well-wishers tried to explain, with the aid of calculations, that under no circumstances could the child be Ram Autar's, she showed no signs of enlightenment. It was the first of *sarh* when Ram Autar went away, the same day she slipped and fell in the new English-style toilet of the yellow house. And now it was *chait*, and during the month of *jeth* she had suffered heatstroke and narrowly escaped death. That was also when the ache in her knees got worse. "The village medic is a bastard, he mixes chalk with his medicines." Then, assuming an idiotic expression she shifted from the main question and continued to babble foolishly. Was there anyone who had enough of a brain to force this old woman to see sense, to make her accept what she had decided not to?

After the birth of the boy she wrote to Ram Autar: "Ram Autar — after love and kisses, may it be known to you that all is well here and we pray to Bhagwan for the best for you — and a son has been born to you. So consider this letter a telegram and come home soon."

People were certain that Ram Autar would burn with rage. But their gratification turned out to be premature because a letter from Ram Autar arrived in which he expressed great joy and happiness at the birth of his son. He also mentioned he would be bringing socks and undershirts for the child. The war was over, he wrote, and he would be home soon. The old woman sat majestically on her mat all day long with the baby propped up on her knees. What better way to spend old age? All the work was being taken care of, the merchant's interest was being paid regularly, and her grandson played on her knees.

Well, people conjectured, when Ram Autar returns, then we'll see what happens. And Ram Autar was coming back from a war which had been won. He was a soldier, after all, would his blood not boil? Everyone waited with bated breath; the servant class, which had sobered somewhat due to Gori's betrayal, now felt invigorated at the prospect of a murder or two that would be committed as honour was avenged.

The boy was nearly a year old when Ram Autar finally came to the village. There was jubilation among the servant class. The cook poured extra water in the pot so the food could simmer at leisure while he was out enjoying the long-awaited spectacle; the washerman removed his pot of starch from the fire and placed it on a ledge in the wall, and the water-carrier set the water bucket against the well.

As soon as Ram Autar appeared, the old woman ran to him, clasped her arms around him and began to wail. But in the very next instant she deposited the boy, who was all smiles, into Ram Autar's arms and beamed, her tears forgotten. Ram Autar looked about him sheepishly as if the boy were indeed his. Then, going to his suitcase, he rummaged hurriedly through his things. People were sure he was looking for a dagger. But when he took out some red undershirts and yellow socks from the suitcase, the collective male ego of the village suffered a deadly blow. What a fool! The bastard thinks he's a soldier! What a eunuch! And the daughter-in-law? Her head-covering drawn about her closely like a new bride's, she came forward meekly with a brass container filled with water, sat down at Ram Autar's feet, took off his smelly boots, washed his feet, and then sipped a few drops of the water.

People did their best to explain the situation to Ram Autar. They taunted him and called him a fool, but he only laughed as if understanding nothing. As for Ram Rati, it was time for him to bring his bride home, so he left. Ram Autar's actions provoked anger rather than surprise. Our father, who generally didn't take much interest in matters concerning the servant class, was also compelled to take note; he too was perplexed and decided to reason with Ram Autar.

"Look here, man, haven't you come back after three years?"

"I am not sure, sir . . . perhaps that is how long it has been."

"And the boy is a year old?"

"He seems to be a year old, sir . . . .he is so naughty, the little devil." Ram Autar was blushing.

"Calculate, you fool!"

"Calculate, sir?" Ram Autar murmured in a sickly tone.

"You damn fool, how did that happen?"

"I do not know, sir . . . it is Bhagwan's gift."

"Bhagwan's gift, you fool? This child cannot be yours."

Abba finally succeeded in overwhelming him with arguments which proved that the child was a bastard, and Ram Autar showed some signs of comprehending the truth. Then, in a stifled voice, speaking like a man half-crazed, he protested, "I gave the strumpet a good beating."

"You're a damn fool! Why don't you throw the strumpet out?"

"No, sir, I cannot do that," Ram Autar stammered fearfully.

"Why not, you idiot?"

"Sir, where will I get three hundred to spend on the family during the wedding?"

"Why should you spend a penny on them? Why should you have to suffer the consequences of your wife's misconduct?"

"I do not know, sir . . . .that is the custom in my family."

"But the boy is not yours, Ram Autar — it's that bastard Ram Rati's." Abba exclaimed in exasperation.

"So what is the difference, sir? Ram Rati is my brother, sir, his blood is the same as mine."

"You're a stupid fool!" Abba was losing patience.

"Sir, when the child grows up he will help out," Ram Autar tried to explain in a pleading tone. "He will contribute his two hands, sir, and he will be my support in my old age." Ram Autar lowered his head with these words.

And who knows why, Abba's head, like Ram Autar's, was also lowered, as if thousands of hands were bearing down on it . . . .these hands were neither legitimate nor illegitimate; they were only hands, living hands that wash away the filth from the face of this planet, that carry the weight of its aging.

These tiny hands, dark and soiled, are illuminating the earth's countenance.

Translated by Tahira Naqvi

Aunt Bichu

WHEN I saw her for the first time she was seated in the ground-floor window of Rahman Bhai's house and was cursing and swearing. This window, which overlooked our courtyard, was kept closed as a matter of principle since there was always the possibility of coming face to face with women who observed purdah. Rahman Bhai was in the employ of nautch girls. No matter what the function at his house, a circumcision ceremony, *bismillah* or wedding, Rahman Bhai always succeeded in getting one of these women to dance at the celebration; Waheeda Jan, Mushtari Bai and Anwari were able to grace a poor man's house at least once with their presence.

But he treated the young girls and women in his neighbourhood with the utmost respect. His younger brothers, Bundu and Genda, on the other hand, were always getting into trouble because of their philandering. Still, his neighbours did not look upon him favourably. He had established illicit relations with his sister-in-law while his wife was still alive. This orphaned girl who had no one in the world to call her own except her sister, was forced to live in her house. She took care of her children and other than nursing them herself, she did everything for them, including cleaning their soiled clothes and washing their filth.

And then one day a woman from the neighbourhood saw her nursing the baby. The secret was out. People suddenly realized that half the children in that household resembled their aunt. Rahman's wife may have castigated her sister in private, but in public she would never admit to any wrongdoing on per part. She always said, "Whoever accuses a virgin of such things will be punished by fate." However, she was constantly on the lookout for a groom for her sister. But who would want to have anything to do with this worm-eaten kabab? In one eye she had a white speck the size of a penny, and because one foot was smaller than the other, she walked with a limp.

A strange kind of boycott had come into effect in the neighbourhood. If someone needed Rahman Bhai's services he was simply given an order along with, "Have we not given you permission to continue living here?" And Rahman Bhai quietly gave in because he considered this indulgence an honour.

For this reason Bichu Phupi sat in Rahman Bhai's window and hurled insults from there. The others were afraid of Abba; who wanted to tangle horns with a magistrate?

That day I discovered that Badshahi Khanum, whom we called Bichu Phupi, was my only real aunt, my father's real sister, and this long-drawn out tongue-lashing was aimed at members of our family.

Amma's face was ashen. Cowering, she sat fearfully in her room as if waiting for Bichu Phupi's voice to strike her like a bolt of lightning. Every six months or so Bichu Phupi stationed herself in Rahman Bhai's window and bellowed at us. Reclining in a chair slightly out of her view, Abba would appear to be totally immersed in his newspaper during her tirade.

Occasionally he sent up one of the boys to her with a message, refuting something she had said. A new burst of anger followed as a result. All of us would abandon our games and congregate in the verandah to hear our dear Bichu Phupi swear and curse. The window at which she sat was filled with the weight and expanse of her body, and she resembled Abba so much, it was almost as if it were he up there, without his moustache, a dupatta covering his head. Unruffled by the force of her diatribe, we continued to stand around and gape at her.

Five feet, six inches in height, thick wrists with joints like a lion's, hair white as a heron, large teeth, a voluminous chin, and her voice — God be praised! It was only one octave lower than Abba's.

Bichu Phupi always wore white. The day her husband, Uncle Masud, made a play for the cleaning girl, Phupi smashed all her bangles with a piece of stone and removed the coloured dupatta from her head. From that day onward she referred to her husband as 'late' or 'dead'· the refused to allow hands and feet that had known the·touch of a cleaning woman's body to come into contact with hers.

This unhappy event took place when she was quite young so she had been suffering 'widowhood' for some time. Uncle Masud was also my mother's uncle. There was somthing strange in all of this. Before they were married, my father was my mother's distant uncle. (In those days my mother was petrified of him.) When she found out she was about to be engaged to him she sneaked some opium from her grandmother's purse and swallowed it. Since the amount she ingested was very small, she recovered after a few days of discomfort. Abba was in college in Aligarh at the time.

he was in the middle of exams when he heard what had happened and, dropping everything, he dashed to my grandfather's house. My grandfather, who was also Abba's first cousin and good friend, pacified him with great difficulty and tried to convince him to return to college. Hungry and nervous, Abba paced up and down not far from my mother's bed. Through the curtains, her eyes half-closed, my mother saw the shadow of his broad, overbearing shoulders shaking with anxiety.

"Umrao Bhai, if something happens to her ..." the giant's voice broke.

Grandfather burst out laughing. "No, no, dear brother, don't worry, she will be all right."

At that moment my little innocent mother became a woman; fear of this giant-like man vanished from her heart forever. For this reason Bichu Phupi used to say, "The woman is a sorceress. She had illicit relations with my brother, she was pregnant before she got married."

When my mother heard these insults being uttered in the presence of her grown children, her face crinkled up and she began to cry. Seeing her weep like that, we forgot all the harsh treatment meted out to us and felt almost maternal towards her. But as for Abba, these foul remarks only made the lights in his eyes dance like fairies. He would send up Nanhe Bhai with an affectionate message for Bichu Phupi:

"Well, Phupi, and what did you eat today?"

"Your mother's liver!" she would exclaim, burnt to a cinder by his response.

Abba would send her another message. "Why Phupi, that's why you have haemorrhoids in your mouth. Take a laxative, I say, a laxative."

She would then begin cursing my older brother with the malediction that his virile body be picked by crows and vultures; she pronounced the curse of widowhood upon his bride-to-be who sat in some room, God knows where, dreaming about her bridegroom- to-be. And through all of this, her fingers stuffed in her ears, my mother would chant the incantation, "You are Might, You are Mighty, rid us of this calamity."

After a short while Abba would give Bichu Phupi another push and Nanhe Bhai would ask, "Aunt Badshahi, is Auntie Sweepress well?" And we would wonder fearfully if Phupi was now going to leap at us from the window!

"Go, you son of a snake! Don't quibble with me or else I'll crush your face with my shoe! This old man hiding inside, why is he sending out the boys? If he is a true Mughal I challenge him to come out and face me himself."

"Rahman Bhai, O Rahman Bhai, why don't you give this wrinkled old hag some poison?" Scared out of his wits Nanhe Bhai said what he had been instructed to by Abba. But he had no reason to be afraid because although he spoke them, everyone knew the words came from Abba. That is why the pain of sin would not be Nanhe Bhai's. Nevertheless, addressing such rude remarks to an aunt who resembled Abba so closely made him break out in a cold sweat.

What a world of difference there was between my father's family and my mother's. My mother's relations lived in Hakimun Gali, while my father's family held residence in Banon Kathre. My mother's forefathers traced their roots to Salim Chishti. By calling himself his *murshad*, the follower, the Mughal emperor had found the way to salvation. They had lived in Hindustan for hundreds of years; their complexions had become darker, their features had lost their sharpness, and their temperaments had mellowed.

My father's ancestors on the other hand, arrived with the last of the troops. Mentally, they were still riding in battle. There was fire in their blood, their features bore the sharpness of a sword's edge, their complexions were fair like those of the British invaders, their statures reminded one of gorillas, their voices thundered like a lion's roar, and their hands and feet were as wide as boards.

And my mother's kinsmen — they were of delicate built, of artistic temperament, and soft-spoken. By profession they were usually hakims or maulvis, which is why their street had come to be known as Hakimun Gali. Some of them had begun to take an interest in business and had turned to professions like gold-lace weaving and perfumery. Because most of my father's relatives held posts in the army, they considered these jobs to be low-class and unsuitable for men. It is true that my mother's people had not developed an interest in any of the competitive sports like wrestling, swimming, arm-wrestling, or fencing. And *pachisi*, a favourite in my mother's family, was viewed by my father's side as a game fit only for eunuchs.

It is said that when a volcano erupts, the lava flows into the valley. Perhaps that is why my mother's family was inevitaly drawn to my father's. Answers to how and when this connection began can be found in the family records, but I don't really remember much. I know that my paternal grandfather was not born in Hindustan and both my maternal and paternal grandmothers were from the same family. But there was one younger sister who was married to the Sheikhs. Perhaps my mother's people had cast a magic spell on my father's family which is why they gave their daughter to 'low class commoners' as Bichu Phupi liked to call them. While she swore at her 'late' husband, she also heaped curses on her dead father who had ground the Chughtai name in mud.

My aunt had three brothers. Two of them were older than her, one younger. Since she was the only sister, she became wilful and headstrong, always getting her way, always forcing her three brothers to do her bidding. She was raised like a boy, rode horses, could use the bow and arrow, and was quite adept at fencing. Although her body had expanded to look like a mound, she still stuck out her chest proudly like a wrestler when she walked. (Of course her chest was the size of four female chests.)

Abba used to tease Amma: "Dear, would you like to wrestle with Badshahi?"

"May I be saved from punishment!" Amma would lift her hands to touch her ears, and mutter. But Abba immediately sent off Nanhe Bhai with the challenge.

"Phupi, will you wrestle with my mother?"

"Yes, yes, why not? Go tell your mother to come here. Tell her to prepare herself and come right away. If I don't make her look like a fool don't call me Mirza Karim Beg's daughter! If you are your father's son, bring her to me, bring that daughter of a maulvi to me . . ."

Clutching the folds of her wide-legged shalwar in one hand, Amma would hastily retreat into a corner.

"Aunt Badshahi, Grandfather was illiterate, wasn't he?"

Perhaps a long time ago Amma's great-grandfather had given Abba's father a few lessons. Abba distorted the facts to provoke Bichu Phupi.

"That man? What could that butt-wiper teach my father? That caretaker who was raised on our crumbs?" This was a reference to the relationship between Salim Chishti and the Emperor Akbar. The Chughtai's traced their roots to the family of Emperor Akbar, who had endowed Salim Chishti, my mother's ancestor, with the title of spiritual leader. But Phupi said, "Nonsense, utter nonsense! Spiritual leader indeed! He was a caretaker at the mausoleum, just a caretaker."

She had three brothers, but she had fought with all of them. When she battled with one, she reviled them all. The oldest was a devoutly religious man; she referred to him as a beggar and a vagrant. My father was a government official so she called him a traitor and a slave of the British (because the British had put an end to Mughal rule.) But for that she would have been in Lal Qila now, drenched in rose attar, a queen, instead of ending up with her 'late' husband whom she accused of belonging to that class of weavers who had a perchant for soupy dal. Her third brother, my youngest uncle, was a scoundrel and a villain. The policeman used to appear at our door nervously to check up on his whereabouts because he had committed innumerable thefts and murders and was a drunk and a debauchee. Bichu Phupi referred to him as a dacoit, a title that was rather insipid when set against the colourful background of his career.

When she squabbled with her husband, however, she would say, "May your face burn! I'm not helpless and alone, I'm the only sister of three brothers. If they hear of this you will not be able to show your face to the world. As a matter of fact, if my youngest brother finds out he will take your intestines out and place them in your hands. He's a dacoit, a dacoit! And should you escape his wrath, my magistrate brother will make sure you rot in jail — he will force you to grind grain for the rest of your life. And if by some chance you slip through his hands, the oldest, who is so pious, will put a curse on your afterlife. Look here, I'm a Mughal woman, not some Sheikhani or a common worker's daughter like your mother." But Uncle Masud knew that he had the sympathy of the three brothers, so he listened to the stream of abuse with a quiet smile. It was this very smile that my mother's relatives had used to torment my father's family for years.

On every Eid day my father went directly from the mosque to Bichu Phupi's house with his sons to hear her curse and swear. On their arrival she hastily withdrew into the inner room and from there, hurled insults at my sorceress mother and her villainous brother. She sent out her servant with sweet vermicelli, but pretended it was from a neighbour.

"There is no poison in this, is there?" Abba would tease. And right away my mother and her family would be torn to pieces. After partaking of the *sewayyan* Abba gave her *eidi* which she would immediately throw on the floor, saying, "Give this money to your wife's brothers who have lived on your scraps." Abba would leave quietly. He knew that as soon as his back was turned she would pick up the money, press it to her eyes, and weep for hours.

Secretly, she would send for her nephews and give them *eidi*.

"Bastards, if you breathe a word of this to your father or mother I'll cut you up into little pieces and feed you to the dogs." But Abba knew how much she had given the boys. If for some reason he was unable to make it to her house on Eid, messages followed one after the other. "Nusrat Khanum (my mother) is widowed at last. Good, I'm glad, I'm so relieved." Insulting messages would pour in all day and then in the evening she would make an appearance at Rahman Bhai's window and start swearing at us from there.

One day while eating *sewayyan* Abba felt nauseous and threw up, probably due to the heat.

"Badshahi Begum, please forgive and forget — my time has come it seems," he groaned. Without wasting a second, her veil thrown carelessly over her face, beating her chest with her hands, Bichu Phupi was at our door in no time. But when she saw Abba laughing mischievously she turned and stormed out of the house, leaving a trail of insults in her wake.

"Because you are here, Badshahi, the angel of death has taken off in fear," Abba said. "I would certainly have died today if you hadn't come."

I cannot tell you what kind of maledictions fell from Bichu Phupi's lips. As soon as she saw that he was out of danger she said, "God willing, you will be struck by a bolt of lightning, you'll take your last breath in the gutter, and there won't be anyone around to carry you to the grave."

Abba gave her two rupees and teased, "We must pay our family entertainers for their buffoonery."

Momentarily befuddled, Phupi blurted out, "Give the money to your mother and sister!" And immediately thereafter she slapped her face and said, "*Ai*

Badshahi, may your face be blackened — you're digging your own grave!"

Actually Bichu Phupi was at daggers drawn only with Abba. If she met Amma by herself somewhere she would draw her close and hug her, lovingly saying, "Nacho, Nacho," and ask, "Are the children well?" She completely forgot that the children she was inquiring after were the offspring of that unfortunate brother she had cursed all her life. Amma was also her niece. What a rigmarole it was! By some odd coincidence I was my mother's distant cousin as well, and by that token my father was also my brother-in-law. There's no doubt that my mother's family caused my father's family much grief, but it was really disastrous when Bichu Phupi's daughter, Mussarat Khanum, fell in love with my mother's brother.

This is what happened. My mother's grandmother, who was also my father's aunt, fell sick and when everyone thought she was about to die, members of both families arrived to tend her. Uncle Muzaffar, my mother's brother, came to nurse his grandmother, and Mussarat Khanum arrived with her mother who was there to minister to her aunt.

Bichu Phupi had no fear in her heart. She knew that she had trained her children to hate and despise her side of the family, and Mussarat Khanum was too young anyway; only fifteen, she still slept with her mother and as far as Bichu Phupi was concerned, was still a baby.

But when Uncle Muzaffar lifted his limpid brown eyes and saw Mussarat Khanum's delicate form, he could not tear his gaze away from her.

During the day, while the elders slept, tired from a full night of waiting hand and foot on Amma's grandmother, the faithful young sat at the sick woman's bedside, keeping less of an eye on her and more on each other. When Mussarat Khanum extended her hand to remove the cold compress from the old lady's forehead, Uncle Muzaffar's was already there.

The next day the old woman suddenly opened her eyes. Shaky, using the pillows to lift herself, she sat up slowly and immediately summoned the whole family. "Call a maulvi," she ordered.

Everyone was perplexed. No one could understand why she wanted the maulvi at this time. Did she want to get married on her deathbed? Not a single person had the courage to question her command.

"Marry these two right away." Everyone was dumbfounded. Who were 'these two?' Just then Mussarat Khanum fainted and fell to the floor. Alarmed, Uncle Muzaffar quickly ran out of the room. The thieves were caught. The ceremony took place. Bichu Phupi was stunned.

Although nothing untoward had happened — they had simply held hands briefly — the old woman thought they had exceeded the limits of decency.

And now Bichu Phupi exploded. She attacked without the aid of horse and sword and laid waste the path before her. Her son-in-law and daughter were banished from the house that very moment. Since they had nowhere to go, Abba brought them to our place. Amma was beside herself with joy in the company of such a beautiful sister-in-law, and *walima* celebrations were held with great pomp.

Bichu Phupi didn't see her daughter's face again and announced that she would henceforth hide her face from her brother. She was already estranged from her husband and now she turned away from the rest of the world. What was it but a poison that had invaded her heart and head? Her life threatened her like a viper.

"The old hag played this little game so she could ensnare my daughter for her grandson," she kept saying; she might well have been right because the old lady lived for another twenty years.

Brother and sister never reconciled. When paralysis struck Abba for the fourth time and the end seemed near, he sent for Bichu Phupi.

"Badshahi, I'm taking my last breath. Come now if you want to fulfill your heart's desire."

Who knows what arrows were concealed in this message. The brother sent them and they pierced the sister's heart. Trembling, beating her chest with her hands, Bichu Phupi appeared at the door she had abandoned for a lifetime and thundered into the house like a white volcano.

"Badshahi, your prayers are being answered." Abba was smiling despite his pain, and his eyes were still youthful.

Although her hair was all white, Bichu Phupi suddenly looked like the little Bichu who used to throw a tantrum and force her brothers to give in to her every request. In her eyes, usually vicious like a lion's, was a fearful, cowering expression; large tears rolled down her marble cheeks.

"Bichu, my dear, scold me," said Abba lovingly. Between sobs my mother begged Bichu Phupi for curses.

"O God, O God," she tried to roar, but her voice quivered and broke instead. "O God, bless my brother with my life . . . Dear God, in the name of your beloved Prophet . . ." She began weeping like a child who is frustrated because he cannot remember a lesson correctly.

Everyone grew pale. The earth seemed to slip from under Amma's feet. O God! Not a single curse fell from Bichu Phupi's lips that day!

Abba was the only one who was smiling, smiling the way he used to when he heard her swear.

It is true that a sister's curses cannot harm her brother, for they are dipped in mother's milk.

Translated by Tahira Naqvi

Lingering Fragrance

In the growing dusk of the room, a faint shadow was advancing ... tip-toe ... towards Chhamman Mian's bed.

Now the shadow was standing with its face towards the bed. Instead of a pistol, the hand probably held a dagger. Chhamman Mian's heart pounded. Toes stiffened. The shadow bent over his feet. But before the enemy could strike the fatal blow, Chhamman Mian had pole-vaulted to the other side and grabbed the assassin's throat.

"Cheeeeen !" A faint squeak was uttered by the shadow. Chhamman Mian dashed the wily opponent to the floor.

Tinkling of bangles and anklets sent Chhamman Mian hurtling towards the light switch. The assassin disappeared under the bed.

"Who the hell ... ?" Chhamman demanded.

"I ... Haleema."

"Haleema ? What ... what the hell are you up to ?"

"No ... nothing."

"Who sent you here ? Dare lie and I'll pull out your tongue."

"Nawab Dulhan," the voice was tremulous.

"O God ! Pyari Ammi is after my life." His imagination was going wild. For several days Ammi had been giving him strange looks and whispering to Nayaab. Nayaab is a witch, she really is. Bhaijan too had been smiling at him insidiously. It's a bloody conspiracy. Not unusual among nawabs. Several times, granduncles had tried to poison Abba Huzoor. Hired goondas to do the job. Wanted to get their dirty hands on the property and devour all of it. Rifaqat Ali Khan was given poison by his own real uncle, administered by the hand of his favourite *kaneez*. To hell with such deadly property and possessions.

Pyari Ammi probably wants it all for her favourite son. After all she has brought her brother's daughter into the house as the daughter-in-law. No wonder she is after my blood.

Chhamman Mian had no love for property. Beating, torturing, squeezing labour for *lagaan*, auctioning their cattle—such displays of power made him sick.

But ... O God! If our own mother turns into a deadly enemy ... no one can be trusted As it is she does nothing but admonish me all the time. "Don't do this ... don't do that. Don't read so much, play so much, live so much!"

"Where is the knife ?" Propped up on his elbows Chhamman was peering underneath the bed.

"Knife?"

"Hands up!" Chamman used his special detective voice.

"Wha-at ?" Halima trembled.

"*Ullu ki patthi*. Hands up!"

When she lifted her hands her dupatta fell aside. Great embarrassment and lowering of arms.

"You rascal ... I said hands ..."

"Why ... Oh!" she chirped.

"To hell with your 'Why ... Oh!' Where's the knife ?"

"What knife ?" Irritably spoken.
"What were you holding?"
"Nothing ... I swear."
"Why ? Then why did you come ?"
"Nawab Dulhan sent me," she whispered, eyes lowered, fidgetting with the bead strung on her thin wire nose-ring.
"Why ?" Chhamman was scared.
"To rub your feet." She leaned on the bed.
"*La haul walaquwwat* * ! Now scram !"
He was unnerved by the mischief in her eyes.
Haleema's face contorted, lips trembled. Thump ... she sat down on the carpet, buried her face in her hands, and burst into tears.
"Haleema ... please. Haleema, don't. Please go. I have an early class ..."
More tears.

Ten years ago, Haleema's tears had fallen at the same rate. Her father was slumped on his stomach coughing up blood and chunks of pink flesh. She was clutching him to her little bosom. Then they all wrapped Abbu in white sheets and took him to the hospital. People never return from hospitals, she learnt. The same rate of tearfall was recorded on the day her mother dumped her beside Nawab Dulhan's bed, filled her empty bags with grain, and left, with never a backward glance at her weeping child.

She grew up in the courtyard of the servants' quarters, nourished on scraps from people's dirty plates. She was never permitted to crawl on the dirt stretch which separated the lowly quarters from the plinth of Nawab Dulhan's verandah. Playing with the

---

* An exclamation corresponding to, "Get thee behind me, Satan !"

filth and dirt with her playmates—the shit-eating chickens and new-born puppies—Haleema had a steady growth and a nondescript childhood.

Shameless, wretched child, she continued to defy mortality. Nayaab Bubu's ten or twelve year old Jabbar used to beat her to pulp. Sometimes he touched a pair of red hot tongs to her soles, squeezed an orange peel into her eyes or thrust a pinch of snuff up her nose. For a long time, Haleema sat patiently and sneezed like a toad, while the household collapsed with laughter. The bullying continued unabated, when she was sent to the door to hand over or receive something; a pinch, a jerk at her nose-ring, a yank at her braid. A rascal, Jabbar. Nawab Saheb's favourite — his own life-blood.

Doesn't make a darned difference, whether or not a maid enters wedlock. Not a single peacock's feather is added to her cap. Nawabzadis would rather be seen dead than allow a maid to sit with them. Two words spoken by the qazi do not have the power to bore a hole in granite, or solve the question of basic survival.

In the mahal, Nayaab Bubu had a very special status. She played her cards carefully and, instead of becoming the Begum's hated co-wife, became her bosom confidante. Her magic stick wielded over the Nawab compelled him into writing a sizeable share of the property in Jabbar's name. Jabbar, her beloved son. All the servants of the household were terrified of him. He swaggered around the house in imported trousers and a *boski* shirt. Supreme Lordship of the Servants, although a chauffeur in name. Bubu inside and Jabbar outside—a pair of millstones. Anyone who dared come between them was instantly pulverised.

And Haleema was still crying.

Chhamman Mian's reprimand devastated her. When he tried to console her she became uncontrollable. When he held her ice-cold hands to pull her to her feet, she clung to him like a vine.

God ! Those daring winter nights ! Deafening thunder-claps. Haleema on Chhamman's inexperienced hands. Cricket buddies had whispered so many ways of laying a girl. But call it misfortune or blunder, Chhamman had always dismissed sex talk as nonsense. He was intimate with only two things, cricket and books. Despite the biting cold, Haleema had scorched him like a brush with live coals. His hands were stuck to her as if she were moulded from glue.

Suddenly a knife seemed to probe his brain. He sprang away from Haleema, trembling with anger.

Storm creating havoc outside, Haleema's tears doing the same indoors !

"Haleema... please... don't !" He was squatting before her crying form.

What he really wanted was to put his head on her bosom and cry his heart out. But he was afraid that the head and the bosom would be glued together. Wiping away her tears with his kurta, he helped her up and, before she could anticipate his intention, he had pushed her out of the door and bolted it from inside.

Sleep had been banished by the force of Haleema's tears. For the remainder of the night, Chhamman Mian shivered in his quilt and cried tears of poison. Outside the frustrated wind lashed through the trees, groaning and moaning in despair.

Finishing her *farz namaz*, Nayaab Bubu raised her hands in prayer. Folding the corner of her *janamaz*, she got off the divan and tip-toed towards Jabbar's room.

Softly opening the door, she peered at her son's handsome sleeping form and tears of maternal pride filled her eyes. Inside she saw the tell-tale signs of Gultaar's dalliances with Jabbar. Gultaar, Chhamman Mian's and Jabbar's father's special maid, left mementoes of her nocturnal visits behind. Today there was her dupatta visible from under the quilt. One day this fool's indiscretions will slice off her nose. She pulled out the dupatta. May God protect Jabbar from the evil eye. A spitting image of his father !

Suddenly it struck her. A father's maid was like a mother. Right ? Best take a *fatwa* from the *alim* Saheb. One shouldn't lose out in both worlds—this one and the hereafter. How could she blame the wretched Gultaar ? Diabetic old Nawab versus this flower of manhood. How she had cried last night. The boy had become so careless. Didn't give a damn that the door was ajar. Had Bubu not been such a light sleeper, any passer-by would have witnessed their love-play. May God protect everyone.

Nayaab Bubu had negotiated the purchase of two proper maids for her Jabbar. Unfortunately, one died of small-pox and the other ran off with the sweeper's son. The harlot ! She had dealt a hard blow. Maids belonging to noble families did not display such depravity.

Many times she wanted to ask Begum for Haleema, but could not muster up enough courage.

"Haleema is marked for my Chhamman." Begum's word was law. Today her persistence will be rewarded. In any case Jabbar did not care for meek, sickly females. Like his father, he went for red-hot peppers !

Muttering under her breath she climbed up to the

terrace. "What?" Her heart stopped beating. Haleema was fast asleep, snuggled in Sarvari's quilt. With the toe of her sandal, she kicked Haleema's anklet and pulled the quilt right off the sleeping girl.

Haleema woke up in a panic and started pulling out her dupatta from under the sleeping Sarvari.

Eagle eyes darted back and forth over Haleema's body. Like a thief she sat with her eyes glued to the pattern on the faded quilt, counting the stitches of the quilting with her finger.

"Well . . . ?" Bubu placed her hands on her hips. "Damn it . . . what did I tell you?"

"Yes . . . Bubu."

"What . . . ?"

Haleema remained silent.

"Say something, you bloody mute."

"His legs were not hurting." Haleema hung down her head.

"Hunh!" Bubu swung around in disgust, her fingers moved faster on the beads in her hand. What a stroke of luck! Her heart was all spring! The lineage would now depend entirely on Jabbar. Her own Jabbar. It is God's will. It is not as if the older son was at fault. That wretched girl, Sanobar. God had given her a short lifeline, that's what. At barely fourteen years of age, she was gifted to the older Sahibzada. What a lovely child Sanobar was. Very frail. If only she had parents to take care of her! In the normal course she would have left her father's house and, with the music of the shehnai ringing in her ears, would have set her delicate foot on her husband's threshold. The mingling of two hearts, and a new world would have been created.

Sanobar loved playing "Brides". Often she would

sit down, pretending to be the bride, surrounded by a cluster of maids. Beautiful child. Small bones, taut body, tiny hands and feet, pearly teeth, and the large eyes of a devi. How she had begged the Begum to bestow her on Jabbar. But Begum was her usual obstinate self. This maid was a gift from her *maika*, she had brought her for the older Sahibzada.

Who says Sanobar's "wedding" was fake ? Bubu was the maid of maids. She was perfectly aware that every girl had a secret desire to become a bride. And a maid had the same feelings as her mistress. Woman first, maid second. During the early evening she had sent Sanobar to the bath. When she emerged, she dressed her in a peach coloured outfit. She had plucked the henna from the bus with her own hands. Sanobar's palms and feet had turned a glorious red. Touching her hair with a fragrant oil, she had twisted it into braids. Friends whispered secrets in her ears and teased her all evening. When Hashmat Mian, Chhamman's older brother, picked her up and took her to his bosom, poor Sanobar had drawn a little ghunghat over her face.

Having seen the face of Hashmat Mian, poor Sanobar, at the age of fourteen had stared at the angel of death. Within the year she became pregnant. The sickly, frail child lay on her stomach all day, puking. Allah, Allah! On such occasions how much fuss is made in normal households. Every member of the clan outdoes the other to please the newly pregnant bride. In pre-pregnancy days Hashmat used to dance to her tune. For every kiss he used to bend his knees and grovel. Now he was showing the first signs of revulsion.

The mahal tradition was that when cattle became heavy with child they were despatched to the village.

As soon as they were relieved of the calf and the milk started flowing, they were summoned back. Maids received identical treatment. Pregnant ones were packed off to the village. There they delivered the brat and there it was left to grow or die. They returned, empty-handed, to the mahal so that the Begums would not be disturbed by the sound of crying babies.

How pathetically the wretches would wail and cry. Like animals they groaned for their young. Breasts filled up with milk, causing intense pain. Often they would burn with high fevers. Sometimes one of the Begums' babies was brought in for suckling. How they would enjoy the pleasures of taking the baby to the breast. But such delights were ephemeral. Ladies of noble birth cannot be expected to breed like animals, just to give their maids the pleasure of suckling! Once their impotent grief had spent itself they were once again put back to work.

Sanobar asserted her will. Refused to go to the village. Bubu tried to reason with her but she fell at the Begum's feet. Bubu had seen too much of life. She hated all maids, hated her own existence. Mostly hated, but was there a streak of love somewhere ?

Sanobar's time in this world was up. She refused to leave and her presence kept souring Hashmat Mian's mouth. If anyone tried to reason with her, she would be ready to gouge out their eyes. One day she suddenly started lashing out at the young man. Sahibzada's blood boiled over. His exasperated kick landed squarely on her stomach and Sanobar was thrown into a running drain. For three days she brawled like a buffalo. To call a doctor for her would have been unthinkable. People have such evil tongues and bad intentions. On the third day, in the darkest corner of the servants' quarters, Sanobar took her last few tormented breaths.

Doubtless, Sanobar was a practitioner of black magic, a real-life sorceress. Four years had passed since Hashmat Mian's wedding but the bride had shown no signs of pregnancy. All types of treatment had been tried. Charms, talismans, offerings at mazars, lamps at mandirs; nothing worked. True or false, the gossips maintained that Sahibzada had kicked a full term pregnancy in the womb, hence his impotence. Day and night Dulhan Begum threw hysterical fits. At the slightest excuse she ran to her parents' house. Her cousin, a renowned doctor, was treating her ... in more ways than one, it was rumoured.

Nayaab Bubu sighed. Dipped her elbow to test the water before carrying the pitcher to Nawab Begum for her morning wash.

At first Nawab Begum had hated the very existence of Nayaab. But after she fell at her feet and professed that as Nawab Dulha's servant, she was equally devoted to serving Nawab Dulhan, the latter showed some signs of relenting. Nayaab assured her that since she had not been bought from the marketplace, she could not be treated like a harlot. Blood of noble generations was coursing through her veins and arteries. Begum had no option but to accept. What the hell! All men of the family tasted a morsel here and there. To give her credit, Nayaab had always remained within limits. She never permitted herself to give credence to a single word of the Nawab's sweet talk. When the Nawab started his affair with Munawwar Mirza, she joined the Begum in the opposition front. Instead of celebrating Begum's impending disinheritance, she cried tears of blood. Her bond was with the Begum and Nawab. Who the hell was this bloody usurper, conniving at the family property ? Men were like gusts of wind, changing direction from moment to moment.

Begum and Nayaab, two teammates, planned a careful strategy. A rakhi tied by the Begum on Tarahdar Khan's wrist pledged them to a brother-sister relationship for life. Tarahdar took Munawwar and departed for Paris. After consigning Munawwar to hell, she proceeded to decorate Begum's bridal bed with her own hands. While slipping on flower bracelets and anklets on her hands and feet, she slipped two words of advice into the Begum's ear . . . how to make the Nawab happy. That night, alone, in the darkest corner of the servants' quarters, she held Jabbar to her bosom and kept an all-night vigil.

To this day, Nayaab had not discontinued her little personal services for the Nawab Begum, not once.

Seeing her downcast look, Begum puckered her brow. "Is all well ?"

Haltingly Bubu related the details. The ground underneath the Begum's feet slipped away. Jabbar was dispatched with the car to fetch Hakim Saheb.

"Nothing to worry about," Hakim Saheb assured them. "The boy is young and inexperienced." He promised to send a "tonic" with complete instructions for the Sahibzada. "It is possible, huzoor, that he may have felt some revulsion. Sometimes the "presentation" does not whet the appetite. That does not mean that the digestive system is defective."

"I had a premonition that the girl was somewhat . . . you know . . . thin, frail, sickly. If you take my advice let Baqar Nawab have her. Hashmat Mian has an eye on the Nawab's English bloodhounds. He will gladly agree to barter the dogs for the girl." Bubu started massaging Begum's feet.

"Heaven forbid ! I would rather poison the wretched girl than hand her to that leper. He is rotting from head to foot."

Never before had the family witnessed such a massive setback. A maid visits the master and returns safe and sound in the morning.

Usually the young masters would take the sexual initiative, without considering the delicacies of distribution and propriety. To prevent rivalries between brothers, the elder Begums made a just division of flesh. Having done that they were assured that each would respect the other's property rights. These domestic dispensations of justice were a hundred per cent legal and binding.

"I am sick of this boy. Eighteen years old and no flirting with the maids. My brothers started at age eleven or twelve. Sixteen, seventeen, and they were stomping and fuming for the kill. Nayaab, did you make sure that she bathed properly? Or did you send her to his bedroom stinking of ginger and garlic?" Nawab Begum was agitated.

"Begum, you still consider me a novice ? How many maids have these hands prepared for the bedchamber? I swear by Imam Husain that he who sees the naked heel of my 'handiwork' won't bother to look at a *pari* from Mount Caucasus. What about Hashmat Mian ? Was ready to fall into the trap of that damned foreigner. Wasn't it my handiwork on Sanobar that saved his skin ?" Bubu was offended by Begum's scepticism regarding her special skills.

"Begum, your son is the flower of youth. But these

are hard days. Recently, Afzal Nawab paid a heavy price for two slave girls. What happened ? The police came and camped at his doorstep. Paid no heed to his assurances that he was looking after these two destitutes as a charity in the name of God almighty. He offered them a generous helping from his coffers. To what avail? The girls were removed to some home. 1500 rupees down the drain. No chance of getting a new maid."

This news created the kind of stir that even a Third World War may not have. Rumours began to hiss and crawl in every corner of the mahal like a clutch of snakes from an open pit. Whoever learnt of it, (and how fast it moved from mouth to ear) pounded his breast.

"God, O God! Poor Chhamman Mian." When he got the news, Afzal Mian headed straight for Chhamman's room, flapping his pyjamas and chewing his tobacco.

"How was I to know ? So this is your inclination, is it ? Had I known why would I have put your Bhabhi's noose around my neck ? Never mind, darling, I am still yours." A few years ago he had fallen head over heels in love with Chhamman. But when Nawab Saheb loaded his pistol, he sobered up. Chhamman Mian hated him.

"Shut up. I have no such taste or inclination. It's just that I don't like such things. Not permitted before marriage."

"But, Sarkar, a maid is permissible before marriage."

"Wrong. Not admissible."

"That means that all our ancestors were fornicators ? Only you are the true adherent of faith?"

"It is my belief . . ."

"Your belief, shit ! Have you ever studied the rules of Din?*

"No. But this defies all reason."

"To hell with your reason. No solid facts. All airy nonsense."

"It is a crime in the eyes of law."

"Who cares for the law of the kafirs ? We only accept the word of God. We treat our slaves like our own children. Nayaab rules the household, her son lacks nothing. Look at the maids—fed with the best grains, they are bursting with health. And if you were handed starved and shrivelled goods . . . my boy, take Sarvari. She's been fattened perfectly."

"Hush !"

"What the hell is going on ?"

"Nothing. Please stop gnawing at my brain."

"Fine by me. If you like being the butt of everyone's jokes, who can stop you. And by the way, Sarkar, in case you didn't know, your fiancee . . ."

"I have no fiancee."

"Well, fiancee-to-be, then! Hurma Khanum is becoming too friendly with that bastard, Mansur."

"So . . . What am I to do?"

"Shall I tell you? I am going towards Sadar—I will send the bangle-vendor. Make sure to wear glass bangles right upto your elbows. What else ?" With his mouth full of betel juice, he let out a roar of laughter.

"Illiteracy . . . damned illiteracy !"

"Our venerable ancestors were illiterate, were they ?"

"Must have been. How do I know ?"

"Nonsense from a convoluted brain. The elders must have thought about this matter carefully before

---

* Tenets of Islam

establishing the tradition. To this day we respect their guidance and adhere to it. This is the best way of preventing young men from falling into worse habits. They become responsible, remain healthy . . ."

"Ways of legitimizing fornication."

"Your words are reeking of *kufr*. Insulting the faith."

"Don't talk about faith. This is its only tenet etched on your heart."

"You are insolent and stupid. To hell with you !"

At night when dinner was served, Nayaab Bubu, with elaborate ritual, presented Hakim Sahib's concoction in a gleaming silver spoon. Already Chhamman had torn up the instruction sheet without reading it and had given hell to Sarvari. He felt like drowning himself in the biggest serving dish on the table. He dashed to the ground the inoffensive silver spoon and stomped out of the dining room. The whole bloody world had branded him impotent, sexless.

So far all the books in his library had used the words "fornicator" and "adulterer" for men who slept with women outside the sanctified bonds of marriage.

Outside the house the wind was raging like a mad demon. The frail branch of a tree was continually tapping on the window-pane, as if seeking refuge from the terror outside. It was a long time before Chhamman fell asleep.

Cool drops of water on his feet woke him up. His heart was pounding.

Haleema's sobbing face was resting on his feet. He quickly drew up his legs.

Again those anguished tears. This girl had teamed up with the enemy. These people would not rest until they destroyed him. Alas !

"Now what is it ?"

"Am I so repulsive that I can't even touch your feet ?" Haleema's voice was choked.

"Stop talking nonsense. Go away."

"I won't. What do you take me for ? I admit I am a maid but I'm not a leper. The entire mahal is cursing the day of my birth. Everyone is laughing at me because I repulse you. I'm not worthy of you. Tomorrow Sarvari will replace me in your service."

"I will kill her. I don't want service."

"You will get used to it. Hakim Saheb says . . ."

"Hakim Saheb is an asshole."

"What should I do ?"

"Go to sleep, it's very late."

"Early or late, what do I care ? Do me a favour. Give me a lethal poison."

"Why should I ? And don't you dare say that again. Suicide is a sin against the Almighty."

"Then shall I go and burn in Baqar Nawab's fire? The man has leprosy."

Another flood had started.

"Baqar Nawab ? Who is talking about that bastard?"

"I am. You get Sarvari. And in exchange for a pair of English bloodhounds . . ."

"Stop this at once!"

"Baqar Nawab is diseased all over. The sweepress was telling Bubu. How Bubu hates me. Jabbar ! My repulsing his advances was a slap on her face."

Haleema's explanation finally began to make sense. Trembling with remorse and anger, Chhamman Mian looked at her. He wanted to dry her tears. But the thought of touching her was terrifying. Once his hand felt her face would he ever be able to withdraw it ?

"Do you want to marry me ?" he asked.

"God !" Haleema could hardly speak. "Hurma ... everyone knows Hurma is your childhood fiancee."

"And you ...?"

"I am your maid."

"Let us suppose you are my maid. Your mother was not. Your father wasn't the son of a maid. You are a Saidani, Haleema, your father was a farmer. Haleema, listen." Both her hands were in his. "I will tell Pyari Ammi. I won't marry Hurma, I will marry you."

"Marry !" Haleema flung both his hands aside with an electrical impulse. "Tauba, Tauba ! Remember Ulfat ? Sadiq Nawab wanted to marry her ... and what did they give her ? Poison. Bari Begum's orders. How she writhed in pain for three or four days. As if the breath was stuck in her throat, refused to let her die." Haleema put both his hands on her neck.

Exactlywhat he was afraid of, happened. Haleema's body was made from glue. Chhamman's hands got stuck.

"Go, go... Haleema ... my dear ... dearest." He enfolded her in his arms.

"How cold, these little hands."

"So warm them..." She undid his kurta buttons and placed her cold palms on his thumping heart. Two sobbing, inexperienced children immersed themselves in each other. The breeze outside was swaying gently like the pleasure-filled gait of a new bride!

Everything Chhamman did was a bit out of the ordinary. Everyone laughed at him. Toys are meant to be played with, they shouldn't become objects of worship. Begum had sighed with relief when, the next morning, Bubu offered her respectful salaams with a meaningful glance at Chhamman's bedroom. Eight o'clock and the door was still bolted from inside.

When Chhamman left for college, Begum saw, with her own eyes, the proof of the night before. Immediately, she offered two *rakat* prayers of thanksgiving. Haleema was a little feverish. She lay face down in her servants' chamber all day. Bubu cracked dirty jokes each time she passed by. The mahal was buzzing, "Chhamman Mian has accepted Haleema." Other maids were green with envy. Lucky Haleema ! What an innocent, handsome groom. Privately, they always referred to their masters as grooms ... it made them feel good.

Girls had always made Chhamman Mian nervous. But Haleema had opened up a new channel of communication. He became good for nothing else. A free period, and he was seen running home. Friends dropped in on Sundays and holidays, and Chhamman was making excuses: "I have to study." And how did the study session go ? Head on Haleema's lap. Kiss stop at every full stop.

"Illiterate. Good for nothing. If only you had studied a bit you could have transcribed my notes." And Haleema scratching ABCD on the floor with a piece of charcoal.

"Can you fill ink in my pen?" Ink on her hands, mouth, nose, dupatta. Topped off with tears ! A proper idiot !

The mahal had superb arrangements. Sons were allowed to stay in a separate enclosure, off the main building. Maids were not expected to do any other work. But Haleema had been trained by Nayaab. She insisted on washing Begum's hands and feet. Never shirked small chores like cleaning and replenishing Begum's paan-dan.

"Go, look after your Chhotey Sarkar." Begum tried to dissuade her from personal service, but she never looked up from massaging Begum's legs. After all, it could not be denied that her beloved son never hesitated to kiss the servant's feet.

Everything was made ready for the "new couple". New clothes, jewellery; almost like a separate existence. A small kitchenette was handy for trying a favourite recipe. Each day the *malan* appeared with her basket of fresh flowers. But Chhamman Mian disliked seeing the flowers sprinkled on the bedsheet.

"Very cruel of our bodies to crush the flowers." He gathered them all into Haleema's lap.

Nayaab Bubu's parrot-like recitation was nauseating." The moment she pukes, she will fall from grace. People can't even stand their own wives, let alone a maid with morning sickness." Chhamman's devotion to Haleema, however, did not leave her entirely untouched.

"I am thinking of arranging the nikah during the month of Khali. These days Feroza Khanum appears slightly peeved." Nawab Begum was now satisfied with Chhamman Mian's manhood.

"To hell with gossips, but I hear Hurma Bitiya has become too liberated." Bubu interposed.

"May live coals burn the tongues of gossip-mongers, but I hear he is a friend of Arshad Mian's. Constant visitor to that house."

"God ! Who told you?"

"Tarahdar Khan's wife. She is a regular visitor. She is related to the seamstress who teachers *sozankari* to Mariam Bitiya. With her own eyes she saw them play with a racket and ball. . . ."

"God forbid that it be an impediment to Chhamman Mian's education, but if you take my advice . . . the sooner the nikah . . ."

"But he runs a mile each time I broach the subject. 'Haleema', he says, 'Haleema or no one'. I have given him my ultimatum. Utter such nonsense again and I swear you will see my dead face."

"Gibberish and rot, Begum, Nawabs and their protestations! Hunh! Never a connection between word and deed! Just keep a close watch. Within a week he will be fine. The girl is already looking sickly."

No secret of the mahal could be hidden from Bubu. Whether it was the buffaloes or the mice, whoever was pregnant, Bubu could tell immediately. By the redness of their faces she could declare that the chickens were ready to lay.

"Pyari Ammi! Is Haleema going to the village?" Chhamman Mian blurted out. Haleema had been crying for the past few days.

"Yes, my love; Nayaab will go along with her. And you know what? I have sent a special message to Ammi Huzoor to send your favourite lime pickle."

"But . . . Pyari Ammi, why are you sending Haleema? Who will look after my clothes?"

"Sarvari, Lateefa."

"If Sarvari or Lateefa touch anything in my room, I will slice them to bits. But why . . . why are you sending Haleema away?"

"Our decision. Who the hell do you think you are? Interfering in domestic matters. . . ."

"But . . . Pyari Ammi . . ."

"Mian! We are still alive. Do what you wish after thrusting us into the grave." Pyari Ammi's eyes were emitting sparks. "Even your father doesn't dare interfere in domestic matters. Have you ever suffered in the past? In all matters concerning maids, Bubu has the last word."

"Pyari Ammi, Haleema is my life. God! She is not a maid ... daughter of a Syed. With loving care, you selected her for me. Now you are tearing off the flesh from raw nails. Why? What have I done?" He wanted to say all this and more, but his throat was choked with tears. Without a glance to the right or left, he walked out of the room.

Haleema was angry with the unending flow of her tears. She wanted to celebrate these last few farewell days. Only four more days to go. Who could predict the future? Four precious days. With great care she had prepared four outfits. Perfume made her stomach heave, but she forced herself to sprinkle fragrance in every fold of the bed. Each strand of her hair was washed and wafted over the smoke from fragrant herbs. Hands and feet were touched up with fresh henna. Dozens of glass bangles were slipped over each wrist, because Chhamman Mian enjoyed breaking bangles. No matter how many he broke, thank God there were always a few left as mementoes of her "married status".

"Not sad about going away"? Chhamman Mian asked, seeing her flushed with happiness. His heart was heavy.

"No." Bubu had strictly forbidden tears.

"Why?" Mounting anger.

"Soon; I will be back soon."

"How soon? A few days?"

"Six-seven months."

"Six months!"

"Shh, softly."

"I will die . . . Haleema . . ."

"God forbid. May all your troubles fall on my head." Haleema warded off the evil spirit. "My beloved husband! Don't let such words escape your lips. God in his mercy will let me return to look after you. Everyone doesn't die. With Sanobar it was different. The older master kicked her womb. O God!" She bit her tongue, clamped her mouth shut with her hand.

"Child!" Chhamman quivered.

"No . . . no, Chhotey Mian!"

"Swear by my soul." Placed her hand on his chest.

"No . . . no. . . no!"

"You liar!" Lighting the lamp he looked at her with probing eyes. Like a criminal he sat with his hands folded in his lap.

His child . . . a real live human being! What was he to do? Leap with joy? Touch the sky and sweep all the stars into Haleema's lap?

"When?"

"Six months." Bashfully spoken.

"My result should be out by then." Chhamman was thoughtful.

And Haleema was thinking about the village. How would the child's crying ever reach his ears? If he was shameless and hard like his mother, he Might survive among the other maid-children, never to be recognized by his father. Grow up to become a servant . . . iron clothes, polish shoes. If it was a girl, she would be given the ultimate honour of rubbing someone's feet . . . to be sent, later on, to the village, to pay off her debt to life.

But Haleema's tongue was clipped to her mouth. Bubu had said, "If you dare incite our Sahibzada, I will slice you into feed for the street dogs."

"Haleema . . . you are not going to the village."

"Please . . . my innocent Sarkar."

He did not permit her to speak any further.

Bubu says men are repulsed by pregnant women. What kind of a man was he? Showering the same kind of love on her as he did on the first night.

Next day Chhamman Mian bunked college. A one-man delegation knocked at all doors.

"Bhaijan — why is Haleema being sent to the village?"

"Tradition of this mahal."

"She is not cattle. She is the custodian of my child!"

Bhaijan's face flushed with anger. "Shame on you for this stupid remark. How dare you utter such nonsense in my presence?" He walked off in a towering rage. Never before had men interfered in the domestic politics of the mahal. Whenever they considered it propitious, Pyari Ammis provided healthy maids for their sons, who massaged their feet and did whatever else was required of them. The moment they were declared a "health hazard" they were sent along with other goods and chattel to the village to be "repaired". No person in his right mind ever got emotionally tangled with a maid.

"Afzal Bhai, please tell Pyari Ammi not to send Haleema to the village." He begged his cousin.

"Are you mad? A pregnant woman — bloody injurious to health. Don't get so worked up. You'll need a new arrangement." He laughed shamelessly. And what about your nikah to Hurma in November?"

"I won't marry Hurma! If Haleema goes to the village that will be the end of my studies", he announced.

Begum's blood vessels were ready to burst. "How dare he? If *he* can be obstinate so can *we*! Now Haleema will stay here only over my dead body. Nayaab... not tomorrow or the day after—take her away *now*. I swear by the Holy Prophet..."

"Najam Bitiya is planning to go to Europe after her delivery?"

"Why do you take her name? May god keep my daughter healthy." Najam was Chhamman Mian's sister.

"Amen! But she won't take the child, will she? And it is not advisable to send Dulha Nawab alone. If that wretched foreigner gets her hands on him, we are doomed."

"God, Nayaab! What are you saying?"

"There are only a few days between Haleema and Najam Bitiya's deliveries. Even if it is a week — no matter."

Begum had begun to understand.

"Najam Bitiya will be saved the bother. When she goes to London, Haleema will continue to nurse the infant. The child will get clean, hygienic milk."

Begum remained silent.

"What if she is not looked after properly in the village? As it is, she appears half dead. Here she will stay before my very eyes. I will feed her nourishing food. And we would have given in to Sahibzada's insistence."

"Precisely what I don't want." Begum appeared firm but her voice betrayed a slight softening of attitude.

"Up to you. All I wanted was for the matter to blow over in a couple of days. Mian will tire of it. We will have had our way and the burden of the favour can be offloaded on to him."

When Nayaab became pregnant with Jabbar, Farhat Nawab cooled off fast. When a woman becomes pregnant, the man loses interest. Law of nature.

But Chhamman Mian was giving the lie to the law of nature and to Nayaab Bubu. He was mad enough to have clutched to his bosom what should have remained grovelling at his feet. Such heroics had never been displayed by any Nawabzada, even for his lawful Begum. All day long his nose was buried in books about pre-natal care and child-raising; all his pocket money was wasted on buying vitamins and tonics for the maid.

Haleema pricked her finger with a needle. She was sitting in the courtyard embroidering Chhamman Mian's kurta. She knew why she was being allowed to stay on, but she did not want to shatter Chhamman Mian's dreams.

Chhamman Mian was panic-stricken. Never before had he seen a pregnant woman at such close quarters. He had heard that Najam Baji was pregnant. But she was always moaning, her enormous form wrapped up in numerous shawls. He was worried about Haleema. What if she burst open like a frog? When he didn't get his answers from his books, he ran all the way to Farkhunda Nawab's house.

Farkhunda Nawab was ostracised by the family because, many years ago, she had burnt her fingers in an abortive love affair. But her husband, Ashraf, was a police officer. Everyone needed to stay on his right side, so Farkhunda could not be ignored or annoyed. The ladies were especially jealous of her. She was very learned. Her son, Naeem, was a close friend of

Chhamman.

Chhamman had no clue that Farkhunda Nawab had been invited by Pyari Ammi to give her advice regarding the bride's jewellery. She reassured Chhamman that she would look up Haleema when she dropped in on Friday.

From the car she walked directly towards Chhamman Mian's rooms.

She scolded Chhamman for his nervousness. "Haleema is fine! She won't burst. Don't feed her so much fat. Milk and fruit should be sufficient."

When she was leaving, Haleema said, "Tasleem Phupijan!" She had pulled her dupatta over her face.

"May god give you a long life, my little doll!" So saying, she rushed out of the doll's house.

Later, when Pyari Ammi displayed the bride's jewellery, she was very quiet.

"Don't sit there like a mute — say something."

"Times are changing, Bhabijan. Hurma is a nice girl, but . . ."

"I know . . . she is fashionable, and the jewellery is old-fashioned. Never mind. I'll order the latest styles from Bombay. Let's talk frankly . . ."

But Farkhunda sat quiet, evidently ill at ease. Then came a string of excuses. A meeting at the club . . . etc., etc. After she left Begum and Bubu had the pleasure of tearing her to shreds.

When Nayaab went to show the jewellery to Hurma, she heard that Feroza Nawab had gone to a friend's house, and that the girl was playing tennis.

Hurma entered, stamping her feet. Nayaab opened the jewellery box.

"Jewellery, Rani Bitiya. Make your choice!"

"Why should my choice be necessary for Haleema

Bi?" she asked, vigorously brushing her short hair.

"God forbid! Haleema is a maid."

"I see. But the child is Chhamman Mian's isn't it?"

"Child!" Suddenly Bubu was hot around the ears.

"Farkhunda Khala was saying . . ."

"Oh no, Bitiya . . . I mean . . . Tauba! Tauba! You are as prickly as a thorny bush! You mother's absence from the house gives you no right to make fun of an old woman. If she was present would you dare fling your shoes in my face by behaving like this?"

Bubu swept out of the house in great indignation.

How the rascal jumps around! Placing his hand on her taut silvery stomach, Chhamman Mian was marvelling at the miracles of nature.

"Why are you so cold, Limoo?" When he was overwhelmed with love for her, Chhamman switched from Haleema to Lima, from Lima to Limoo. He wrapped her lovingly in a quilt. Burying his face in her body, he took several deep breaths. How fragrant Limoo is! Like a fully ripe mango. Ever inviting. A bowl of cool water, full to the brim, drink from it every day and the thirst is everlasting. It was selfish of him to make so much love to her. She will wilt away with excess. No . . . from now on he won't touch her. If only he could make time stand still! Don't look ahead, don't look back. Darkness has been left behind . . . but what lies ahead? Who can trust the future?

"God's curse on her. How Haleema has betrayed us!" Begum dipped her finger in honey and thrust it into her newborn grand-daughter's mouth.

"Nayaab, your mouth is a pit of coals. You said they will deliver together. Najam has been crying since morning. Doesn't want to start the baby at her breast. And your Haleema! No sign of delivering. You promised to send Haleema's baby to the village and hand her Najam's for nursing. Now what?"

The world can stop rotating, but Nayaab's word, once given, could not be belied. That cheap Haleema, how dare she defy her prediction?

Haleema was squeezing oranges. Chhamman Mian would soon return after winning the match. Bubu glanced at her like an eagle sizing up its prey before pouncing on it. Today she was full of venom.

"Haleema!" Her voice was cruel. Haleema trembled.

"So? What have you been harbouring?" Her eyes scorched Haleema from head to foot.

"Speak, bastard, whose is it?" As if it was the first time she had seen her swollen stomach.

"This orange . . . ?"

"No, wretch, this melon." She whisked at the full term pregnancy with the end of her fan.

Haleema was dumbfounded! No one had ever remarked on her pregnancy. She stared, open-mouthed.

"Will you speak or shall I take my shoe to your face? Bastard, whose is it?"

When Gori Bi, the maid of Manjhley Nawab, had asked Nayaab the same question many years ago, she had flung the reply right at her face!

Haleema's tongue was frozen. If someone had cut her into little bits, she would never have uttered Chhotey Saheb's name. His sin was her sweetest benediction.

"Why don't you say something, you damned wretch?" A resounding slap landed on her left cheek. A gold ring tore her flesh and drew blood.

Chhamman Mian was scoring hit after hit. The

entire field resounded with applause. When he lifted the silver cup in his hands, he felt as if Haleema's taut silver stomach was throbbing.

By force of habit he came running to the room looking for Haleema. When he got no response, he ran across, drenched in sweat, into Pyari Ammi's room.

"Where did you get this lota? It is quite unique."

"Bubu, this is a cup, not a lota!"

"Phone Hakim Saheb, my love." Pyari Ammi was groaning. "My legs are getting stiff again."

"I will. Bubu, ask Haleema to take out a cotton kurta. It is very hot."

When he returned after phoning, Bubu motioned with her hand, "She is sleeping."

"My clothes ..." Bubu nodded her head.

When he came out after his bath, Sarvari was drawing the cord in his pyjamas.

"I am asking about Haleema and you are talking bloody nonsense." Chhamman growled.

"Allah! How do I know? Must be in the servants' quarters." Sarvari was dolled up from head to toe.

"Servants' quarters? Get her here." He snatched his kurta and threw it across the room.

"You heard me, witch. Go! Run!" He yanked the pyjama from her hand. Sarvari giggled.

"Bubu sent me."

"Sent you ? Why ?"

More giggling.

"*Ullu ki patthi.*" Chhamman raised his racket. With great coquettry, Sarvari left the room, tinkling her anklets and jangling her bracelets.

For five or ten minutes Chhamman was very agitated. Wrapping a towel around his waist, he flipped the pages of a magazine. After fifteen minutes he became restless.

"Anybody there?" This was his typical way of calling for Haleema. Once again, Sarvari descended, armed with the apparatus of heavy flirtation.

"Tell me the truth, witch." He caught hold of her braid and gave it one twist around his wrist.

"You are killing me ! Oh God ... please! There ... there in the servants' quarters."

Chhamman let go of her braid. Trembling from head to foot, he thrust his feet into a pair of slippers and ran out.

"Where are you going, Mian ? Don't. This is not the time for men to go." Sarvari ran after him. But Mian did not hear a single word. Met Nayaab in the verandah.

"Bubu, get the lady doctor."

"Oh God, Chhotey Mian ... your clothes. You bastard!" she yelled at Sarvari. She was sending Lateefa, but Sarvari fell at her feet.

"Bubu, let Jabbar take the car. Telephone won't do."

"Whatever for ?"

"Haleema ... !" His throat was dry.

"Haleema? She doesn't need a doctor. She ... needs a memsaheb from London! Shameless corpse. These niceties have given a long rope to the maids. Go, Mian. There was a phone call from your friend, Naeem Saheb. He is having a birthday party. Sarvari, miserable wretch, take out Mian's special churidar-pyjama and sherwani." She started to walk away.

"What had I come to say, Mian? You made me forget. Your Pyari Ammi is not well. On your way to Naeem Saheb's, look up Hakim Saheb. I'll ask Jabbar to get the car." Walked away quickly before he could open his mouth.

Bewildered, Chhamman returned to his room. Then got up with a start and threw on a few clothes. How many times had he seen a maid's death ! For months his dreams were haunted by Sanobar's corpse. Haleema is like a flower. Anaemic. Tubercular. He ran to his elder brother's room.

"Bhaijan !"

"What ?" He was engrossed in a game of chess with his friend.

"I have to talk to you." With trembling hands he tugged at his sleeve.

"Wait a minute. What a superb move ! Watch us. Well, Mian Qudoos. Save your castle, otherwise. . . ."

"Bhaijan." Chhamman felt death all over him.

"Sit for a few minutes. Your move, Mian Qudoos."

Twenty minutes passed. Twenty decades for Chhamman.

"By the way, congratulations ! What a superb cup." He looked back at Chhamman and spoke with warmth.

"Bhaijan . . . Haleema . . . please call the doctor !"

"She will be called if necessary."

"No, Bhaijan. This will kill her. Please *do* something."

"Let her die then. Am I God to prevent the inevitable? And you? . . . Shamelessly blubbering for a slovenly maid. Have some decency, man. She is a bloody whore. Don't indulge in her whims. With a bastard in her stomach, is she a whore or a nun ?"

"Bhaijan . . . I . . . Bhai . . ."

"Stop stammering. Without a nikah a woman is a harlot, a whore, an adultress. She should be stoned in the market-place. Better dead than alive. The world would become a cleaner place."

"I share her blame."

"So? What do I care? Go and repent. Don't waste my time !"

Hellishly difficult. Reasoning with such a bloody blockhead. If it were anyone else Chhamman Mian would have broken his jaw. But he had always respected his older brother. Childhood habit. Gulping down his rising blood, he strode back.

Like a maniac he banged his head at every door. Begged his father, but Gultaar had taught him such a lesson, that at the mention of the word, "maid" he jumped three feet in the air.

"How dare you confess your dirty deeds with such shamelessness? First you poke your nose in the shit-drain, then you want to drag your family into the same mire."

Chhamman rubbed Pyari Ammi's feet with his eyes. But she managed to throw a hysterical fit. Why hadn't she lost her hearing before such evil words struck her eardrums ? Why didn't blindness strike her before she saw the dawning of this disastrous day?

He sank to his knees before Chacha Abba. *"La haul wala quwwat*! Let her die, the dirty rag. Don't *you* worry. I will give you my Mahrukh. A real fire-cracker ! Shame on you, boy... dying for a sickly maidservant. Your indiscriminate reading of worthless books has resulted in this."

People were laughing openly, joking. The target of their jibes was sitting on the cold and moist floor which skirted the servants' quarters. Chhamman Mian was crying. An eighteen year old crying like an infant, whimpering like a child.

Abba Huzoor was furious. If Pyari Ammi hadn't

gone into a state of hysteria, he would have skinned the boy with his own knife. Traitor. The day he heard that his beloved son had successfully copulated with the maid, his mutton-chop whiskers had ridden up and down with an irrepressible grin. How disgracefully the older son had let him down. If the younger hadn't performed, who would have inherited the vast family fortunes?

Never had such melodrama been witnessed. Servants were tittering, maids were giggling. In the darkness of a semi-room, on a rough bed of jute string, Haleema was cooing like a pigeon. Her palms were bleeding from the tightness of her grip on the rough hemp.

"Sarvari, you wretch! He is sitting on the damp floor. He will catch cold. Oh ... Oh." If only these painful contractions would stop ... for one moment ... she would make him swear by her head to get up from the wet floor. But ... but ... before God Almighty, she held nothing ... nothing against him.

Excruciating waves of pain were racking her large, shapeless, sweat-drenched body. She had bloodied her lips, so that no sound reached Chhamman. Her shrieks of pain would have driven him mad. But the soundless waves were registering on his heart. Chhamman was almost delirious with fear. He wanted to lift a stone and break open his skull ... perhaps the steaming tension would be released. Suddenly he heard his name uttered in an agonizing shriek. He was yanked out of his depression. He hurtled towards his cycle and, in his mud-splattered clothes, dashed out of the gate, barely missing a head-on collision.

"My son!" Regaining consciousness, Begum

started beating her chest.

"My God, Chhamman, is all well?" Eyes shot red, covered in slime, Chhamman was crying like a baby. "Phuppo... Phuppo...."

"Is she...?

"Dead. Dying. No-one listens to me. No-one."

"You are stupid. I asked you to inform me. Let me call an ambulance. No-one has the stamina to fight with your elders at the mahal."

"I will phone." Ashraf lifted the receiver.

"I was playing my cricket finals. When I returned, I discovered... Phuppo, she will die. Maybe she is dead already...."

"No... she won't."

When Farkhunda Nawab's car, followed by the ambulance, entered the mahal, the commotion that ensued was deafening. Begum Sahiba threw another fainting fit. Nawab Saheb came snarling towards the door with his revolver loaded. On seeing the police car behind the ambulance, he turned right back. The family had never seen such public insult; not even when Manjhley Nawab's property was confiscated by the court.

Farkhunda Nawab looked neither to the left nor to the right. She marched straight in the direction of the servants' quarters.

Chhamman Mian swooped up the bleeding Haleema in his arms. In the mahal, the mourning-carpet was spread out. Miraculously, the Begum rose from her fainting fit and started on a litany of curses.

The next day, with a stroke of his pen, Chhamman Mian abdicated his right to the family property. It wasn't a fortune that he had earned by the sweat of his brow... so who cared? Whatever Abba Huzoor dictated, he wrote—most willingly.

Chhamman Mian now lives in a dirty old house in a narrow gali. It is said that he teaches cricket at some school or another. Attends college in the evening ... Often he is seen on his bicycle dressed in worn-out cotton trousers and an old shirt. In the basket attached to the handlebars, among the fruit and vegetables, sometimes one may see a child, sitting quietly, with large limpid eyes.

What a story! Lost his entire family for nothing. All this education for nothing. They say he has a woman in his home. Who knows whether he has married her or not. God! What bad days have befallen us!

Translated by Syeda Hameed

Glossary

adwan	:	the strings at the foot of a bedstead by which the cross-strings are tightened and braced
alim Sahib	:	a learned man
Ayat-ul Kursi	:	an ayat in the Quran
babua	:	doll
bismillah	:	a ceremony to mark a child's first reading of the Quran
chait	:	twelfth month of the Hindu calendar
chillas	:	a forty-day observance
eidi	:	money given to younger people during the festival of Eid
farz namaz	:	essential prayer
gurdhani	:	a sweet made with sugarcane
janamaz	:	prayer-mat
jeth	:	the second month in the Hindu calendar, corresponding to May-June
kaneez	:	female servant
khali	:	the month between the festivals of Id-ul-Fitr and Id-ul-Zuha
kheel	:	puffed rice
kholi	:	a small room
kibla	:	direction of the Kaa'ba which

		determines the direction of the Islamic prayers
kufr	:	heresy
lagaan	:	rent or revenue from land
maika	:	maternal home
malan	:	a female gardener
malida	:	a cake made of pounded meal, milk, butter and sugar
mannat	:	a promise or vow
mazar	:	shrine
niaz	:	offering of food and alms in the name of the Prophet
rakat	:	the divisions of the Islamic prayer
sozankari	:	special embroidery
ullu ki patthi	:	common abuse, roughly corresponding to, "You idiot"
walima	:	party given by the bridegroom the day after the wedding
wazifa	:	repeating a daily prayer

The Heart Breaks Free
&
The Wild One

Translated by Tahira Naqvi

The Heart Breaks Free

What a strange and mysterious moment it is when you suddenly open your eyes and can't tell whether the sun is setting or just rising, which way your feet are or where your head is, and you don't know where you slept and what this place is where you've awakened! It becomes imperative then, to determine where your head and feet are and you have this feeling that if you don't find out immediately you'll be lost forever.

When we were children our first reaction to this was tears, but then a flash came down from some unknown source and right away we were able to place ourselves, to determine where everything was. All at once fountains of mirth burst forth and to provide further proof of our existence we ran after the chickens or began grappling with one another like dogs. At that point Amma would order us to make ourselves scarce and this we happily did. Making a run for the garden we proceeded to pluck off half-opened buds from the bushes and gathered them in our laps.

Thus we occupied ourselves until it got dark. Then Ali Bakhsh would slip in a bunch of lanterns from behind the curtain on the front door. The wicks were raised and lighted and the lanterns dispatched to every corner of the house so that the walls and doors which had been engulfed in darkness were visible again.

The watchman climbed a ladder and lighted the boxed lamp on the front door. Frightened, the bushes hastily retreated into the darkness and the buds we had collected in our laps began to flower. At that time, and for no apparent reason, we were assailed by feelings of dread. A stealthy chameleon, its cheeks ballooning as it manufactured poison in its mouth, turned red like an ember and then scampered up the tamarind tree. And we felt as if our feet were melting like wax.

This was when that mysterious voice floated and vibrated as it travelled across the water:

"*Kanhayya, your flute has become my enemy …*"

We ran without a moment wasted, dashed through the curtain on the front door, threw the flowers down on our grandmother's prayer mat and took refuge under her dupatta.

"Dadima, please read *ayat-ul kursi* quickly and blow on us!"

Only when we felt Dadima's "Ahmed Hussain, Dildar Hussain," soaked in tobacco and betel juice blow on our faces did we breathe sighs of relief.

"*Kanhayya … yo…u…r … flooote … has become my … enemy…*" The sound weakened and then disappeared altogether, leaving behind only the rustling of the wind.

Our father had been transferred recently to Bahraich. Situated across from our spacious, two-storied bungalow was the shrine of Sayyed Salar Masud Ghazi. Adjacent to the house was a garden where we spent the major part of our waking lives. At the end of a long line of modest-sized quarters was a large well, in the back, fields of corn. On the other side was a white mosque and rows of *har-singhar*, jasmine, *chameli* and *mogra* trees that extended as far as the eye could see. Not too far from the mosque was a Muslim cemetery and on the banks of the river, some distance away from the mosque, beyond the melon plantation, was a crematorium. We dreaded these two spots the most. The mysterious voice appeared to come from this direction and anything coming from there struck fear in our hearts.

Whenever we stepped out of line, or if we made a row, we were frightened into docility by references to that voice. "She's a demon, she'll eat you up alive, she's a ghoul, if she lays hands on you she'll cast a spell on you. Don't you know what they say? A wedding party once drowned in the Ghagra stream but the bride didn't die, she turned into a demon and floats about in the stream to this day."

There was another factor associated with this voice. No sooner was it heard than Aunt Qudsia suffered a paroxysm; her jaw locked, she'd begin to foam at the mouth and the house turned into an abode of anguish.

"O Mighty Qadir, bring us Qudsia's husband," Nani Bi (our maternal grandmother), chanted, swaying. But Mighty Qadir seemed to have clogged his ears with oil; he paid no heed to anyone's pleas. Perhaps he was ruminating on the matter of returning Aunt Qudsia's husband to her.

She had been married for nearly ten years. Her father packed her husband off to England soon after the wedding — that was one of the conditions of the marriage. In keeping with custom, he returned from there with an English wife, a *mem*. Now he had a clinic in Mainpuri. This is why Aunt Qudsia endlessly chanted verses from the Quran, spent long hours in worship and prayer, and when all of this proved fruitless, suffered from attacks in which her jaw locked and foam gathered at her mouth. Unfortunate woman, what else could she do? She penned several letters beginning, "My master, may you live long." She wrote: "Give me a spot in a corner of your house as a maid of the memsahib, I'll serve you both, I'll eat your left-overs, wear your cast-offs, and if I utter one word of dissatisfaction, you may punish me as one punishes a thief. You are the master, I your slave, what better fate can I ask for than dying at your feet," etc., etc., but the master apparently thought it foolish to bother with a reply.

Usually Aunt Qudsia was introduced to people like this: "This is Qudsia, her husband has taken in a white woman." People were quite impressed. At that moment Aunt Qudsia, too, would forget her own misfortune and experience a certain degree of pride. Her rival was the daughter of the rulers, who knows, maybe she was even distantly related to the King! Not everyone can take in a white woman. In a way her husband had honoured her by bringing a white woman to be her rival; he could have taken in a washer woman or a sweeperess.

Aunt Qudsia was married at the age of fifteen. Six months after the wedding her husband left for England. For two years a fervid romance flourished. Her face lowered she was seen either writing to her husband or reading one of his letters. Gradually the letters cooled off. She continued her frenzied writing, but replies there were none! Then all kinds of bad news started trickling in. After the First World War white women diminished in value and whoever went abroad returned with a catch from the free-flowing Ganga. But Aunt Qudsia's husband turned out to be rather strange. There were other men as well who were bringing home white women, but once every six or seven months they also showed their faces to their Hindustani wives. Her husband, on the other hand, maintained absolute silence and made no effort to find out how she was doing.

And that's why Aunt Qudsia became hysterical during Urs (the celebrations at the shrine), that's why whenever there was a wedding in the neighbourhood her jaw locked, or when, in the darkness of night someone sang a song of separation, she frothed at the mouth. The mysterious voice affected her the most, so much so that she paced restlessly, cracked her knuckles, nervously twisted the corners of her dupatta, and suffered an attack of hysterics.

We were picking off buds. Our laps were full, but we lingered to see the lighting of the boxed lamp on the front door. Suddenly the voice floated up right behind us. Our hair stood on end. We turned in surprise. She was sitting on a fallen fig tree trunk that had come down during a storm and now sat among crumbling gravestones in the cemetery behind the mosque. Her face wore a sad look. She paused in her singing. Our feet weighed heavily like sacks stuffed with straw.

"Let go of my dupatta," she murmured petulantly as if addressing someone behind her.

Terrified, we ran wildly from there. No one was holding her dupatta, there was no one there.

She stood up hastily, and tugging at a corner of her dupatta ran away laughing as though she were being pursued playfully. Soon she had disappeared into the trees.

Fear gripped us, our feet seemed to drag us down.

"We'll meet in Meerut." Her voice echoed in the distance and we ducked around the curtain and into the house.

"You, beloved, so dark, and I so fair / We shall gaze at each other in the mirror."

Her voice vibrated again like a top and we felt as if there were beadwork-needles running down our backs.

"You, beloved, so stout, and I so thin / On scales we shall both be weighed."

What a coincidence! Aunt Qudsia's husband was both stout and dark, but there was not a ghost of a chance of meeting him in Meerut. What could she do except have an attack of hysteria?

Nani Biwi was busy with something else. Dadima, who was still murmuring over the prayer beads, blew on us, but our fear did not abate. Off! How many grandmothers there were, and aunts, both maternal and paternal, but what good were they? There was no vigour in their blowing.

"Stay away from her, child," the attendant at the shrine said one Thursday when we arrived there with our usual offering of flowers. "She's very dangerous."

"Why?"

"She brings bad luck, she ate up her parents and her husband."

"She ate them?" We thought she had sprinkled salt and pepper on them and really eaten them.

"If she catches you alone she'll pull out your heart and eat it," he frightened us further.

"Is she a demon?"

"Of course."

"May God help us!" Chacha Mian, who had come with us, interjected. "What nonsense is this. No, dear children, she's just insane." He glared threateningly at the attendant.

"Insane?" We didn't like Chacha Mian's explanation. All the romance was gone. She's just insane? And not insane in an amusing way, either, she doesn't smell, or rip her clothes, nor does she throw stones at anyone. Instead, whenever you chance to run into her you find her singing.

"Beloved, I'll be a flower in your lap/ A flower in your lap, beloved."

What a melodious voice. That's why Aunt Qudsia became so agitated when she heard her sing.

"Amma dear, please send for her, we'll hear her sing."

"No, child, I'm not going to send for that mad wretch. She's from a good family and look how she wanders all over the place without restraint, her purdah forgotten. She's possessed, you know; everyone drowned in the Ghagri stream, but she remained afloat for three days as if there was something holding her up."

"But the unhappy creature sings well." Aunt Qudsia nursed an obsession for songs. When Uncle Shabir sang devotional songs, streams and rivulets flowed from her eyes.

"O Rasul-e-Arabi/ To you I offer my life," he sang and Aunt Qudsia, her dupatta held to her nose, sobbed as she swayed to the rhythm of his song. Everyone sat at attention, waiting for the paroxysm that invariably overtook her when Uncle Shabir sang. Her hands would rotate, her eyes roll up in their sockets, and foam bubble at her mouth. Nani Biwi and Dadima would run toward her to blow holy incantations on her while Uncle Shabir, seated on the wooden divan, tried to conceal the shaking of his hands. Until Aunt Qudsia calmed down, he would pace up and down outside the front door.

Uncle Shabir was related to Aunt Qudsia by marriage, he was a brother-in-law. The only child of poor parents, he was a timid, uninteresting and ineffectual man and it was indeed lucky he was an only child or we might have had to contend with several uninteresting and ineffectual uncles instead of one. He was very thin, and nearly three feet taller than Aunt Qudsia. Humped over like a camel, he was in the habit of taking long strides when he walked.

"Shabir Bhai, please sing something," Aunt Qudsia would entreat in a melancholy voice, "please, it will calm my nerves."

"What can I sing, I have a scratchy throat today." He always presented the same excuse. Then he cleared his throat, blinked his eyes a few times, flared his nostrils, pressed both hands together between his knees, and:

"O east wind, if you travel to Tayyabba/ Promise that you will embrace the curtains of the sanctuary."

He sang in a clear, unsullied voice. You felt sorry for him. The east wind had also clogged its ears with oil it seemed; it didn't hear him nor did it travel to Tayyabba at his behest.

It was common knowledge that Uncle Shabir was in love with Aunt Qudsia. But what a sluggish, timid love it was. Other young men and women in the family also loved and what a sprightly and energetic love it was! Amorous embraces in secret, or a tussle during a game of pachisi, grabbing hold of each other in dark corners! Grandmothers, uncles and various aunts cursed and remonstrated endlessly but the laughter and giggling continued unchecked.

Uncle Shabir, on the other hand, never sat close to her, never allowed even his little finger to touch her; she was forbidden fruit which belonged to another, to a man who had put her somewhere and forgotten about her. She had recently turned twenty-five and already there were silver strands gleaming in her hair. Everyone hoped she would age quickly so the matter would end once and for all.

"No, I'm not going near that mad wretch," the old smelly crone, Pathani Bua, retorted when Aunt Qudsia solicited her help. "That husband-eater threatens you with a stone every time you go near her."

"What's amazing is that the ruffians out there don't harass her. If it had been some other girl she'd be in shreds by now. The wretch, she roams around in the woods all night dressed up in her finery. Isn't she scared?" Chachi Bi asked.

"Why, what's she got to be scared of?" Pathani Bua said, "no one dares to look at her with a crooked eye."

"Why? Is she a lioness, will she tear you to pieces? She's always alone, isn't she?"

"No, she's not alone, her husband is with her."

"What husband?"

"Bale Mian . . ."

"What nonsense! Don't be a fool, woman."

"This isn't nonsense, I swear, she's the beloved of her husband, she's a true faithful of our Ghazi Mian."

Pathani Bua proceeded to explain in greater detail. She was Ghazi Mian's beloved and this despite the fact that Ghazi Mian was martyred four hundred years ago. Love is not fettered by the chains of time.

There was an Urs at Ghazi Mian's shrine every year. Qawwali singers and others came from far and wide. People of every religion and caste, old and young, children, women and men, all made the pilgrimage to the shrine, offered vows and received answers to their prayers.

Every Thursday the dancing girls from the town and its neighbouring districts arrived with their offerings. They sang thumries, dadras and ghazals in honour of Ghazi Mian. When a dancing girl was about to surrender her virginity she would first sing and dance at Mian's shrine. A fair was held during the flame-ridden heat of May and June and the faithful came months ahead of time and set up camp. Such enormous crowds gathered during the actual days of the fair that you couldn't find an empty spot anywhere. Stretched in front of the main entrance to the shrine was an over-sized marquee on which the arriving pilgrims threw garlands, sweetmeats and money.

Flags were transported here from neighbouring towns

and districts. There were sixty-foot high bamboo poles with clusters of black or white hair attached to the top, while just below them hung streamers made from rupee notes. Anyone whose wish was granted offered the standard at the shrine. Dancing and leaping to the beat of kettle-drums, the men arrived at the entrance of the shrine and formed a circle; a muscular man built like a wrestler, balancing the standard, stationed himself in the middle of the circle; in order to keep the banner steady, to prevent it from tipping, four other men held on to ropes extending from the spire of the standard. Then, lifting up the standard, the man danced and executed tricks with it. Sometimes he'd place the base of the standard on his forehead and wriggle his body, at other times he'd catch it between his teeth and sway. Finally, when everyone began sweating, or maybe when the group ran out of time (there were other groups with standards waiting their turn), the weary flag was furled around the pole like a sail tied to its mast, hitched on shoulders and carried into the shrine through the tall entrance-way. And then another flag dance began. At the end of the fair days all the flags were auctioned off.

Our mother bought flags every year for use as floor cloths — these were the best examples of tambour-work. Embroidered on the rough cotton fabric were colourful designs in the shape of elephants and horses. Here you could see whole armies on the march with their spears hoisted, there a caravan of camels; in another corner were flocks of sheep and goats, herds of cows, along with groups of men and women exchanging secrets. We would roll around on the divans all day long, observing the scenes below us, never tiring of what we saw.

Besides the flags, those whose prayers had been heard also offered, in accordance with what they had promised, gold and silver figurines, tables, chairs, beds, and pots and pans. All this was followed by Ghazi Mian's wedding ceremonies. A kettle-drum was placed at the entrance. Early in the morning the playing of the drum commenced to one's annoyance and continued late into the night. All day one group after another came and surrounded the drum players, and sometimes one or two men broke into sad songs about lost love. As soon as one group had exhausted itself another took its place. Women possessed by evil spirits came to Mian's door to be rid of them; they loosened their hair and shook their heads rhythmically from side to side, and when the person chanting holy verses blew smoke over them, they screamed and fainted. But it wasn't long before they regained consciousness and started swaying again. If the spirit were a stubborn creature it would not budge for days; red and green clubs were used to punish it and only then, after a terrible struggle, did it depart. Happy and contented, the women who had been healed then made offerings at the shrine and went their way.

On the fifth of the month came the ceremony of the fan, on the seventh the sandalwood ceremony and on the ninth, the henna ceremony. At night on that day Ghazi Mian's kurta, on which the Quran was etched in its entirety, was brought out for viewing. Frenzied crowds engulfed it. On the eleventh, the ceremony marking the readying of the marriage procession took place.

A long time ago, Radha Bai, alias Zehra Bibi, a child widow from a family in Raduli, lost her heart to Mian. Ghazi Mian appeared to her in a dream and accepted her love. She made her home in his shrine. She was known to wash the tomb with her tears and sweep the floor of the shrine with her hair every day. Her father was an oil merchant. He forcibly dragged her away from Ghazi Mian, but Radha refused to give in. All girls with the name 'Radha' are stubborn; boldly and fearlessly they announce their love, suffer every dishonour and stigma happily, and put life and soul on the line. And the dice rolls in their favour. Unfavourable winds are compelled to give in when confronted with the ardour of their love, people begin to worship them, sing songs about them, and finally worship them as goddesses.

Ghazi Mian's Radha also had to walk on coals. She too had to drag herself through thorns. Her mother beat her senseless, her father whipped her with moistened rope and tied her to a peg in the cow shed. And the whole village spat at her. In the middle of the night, when poor Radha, starving and thirsty, weary from her wounds and splattered with cow dung, was taking her last breath, Ghazi Mian came to her. He washed her wounds with his tears, clasped her to his sacred chest, and dipping his forefinger into his heart's blood he made the bridal mark in the parting of her hair.

When the demented Meera fell in love with her Girdhar Gopal the world let vipers loose in her life and gave her a cup of poison to drink and then — Krishan Murari's flute came to life and the viper turned into a garland of flowers, the cup of poison brimmed over with the elixir of life.

The next morning the inhabitants of Raduli awoke to the sounds of temple bells and the *azan* echoing from the minaret of the mosque. Immersed in the fragrance of sandalwood, dressed in majestic clothes, Radha lay on a bed of flowers in everlasting sleep. There was not a single scratch on her, her body glowed like burnished gold, her hair shone with *sindhur*.

People in Raduli were thunderstruck. A meeting of the village elders was called. It was decided that the girl now belonged in another's house, there was no reason for her to stay in her parent's home. So she was delivered to her groom's dwelling.

The Hindus called her Radha, the Muslims referred to her as Zehra Bibi. Her plain, unpretentious grave sat at the foot of Mian's tomb. At one end of her grave grew a tamarind tree whose bark was known to exude the fragrance of sandalwood when burnt.

Since Radha's death the Raduliwallahs had been bringing an offering of Mian's *barat* to the shrine every year. Children were put to bed early so they could be aroused around three o'clock at night to witness the arrival of the wedding procession. As soon as the familiar sound of trumpets was heard everyone was awakened. Quickly splashing some water on our faces, we all ran up to the roof to see the wedding procession enter the village.

It's been so many years, but to this day my eyes are blinded with the memory of that *barat*. A white steed in front, heavily laden with silver and gold ornaments, covered with flowers, the silvery strands of the *sehra* kissing the hooves.

"Look, there's Bale Mian!" We thought we could really see him seated on the horse.

Behind the horse was a palanquin with fine red muslin curtains and inside it was the Quran with a candle burning alongside it.

"The bride, the bride!" We were spellbound. The trembling flame of the candle behind the red muslin curtains appeared to take the form of a shy, reticent bride. Following the bride were the wedding guests carrying tiny umbrellas. These were decorated with small stars between embroidered bands and beaded silver and gold tassels hung from their edges. Twirling these umbrellas like reels, swaying, dancing, the members of the wedding procession filled the streets. It was a dazzling sight. For days afterward little umbrellas continued to dance in my vision.

Sometimes when you see something very beautiful you feel a lump in your throat. Aunt Qudsia always had a lump in her throat and all she needed was an excuse to start weeping. Resting her head on the window sill, she shed voluminous tears; seeing a wedding procession always cut her to the quick. But everyone was saddened by this *barat*. Was it a *barat* or a funeral? Life's doors are shut on a young, frail girl, she wants to create a world of dreams and open a small window in it. But the stupid people around her don't allow it because she threatens their beliefs. And what happens? She shatters all their beliefs and turns away from them.

Now Uncle Shabir was neither Krishan Murari nor Ghazi Mian. He was an incomplete, hollow man. He could not turn the snarling vipers in Aunt Qudsia's life into garlands with his flute, nor could he change the cowdung that enveloped her soul to sandalwood by sheer dint of his faith. His total assets were his two trembling hands which he could use well to stifle turbulent emotions. And Aunt Qudsia, at the age of twenty-six, was fading away like a forgotten remark. She didn't even have enough courage to be like Bua and lose her sanity. At least then people would fear her. As things stood now, her Ghazi Mian was ridiculed and pitied. There are those who are more alive in death than the living.

Bua was probably just a few years older than Aunt Qudsia. From the time she is young, a woman's heart is filled with a thousand fears so that when she reaches puberty she thinks of herself as a fragile, unbaked clay pitcher that must encounter stones at every step. Because she had lost her mind, Bua's fears had vanished, especially her fear of losing her honour. She was no longer a hollow clay pitcher, she was solid rock. In a manly fashion she went where she pleased, regardless of whether it was night or day. Somehow she had managed to make people fear her. Nobody really knew how, but one or two miracles came about and people began to believe. Once a ruffian, finding her alone, tried to grab her. Ghazi Mian slapped his face with such fury that it caved in. At another time an unfortunate fellow tried to force himself on her and it is believed that the hand which he fastened upon her wrist decomposed and fell off.

Our uncle, Chacha Mian, was an apostate. He used to say, "Every year thousands of lepers throng to the shrine with hopes of being healed. Decomposition of limbs and their subsequent falling off is not a miracle, it's a disease. And it's not unusual for an alcoholic to suffer from an attack of facial paralysis."

But we were afraid of doubting Bua. What would you do if your whole face fell in and collapsed? She had the temperament of an ogress. However, ever since we had discovered that she was not a ghoul or a spirit and was only a little mad, we ceased to be terrified of her.

One day we found her standing under the oak tree, wiping mud from her slipper. I gave her Aunt Qudsia's message.

"I'm not coming," she said rudely. "I'll come when I feel like it." Muttering, she walked away toward the path across the small bridge.

Finally, after a long time, she felt like it and there she suddenly was. Without standing on ceremony, without saying a word to anyone, she went directly to the water pitchers, poured some water in a brass cup for herself and sprinkled some on the chameli buds she had tied in a corner of her dupatta. Then she drew the dupatta over her head, placed her hands on her hips like a nautchi and started smiling. Amma had always warned us that girls from good families don't stand with their hands on their hips, only nautchis do that. While you're growing up there's a time when your hands become a nuisance, you don't know what to do with them. So, driven by the fear that I might become a nautchi if I weren't careful, I would sometimes place both hands over my head.

"What is this, you wretch, why are you slapping your head?" vexed, Amma would scold me.

"Where should I keep my hands then?" I would wearily ask.

"In the fire!" She'd get more irritated. "Get out of here." And I would quickly slip away.

Suddenly Bua laughed. Then she came and sat down on the divan and proceeded to adjust the folds on her tight pajama. Her clothes were clean and spotless. A starched pink dupatta was draped neatly across her shoulders while the bunch of chameli buds tied in a corner swung next to her cheek.

Unable to withstand her stare, Aunt Qudsia lowered her eyes and pretended to busy herself by adjusting her dupatta over her shoulders.

"*My eyes are red from weeping...*"
She seemed to be teasing Aunt Qudsia.
"*Smoking, chewing paan, my beloved/ My cruel beloved didn't come today/ My eyes are red from weeping...*"
Aunt Qudsia was holding her tears in the palm of her hand; she began sprinkling them. But before she could bring on an attack of hysteria, Bua leapt up and was gone out of the back door in seconds.

Her voice glided in the distance: "*My eyes are red from weeping...*"

Everyone was impressed. Bua had knowledge of hidden things, she knew how to handle Aunt Qudsia.

"She must have heard it from somebody," Chacha Mian said. He was an apostate, you see. But no one paid any attention to his remark. After this episode Bua became a frequent visitor to our house. She'd come, sit down, and if she felt uneasy she'd just get up and leave.

"Come, stay," Aunt Qudsia cajoled pleadingly.

"No, no I can't... he'll be waiting for me..."

And I'd imagine Ghazi Mian actually standing under the shade of the *kadamb* tree, waiting for her.

"She's lost her wits, the unfortunate creature, and she's from such a good family, too."

"You know, she doesn't look mad to me."

"Why, you'll think she's mad only after she picks up stones to throw at you? Doesn't she have that low caste woman in her house, and what does she know of the value of money? Anyone can come in and steal all she's got and she'll never know."

"Don't say anything about her, please, I'm not sure it's safe."

"Why, I'm not saying she's a bad person, am I?"

Once Maulvi sahib, the village cleric, said to Bua, "You had better get married, girl. What's the good of roaming around like this?"

Enraged, Bua pounced on him: "Why don't you get your mother married to some ruffian walking on the streets!"

"A woman is not safe without a man by her side," Maulvi sahib explained.

Bua exploded: "I have a man by my side, your father's father ... if he hears you talk like this he'll set your beard on fire."

Who could chide Ghazi Mian's cherished beloved without incurring his wrath? While returning from the well with a bucket of water Maulvi sahib's son was bitten by a snake. Maulvi sahib's wife fell at Bua's feet, rubbed her nose on her shoes and it was only then that the boy's life was spared.

"It must be a water snake, they're not the poisonous type," Chacha Mian remarked. But who will listen to talk that mocks belief? Fear of Bua grew in people's hearts. She wasn't just anybody, she was Ghazi Mian's most treasured beloved, Ghazi Mian, who made it possible for a barren woman to conceive, who healed a leper, who turned beggars into kings and kings into beggars in seconds. Was it any wonder that he cared so much about his favourite girl?

Since she hadn't produced even a mouse as yet, Aunt Qudsia was sure the *mem* was barren. Nani Biwi's fasting and prayers had surely put a lock on her fertility. Allah could change everything in no time. Nani Biwi had also made a vow at Mian's shrine that when, with Allah's grace, Qudsia's luck changed and she became pregnant, she would make an offering of a silver figurine.

For three years Nani Biwi's silver cradle had been placed at Mian's feet with the entreaty, "Ghazi Mian, please fill this cradle." And along with that continued the pleas to Qawi Qadir to bring Qudsia's husband back to her. But all the vows, prayers and fasting came to nought. The cradle was filled up, but it was the *mem* who became the instrument. The day she heard the news that her rival had given birth to a daughter, Aunt Qudsia was weighed down, as if a marble tomb had been erected over her soft, newly-dug grave. On the day of reckoning the angels of death, Munkar and Nakir, would be slow to breathe life into her.

Bua, who had been absent for many days, suddenly

appeared. Nani Biwi was busy scolding the *nain* who had arrived with sweets to offer felicitations on the occasion of the baby's birth. Tossing the ladoos into the gutter, Nani Biwi threatened to shave off the *nain's* hair; the woman clasped her lehnga about her legs and bolted from there.

On hearing of the arrival of the baby girl, Bua began twittering.

"Listen girl, your *soutan's* lap has been blessed, aren't you going to distribute sweets?" Then she took down the drum and embarked on silly songs about childbirth.

"*With bells on his ankles / The little tot will play* cham, cham, cham . . ."

There was no little tot, what cursed *cham, cham* was there going to be? This uncalled for singing angered Nani Biwi. She railed and ranted at Bua who dropped the drum, left the house and trudged off to sit behind the mosque. She was gone for many days. This was not unusual. Not caring whether it was night or day, she started off on foot, wandering from one village to another. Somewhere along the way, standing on the edge of a well to catch her breath, if she heard a new song, she'd include it in her repertoire of lyrics. Then she moved on. Often she travelled without food for days. The crazed have great strength. We had never seen her sleeping. She wasn't bothered by either snakes or scorpions or wild animals. In the village on the other side of the stream a lion was spotted, but it stayed out of her path. We had heard rumours that the lion offered her salutations by placing its head on the ground before her.

Bua told her stories of Ghazi Mian's playfulness with such aplomb that it became difficult to doubt her word. When you live next to a shrine everything seems to make sense. Mian was very stubborn and mischievous. He teased her always, tugging at her dupatta, clutching her bangles.

"Now listen, how did he fall in love with you?" Aunt Qudsia asked.

"His heart led him to me," Bua replied, smiling proudly.

"That's what I'm asking, how did his heart lead him to

you?" Aunt Qudsia was always anxious to find out how one could win someone's heart. Although she had sacrificed her body, soul and everything she possessed, she had not succeeded in winning anyone's heart.

"I don't know, why don't you ask him yourself, he's standing in front of me, smiling." She pointed to the wall with her finger and all of us followed it fearfully. Our eyes could see nothing, but for her the world around was filled with blinding light.

"How did you meet him?"

"I was on my way to the well, to draw water, he stood in my path, blocking my way."

"And then?" We all moved closer to her.

"I tried to run, he clasped my wrist."

"And then?" We edged closer still.

"My father was very angry." She was in a world of her own already. "He said, we won't give him our daughter, he's a boatman's son."

"A boatman's son?"

Bua explained that Mian had taken the form of a boatman's son in order to beg for her hand; he fell at her father's feet and pleaded. But her father got angry and rejected him and arranged her marriage to someone else. A terrible storm arose while the wedding party was attempting to cross the Ghagra stream in the middle of the night. It was Mian, transformed as the boatman and oaring their boat, who had summoned the storm. He ignored everyone else and made an attempt to save her from drowning, but the others tried to interfere. Enraged, he tipped the boat and let everyone drown. Surrounded by flowers, Bua floated for three days on the surface of the water in her bridal clothes.

"And then?" We had moved practically into her lap by now.

"And then nothing!" Exhausted, she pushed us away and left the house to wander in the cemetery in a daze, lost, singing love songs.

Bua was a virgin. No man had touched her. After the *barat*

drowned she managed somehow to get to the banks of the stream. For days she strayed in the woods. When her parents heard she was alive they came after her to take her home, but by then Bua had retreated into a world of dreams. She refused to shatter her bridal bangles; she was a bride, and Bale Mian was her bridegroom. No one had the courage to tangle with Bale Mian.

"He's calling me," she'd suddenly say and wander off into the woods, singing songs of love. Considering her desire to be Bale Mian's, no one dared stop her. Gradually, as time passed, certain miracles came to be associated with her and people seemed to be more and more intimidated by her. Then they began to worship her. If someone needed to ask a favour of Mian, she was the one who was pampered first. Wherever she went she was treated with deference and to have the opportunity of doing something for her was regarded as a stroke of good fortune. When a prayer was answered, a pink dupatta, fragrant oil and attar, bangles and flowers were offered at Ghazi Mian's shrine for her, along with the offering that had been promised for Ghazi Mian. How much did she eat? She could stay without food for days. People filled large decorated trays with food and brought them to her house and she distributed the food among beggars. She had been living alone since the death of her parents. A low caste woman took care of the house. The village washer woman, who was careless with everyone else's clothes and frequently lost or misplaced laundry, washed Bua's clothes with the utmost care, giving them the best crispness and lustre. Bua owned some land, but never bothered to take any profit from its tilling. Perhaps that was why people had begun to view her as Ghazi Mian's cherished beloved; they too cherished her. She had no reason to fear anyone, there were hundreds who were ready to surrender their lives to her. Therefore, although she was a weak woman, she was not handicapped or helpless; she claimed all the rights of a man. She moved about alone, as she fancied, declared her love in a loud voice, sang boisterously, made bold comments without reserve, swore unabashedly, sat in the company of men while a qawwali was going on and generously threw money to the singers.

During the annual fair at Ghazi Mian's shrine, thousands of ruffians and scoundrels trooped in along with the lakhs of pilgrims and worshippers; every other day you heard about kidnappings and rapes. Upper class ladies considered it dangerous to come out even in enclosed palanquins or guarded carriages. And Bua, all the while, sailed about without a care among the crowds, her dupatta floating behind her.

"My word, Bua, the world is a dangerous place, don't go to the fair," Amma warned her. "Aren't you afraid to wander around all by yourself?"

"But I don't wander by myself, I'm not alone, he's with me." In other words, her *he*.

There was no one among us who could contradict her. What could you say? And if we said something she didn't like we'd be in trouble; who knows what miracle might follow.

"She's a degenerate, the wretch!" In the beginning Chacha Mian didn't like her at all. "And she's not mad either. She's just making a fool of all of us."

That very night Chacha Mian suffered an attack of liver pain that left him gasping for breath. He kept insisting that he'd had a liver ailment for many years, but who was going to pay any attention to what he said? "He's an ignorant man," Amma admitted to Bua in an attempt to win her over. She secretly begged her to speak to Ghazi Mian on their behalf.

The pain would have subsided on its own, but Amma was sure he had been cured because of Bua's intervention. And she warned Chacha Mian that if he ever said another unfavourable word concerning Bua again she would beat her head with her hands. What did he have to lose? He had no children and no God, while she, by God's grace, was a mother and could not afford to antagonise anyone. As for

Abba, she had already sworn that if he said anything hostile with regard to Bua he would surely see her dead. Abba had often maintained that this business of believing in spiritual leaders and their followers was a sinful undertaking. But Amma's family was dearer to her than concerns about the next life.

When our friendship with Bua grew it seemed as if we'd come to terms with God; because of Bua we felt as if we too had some connection with Ghazi Mian. Sometimes when she was in a good mood she spent the night at our house and all of us quarrelled for the opportunity to sleep with her on the same bed. She exuded a wonderful fragrance of soft-smelling, freshly-dug earth. When, after several days of absence, her voice floating in song reached our ears, we became frantic with excitement and ran to fetch her. Like ants we clung to her, dragging her home. The very same voice which used to strike fear in our hearts now fell on our ears with the magic of an ancient melody.

As soon as she stepped into the house, everything brightened and came to life, the drum beat vibrated:

"*Ho, my raja, bring me some medicine from Dilli/ So I can be cured.*" She sang the new songs and new tunes she had picked up.

"*The rains are here/ My brother, will you not put up the swing?*"

Dark clouds swirled, rain drops fell, young hearts stirred with emotions, flames smouldered in Aunt Qudsia's eyes. Who was going to put up a swing? Aunt Qudsia became dizzy and nauseated when she saw anyone swinging. But Bua brought a length of rope from somewhere, we made a swing and with a down pillow for a seat we swung high and low. Bua sang long, high notes and Aunt Qudsia, from her place on the divan, joined in:

"*My heart yearns, the clouds pour/ My friend, how will I endure these days of spring . . .*"

Sitting at a distance Uncle Shabir stared at the floor like a criminal, as though he had a hand in making the clouds pour and the heart yearn, as if Aunt Qudsia's spring had soured because of him. Qudsia belonged to someone else, she was forbidden fruit. Secretly he consulted maulvis, talked to lawyers, but we're talking of the time when the Khul'a Bill hadn't been passed. At first no one thought of divorce because of the fear of bringing dishonour to the family. Then, after some of the rebels in the family succeeded in bringing Nani Biwi around to the idea of divorce, Aunt Qudsia's husband stubbornly refused to give in.

Rejecting our world, Bua had created a free world of her own where she ruled. She had sealed all doors but after all she was a woman; a chink remained somewhere. We became very fond of her and sometimes affectionately made obstinate demands; when she got ready to leave we trailed her tearfully, forcing her to turn back.

"Bua, these silly children are crazy about you, why don't you take them with you," Amma would say, and Bua would cancel her trip.

If she hadn't been slightly demented, Bua was fit to be weighed in gold. She had started helping out with chores in the house. Cleaning was her particular obsession. Accompanied by an army of kids she went about tidying up and threw out basketfuls of rubbish. If only she could come back with us to our hometown after Abba's retirement.

"Can't she be cured?" Amma asked Hakim sahib who used to be called in to treat Aunt Qudsia. He came to our house once or twice every week.

"Of course she can, begum sahib. There is no ailment in this world for which medicine doesn't have a cure. Start giving her a laxative and God willing, her mind will return to its normal state."

Hakim sahib had only one medicine for every ailment: laburnum purgative. When Aunt Qudsia felt unwell, it was this very laxative that was administered to her. Not only did you feel that your life was slipping away but your body also seemed to be threatened by the effects of these laxatives. She had no recourse but to be cured and for days afterward she was afraid to blink an eyelid for fear that it might be mistaken for an oncoming attack. Chacha Mian, too, had been given these laxatives for the pain in his liver. After the first dose he threatened to kill Hakim sahib.

"The heat from the body travels to the brain. Purging the stomach helps get rid of all noxious matter." Hakim sahib proceeded to throw light on the advantages of purgative therapy and everyone was convinced. Bua, however, ignored his advice.

"Come now, what's this silly hakim going to do for me." Irritated by all this talk, Bua made off. No one could discuss her illness for any length of time.

It was while a treatment for Bua was being sought that something tragic occurred which clearly confirmed her unbalanced state of mind. One of our cousins, the third among her siblings, was rather homely and the family faced constant hurdles in finding her a suitable match. After much hard work an aunt from Saharanpur finally got something going. The boy's mother arrived to talk things over. The house was cleaned so thoroughly to impress her that we began to feel like guests in our own home. Displayed all around us were items which we had never been allowed near for fear that we might break or tarnish them.

Bua had not made an appearance for many days. After a frantic search lasting three or four days, we gave up on her. A lengthy menu was being prepared for the mother-in-law, the *samdhan*. Suddenly, chameli buds dangling from a corner of her dupatta, a new song on her lips, Bua arrived in her usual way. First she was taken aback by the manner in which the house had been cleaned and decorated. Then she spotted the guest and lost control altogether. Going up to the woman, Bua flicked her eyelashes and knit her brows as if searching for a microscopic tic. The *samdhan* was not invisible. True she was short, but her lack of height was amply made up for by her massive bulk.

Amma was perturbed by Bua's behaviour and made an

attempt to distract her with some silly chatter. But, pushing aside Amma's restraining hand, Bua asked the *samdhan*-to-be:

"I say, sister, what kind of grain do you eat?"

The *samdhan's* face came alive with a variety of emotions. The diamond nose bob vibrated in the smooth, black nose, and it seemed as if she were about to explode with a loud bang.

"Bua dear, will you take this ice-water to the men's quarters?" Amma pulled her away from their guest. "Number Three has received a proposal, why don't you go and see the groom and tell us what he's like—he's outside." Amma managed to get her to leave.

"She's mad, the wretch," Amma apologised.

But the *samdhan* would not be appeased.

Bua left the room and returned within seconds. Dumping the tray with the ice-water on the divan, she beat her forehead with her hand.

"O my mother! Is that a groom or a tobacco leaf and a dwarf to boot!" She placed her right hand over her left, fingers extended, thumb to thumb to show them what she meant.

Bua continued: "I tell you, they don't make a proper pair. The groom is no good, you'll only ruin the girl's life. I say *samdhan*, go and find someone who's a fairy like yourself for your son, and leave our girl alone."

The *samdhan* didn't explode, but she did leave Number Three alone.

Vexed, Bua kept swearing; Amma could not calm her down. Taking the drum down from the peg she began a song on a high note:

"*A dark lover I won't take, sister, a dark lover . . .*
When my groom sits beside me on the nuptial bed, I'll kick him so he falls, sister . . .
A dark lover . . . I won't take . . ."

Poor Number Three was fated to live with hurdles. The whole household reprimanded Bua for her actions, but thrusting the drum to one side, she continued to mutter: "Is she unwanted baggage, hunh?"

She was gone for many weeks this time. We thought she wasn't coming back. The house was lonely without her and Aunt Qudsia's attacks recurred with greater frequency. Her temperament also soured. In the past she had complied with everything Nani Biwi said.

"Qudsia, child, drink some milk."

"Yes, Bi Amma."

"Child, lie down, give your back a rest, you've been stretched like a rod all day."

"Girl, how long are you going to remain in bed, get up now."

In other words it was always "Get up," "Eat this, drink that." Like a disease Aunt Qudsia was affixed to Nani Biwi who constantly expressed her grief at her daughter's fate and continuously scrutinised her. What else was there for her to do, anyway? And Aunt Qudsia answered with, "Yes, Bi Amma," to everything.

Suddenly, no one knows why, Aunt Qudsia began to get irritated with Nani Biwi. The two would quarrel with each other, sometimes Aunt Qudsia would cry, and sometimes Nani Biwi. And Dadima invariably jumped in. One by one all the aunts in the house would also be embroiled in the battle and before long two separate parties emerged. It all started with one thing and ended somewhere else altogether.

Members from our mother's side of the family formed one group while those from our father's side formed another. Attacks directed at seven generations of each party commenced. And later, their faces swollen, all the women stiffly avoided each other for days.

Every skirmish originated from Aunt Qudsia's camp. The bitterness in her temperament grew with each passing day; she seemed to derive pleasure from hurting those around her. Her behaviour towards Uncle Shabir also became chilly.

"*Why, when I called for you, did you take so long,*" he began with one of Aunt Qudsia's favourite pieces. She turned her back to him. The poor fellow squirmed uncomfortably.

"You should go, it's getting dark and it's the rainy season," she said dryly, feeling sorry for him. Grateful that she was thinking of him at least, he got up and left.

And then one day we went mad with joy. We found her. It was spring, the woods were blazing with *palas* blossoms, our eyes seemed to be brimming over with the red of the flowers. She was standing next to an amber-laden tree, dusting sand from her slippers. Her pink *dupatta* glowed from the fiery reflection of the flowers, spring blossoms danced in her eyes as if she had just come from a visit with her beloved or was on her way to meet him.

We were all over her. Love makes one so helpless. Our exuberance filled her with a glow, the beads in her throat began to tinkle.

"Wait, wait a minute, I'm coming." We dragged her. Suddenly she paused, cast a glance behind her and said, in a pleading tone, "I'll be back soon."

We were nonplussed. To whom was she making a promise of return? There was no one there. She took a few steps, then stopped. Angrily she said, "Don't put on an act with me, I'm warning you." Then she made as if to walk on. Once again, as if she had heard some objectionable remark, she knit her brow and scolded: "All right, you can go, I won't come back . . . . I'll see what you'll do . . . you don't trust me . . . I don't care . . ." She was fighting the air and our legs seemed to be melting. If we hadn't loved her so much we would have made off from there a long time ago.

Bua's arrival caused a stir in our house. It was a strange co- incidence that whenever she came a parcel containing fruit or sweetmeats arrived or we received some good news. Her appearance livened everyone's hearts; if a fight was in progress, it ceased, or maybe in the ensuing commotion people forgot what they had been fighting about. Shrugging off her despondency, Aunt Qudsia also got up and took note of what was going on.

"I'm not coming," Bua scolded the air in front of her. Everyone became fearful.

"What's the matter?" Amma asked.

"Such grief. He's pestering me, he doesn't trust me, he says I have another lover, I have eyes for someone else!" She screamed as she complained about Bale Mian. "Who does he think I am . . . a hussy?"

"Ahhh . . . you crazy girl," Amma said sadly and sighed again.

"He's burnt to a cinder with jealousy, he says I'm fickle."

Her imaginary lover was an odd composite indeed; a little bit of James Bond, a little of Krishan Murari, you might say. James Bond is a hero for every age, whether he appears as a hero from *Dastan-e-Amir Hamza* or as Hatim Tai. And her beloved was also a reflection of Krishan Murari because people generally sang songs about Krishan. As a matter of fact, Bale Mian's antics reminded you of him: tugging at her dupatta, twisting her wrists so that her bangles broke, and when moved to anger, resorting to slapping, or upturning a boat.

He exhibited all the traits of a suave young man. No matter what anyone might say, Bua's Bale Mian was undoubtedly more colourful and vibrant than Aunt Qudsia's Uncle Shabir. We believed everything Bua told us. Why was it so surprising that she could see Bale Mian? Didn't we observe elephants and stallions in the clouds, and Raja Inder's court in all its glory in the peeling plaster of the crumbling, saline-ridden walls? We didn't think she was deranged. If there were a few deranged people like her in every household, life would certainly be more tolerable.

"I say Bua, won't you come here for a minute," Amma cajoled; she had something to say to her that was important. Perhaps because Bua was angry with Mian, she didn't bolt when Amma brought up the question of Hakim sahib's treatment. It seemed that she was listening intently.

"Ahhh . . . what treatment . . . my suffering at his hands will take my life . . . he grumbles at every step, then he tyrannizes me . . ."

Taking the drum from its peg she gazed at it ruefully.

"*Little mouse, why do you gather all this treasure/ Soon all will be taken away . . .*"

When the drum failed to perk her up she began quarrelling with Bale Mian:

"*Beloved, your tantrums I won't tolerate anymore . . .*
I tell you, if you climb a horse, I'll climb an elephant . . .
Beloved, your tantrums . . ."

She wore her beloved out. If he climbed the roof, she climbed a mountain, if he followed her to the mountain, she darted into the infernal regions under the earth; in other words, she made him huff and puff.

"Look, here he is, touching my feet, begging forgiveness."

The insane are like kings in their own realm. What confidence Bua had in herself. The king of kings bowed at her feet, one smile from her and he was no longer himself. If you can find someone who cares for you like this why should you not discard the life of reason and good sense?

When birds who are caged gaze at the flight of those soaring freely in the skies, they are compelled to dash their heads against the wooden bars of their cages. And, unable to find escape, they conspire with their captors. Isn't it true that domesticated fowls or birds with clipped wings are used by hunters to ensnare their own kind?

The good women enclosed in the four walls of their home, tightly bound by the constraints of society, also could not tolerate Bua's freedom. She was a woman, but she enjoyed the rights of men, and everyone resented that. Bua didn't refuse to take the laxative, but she also did not protest strongly.

Amma said that the wretch's yes or no was all the same; after all, the treatment was for her own good.

All night long *amaltas* pods, *amla*, *har*, *bahir* and other items from the same disgusting family continued to be emptied into a large, unpolished copper pot. After her morning prayers Nani Biwi raised the heat under the pot again. Bua had been detained under some pretext.

The first dose had to be taken on an empty stomach, first thing in the morning. We also awoke. The whole house was putrid with the smell of *amaltas*. The sight of the large tin bowl filled with a mixture that looked like rotting cow-dung, made my stomach turn.

Bua tried to shake her off, but Amma pressed on with pledges on her own life. Nani Biwi pleaded on Mian's behalf. They brought her to the edge of the water drain and told her to squat.

"Hold your nose with your dupatta," Dadi Amma suggested.

The entire family had gathered as if a fighting match between rams was about to commence. Bua pressed her nose with her dupatta and with Tai Amma's help she balanced the large bowl with one hand.

"Don't make her drink this ... Amma bi ... O God, Apa bi, leave the poor wretch alone." Suddenly Aunt Qudsia was pleading with everybody. "Please, you're so nice, Tai Amma ..."

She had suffered the tortures of this laxative.

"My word, girl, are you out of your mind!"

"*Aakh! Aakkh!*" We made gagging noises as we sat close by with our noses pressed between our fingers.

"No, Apa bi ... please, don't make her drink this. I've had it, may God help us!"

"Because you've had it you're still in one piece. You might have been picking at straws by now if you hadn't."

With great ceremony Bua took one sip from the cup and "*Phurrr!*" she spat it all out on Tai Amma's breast. Throwing the bowl into the drain, she made a beeline for the tap and gargled until she was spent.

"May he die, that bastard hakim, it's his mother's crushed liver in this drink."

Each time she washed out her mouth she delivered a heavy invective intended for Hakim sahib. "May his mother's grave be filled with worms!"

"You foolish girl, you've dumped such valuable medicine into the gutter. If you didn't want it you should have said so in the beginning so we could have saved it for Qudsia."

Aunt Qudsia winced.

"I didn't throw it, he pushed it out of my hand." Placing the blame on Bale Mian, Bua calmly began chewing cardamom seeds.

"But he was not speaking with you," Tai Amma said irately.

"Oh, he is such a vagabond! Who can fight him? Last night he wouldn't leave me alone, he clasped my feet, begged forgiveness and cried."

May God forgive us!

Bua rose nonchalantly and got ready to leave. "Why, where are you off to?"

"I have to go, he's getting angry with me again. *Beloved, I'll be a chameli in your lap* . . ." She was one with her beloved again.

A travelling theatre was in town, we were all longing to go. Bua went without a ticket every day and picked up new songs of burning love.

Aunt Qudsia's behaviour was changing. Instead of reading Rashid-ul Kheri's *The Morning of Sorrow* and *The Night of Life* and sobbing, she now surreptitiously read *The Poems of Love's Poison* and at night she paced the courtyard.

"Sir, the wretch will absolutely not take the laxative." Amma complained to Hakim sahib.

"No matter. By Allah's grace, I have other drugs; she will never guess she is taking anything. Here, give her these three tablets rolled in paan or some sweets. Continue this treatment once every three days and God willing, she will be completely cured."

"Here, Bua, have a paan." As soon as Bua appeared Amma would open her paandan.

"No dear, no, my breath will smell." Bua dodged Amma adroitly.

But if women don't have anything better to do than meddle, how long can you escape from them? Perhaps she had a quarrel with Bale Mian or maybe his attention strayed, but somehow the first dose finally went down Bua's throat. And everyone waited for results. Nothing happened. Except that Bua placed a rope cot under the neem tree and went to sleep, something we had never seen her do before.

Everyone was convinced that Bale Mian had played a trick by impeding the progress of the tablet, or possibly it hadn't been administered first thing in the morning and that was why no results were in evidence. Suddenly Bua awoke with a start. For the first time we saw a strange expression of undefined fear on her face. She undoubtedly had knowledge of the unknown. She got up and left angrily.

"I say, to hell with all this wretched treatment! What if she leaves a curse or two behind, where will we be? One shouldn't tangle with the pious." Amma made her decision.

"It is truly amazing, the tablet had no effect on her," impressed, Nani Biwi proclaimed.

But in the evening surprise fell upon us like a mud slide. Bua's sweeperess came running to our house with the message that Bua had been suffering from dysentery all morning and now she was also vomiting. Bewildered, Amma sent off a servant to Hakim sahib.

"It's the heat flowing out," Hakim sahib remarked, and handed the servant a potion which reduced the flow of the heat, but caused Bua's temperature to rise at an alarming rate.

Amma sent for her several days in a row, but she refused to come. She hardly ate much earlier and now her sweeperess came and fetched some watery rice and khichri and sago pudding, but Bua didn't touch a thing. All she did was drink large quantities of water.

When she came after several weeks, we felt as if she was

distanced from us, as if we had remained children while she had matured. When we tried to put our arms around her neck she tottered and sat down.

"Come now, what silliness is this." She spoke in a brusque tone, as though we had never draped our arms around her neck like a garland before this. Her clothes were rumpled, her hair dry and bedraggled. She had always been thin, now, after the illness, she was worse. When we requested her to play the drum she hedged. Amma placed a tray of pea pods before her. She started shelling them.

Nani Biwi and Amma exchanged meaningful glances above her head. They both expressed relief; if the remaining two tablets could also be administered, no signs of the illness would remain.

"I say, Bua, Mian isn't upset with you, is he?" Amma probed.

"Am I the one to fight?" This meant that a dispute was in progress. "I don't know what he thinks of himself, that son of a *lat* sahib!" She seemed perturbed. There was, without a doubt, a falling-out between them.

Bua's sweeperess had gone to a neighbouring village to perform an abortion. Her usual trade was rolling twine, but occasionally, as a side business, she helped the needy. Amma persuaded Bua to spend the night at our house.

Amma was ready to swear on the Quran that she had not given Bua the second dose, but Dadi Amma insisted that she and Nani Biwi had been conspiring; the second dose had been given and had acted as an acid bomb. Bua collapsed from a wave of diarrhoea that seemed to have no end. That night things became so bad that Abba also got wind of what was going on. The doctor was sent for, he prescribed medication, but Bua suffered helplessly from loose motions all night long.

Abba thundered that the Hakim sahib ought to be whipped, he was a fool, and that if he prescribed any medicine for anyone again he would be handcuffed.

Dadi Amma had been kept out of all this good work. It

was Nani Biwi's special case and she wanted to man her position herself.

"I say, girls, what is going on?" Dadi Amma, who was quite deaf, would occasionally repeat this question.

"Nothing, sister dear... mind your own business!" Nani Biwi uttered the first part of the sentence loudly and the second almost inaudibly.

"Nobody tells me anything," Dadi Amma muttered. The two were always at odds with each other. They were *samdhans*, but were also sisters-in-law by marriage. However, the real reason for their dissent lay in the fact of their beliefs. Nani Biwi belonged to the Sunni sect while Dadi Amma was a Shia. Their cantonments were set up in different verandas. Amma came and sat in Nani Biwi's veranda early in the morning. Amma was the nucleus around which our household revolved; it is obvious that her veranda assumed greater importance. After offering salutations to Dadi Amma, Amma came and sat here. The door to Aunt Qudsia's room also opened on this veranda, Aunt Qudsia, who was the family's most urgent social issue. Her comings and goings caused the place to bustle. Uncle Shabir too sat there. And as for the children, they will be where all the activity is. Dadi Amma was jealous: because the children's paternal side of the family was Shia, they should be raised as Shias as well. However, Nani Biwi had all the power; at every step she praised the tenets of the Sunni sect.

We were backed by Amma. When we didn't heed Dadi Amma's injunctions, Amma reprimanded us with a smile and we were emboldened. But if we ignored Nani Biwi's orders, we had to listen to threats of bones being shattered.

Both sides attempted to show us the straight road leading to heaven. Dadi Amma taught us one *kalima*, while Nani Biwi taught us the other. Confused, we jumbled them up, something that had an effect on us similar to that of Hakim sahib's tablets; we felt as if we had taken a mental purgative.

The keys to heaven got all mixed up and both sides showered us with damnation.

Nani Biwi held *milad* in answer to Dadi Amma's *majalis*; we got fine-grained sweets in earthen cups and immediately became Sunnis. But when the coverings were removed from the chandeliers in Dadi Amma's veranda, and the *taboot* was brought out, we became hers completely; when *nohas* were recited in tremulous voices, we donned black shirts and beat our chests with vigour. Nani Biwi pummelled us and tempted us with colourful sweets, but it was wise to be a member of Dadi Amma's party during the holy month of Muharram. For us the doors to heaven opened on the side where goods were most plentiful.

"Girl, are you Sunni or Shia?" Dadi Amma would frequently ask.

"Shia," I would reply promptly.

"Are you Shia or Sunni?" Nani Biwi usually queried before handing out sweets. Thank God the two verandas were at some distance from each other and both grandmothers were somewhat hard of hearing.

The question of Bua's treatment took a rather unpleasant turn. Dadi Amma filled Abba's ears with gossip, he scolded Amma, Amma cried heartily.

Abba's retirement was approaching. Prosperity makes you large-hearted and you feel great affection for your relatives. But with the onset of hard times, the fountains of love also dry up. All his life Abba had spent money indiscriminately. Now, with only a few years left before retirement, he wanted to make up for all that careless spending.

Everyone stiffened when a crow cawed. Here comes another guest. The crow cawed at our house every day; when our relatives from our father's side poured in, our mother's relatives, not wishing to be left behind, arrived as well. If paternal aunts showed up with their spouses and children, the maternal aunts also made an appearance with their entire families in tow.

The guests fell into two camps. Two tables were set up

and spies were sent out to make sure that the opposing camp was not receiving preferential treatment. Usually Nani Biwi's party had the upper hand since Amma was in her camp.

Abba had no time to involve himself in party politics. In addition, he was the one who made the money and Amma the one who spent it. The situation was very similar to what it's like in America these days; everyone, regardless of what party each person belonged to, pampered her. Abba, on the other hand, was neutral. He treated both parties in the same way.

However, Chacha Mian, my father's younger brother, was the one who was always looking for an opportunity to make trouble between the two parties.

Amma entertained her in-laws well, but in a way that smelled openly of disaffection. If there was a shortage of food she would announce the fact in a loud voice: "Send it over there, we'll eat with chutney and pickle."

But Chacha Mian was a sly one; he ate with Amma's party, partaking of whatever special dish it was that had proven unplentiful, and then went over to Dadi Amma's camp and said, "The liver and kidneys cooked today were excellent."

There were no liver and kidneys cooked that day.

Dadi Amma grumbled: "My word, I've had a hankering for so many days; no one bothered to send us any, they wolfed it all down themselves!"

And the following day when Abba came home from the court and went to greet her, she immediately complained about the liver and kidneys. Abba said to Amma, "I say, why didn't you send some liver and kidneys over there?"

"My word! When did we have liver and kidneys?" Amma would stand up in a huff.

"I swear I saw it with my own eyes, Bakreedan took over a bowlful," Dadi Amma declared depending on Chacha Mian's word. Oaths would be taken, faiths dragged in, and finally Chacha Mian would be called. He would say innocently, "What liver and kidneys? I've said so many times we shouldn't eat watermelon with rice, now I have a pain in my kidneys and once the pain starts..." Chacha Mian tried to avoid the subject. "Did you eat liver and kidneys over there or not?" Dadi Amma persisted.

"When? I didn't get any. This is not fair, such rich foods being cooked and eaten by others."

No one really knew what was going on. Witnesses were brought forth, then someone who was feeling heavy-hearted burst into tears, in answer to which another person broke down; old wounds were rubbed anew:

"All I did was ask for a tiny morsel and she was downright evasive..."

"Such a blow it was, the fingers left a mark on the poor wretch's face..."

"I say, sister, it's quite another matter when it comes to your own kin..."

"Yes, indeed, and we're just enemies..."

When all of them were exhausted, Chacha Mian stepped in.

"What's all this bickering? You sound like butchers and common people... what kind of decency is this... fighting over morsels like dogs."

Hearing him scold, everyone, exhausted and worn out by now, felt contrite and went off to bed. Members of the paternal side of the family were glad that Nani Biwi's party had been severely reproached on account of Bua.

Bua was very sick. The time for the third dose never came; she was no good to herself after the second. If Qais had been administered all three doses prescribed by Hakim sahib, he would never have become Majnun, the crazed lover. He would have lost the vigour needed to roam the desert and the energy to cry out 'Laila! Laila!'; the poor fellow would have forgotten all about love's sprightliness.

The fever subsided, but for several days afterwards Bua was so weak she could barely talk. Because the second dose had produced immediate results, she was still at our house.

All day long she sat silently in a corner, her eyes shut. Her reason had made a comeback; she seemed quite sensible now.

Bua's sweeperess had not yet returned. Amma pampered Bua no end and personally prepared soup for her. But Bua, her face drawn, would not budge. After much coaxing she would take a few sips but immediately throw up; either that, or she had to set up her cot next to the toilet. Her digestive system was permanently damaged; heat seemed to flow out without the aid of medicine.

Where has Bua gone, I wondered sometimes. That jaunty, proud Bua who ran about with the children shaking the branches of the jambolana tree for jamuns, our mad Bua who stole melons and cucumbers from the fields! Why did Allah give her back her reason? She had even forgotten to laugh.

And singing?

After the second dose her throat became hoarse.

O God, she'll never again put up a swing on the neem tree and sing songs about the rainy season.

Amma had appointed herself Bua's guardian. She arranged to have her house rented and Bua began to live with us. When the sweeperess returned, she came to Bua distraught. Bua's health was relatively better at this time. She was peeling potatoes for potato *bharta*. Because winter had begun, she spent most of her time in the kitchen.

There was a time when during the coldest winter months Bua went around with just a light shawl draped over her shoulders at night. But that was when she had been filled with warmth.

Amma scolded the sweeperess and sent her off. Bua continued to sit quietly with her head lowered. As soon as the rent from the house started coming in, Amma put it all together and ordered a pair of gold bracelets for Bua. When the bracelets, decorated with carved lion heads, arrived, Bua turned them over a few times in her hands, then handed them to Amma.

"Keep them."

"I say, girl, put them on," Nani Biwi insisted.

"My word, no, what's the occasion for wearing bracelets?" she replied tartly. Bua had also developed the ability to tell the difference between what was proper and what was not.

"Do you see her? Who can say the poor girl was once mad. How mature she is now." Nani Biwi called her dullness, maturity.

Bua did not mention Bale Mian either. If one of us asked, "Bua, how is Mian?" she pretended he had been nothing to her, as if he were a stranger. We teased her further.

"Don't eat my brains!" she'd snap at us and Amma would censure us and shoo us away.

"I say, don't remind her, the wretch, she'll lose her mind again." Nani Biwi also scolded, but she too teased Bua sometimes.

"I say, it seems your Ghazi Mian has forgotten you altogether."

Bua sat still as if she were deaf.

But one day she showed some of her old spirit.

If she watched her diet carefully she was able to keep everything down. By now she had taken over most of the housework and had graduated from light jobs to frying garlic in ghee and pouring it over the dal. Every day she kneaded five seers of dough and before long she was also cooking rotis.

"He's unfaithful," Bua said archly. Then she became emotional. She had been drying her hair after a bath. She looked a little like the Bua of old. Suddenly she broke into song in a lifeless voice:

"*Ho, raja ji, my rival has long tresses/ Don't get caught, raja ji . . .*"

The old passion was gone from her voice. Bale Mian had been unfaithful to her or was about be unfaithful to her. Seeing her own dry hair she was suddenly threatened by her rival's long tresses.

"*Ho, raja ji . . . my rival has pink cheeks . . .*"

Bua's once wheatish complexion had become muddy and lustreless. All of a sudden she was stooping like an old woman. When she got to her feet she braced herself by putting both hands on her knees. The old vitality and sprightliness had disappeared; after forsaking Bale Mian's love, she was dispossessed and vacant, a ruin.

Childhood never mourns any loss for long. We moved on, leaving her behind as she lagged. Aunt Qudsia was no longer the same either. Instead of constantly complaining about the noise we made, she now called us to her and resolved our disputes, tutored us, scrubbed our dry, chapped hands and feet and massaged them with vaseline. It wasn't long ago that she had wandered listlessly and morose, her hair uncombed for many days, her clothes filthy because she would forget to change. Why would a woman adorn herself if the person whose gaze matters the most turns away from her? However, in consideration of her married state she had continued wearing two glass bangles on each wrist. People recounted tales of her patience and loyalty with awe and wonder.

A soft, delicate change had begun to appear in her. Instead of staying in bed for hours she started to walk regularly. Her complexion blossomed, perhaps because she used a turmeric paste prepared from a fine selection of herbs. In the past when Nani Biwi combed her hair, big clumps would fall out. Now her hair was silky and shiny, probably because it was washed with *shika kai*, *nagar motha* and other fragrant roots that are generally used by brides. Or maybe now we liked everything about her because she no longer considered us a curse from God but thought of us instead as mischievious children.

In the past she carelessly dipped her dupattas in any odd shade of purple or yellow dye (in deference to her wedded state), and threw them out to dry on the line. Now, ever since she had sent for the bale of muslin # 26 from Agra, the dupattas were dyed in soft, sober colours. First the clothes were tailored to match the season and then matching gold or silver lace was stitched on to the dupattas. For Muharram the colour was green, and for spring they were dyed in five-toned, wavy stripes. We happily transported bucketfuls of water to her, flung her gold-embroidered dupatta up and down, this way and that in the sun to dry, and dumped heaps of half-opened buds next to her pillow.

We looped her earrings with clusters of buds, wrapped the earrings in moist cloth and left them by the water containers. In the evening she bathed, donned a soft-hued, crisp gharara along with an embroidered muslin shirt with which she wore a gathered dupatta, put on the earrings laden with flowers, and smilingly gazed into the empty air before her as if she too had a Ghazi Mian standing there, teasing her.

The responsible women in the household were a little concerned about the changes they saw in Aunt Qudsia. The attacks of hysteria she had suffered from were understandable; every unfortunate woman who is rejected by her husband occupies herself thus. But dressing up and wearing flowers does not become a woman whose earthly God has turned away from her. She must thank God for whatever meagre clothing she can obtain, cover herself with it, and eat whatever little comes her way. What would people say if they got a glimpse of her fanciful behaviour?

Surely she would be spat at.

All this adornment, these rosettes, they enflame wicked thoughts, the devil gets encouragement from them.

"I say, Qudsia, you don't look well, should I send for Hakim sahib?" Nani Biwi, fearful of her daughter's well-being, suggested.

"No Amma bi, I'm feeling fine." Aunt Qudsia guiltily evaded her mother's gaze.

"My word, sleeping late again! Why, you've missed your morning prayers, girl!"

"I've said the make-up prayers, Amma."

"God knows what rubbish you read all night. Is it any wonder you can't get up in time for morning prayers?"

Every other day Aunt Qudsia received a fresh batch of novels in the mail. Not once did she show them to anyone. As soon as a fresh shipment arrived, she immediately hid it under her pillow.

These days when Aunt Qudsia wore earrings or bangles, Nani Biwi reacted with indignation: "What's the occasion for these earrings?" she'd ask.

"No occasion, I just felt like wearing them," Aunt Qudsia would reply, tossing her head, making the earrings swing.

"My oh my, what feeling is this?" Nani Biwi grumbled.

There was a time when Nani Biwi mourned, expressing sorrow at the sight of Aunt Qudsia's unadorned wrists, lamenting that she couldn't wear earrings. "Ahhh, what hopes went into all this jewellery . . . the poor girl wasn't destined to use any of it. I say Qudsia, put on a thing or two at Eid or Baqr-Eid at least."

"Who shall I wear it for, Amma?" Aunt Qudsia would respond with a deep sigh.

But all that was in the past. And now? No, the signs were not at all good; reading those wretched, cheap books all night long, pacing the veranda and sighing, looking up at the sky and smiling to oneself . . . no, these are not the ways of girls who sacrifice their lives for the family. Why were buds sprouting from this old, dried-out trunk?

No longer did Nani Biwi pray with the same zeal for Aunt Qudsia's husband's return. The groom didn't show his face, but Uncle Shabir, on the other hand, came regularly. He seemed to be getting taller with each passing day; he gave the impression that, like a juggler, he had stilts attached to his legs.

Assuming an air of indifference, he would come and sit down at some distance. Aunt Qudsia nonchalantly played with her dupatta which kept slipping from her shoulders, and the gold buttons, in the meantime, became heavier and sunk deeper into her chest. These two didn't need to use their eyes to gaze at each other.

Soon she'd prompt one of us to ask Uncle Shair to sing

"*Sarkar Madine-walle.*" We preferred "*The eyes spoke/plunging a dagger into the heart*". However, in order to make Aunt Qudsia happy we would pester Uncle Shabir to sing the *na'at*.

"Let him sit on the stool here," she would say encouragingly and we brought him over to the stool.

He would start singing, and if, impelled by boredom, we tried to slip away, Aunt Qudsia caught hold of us and whispering promises of carrot halva and laddus into our ears, made us stay. It was as if she were guilty and could not be left alone with him. Our presence gave them an opportunity to say God knows what to each other; we never understood much. Often, Aunt Qudsia suddenly broke into a laugh for no apparent reason and continued laughing. We too joined in; children don't always have to know why they're laughing. Auntie's complexion glowed and the flower-laden earrings swayed and kissed her cheeks. With everyone laughing, Uncle Shabir's eyes also brimmed with light and his wooden mouth came to life.

"You're laughing for no reason, you silly girl!" he'd say ever so softly. But Auntie heard him.

"So do you want me to weep all my life?"

"No, Qudsia! I . . . I want . . ." he fumbled.

"Whom do you want?" Aunt Qudsia interjected, twisting his words to suit her meaning.

"Qudsia . . . " Mumble, murmur . . . whatever he said was unintelligible to us.

We stared at them like idiots.

Mumble, murmur . . . Aunt Qudsia was saying something. We didn't know what they were saying to each other. But we were aware that a delightfully sweet conversation was in progress. The expressions on their faces filled us with joy; children often understand unspoken words, feel them. We giggled loudly and they used our laughter as a screen behind which to hide.

"Liar! Swear on my life!"

"But how can I swear on *my* life?" he would reply so softly that stone-deaf Nani Biwi could not hear a thing. Dadi Amma's encampment was some distance away.

The two parties were embroiled in battle these days. Dadi Amma sent over some sweetmeats.

"It must be impure."

Nani Biwi maintained that Shias spat into food before handing it out to others or else mixed excrement with it. She threw the grainy, sugar-sweet laddus to the ducks in front of everyone, leaving Dadi Amma fuming with anger. But when Nani Biwi sent her some loquat that had arrived from Saharanpur, Dadi Amma immediately handed the fruit over to her sweeperess.

"Be sure to wash them," she said loudly to her hoping to rile Nani Biwi.

Anyway, Aunt Qudsia would say something and the atmosphere would become taut. She insisted on forcing Uncle Shabir to look into her eyes. However, he avoided her eyes, pinning his gaze instead on the bricks on the floor with an intensity that made one think that if he looked away the bricks would jump up and run from there.

When it was evening Uncle Shabir left, but lights continued to glimmer in Aunt Qudsia's eyes, and the smile that played on her lips was reminiscent of the cocky smile that hovered on Bua's lips when she saw Bale Mian. That was when she and Bale Mian hadn't quarrelled. But now Bua's eyes had an empty look, like dried-out, smoking oil wicks. A staleness hung about her. Some time had passed since her treatment, but Hakim Sahib's tablets seemed to have become permanently glued to her stomach lining; she would get the runs frequently and was always burping.

There was a time when Bua had the appetite of a bird, but now she heaped her plate high with maize bhat and arhar dal and constantly complained of heartburn. She also spent the better part of the day asleep; leaning against a wall, her mouth open, she could be found sleeping quietly most of the time. In her state of madness she didn't seem to need sleep, now she dozed all day. She had also become quite shrewd. Every day she visited her tenants and bickered with them.

"The bastards aren't paying rent on time, they're out to rob me."

As soon as Bua regained her sanity, she saw that the world was full of thieves and brigands. Her vision cleared and brightened, as if someone had applied a magical kohl to her eyes. The roof was leaking, but who can you get to repair it? All the workers are thieves, they'll clean you out.

After the bracelets came a matching gold necklet with the same lion's-head and this too was immediately placed in Amma's steel safe. Still she wasn't satisfied; every once in a while she'd ask about her jewellery.

"You're sure the lock's working?"

If a robbery took place in the neighbourhood, Bua felt the world was coming to an end. Right away she would have Amma open the safe and check its contents. No longer was she our dear, sweet Bua; she seemed to us now like all other stupid women.

All old associations slowly slipped from our minds. We were irritated by the sight of Bua grinding spices. Clamouring to sleep with her now seemed like a foolish thing to do. Instead of the fragrant odour of freshly-dug earth, her body now gave off an offensive smell of garlic, onions and stale food.

Meanwhile, Aunt Qudsia blossomed some more.

Nani Biwi tried every trick in the book, but Aunt Qudsia did not take the laxative and openly solicited Uncle Shabir's help in reading Mir's poetry. Evening came. No sooner had Aunt Qudsia turned her face to the left with the salam at the end of the *asr* prayers than Uncle Shabir appeared magically like the storybook giant at the front door. He would explain and she would understand; their eyes remained lowered, their faces wearing masks of strangeness. Their eyes met just once or twice and, for no apparent reason, our hearts raced like colourful kites entwining cords in the sky.

If we, the children, could guess what was going on, surely Nani Biwi, who was exceedingly clever, was not fooled. Dadi Amma, meanwhile, did not spare her meaningfully judgemental smiles.

"I say, woman, if something untoward happens, the head of the household will have to face dishonour," Dadi Amma proceeded to explain the intricacies of philosophy to smelly, old Pathani Bua while the woman pressed her feet. She raised the subject as if they were discussing everyday politics. God help her, she wasn't pointing to anything specific, but it wouldn't be her fault if suspicion was raised by what she was saying.

Nani Biwi heard all this and fumed.

"Please, break off some tamarind pods, won't you? We'll make some chutney." Aunt Qudsia was playing with the buttons on her shirt front.

Uncle Shabir had just arrived.

"What shall I break them off with? Is there a stick or a pole around here?"

"My word! You're no less than a pole yourself, why don't you just reach up and break some?"

For a split second a rod of brightness flashed in Uncle Shabir's eyes. He appeared alive and if no one had been around he would certainly have done what Manjhuji's fiance did when he found himself alone with her . . .

After Uncle Shabir left, Nani Biwi reprimanded Aunt Qudsia for her flighty behaviour.

"Why, have I committed adultery?" snarled Aunt Qudsia.

"Tsk, tsk, you wretch! What will people say? Agreed that Shabir is a decent man, he's not an outsider, he's your brother-in-law, but the world is an unjust place. It doesn't take long for a mole-hill to become a mountain."

"What do I care about the world? For ten years that man—may he die—has been making me weep and no one says one word of reproach to him."

It's true, girls should not read such peculiar books. There's all kinds of rubbish in them.

"Child, he's a man, no one can harm him. A woman's person is like a mirror, once there's a crack in it you'll forever see a crooked image of yourself."

"Hunh!" Unable to pursue the argument further, Aunt Qudsia turned her attention to the box of bangles. "*My Girdhar Gopal/ There is no other . . .*" she began humming as she selected bangles to match the colour of her shirt.

"*The vine has spread, what can anyone do now . . . My Girdhar . . .*"

"My word, child! How many times have I told you not to sing these dreadful, impious songs? And you neglected the afternoon prayers, too. I tried to wake you up, but you were too lazy. Of course, when you stay up so late at night you're sure to sleep late in the morning, like a bat."

Aunt Qudsia rose to her feet so abruptly her dupatta fell to the floor and the tiny bells on her buttons jingled. Picking up the *lota* she went to wash for prayers. Nani Biwi was not the only one who was upset; all good women were disturbed by the sight of girls walking about brazenly. Decent girls walked respectfully, taking small steps. Aunt Qudsia's newfound agility had shaken Nani Biwi to the core.

"I say girl, what kind of a gait is this, like a singing girl's, the front and back all sticking out?"

Trying to talk to Aunt Qudsia was like hitting oneself with a shoe. Nani Biwi conspired with Amma.

"This wretch Shabir just won't leave us alone. I've told him off so many times, but I think he's not budging because of encouragement from Qudsia. I'm very worried."

"I say, Amma, you're just imagining things. Now you're suspicious of poor Shabir. Because of him the unhappy girl gets to laugh and relax a little. She must have a reason to continue living, don't you think?"

If Amma was in a good mood Nani Biwi became more agitated.

"To hell with such living! What is she planning anyway?

And seeing your sister's false tears you're melting too?"

"I ask you, why would such a thing be so terrible?" Amma said after a pause.

"What do you mean?"

"Machu was saying, he had consulted with a lawyer friend of his, he was saying . . ."

Uncle Machu's real name was Mustaqeem and his nickname was Machu. *Mustaqeem* means straight; but Uncle Machu didn't have a straight bone in his body. He was crooked beyond measure.

"May the contemptible wretch's mouth burn! What is he but a good-for-nothing raised on the crumbs of prostitutes!" Nani Biwi went so far as to dig up his grave. He, in the meantime, alive and well, was receiving a hair massage from Aunt Qudsia.

"All right, please . . ." Amma fumbled for words.

"How dare you! Do you want your sister to have a second husband?"

"Get out of here!" Finding me listening intently to this conversation, Amma smacked me.

Unaware of what was going on, Aunt Qudsia, at that moment, was blushing in response to something Uncle Machu had asked. Just when her glowing, white cheeks seemed to disappear into the folds of her pink dupatta, the curtain moved and Uncle Shabir erupted into the room.

The air around us seemed to hold its breath. Gathering the front folds of her wide-legged pajama, Amma tucked them in at the waist and, ready to serve her lord and master, left the room. The bell on Abba's cycle could be heard from a distance. On his return from the club he usually went straight upstairs to his room, calmly keeping to himself on the second storey, very much like the leader of a caravan. Her keys jangling, Amma strode off to wait upon her husband and Nani Biwi took charge of the fort.

Uncle Machu generally slipped away as soon as he heard the sound of the bell. He was terrified of his serious, sober older brother and made every effort to stay out of his way in order to avoid being questioned on one matter or another. Considering the sort of thing he was involved in, it was certainly prudent for everyone to refrain from questioning him.

Placing the bundle of books on the bed, Uncle Shabir mumbled something, Aunt Qudsia inaudibly mumbled a reply, and off he went to pay his respects to Dadi Amma.

Nani Biwi was on guard for him like a cat waiting to pounce on a mouse. As soon as he emerged from the veranda, she grabbed him.

Aunt Qudsia, feeling a little bashful, walked off to the kitchen to prepare a tray for Abba. Food was being dished out and presuming that Nani Biwi was sharing some pleasant secrets with Uncle Shabir, she stared humming.

The drum had been refurbished. Aunt Qudsia sat down on the divan, picked up the drum and proceeded to tighten its rings. Leaning wearily against a wall, periodically spitting on the floor to one side, was Bua; perhaps she wanted to spit out the taste of *amaltas* from her mouth. These days she would start spitting wherever she was sitting.

"Bua dear, please play the beat you heard at the theatre, show me how the man struck the drum with his palm."

Bua cast a glance at the drum as if asking, "What *is* this thing?" and then, turning, spat on the floor.

"Oh, Bua! For Bale Mian's sake," Aunt Qudsia implored, pushing the drum toward her. She reached for Bua's hand, pulled her, then hastily let go. "Bua! You have fever!"

When she touched Bua's forehead she discovered it was burning.

Nani Biwi had been complaining for many days that Bua had stunk up her veranda. "I can't breathe," she said, "tell her to go back to her own house, the tenants have gone, we'll send her two meals a day."

She egged on Amma who had also lost interest in Bua by this time. Whatever they had all done for her had been done for her own good. Abba had been warning us about tightening our belts. This constant waiting upon guests was taking its toll; we had guests every day, elaborate dishes were prepared, clothes were made for them depending on whether it was summer or winter, and in the end the guests, barely escaping indigestion, grabbed their gifts and left, vacating their beds for a new set of visitors.

Bua's future had been satisfactorily taken care of. It was no one's fault that she wasn't well. Why, didn't she eat everything and anything that came her way? Her sweeperess had been gone a long time. The woman did visit once, pressed Bua's feet, crying all the while at her condition, but she was scolded and again driven away. She made her home under a peepal tree and eked out a living by begging.

But now they had no choice.

Manjhu was coming to attend Urs along with her in-laws. Her mother-in-law wanted to pray and make an offering at the shrine for a grandchild. So Bua returned to her house. However, her precious sweeperess became a constant presence on the veranda again. Three times a day, tea and food were set in a tray and sent out. If Bua was feeling well, she'd come herself and stay for several days in a row. Since Nani Biwi had had her veranda whitewashed, she had become extremely cautious; Bua hesitated to be about in such a clean and tidy place. There was a time when Bua's clothes were whiter and cleaner than those donned by the lady of the house and when she visited she sat with the other women. Now when she appeared, a small wooden stool or a bamboo chair was quickly pushed toward her. She either sat on the stool or if one wasn't around, she'd seat herself in the doorway, just like the sweeperess, washerwoman, or any other low-caste woman.

Sometimes, when she didn't have the energy to make it back to her house, Bua slept in the cowshed, a part of her cot inside the shed, the rest sticking out. The foul smell from Bua's body was lost in the stench of cow-dung and chicken droppings.

Uncle Shabir disappeared after his talk with Nani Biwi. Aunt Qudsia paced about restlessly and it seemed that she had vowed not to sleep; all night long she tossed and turned. Nani Biwi was beside herself with anxiety.

About this time Sanjhli's fate once again showed signs of changing. Her prospective in-laws had come and were being appropriately entertained.

"I say, is she the one whose husband brought in a *mem*?" the prospective sister-in-law inquired in a sorrowful tone.

Instead of trembling with pride, for the first time in her life Aunt Qudsia laughed crudely at this remark. "Yes sister, my rival is a *mem*, but I hear yours is an oil-manufacturer's daughter."

This was true, but it was something that had been covered up like cat's shit. The sister-in-law burst into tears.

When the guests left it was discovered that the young man in question had a squint in one eye. But everyone was sure it was Aunt Qudsia who had created a hurdle for Sanjhli this time. When Hakim sahib was consulted on the matter of Aunt Qudsia's condition, he presented the same diagnosis as before: an excess of melancholic matter in the body. As for treatment, it was that same wretched *amaltas* prescription, the only cure for heat in the blood!

Nani Biwi ignored Aunt Qudsia's protests and setting up a brick stove in her veranda, she prepared the elixir with her own hands.

"Child, say 'Allah is all, Allah will help' and toss it down." Nani Biwi handed her the copper bowl and patted her back.

Aunt Qudsia calmly flung the bowl exactly where Bua had thrown it that day in the gutter.

"A curse upon you! What are you doing!" Nani Biwi screamed, but Auntie walked away, calmly took the drum off the peg and began humming a song she had learned recently from the sweeperess.

Furious, Nani Biwi tried to snatch the drum from Auntie, who pushed her away with such force she nearly lost her balance and fell.

"If I'm a burden for you why don't you bury me alive, why do you want me to die like a dog? I will not drink this poison, I will never drink it!"

That was the day Aunt Qudsia discovered how Nani Biwi had instructed Uncle Shabir, in very polite tones, to stop coming to the house.

"You consider her your sister, dear boy, but people are very narrow-minded . . ." she explained to him and Uncle Shabir understood.

"Are you out of your mind, wretch!"

"Yes, why shouldn't I be out of my mind? I'm human, I'm not a stone. You hurled me into hell when I was fifteen, the colour of my wedding henna hadn't faded yet when he crossed the seven seas to a faraway place, and there he was stung by a white snake. But tell me, is this all my fault? Did I dally with anyone, did I give a thought to another man?"

"You were destined for a tragic fate. Who can interfere with God's will?"

"What sin have I committed that I should be punished while that scoundrel continues to live a happy life?"

"You miserable creature, aren't you ashamed to call your husband a scoundrel . . . he's your earthly God."

"A curse upon his face, the worst villain that ever lived!" Aunt Qudsia advanced threateningly.

"You wretched girl! Have you no pride in your wedded state? He hasn't done anything wrong, the Shariah allows a man to have four wives. You are not the only one in this world, there are thousands who suffer like you, but they endure hardship gracefully. A man is unfaithful by nature."

Finding that she was losing ground, Aunt Qudsia began to curse herself.

"O Allah! Please take me from this world! Mighty ruler, make my body dirt so I can at least be rid of this hell, or else take his life so I can be rid of the vile creature."

"You witch! Who is this you're cursing?" Nani Biwi shuddered. A husband is, after all, a husband.

"Baqar Hussain, your beloved son-in-law, the bastard,

the son-of-a-bitch!" Aunt Qudsia was slipping away. "May he burn in hell! May worms gnaw at him in the grave!" Spreading out her dupatta, she swayed as she cursed.

"So, will you go after a second husband?"

"Yes I will .. I will . . ." No, this wasn't Aunt Qudsia, this was an ogress.

"Then go and sell yourself in the bazaar."

"I will do that, I dare anyone to stop me."

Aunt Qudsia had no intention of selling herself, but anger led them from one thing to another. Nani Biwi remembered Nana Mian and cried bitterly. Ever since Uncle Shabir had stopped coming to the house mother and daughter engaged in altercations of this nature nearly every day. Finally Aunt Qudsia's in-laws received news of what was going on. Her father-in-law expressed alarm.

"Amma has spoiled her thoroughly. If this continues any longer the girl will no doubt bring dishonour to the family. It's better that we send for her, she'll come to her senses when she's here."

Nani Biwi agreed to send her. She could no longer bend her to her will. "Yes, this is how it should be," she decided, "it's between them and their daughter-in-law. How much longer can I beat my brains, anyway?"

But as soon as she heard that her in-laws had sent for her, Aunt Qudsia became enraged.

"Why doesn't he rebuke his son, the hypocrite! May his beard go up in flames, may his face burn!"

"You wretch, he's your uncle!" Nani Biwi screamed.

"To hell with such an uncle! Couldn't say one word of reproach to his own son. I say, they're very happy, there's a *mem* in the house, they butter her up, sit down at a table to eat dinner with forks and knives. After all, they're living on the crumbs their son throws them, they have to wag their tails in the *mem*'s presence. She's going to make God bless them in the next life no doubt, they're sure to follow even her shadow into heaven."

"You won't stop this nonsense, wretch? Oh God, save this

miserable creature from dishonour. May your tongue burn!" Nani Biwi picked up a shoe and crushed Aunt Qudsia's lips with it.

That was when Aunt Qudsia became like a woman possessed by a ghoul from the cremation grounds. She gnashed her teeth and, grasping both of Nani Biwi's twiggy wrists, she twisted them.

For a split second Nani Biwi peered into her raging eyes. Her heart convulsed. She could not see her dearer-than-life Qudsia Bano there; instead she saw a wounded lioness, a female cobra whose hood had been crushed, and she felt her own life was being wrested by that steely grasp. The old woman doubled over in fear. Everyone ran toward them with cries of "Hai! hai!" Nani Biwi was trembling from head to foot like a doe surrounded by hunting dogs.

"Oh God, Qudsia, what have you done? You raised your hand to Amma!"

Feeling completely helpless, Aunt Qudsia struck her hands against the stone slab lying on the terrace, smashing her bangles to pieces.

"I say, people, what is going on?" Dadi Amma, who was deaf, asked impatiently in a stifled voice. "Girls, will someone turn up the wick on the lamp. What is happening?" She was surrounded by lanterns, but who could dispel the darkness in her eyes?

The whole house was in an uproar; all the servants crowded near the front door, the women lifted their pajama folds and ran, the children began to whimper, the hens cackled.

"If anyone comes near me, I swear upon the Quran, I'll split her head open." Aunt Qudsia lifted the stone slab above her head. All the women valued their lives; they continued to rant and rave, but no one dared take one step in her direction. Aunt Qudsia started crushing the broken pieces of glass. Before she could bring her hand to her mouth, Uncle Shabir calmly placed his hand on her shoulder.

For ten years no man had touched her. Her hands fell

helplessly to her sides. She turned and looked into Shabir Hasan's eyes. This was the moment when she would have even returned from heaven. Shutting her eyes, she swooned and fell upon his chest.

Shabir Hasan's worthless hands hesitated for a split second. Then, in front of everyone, he clasped her to his breast with a force that made his ribs crack. The whole family was silenced as if a snake had been spotted. We forgot our play and gaped with our mouths hanging open. The air around us was stilled. Nani Biwi collapsed like a weak roof.

"What is going on, people, why this sudden silence?" Dadi Amma felt under her pillow for the *sajdah-gah*. "Is everyone getting ready for prayer, is that why no one says a word?"

Shabir Hasan gathered Qudsia Bano's slender body in both arms. It seemed as though he would never let her go, that he would carry her off somewhere. We were all holding our breath. Steeling himself, he gently put her down on the bed and calmly stationing himself some distance from her, he proceeded to stare at the floor as if to say, 'Well, here lies Qudsia Bano, she's unconscious, this is a good opportunity, come quietly and quickly strangle her, but don't kill her slowly, agonizingly.'

Hakim sahib checked her pulse and immediately came to the conclusion that the heat had travelled to her head, causing her brain to become numb. No one has any say in what Allah has fated, he added.

"The hakim speaks nonsense," smelly Pathani Bua remarked as she dusted her lehnga, "it looks like something else to me."

"Yes, I suspect that the spirit that had bewitched that wretch, Bua, has abandoned her and taken over the poor girl instead. Don't you see sister, as Bua's condition improved, poor Qudsia Bano's ways deteriorated." Aunt Baqar did her best to convince Nani Biwi. "What a terrible thing it was to see — the girl would wear white clothes, attar and aromatic oils and wander in the garden at all times of the day."

Aunt Qudsia's status began to improve. She was no longer alone. A spirit, demon, jinn, or some saint was with her. My poor Amma was taken in right away. Amma was a simple soul, anything she didn't understand she feared as a matter of caution.

Saint, demon, spirit or jinn, whatever it might be, she was reluctant to lock horns with any one of them. This was why she regularly sent a donation to the temple for Vishnu and, every now and then, made arrangements to provide fodder for a five-legged cow and milk for snakes.

"Daughter, this is blasphemous," Nani Biwi used to warn her, "offerings and *niaz* is one thing, but don't ruin your chances of going to heaven by getting involved with these good-for-nothing rituals."

But Amma was more concerned about her husband's life and the well-being of her children than she was about life after death. Now, who was to say that you could do anything if the gods and goddesses got upset? Right next to the cemetery were the cremation grounds and the children wandered around all day like bulls let loose. One day they went into a temple and showed disrespect to Bhagvan. Mahantji came to the door with complaints and to make amends Amma immediately made arrangements to feed a few Brahmins so that the god would not turn things upside down in anger. Whenever prasad arrived from the temple, all the women in the house said "*Thu, thu*, throw it to the hens, it's impure." But Amma would set it down on one of the shelves and in a twinkling the children gobbled it up. Only then was she satisfied. Anyway, children can digest even stones and who knows, maybe there was something propitious in the prasad.

And now she set out to serve Aunt Qudsia. Agreeing to everything anyone said, she arranged incantations and invocations to get rid of jinn, spirits and demons. She also offered *niaz* in the name of holy saints and began treating

Aunt Qudsia with undue regard. She was afraid of this new Qudsia. On the question of madness, she was neutral; who knows, maybe the insane also held special powers. Someone with children and a family had to exercise extreme caution in order to avert the threat of danger from any source. And jinns were known to be temperamental; after all, God Almighty made man from clay and the jinns from fire; if the fire was ignited who was to say what the consequences might be.

It was quite obvious that the spirit or demon that possessed Aunt Qudsia was not the type that would instruct her to throw the shit around. No, she seemed to be under the influence of some very cultured, fashionable, extremely fanciful saint. Uncle Machu writhed when he saw the way Aunt Qudsia was pampered; true, God had not shaped him from fiery flames, but he must surely have used embers.

"I say Qudsia Bano, what a clever one you are! You're fooling everybody, aren't you?" Uncle Machu smiled, but it was common knowledge that he was a worthless person and an apostate. Everybody cursed and chided him.

"The saint will convulse and collapse as soon as you administer three of Hakim sahib's racking purgatives." He made sinful remarks, causing Nani Biwi to beat her forehead in distress.

"May your tongue burn! That unfortunate girl has lost her senses and all you can think of is this gibberish." She felt very maternal toward her daughter these days. At the slightest provocation a lump would form in her throat and she would start reminiscing about Nana Mian. "If he were alive would the poor girl have had to listen to such nonsense from people?" she complained one day while preparing a fruit drink for Aunt Qudsia.

"Ah, I understand her wiles. Shabir Mian is the reason for . . ."

Aunt Qudsia, in the middle of combing her hair, turned to spar with him. She looked into his eyes and sneered.

"Why, did Mushtri Jan beat you with a shoe and throw

you out of her house?" she quibbled. Everyone was aware that Uncle Machu lived off the earnings of the nautch girls.

"Let's not talk about me, let's talk about you instead . . ."

"Qudsia, my child," Nani Biwi handed her the glass of sharbat and, turning her face away from Uncle Machu, said, "Don't bother with this wretch, he's a worm from the gutter and he thinks everyone else is like him." After the accident Nani Biwi had become extremely pro-Qudsia.

"The young lady is under the spell of a very powerful saint, he should, under no circumstances, be antagonized," Nani Biwi's Maulana from Lucknow stated emphatically. And Hakim sahib ventured that in his humble opinion the purgatives should be postponed for the time being; it was important, he maintained, that emotions not be inflamed, otherwise more heat would travel to the brain. But how could you explain all this to Uncle Machu? Ever since she had become unstable, Aunt Qudsia had been enjoying a life of ease and comfort. It was as if she were living on a soft, cottony cloud. Like a princess she reclined all day on a bed that was draped with clean, sparkling sheets, and enjoyed the poetry of Zauq and Sauda; Uncle Shabir sat nearby and recited verses in sweet, melllifluous tones. Once in a while, just to make him uncomfortable, she asked him to explain a suggestive verse. He came regularly now as he had done in the past, and if he were even a few minutes late Aunt Qudsia became restless.

Uncle Machu frequently stooped to low tricks, but that day he went too far. Aunt Qudsia was holding the glass of sharbat to her mouth, but hadn't taken a sip as yet.

"What a silly one he is, your Shabir Hasan. Now if it had been me . . ." He spoke softly in order to avoid being overheard by Nani Biwi.

"If it had been you . . .?" Aunt Qudsia gnashed her teeth.

"I'd run off with you," Uncle Machu said, stretching his long arms.

"You miserable wretch! Do you think I'm like Mushtri Jan?" Aunt Qudsia was like an unsheathed sword.

"There's a Mushtri Jan hidden in every woman and when the opportunity arises . . ."

Aunt Qudsia flung the glassful of sharbat at his face and then, taking off her slipper, she attacked him.

If one can obtain the kingdom of heaven and earth by losing one's mind, who would be stupid enough to want to regain sanity? In the past if Aunt Qudsia happened to raise her voice she was immediately taken to task. Today she was hitting a six-foot tall man built like a giant, cursing him a hundred times in one breath, and everyone was silently applauding.

"Wait, wait, good woman, I was only joking," Uncle Machu said, trying to ward off her blows with his hands. This was the Uncle Machu who had once, for the sake of Mushtri Jan, lifted Sadeeq, the wrestler, and thrown him over a wall as if he were a bunch of flowers, not a man as big as an elephant. This same Uncle Machu was being beaten by Aunt Qudsia. We too were convinced that day that it wasn't delicate little Aunt Qudsia who was pounding Uncle Machu with the force of a wrestler, but indeed the jinn who was in love with her. And who could take on someone who is the beloved of a jinn?

In the twinkling of an eye the different domains of the house became disconnected like unrelated districts. The time for Urs was approaching. In addition to other festivals and celebrations, this too, was an excuse for visitors to appear. Relatives and far-off acquaintances began showing up months in advance. But it didn't make much difference since no one was given separate bedrooms or bathrooms. Additional cots, beds and wooden divans were set out and that was all. The tablecloth was lengthened and two people were served in one plate. None of this was a nuisance, except that the atmosphere that prevailed was like that of a noisy, crowded bazaar. Which was a lot of fun. Our maternal camp and that from our father's side of the family were split into smaller groups. It was a strange spectacle. The women who congregated in Dadi Amma's camp were mostly elderly ladies who became agitated if you made the slightest movement in their presence. In Amma's camp were women of her own age, giddy and worldly. Those with husbands and nursing infants were cloistered in a far corner on two beds each, while young girls slept on the opposite side of the verandah, two to a bed. When they were not sleeping, these girls traipsed about like a herd, whispering in each other's ears. Children, hens, pigeons and dogs gathered in the centre of the courtyard and noisily jumped up and down on empty rope cots. If an accident occurred in one part of the house, it would be quite a while before everyone got wind of it.

This was why there were very few eye-witnesses to the beating Uncle Machu received at Aunt Qudsia's hands that day. By the time the females donned their shoes and, grabbing the folds of their pajamas, arrived on the scene, there was no trace of the accident that had taken place with the speed of lightning.

When everyone finally gathered, all they could see was Aunt Qudsia snarling, her face covered with her dupatta, and Uncle Machu ducking out of the door, laughing, as if he had just received sugary sweetmeats, not a beating.

"Is anyone listening? What is going on, girls, no one tells me anything." Dadi Amma groaned. All the tired, elderly women in her veranda turned over on their sides once and then continued dozing.

"What is it, what happened?" everyone was asking.

No one knew if smelly Pathani Bua had had an altercation with the cleaning boy upstairs, or if a snake had been spotted somewhere in the house.

"Who was beating whom?" they turned and asked each other again. Mothers were counting their children, while Amma, oblivious of all this confusion, her pajama tucked in, had heard the bell on Abba's carriage and was off to meet her beloved.

"What could have happened? Lot of fuss about nothing, that's all!" Although she was one of the few eye-witnesses,

Nani Biwi disclosed nothing. "Whoever tussles with these people will suffer," she added mysteriously. She was obviously not referring to Aunt Qudsia. That slip of a girl, so frail and delicate, where could she get the strength! All this was the doing of the saint.

It was a very melancholy evening. A thin layer of dust and fog stretched across the sky and swallows scissored the air. The qawwali groups were arriving, all day long workmen repaired large, sprawling marquees, and the shrine, spotlessly white after being whitewashed, looked like an untarnished marquee that had been thrown open and spread out unevenly.

During this time we forgot about home and spent the better part of our day at the shrine. The sermon made us cry, but we found the qawwali extremely enjoyable. We didn't understand a single word of the verses sung, but the mention of Mecca and Medina impressed us greatly. Somewhere along the line one of the spectators worked himself into a state of frenzied ecstasy which resulted in widespread commotion. At this time the qawwali singers got stuck at one verse, repeating it over and over again until the person dancing in ecstasy lost his momentum. Then the singers began with a new verse.

"What's the matter, people? Why don't you tell me anything?" As soon as we walked into the house we found Dadi Amma muttering in a confused tone.

Bua's sweeperess was touching everyone's feet, begging, "Please come with me, Ram only knows what's happened to her."

"Now calm down, woman, who are you talking about?"

"What happened?" people were asking each other. Finally it was revealed that Bua had been running a fever for several days. The previous night she had left the house and in the morning was discovered lying face down in the cemetery. Since then her windpipe had been rattling.

"Tsk, tsk, the poor thing," the women said sorrowfully and returned to their chores.

"When I ask, no one tells me anything, am I a dog, barking away with no one to hear me?" Dadi Amma retrieved her *sajdah gah* from under her pillow and murmured her *niyat*. Nani Biwi was appalled by the manner in which she recited her intent and also objected to the way Dadi Amma bowed during prayers, claiming she looked like a frog ducking into water.

Aunt Qudsia, the only person who seemed to be in distress, ran anxiously from one corner of the house to another. "Will someone send for the doctor?"

The doctor responsible for cases at the shrine treated patients free of charge. No one was surprised at Aunt Qudsia's perturbation, and no one had the temerity to ignore her command. All night long Bua's windpipe continued to rattle. The doctor diagnosed her condition as double-pneumonia. The next morning we also went to see her, not out of concern for her health but out of curiosity. Stretched out on a worn-out rope cot was Bua struggling for life. The air was so putrid you couldn't breathe in there. It was only on the third day that the rattling of the windpipe ceased.

May God forgive us! Her body stiff in the white shroud, Bua looked so terrifying! How woebegone and miserable her face looked—those half-opened eyes, the purple colouring, that pinkish fluid oozing from her nose and mouth. For years to come she appeared in my dreams to frighten me. I'd be scared to go in the dark, fearful that Bua might suddenly appear and devour me; as soon as it was twilight my spirits flagged and I'd be afraid to go out and pick buds. It seemed as if she was behind the mosque, standing under the banyan tree, dusting off sand from her slipper and I almost expected to see her appear suddenly singing, *"Beat the drums/ We'll meet in Meerut . . ."*

She was always cross with Bale Mian, but when he turned away from her the whole world rejected her. Bua suffered in this terrible manner and not once did he bother to turn around and ask how she was doing. Ah, poor, unfortunate Bua! The world polices dreams as well, the very reason for living becomes a sore point with people.

The terror of Bua's death hung over the entire household. Everyone's hands were stained with Bua's innocent blood. In order to rid the house of evil spirits, two maulvis were immediately stationed in the outer courtyard. All day they rocked while reading from the Quran, and then proceeded to stuff themselves with trayfuls of food.

Bua's death completely unsettled Aunt Qudsia. For two days she ate nothing. All night she paced about restlessly, stared at the floor in the veranda in the dark with her head lowered as though in search of a crack that she could disappear into. She gazed about her, wide-eyed like a starving bird, as if afraid that some bloodthirsty animal might spring at her and grab her throat. All around her she saw death. Nani Biwi prepared glasses of sharbat and left them with her and she emptied them into the spittoon when no one was looking. Holding the paan in her hand, she pretended to chew but later threw it into the toilet. She took a morsel or two only from Amma's plate. She no longer trusted anyone.

That evening Uncle Shabir came. For a while he sneaked glances around him like a thief, then, avoiding Aunt Qudsia's gaze, he handed her a copy of *Diwan-e-Ghalib*. After this he greeted Dadi Amma and then left without casting another look at Aunt Qudsia. Tightly clasping the book in both hands, Aunt Qudsia sat still as though a cobra might leap out of it and devour her if she opened it. Nani Biwi was straightening her bedsheets. She lovingly arranged some flowers on her pillow and turned back the quilt.

"Here, daughter, why don't you rest for a while. I'll bring your food here, there's a lot of rubbish over there." She pointed to the crowd eating at the tablecloths laid out on the veranda floor.

"I'm not hungry, Amma bi." Aunt Qudsia placed the book under her pillow.

"Why child? You didn't eat anything at lunch either, and . . ." She had no idea that her daughter was distrustful of her. After all, she was a mother. She had always doted on her favourite daughter, whatever she did was for her own good.

All at once Aunt Qudsia's heart jumped into her mouth. Uncle Machu was picking up the book. She felt as if she were in the grip of a fever. A tiny fragment of paper fluttered and fell at her feet. Before she could retrieve it, Uncle covered it with his shoe, bent down and picked it up, turned it over a few times, then handed it to Nani Biwi. Aunt Qudsia shut her eyes.

"What is it?" Nani Biwi took the fragment from him, glanced at it cursorily and threw it down. "Don't be silly!" Nani Biwi was illiterate, she couldn't read a thing.

"Wait a minute, this is a charm, don't be disrespectful." Uncle Machu took the paper and placed it on Aunt Qudsia's pillow.

"What kind of a charm?" Nani Biwi asked in a serious tone.

"It's for getting rid of evil spirits."

"Hunh! I'm not your playmate that you should tease me." Muttering angrily, Nani Biwi left.

"And those who are playmates don't care either," Uncle Machu mumbled softly as he walked off to pay his respects to Dadi Amma.

"Amma Begum, please give me the Fatehpur land or, I swear by Imam Hussain, I'll become a Sunni."

"Some religion!" Nani Biwi grunted under her breath.

"If you give me the Amethi mango gardens right away I promise I'll become a Sunni," he wrangled with Nani Biwi next.

"Goodness! Those are in Qudsia's name!"

"That's all right, I'll take Qudsia too as a gift, and I'll shut everybody up, don't you worry."

"Dust in your mouth!" Nani Biwi ran after him with her shoe and he went off to one of our other aunts.

"If you give me these bracelets I'll cut the noses and plaits of all your rivals and place them at your feet." But no one gave him anything because everyone knew he had wasted his entire inheritance on dancing girls.

Nani Biwi awoke in the middle of the night for *tahajud* prayers and the hands that were raised for ablution remained suspended in mid-air. Aunt Qudsia's bed was empty. The flowers were still on the pillow, untouched, fragrant, not a petal out of place. The front door was ajar like a gaping hole, its latch still swinging. Nani Biwi's screams roused the whole household. She was running around from one corner of the house to the other, yelling Aunt Qudsia's name. Soon everyone took lanterns and began a search.

"Will you listen, what's going on, I ask?" Dadi Amma's whimpering query compounded the confusion.

Her arms around her as if she were a little girl, Amma tried to comfort Nani Biwi.

"What's happened?" The question came from all sides. Children began to whine, the hens started cackling.

"Oh, I think someone left the chicken coop open." In her state of drowsiness Dadi Amma came to the conclusion that the cat had made off with one of the hens.

The imprints of Aunt Qudsia's small, bare feet were traced to the edge of the large well where they disappeared. On the left the path leading to the railway station was full of marks made by animals and people, but there were no signs of Aunt Qudsia's tiny, white feet. The well was searched thoroughly but Aunt Qudsia's body was not found. Had the earth devoured her, had the sky swallowed her?

"My daughter was meant for heaven," Nani Biwi wailed, weeping uncontrollably on the third day of mourning.

"Why do you cry? May Allah bless her where she is," Uncle Machu said, drying false tears. What a vile man he was, our Uncle Machu!

"Amen." Dadi Amma proceeded to recite verses from the Quran under her breath.

In a few days some rather strange stories began circulating.

When Aunt Qudsia jumped into the well a window suddenly opened in its floor. She saw a vast expanse of open space. Absolute silence reigned around her and there wasn't a soul in sight. All at once a cloud of dust rose in the distance. When the dust settled she saw a golden throne arrayed with richly-embroidered cushions. Four fairies, holding the throne aloft, stood before her respectfully, their heads lowered. Aunt Qudsia was escorted to the throne which then ascended into the sky.

It was Uncle Machu who invented these tales. Some tactless people also suggested that she had run off with Uncle Shabir. Anyway, the mention of Aunt Qudsia's name became taboo in our house from that day on. As long as Nani Biwi was alive no one dared mention her name for fear of a rebuke from her. Then everyone forgot everything because forgetting is profitable; your conscience doesn't torment you.

About two and a half months ago I received a telephone call.

"My name is Rafiah Hasan. I'm calling from the Victoria Terminus. Tomorrow I'm leaving for London by a morning flight. Do you think you could see me . . . I won't take too much of your time."

She was going abroad for her Ph.D. I didn't feel like seeing her. She was probably a literary enthusiast and she would reiterate the usual trite views and upset me : well-established writers don't give newcomers a chance, they keep to themselves, they praise only each other, etc. She would attempt to prove I was biased, that I was an opportunist.

"As a matter of fact . . ." I tried to hedge.

"I promise I won't stay long, just ten minutes will be sufficient." I could see she was clever.

When she arrived she smiled affectionately at me and for some reason I felt a burden lifting.

"I obtained your address with great difficulty. You probably don't know this, but you're my cousin. My mother, Qudsia Shabir Hasan, is your aunt."

"Aunt Qudsia? You're Aunt Qudsia and Uncle Shabir's daughter?" I stuttered like a fool. *'We'll meet in Meerut/ The two of us.'* Bua's melodious voice rattled the doors of memory. So they did meet. Some people die so that others may learn how to live!

"And just then Ammi's courage gave out. She fought with Abba, accused him of trying to lead her astray, but Uncle Mustaqeem . . ."

"Uncle Machu!" He was not destined for heaven, but God works in mysterious ways.

"Ammi lost her nerve when she saw him. She was on her way to jump into the well and kill herself. But Uncle Machu said, 'You left your shoes behind, you'd better put them on or else you'll catch your death of a cold.'"

"Uncle Machu said that?"

"Yes, and took out Ammi's shoes from his pocket and gave them to her. But Ammi insisted she wanted to die."

"But the imprints of her feet?"

"How could anyone find those? Abba lifted her up in his arms." She burst out laughing. "Whenever I think of this story I can't help laughing. Ammi is so fat now. Well, from there they went to the railway sation."

"And from there to Meerut." I was tormented by Bua's memory.

"Meerut? No, to a friend's house in Raduli."

"Raduli? Her in-laws. Well-done!"

"Whose in-laws?" She was confused.

"Never mind, continue."

"Abba's friend, Abrar, was a lawyer. They tried very hard to obtain a divorce, but he said, 'I'll die before I divorce her'."

"And how could fate be so cruel — he didn't die."

"It didn't make any difference. He was never really alive anyway."

"You're right, it didn't make any difference."

When all efforts to secure a divorce failed, Uncle Machu's friend came up with the idea that there was a chance of getting a divorce if Aunt Qudsia became a Christian. A priest in Kanpur was consulted. But when he was given the reason for the intended conversion, he was furious. Also, if Aunt Qudsia reverted to Islam later the divorce would be nullified.

Uncle Machu, when he got news of this muddle, arrived on the scene and threw a fit. He threatened to kill everyone and run off with Aunt Qudsia himself. He also threatened to bring Uncle Shabir to task. That same evening a maulvi was sent for and the nikah took place.

"'This is not a proper marriage,' Shabir Hasan's friend, Abrar, said. He was a lawyer."

"'Why not?' Uncle Machu was ready to twist Uncle Abrar's neck."

If Aunt Qudsia's husband had got wind of this he could have brought charges of fornication against them.

Aunt Qudsia and Uncle Shabir went into hiding like thieves for the rest of their lives. It's true ordinary people generally lead anonymous lives, but there's always fear, this despite the fact that Uncle Machu had warned Aunt Qudsia's husband that if he gave them the slightest bit of trouble he'd kill him.

"And how will I face God?" Aunt Qudsia used to say.

"You just fall down and faint when you're there, and I'll take care of the rest," Uncle Machu comforted her.

"And when the Divorce Bill was passsed he and his English wife were in England. They had settled there after he obtained British nationality. Also, I wasn't a child anymore. My parents didn't think it was necessary to start a commotion all over again." She became pensive for a few moments. "When I think of Ammi and Abba's love I feel like laughing at the importance that is attached to marriage and divorce. Perhaps this is because I'm not like everybody else."

"How do you know you're not like everybody else?"

"Because I think what Ammi and Abba did was what they should have done. I consider myself fortunate to be the fruit of their love."

She had come for ten minutes only. But the thought of wishing her goodbye had still not occurred to me and she hadn't mentioned leaving either. A few hours earlier I had had no knowledge of her existence. She was a stranger to me. After dinner we strolled on Marine Drive late into the night, hand-in-hand, like children. A fragrant flower blossomed between us and kept blooming.

"It seems as though we've known each other for years." We were both experiencing the same feelings.

"Sometimes one tiny moment becomes a heavy burden for all of life."

"For what crime did Ammi suffer so much?"

A silence hung between us for some moments.

"And why was Bua separated from Bale Mian?"

"Why do people snatch someone else's dreams and crush them?"

"Because there are no dreams in their own barren lives."

"And so they murder others? Why?"

"In order to get rid of their feelings of inferiority they scream and say, 'My country is great, my religion is the most supreme, my city, my house . . . my world are the best and of the highest order, my consciousness, my beliefs, my way of thinking are right'."

"But forcibly?"

"Yes, forcibly. These are the people who regard freedom of action and freedom of thought to be the right of every individual, who advocate democracy, who use swords to stuff democracy down your throat, or call it a divine right, or force it on the pretext of some emotion or principle, some cultural or social standard. And if all else fails, they blame spirits and demons."

At the airport the next day we embraced and she clung to me for a long time as if she wanted to imbue my very being with a special message.

"There's only one thing I hope for."

"What?" The line of passengers was diminishing.

"That we should also have someone love us with the kind

of dedication with which Abba loved Ammi . . . and . . ." She lowered her eyes.

"And?" I stopped her at the stairs leading to the boarding gate. If she left without telling me I'd be tormented by the sharp pain of this unfinished sentence for the rest of my life.

"And like Uncle Machu who . . ."

"Uncle Machu!" Uncle Mustaqeem, that crooked, devious Mustaqeem, the lecher, libertine, apostate, drunkard, liar, who was a gruesome sore on the family's lustrous, elevated forehead, whom no girl in the family would allow to touch even her soiled hem. He had loved Aunt Qudsia, loved her in such a way that today her daughter held in her heart a longing for such a man.

"But he knew Ammi didn't care about anyone except Abba. Poor Abba, he was such a wishy-washy person. The entire scheme had been devised by Uncle Machu."

She left. Suddenly I was engulfed by an immense loneliness.

"Uncle Machu! Did you hear? Right now there must be little fireflies glittering in your grave."

When will people learn to recognize each other's true worth?

The plane shuddered like an irate giant, thundered, and flew off into the lofty sky.

Go, Rafiah Hasan, you can go without fear where you want to go. You have your own tape measure, your own weights, your own scales to plot and gauge life's values. No one will be able to cut you down, your dreams will never be crushed.

The Wild One

Puran

Rain fell with unflagging tenacity. The sky seemed to have developed holes, but was it any wonder really that having stretched taut for this long it should now rot and wear out? It had rained several nights in a row and today, beginning early in the morning, it had continued to come down all day. It was as if oceans of water were being hurled with great force at the earth. Defenceless now, the mud walls of many of the houses had started collapsing from the impact of the water; roofs swung like soggy beards from the weight of the poles and bamboo rafters, forcing the inmates of these dwellings to seek shelter under trees. But the water appeared to mock them. The trees were not canopies of stone, so why should it not find its escape through branches and leaves ? The sound of overflowing drains sharpened the mood of anxiety that prevailed, while darkness, fast approaching, threatened to further exacerbate the situation.

Asha was trying to give Amma a last drink of water. Her own mother had died early, while her father, a good-for-nothing fellow, was found dead some years later near the railway station. Since then Asha's maternal grandmother had been both father and mother to her. But her grandmother was also about to depart. She had been good to her, but now she was old and sick. It was true that at one time she had been Raja Sahib's nurse and after he passed away she had continued to straddle his children on her shrunken, bony knees and sing the same old worn-out lullabies that she had once amused him with. But she was a servant after all; she hadn't been left with an endowment of land. As for her jewellery, she sold the pieces off one by one when she fell on hard times. She had always lived in Raja Sahib's palace, and anyway, who needs gold trays in one's old age? Slowly she crumbled away in a corner of the palace until finally, as an act of kindness, Raja Sahib ordered a subsidy for her and sent her back to her village. Whatever else might happen, she was glad that at least she would die in her own place. But it wasn't her village really, it was Raja Sahib's.

"He's not here? He's not here yet?"

Asha thought the old woman was referring to the messenger of death, but in fact she was thinking of Puran. Puran was Raja Sahib's youngest son. He had slept in the old woman's bed until he was seven. Every Sunday he came to village with his older brother and today was Sunday, wasn't it? Why was the old woman waiting for him? If it hadn't been for this, her breath might have abandoned her body a long time ago.

"Where is Ranji's mother?" The old woman came out of her stupor.

"Yes, Amma, shall I get her? It's raining."

"No ... but she ... shouldn't have left ... like this."

Her own breath seemed to be strangling her. "Is it raining hard?" She was worried the rain might hinder the lighting of her funeral pyre.

"Yes." Asha nervously twisted a corner of her dhoti.

"And where is Ranji's mother, the wretch!" Why was she so preoccupied with Ranji's mother?

Ranji's full name was Ranjit; the 'Singh' had been added on to veil the stigma associated with the trader caste. But everyone called him just Ranji. His mother had been known at different times as Kirya's bride, Moti's daughter-in-law and Ram Bharosa's wife, and had changed roles quite often. All the men she had been associated with died one by one. Ranji was the offspring of one of these men and as such his place in society was akin to that of a *thor* tree; he expressed no desire to be useful. As a teenager he joined a band of singing eunuchs for a period of time. This caused his mother to spend the better part of her day cursing and swearing at the people in her neighbourhood; persistent in her refusal to believe he had anything to do with the eunuchs, she kept telling everyone he was with a nautanki troupe. Whatever it was, after a few weeks Ranji returned to the village and soon thereafter, gained notoriety for this singing. Also, he suddenly developed a defiant streak; whereas he had once been associated with eunuchs, he now kept company with the worst kind of ruffians. His mother, despite all this, went around the village with her head held high.

The old woman's anxiety bore fruit; Ranji's mother arrived under cover of a gunny sack.

"Where did you go?" the old woman roared like the angel of death.

"It's all right, I went to see if Ranji had returned. I stopped over at Lachmi's mother's place — I don't know where that wretch has taken off to!"

"Hunh! And what if I had died?" The old woman didn't want to frighten Asha by dying when the girl was alone with her. And she was justified in scolding Ranji's mother. After all, Ranji had professed love for Asha. The old woman's first reaction had been indignation. Then she examined her surroundings closely and realized there weren't any wonderful young men forthcoming. Also, although Ranji behaved like a scoundrel in his own home, he had certainly never had the courage to tease Asha. But then Asha rarely left the house. Like a snake the old woman had sat guard over her all these years. Whatever Ranji's mother did for the old woman was in the nature of a bribe. And whenever Ranji came over, he'd sit in a corner like a donkey with his head lowered. The old woman felt inclined to consider him for Asha, but she hadn't quite made up her mind yet. Anyway, Asha was still too young. It was only two years ago that she started wearing a proper dhoti; until then, dressed in a lehnga, she looked like a little girl. But Ranji's mother maintained that the lehnga or dhoti had nothing to do with anything — at Asha's age she had already had two miscarriages and was pregnant for the third time.

"It depends on how one is built," impressed by Ranji's mother's pluck, the old woman used to say. "My Asha is so delicate." And then she would take a look at Ranji's massive physique and shudder fearfully.

Ranji was not a bad man. But who was conducting a beauty contest? True, he was short and his teeth were slightly inverted; the lower line of teeth protruded while the upper row was pushed in, making his jaw stick out somewhat and when he laughed it seemed as though his throat had been turned upside down. His lips were flat, his nose was broad and bent, and the little hair left on his head was constantly bedraggled from lack of washing. But he had soulful eyes.

"Isn't Puran here yet?" Tired of hearing about Ranji, the old woman asked.

"What? Do you think he's going to come in this downpour? Let me tell you, these high-class people don't really care about anyone."

If the old woman had had any spirit left in her she would have come down hard on Ranji's mother, forcing her to swallow her words. The blind wretch! Did she not see him come every Sunday? As soon as he came he would ask for pure butter and pickles. Pure butter in war time ? Why did the war make butter disappear? They must be using it to fire their canons . . . but why don't they use gasohol instead? People have to subsist on gasohol while the canons . . . yes, these canons, these blazing canons . . . no sooner do you speak than they start spewing flames, these white men! What is this? What do white men have to do with butter?

Anyway, Puran came every Sunday. Today the old nurse waited anxiously for him and the rain wasn't letting up.

"What do you know? Of course he will come . . . look, is that him?"

"No, that's not him." Afraid of having to get up and go to the door, Ranji's mother answered quickly. "Now, have you eaten anything?" she asked, making an attempt to change the subject. "Just look how weak you are." She tried to frighten the old woman by reminding her of death.

A few minutes later they heard Raja Sahib's car. The old woman perked up. She recognized the sound of the car well. When did any other car ever come to the village? In a few minutes Puran was sitting beside the old woman on the soiled, foul-smelling bed.

"Amma, you're not getting the proper treatment here," he said lovingly, "I've come to take you home."

The old woman was willing to go with him, but a hand stronger than Puran's was pulling her with increasing force.

"I'm going to be with Pramatma soon, son . . ."

"What kind of talk is this? You're the one who used to say I'll bring home Puran's bride, I'll sing songs to his son, I'll get leave from Pramatma if I have to . . . Let's go then, let's go today. You'll get treatment like this!" he said, snapping his fingers.

"No doctor can cure me now . . . listen, son . . ."

"No Amma, you . . ."

"Listen, my dear child . . . Asha, my daughter, she's a very good girl, I've taken special care of her . . . take her to Raja Sahib, don't make her unhappy, find a nice boy for her to marry . . . people are all the family she has now."

Puran failed to recognise the signs of death. "No, you have to come along."

"I'll go . . . if only Ranji had been a decent . . ."

"Ranji is making plans to start his own business with the village lender's help," Ranji's mother spoke up. "It will get going in no time." Although Ranji had made several attempts to run his own shop, the business lasted only as long as the goods in the shop did. When he and his friends consumed whatever was in the shop, Ranji would move on to another enterprise. He set up a *dahi-bare* stand and finished everything off himself; the paan and cigarette shop was done in by freeloading friends and acquaintances. The initial investment also went down the drain.

"Yes, if Ranji settles down he's not a bad sort at all."
"We'll see, Amma. First you must concentrate on getting well."

But the old woman was not the slightest big interested in getting well, and even if she was death had no mind to wait any longer. Puran's request became futile when the old woman departed, leaving a sobbing Asha behind.

Ranji's mother let out a fearsome wail which frightened Asha into silence. Who was left to mourn like this? When the tree dried up, the leaves were scattered here and there. Asha got into Puran's car to begin a new life at Raja Sahib's house. All the way there she cowered in a corner, silently wiping her tears. Afraid that her sobbing might increase if he talked to her, Puran left her to herself.

But when Asha arrived at the palace, her wildly thumping heart quietened somewhat. Raja Sahib patted her head lovingly and Mataji made her sit next to her. But Bhabi — Bhabi clasped her to her bosom.

Asha was too young to grieve forever for an old grandmother. In a few days she forgot her pain. The company of the other servants, her own work, and the love she received from Bhabi and the children made her forget everything else as well. Soon she embarked on a simple, peaceful life.

Bhabi

Asha had no brothers or sisters so there was no question of having a bhabi. But whenever she saw the impish, good-natured daughter-in-law of this family, her heart stirred with love. Although petite like a doll with hands that were small and helpless-looking, Bhabi was mischievous indeed! And how her laughter rang, like silver beads striking against each other. It was difficult to imagine she was mother to these children. Judging from her looks you would think she was only a little older than Nirmal. As a matter of fact, when

Nirmal was born, she didn't quite know how to wrap a sari. And Sheela! What a cow she was, the stout daughter of a dainty, slender mother. What she ate in one day her mother would not be able to consume in three. And the youngest, he was remarkable! Yes, it wasn't difficult to imagine him as Bhabi's son because he was the one she doted on the most. Such strange children, and then her husband, the image of Buddha! The more she laughed, the quieter he became. A bania's spirit seemed to have invaded his body; he appeared to spend most of his time managing the affairs of the estate. Yes, sometimes he smiled, but that was all. And Bhabi? She soared like a butterfly all day long. Although she and her husband were as different as the sky and earth, they got along well, just as the sky and earth have been getting along since eternity. He wasn't concerned with the fact that his wife was young and stubborn, or that she was temperamental and easily upset by some little thing her mother-in-law might say. She would shut herself up in her room and cry for hours afterwards, or complain to her brother-in-law, and she was such a favourite among her in-laws that her mother-in-law's alleged mistreatment of her was also reported to her father-in-law. As for Puran, she quarrelled with him constantly. He was the first one to win her affection after she was married and came to this house, and he was the one she fought with the most too. She had never learned to be timid.

This Bhabi, spirited and lively, began her day early in the morning with orders that the children bathe and dress. Then she supervised breakfast until she was out of breath.

"Mummy, my toast!" Nirmal screamed. Skinny little boy!

"Where's my milk?" All the milk she drank made Sheela as round as a *kachori*.

And at this point the baby would emit a scream from some remote corner of his throat. Bhabi wrestled to keep peace between them.

"Look Mummy, she took my papad," Nirmal bleated.

"Here, take your *papad* back, you beggar!" Sheela threw the *papad* at him.

"Mummy, look," Nirmal wailed.

"Dried insect!"

"Fat cow!"

"You dried up insect, the wind's going to blow you away one day."

"You fat cow, one day you're going to burst with a loud bang."

"Dog! Cow!" The two ended up scratching each other's faces. Before long milk spilled on to Sheela's beautiful embroidered frock and a piece of toast got stuck to Nirmal's elbow. This was when Bhabi yelled at them.

"Nirmal, what silliness is this?" Nirmal would receive a couple of smacks on his thigh and Sheela a wallop or two on her back.

And if by any chance Puran happened to wander in, all hell would break loose. He would make Nirmal choke on his food, tickle Sheela in the stomach and squeeze the baby's chubby cheeks until they were red.

"Get away, who do you think you are," Bhabi would protest, pushing Puran away with her small hands. "My poor baby, his cheeks are sore from all this pinching."

But Puran proceeded to crush him and the baby continued to giggle.

"Look, Bhabi, he's laughing," Puran would say.

"He has no shame."

"Yes, he's like his mother." Puran would fling the baby in the air, making Bhabi's heart convulse.

"Puran, O Puran, my baby!" She would hold her breath, but when Puran turned the baby's face around she'd see he was still smiling.

And if Asha were given a chore to do Puran would protest: "Asha is not our servant, Bhabi, why do you make her work?"

"Why, don't we do any work?"

"Oh yes, you really work very hard, smacking the children all day long. What else do you do? But Asha is not a servant..."

"You don't become a servant simply by working. And anyway, Asha has to get married one day, she's from a poor family, do you think she'll have servants in her home?"

"So what if she's from a poor family. Why does she have to be married to someone poor?"

"If she won't marry someone poor, then you had better find her a prince, Puran Singh *ji*," Bhabi spoke in a loud voice so everyone could hear her. Puran lost his nerve.

"That's not what I mean, you're raising your voice for no reason. Why do you have such an enormous throat?" Puran muttered and took his revenge by turning again to Munna's cheeks and Sheela's stomach.

Chote Bhaiya

There is an old saying that if you eat fiery hot peppers while you're pregnant, your baby will have a peppery temperament when he grows up. Perhaps when Bari Bahuji was carrying Puran she had chewed on some hot peppers. He could not be still for a moment. There was no problem when he was away at college, but when he came home during the holidays, he brought a storm in his wake. Having finished college, he was permanently home now, preparing for the civil service exam. Who knows why he had taken this silly notion into his head. The family's land holdings and assets were enough for seven generations of comfortable living. But once boys go to college their attitude towards life in the village changes. Actually, the fault lies with the villages themselves. What can they offer besides land cultivation and management to hold misshapen, dilapidated cottages, muddied paths, putrid streams, revolting rows of cow-dung cakes, sickly-looking livestock, and soiled children. How can one be happy there?

Anyway, Puran didn't have a quiet bone in his body. All day long he locked horns with Bhabi, teased the children, clowned around with the female help, and sneaked in sarcastic comments about Bare Bhaiya.

"Bhabi, I've heard that a black cat crossed our mother's path when Bhaiya was about to arrive in this world."

"Hunh! Do you think he should be a good-for-nothing like you? And stop tickling my daughter, her stomach's not made of stone."

"All you ever think about are the children. Do you give any thought to their father? It's true that the children can't be ignored, but what about your dear husband? He putters around with the accounts ledger all morning. I'm sure he laughs sometimes, perhaps when he's by himself . . ."

"I am going to hit you Puran, you wretch!'" The idea of Bhaiya laughing in private proved to be funny and Bhabi blushed.

Bare Bhaiya was not the only one who bore the brunt of his teasing. Puran went after the servants as well, especially Chamki, who often received a playful smack from him. Sometimes he splattered her face with shaving cream while he shaved, or tied her braid to the bedpost. Alright, she was a young woman so she enjoyed his teasing, but what did he have in common with Bhola's aunt ? Frail of mind, she lay in a corner of the veranda all day long like a pile of abandoned debris. In winter she covered herself with an old coat or sweater, but in the sizzling summer heat even her kurta became too much for her. Since she couldn't tolerate the humidity in her room she chose to doze on the veranda instead, fanning herself with a broken fan. Puran often went and sat beside her.

"Do you hear me, Bhola's aunt? Why throw your youth in the dust?"

The old woman glared at him in the hope that he would take her indifference as a hint and leave her alone.

"Do you hear me, you're still so young."

"Go away, boy."

"Now this is what I don't like. Listen to me . . ."

"What do you want?" Bhola's aunt's voice was like that of an old man's.

"What I'm saying is, why don't you wear a kurta?" Puran said, unable to come up with any other criticism.

The old woman stubbornly ignored his remark. The young servant girls blushed at this, and Bhabi also pretended she hadn't heard anything.

"I'll get you something, if you like I can get you three or four blouses."

"Be off, you and your blouses!" There was no change in the old woman's bad humour.

"How many times have I said, Bhola's aunt, you should apply some mehndi and kajal." The young girls giggled and Bhola's aunt muttered coarse invectives under her breath.

"These witches are jealous of you, Bhola's aunt." And slowly Puran inched closer to the old woman.

"What is this? Get away, son."

"You're calling me 'son'?" Puran pretended to be seriously offended.

"Yes, brother, now be a good boy and sit over there, it's too hot."

"Now you're calling me 'brother'?" Puran feigned further indignation.

"Shouldn't call you son, shouldn't call you brother, so should I call you husband?"

And once again the old woman let loose a tirade of invectives.

"I suggest we get married. Now, how old are you?"

"Wretch! Don't court trouble, bastard!" The old woman roared in a heavy voice.

"Bhola's aunt, when you start swearing, I want to kiss you. Wonderful! Excellent!"

Finding that her swearing was ineffective, Bhola's aunt resorted to physical retaliation. All the young servant girls became involved in the scuffle, the old woman continuing to spew a torrent of such foul language that even Puran finally ran off from there in embarrassment. When she took her complaints to Bari Bahuji, Bhabi teased:

"Well, why don't you, Bhola's aunt? He's not such a bad boy."

And Bhola's aunt retorted with something that made Bhabi bolt from the room.

Chamki

Chamki came from the same village as Asha. Her name was Chamki because every other girl in the village was called Chamki. If you saw a girl who had a squint, was small and dark, you would think her name might be Kallu or Radhu or something similar. But no, she would turn out to be Chamki. Chamki, however, was indeed Chamki; her cheeks shone, her eyes shone, and as for her hair, it shone like strands of polished steel. As a matter of fact, her waist shone too as did her hands, and when she danced, it seemed as though she was surrounded by dancing stars. Her voice was loud and melodious, not meek and cowering like Asha's which could put you to sleep. Her voice roused people from their dreams, and if she went out, all the orderlies, stewards and gate-keepers began humming; not only that, the dhobi's arms pulsated with renewed energy and the sound of his humming grew louder. But she wore an angry look when she was out of the house and ignored everybody, so that if the Munshi, who at least had an F.A., ogled at her, she abruptly turned away from him as well. Of course, when her back ached from Puran's pummelling, she seemed to bloom. And what a disorderly person he was. None of the menservants could keep his room in order. He turned the whole cupboard upside down when he took something out, and while looking for one pair of shoes, he would toss out five or six others, scattering them all over the room; his books would be strewn about like a scattered deck of cards and his dressing table was always dripping wet and splattered all over with shaving lather. If Chamki cleaned his room, he rewarded her by spanking her and tweaking her cheeks.

Like a diligent supervisor, she began making preparations

to clean his room early in the morning, and if there wasn't anything to be done, and while Asha was busy helping out with rolling puris, Chamki would spend her time arranging fresh flowers in Puran's room so that it resembled a garden.

First these young women throw themselves before an oncoming train, then you have moaning and groaning followed by complaints that they have been disgraced, dishonoured and robbed. Thus they hold society responsible for their own weaknesses, and how strange that the world chooses to participate in their mourning and proceeds to join in their condemnation of society. So Chamki, too, threw herself before the train. Luckily this engine changed tracks and went its way. Puran's games didn't go beyond pummelling and occasional pinching. But thunder will bring down rain some day. Anyway, the other female servants in the house didn't approve one bit of Chamki's tomfoolery with Puran. Cutting remarks and comments were exchanged all day long:

"Well, haven't you seen a cat playing with a mouse, and the stupid mouse thinks it's just play?" Lata was very philosophical and why not, she was the mother of six children.

"Wait and see, she's always in there with him, she'll not forget, these princes are no good . . ." Bhola's aunt was not Chamki's rival.

Asha paid little heed to what was being said, but there was no doubt that she was afraid of Puran. She remembered one day he had sauntered in while she was mending Sheela's frock and started a conversation with her.

"Work, work! I say Asha, why don't you ever do something for me too?"

"What do you want me to do?" Asha bent over the machine.

"There are thousands of things to be done. For example, the dhobi brings back my wash with nearly all the buttons missing and I have to go around with my shirt-front open."

"What buttons?" Chamki interjected sharply. "I stitched on every last one."

"I'm not talking to you. You see Asha, you've never done a thing for me. Anyway, why should you be working at all? Are you a servant?"

"Everyone has to work — you don't work, you don't eat." Chamki vied for Puran's attention, but he was only interested in Asha.

"You're so frail and thin and you have to do all the work. I'm going to speak to Mataji, I'll tell her she shouldn't make you work so hard, and ..."

"No, please ... I like working."

"And why don't the others do some work too? This Chamki, for instance, such a cow, why isn't she sewing?"

Chamki was sitting nearby hemming Bhabi's sari. Asha cowered under the weight of Puran's burning gaze.

"That's enough now," Puran said, snatching the frock from her hands.

"No..." Asha wished she could disappear into the machine.

"I forbid you to continue sewing."

"Sheela is going out, she's in a hurry."

"There's no hurry."

Asha remained silent.

"All right, there, go ahead and sew right over this." Puran placed his finger next to the needle on the machine.

"A curse upon these scissors!" Chamki flung her scissors and left the room in a huff.

"What is that witch so worked up about? Here Asha, let me see, did she hurt your hand? I'll see to that miserable creature in a minute . . . ."

"Chote Bhaiya, we'll never be done with housework if you keep meddling like this." Chamki's defeat had amused Lata.

"What a grouse you are, Lata. Am I talking to you or ..."

"I wish you had been outside instead of sitting here wasting your time with these girls." It was Bare Bhaiya, standing in the doorway.

Embarrassed, Puran quickly busied himself with extinguishing his cigarette.

"For two hours Seth Tikka Ram ate my brains out and I couldn't do any work at all. If you had been there I would have gone to the office for a while."

"Bhaiya, I don't have the energy to take Seth Tikka Ram's nonsense," Puran said, making a face.

"Nevertheless, you had better come outside."

"There, that serves him right," smilling, Lata whispered under her breath.

On his way out Puran bumped into Chamki. She looked upset and angry. Puran reached out and pinched her in the ribs. She felt cleansed, she was shining again, but not with anger.

Flowers

"The dining room, the veranda, Bhabi and Bare Bhaiya's bedroom and . . ."

"And what about me?"

Startled, Asha turned and saw Puran chewing on a match. She had been counting vases.

"You're not putting any flowers in my room."

"But Chamki is the one who puts flowers there . . ."

"That Chamki again! So what if she puts flowers there. You are arranging flowers in every other room except mine, I'm going to lodge a complaint."

"I'll take a vase to your room too . . ." Asha quickly began sifting through the remaining flowers.

"No, not these dead white flowers that look like they belong on a corpse. I want those red ones."

So Asha took the red flowers to his room and arranged them in a vase. But all the while her heart thumped violently, as if she were stealing. Unless it was absolutely necessary, she never stepped into Puran's room. And what if Chamki appeared without notice?

During dinner Puran thanked her quietly for the flowers

and she ran from there with the food tray in her hands. Later in the afternoon, when she happened by the veranda on the way to her room, she felt as if someone had kicked her; scattered about near the drain were the red flowers. She hastened to her room.

'This is the punishment for your boldness,' lying on the floor she scolded herself, as if some earthshaking event had taken place. Humiliation, anger at herself, and a host of strange feelings invaded her thoughts and left her troubled and depressed. They had wilted, who knows how long they had been lying near the drain, and how they must have suffered the cold, she thought. All at once the sound of whistling startled her. Usually, because of all the work she had to do, she did not have time to see who was doing what, but from her place on the floor in her room where no one ever came except herself, she could peek at him through the chink in the door. What was that smiling, mischievous face like? She saw it a hundred times during the day, but she couldn't recall a single feature. Why? The reason was that she had never really looked at him closely.

She saw a pair of large, fair-skinned feet encased in sandals and topped by striped pyjamas abruptly come to a halt near the flowers. Asha held her breath. Two hands were lowered and the flowers were swept up. Asha's eyes closed and she clung to the earth on which she lay as though she wanted to be swallowed by it; after all this was the earth that had given birth to those red flowers.

"Who threw these fresh flowers here? This isn't a public garden," a voice said and the sandals disappeared.

For a long time Asha remained prostrate on the floor with her forehead glued to the earth, the very earth which had given birth to those flowers.

In the evening when she was returning from a walk with Chota Munna in his carriage, Puran came up and started kissing the baby.

"Munna, oh Munna! I feel like swallowing up your cheeks, and you're so naughty, pretending to be so quiet, I know you well now. All this talk of work, work, work. I wish Bhagwan would take work out of this world. Why don't you ever talk to anyone?"

Asha, twisting the knob on the handle of the baby's carriage, stood quietly nearby.

Puran continued, "I know what it is, you think I'm not a very nice person, I'm an orge, I'll devour you."

Puran lifted his face and looked at Asha. She was frightened by the intensity of his gaze. "You think I'm a lion, I will tear you into pieces and swallow you?" He continued looking at Asha. "And who knows, if that's what you wanted, I could indeed devour you this very minute." Asha's discomfort made his heart melt and he bent over the baby again.

"And Munna, do you know that I picked up those flowers? Chamki's a wretch, isn't she? Yes, she is. Those beautiful red flowers, red just like Munna's cheeks, I've stashed them safely in my drawer. Well, you must have a lot of work to do, right? You may leave now, yes, please go."

When Asha went past the bush with the red flowers she felt the flowers were smiling quietly, smiling with their eyes shut.

Holi

The weather never ceases to toy with humans. In summer you feel like jumping into a sea of ice and if someone speaks to you, you can do little more than snap back in response. Tenacious heat, a dull ache, and without a fan a feeling that you're simmering slowly. And if the fan is turned on, your head swims. Oh God! And winter? Lethargy, lassitude, cold, cold, everything so cold. Even the heart turns cold. When spring arrives, everything blooms, all that has been lying dormant, stirs. For no reason at all you feel mischievous and playful, tickled by a strange restlessness. And then comes Holi and it's as if a volcano has erupted. If Holi didn't come around every year, this heart would burst out of its cage in frenzied madness. How long can a river be held back by a dam? Only so long as the dam can hold. But why hold back in the first place? On the day of Holi Asha's spirits danced too. Bhabi had been tormented all morning; she was like a little nugget of coloured powder. Already she had changed her sari thrice. It seemed as if the colour from the powder had penetrated her very skin. What does vermilion do? Does it contain some secret ingredient which affects you like alcohol? The more it is rubbed on the more delirious you become.

Today even Bare Bhaiya was not spared. His turn came after Bhabi's. Asha emptied bucket after bucket over him and also splattered him with vermilion powder. As for herself, so far she had managed to slip out of everyone's hands like a slithery snake. Puran, meanwhile, had succeeded in creating havoc. When Bhabi finally fell down in exhaustion, he turned his attention to Bhola's aunt.

"You bully, why do you lock horns with me?" she roared in a masculine voice.

"Dear Bhola's aunt, we are fated to be together. In my past life you must have belonged to me, why else . . ."

Her shrivelled hair glittered and bloomed with vermilion- coloured flowers, while suggestive, full-bodied invectives rang out as further embellishments.

"Hey, Puran, here's Asha," Bare Bhaiya said, trying to get rid of Asha, "let's see if you can cope with her."

Everyone egged Asha on. She became nervous. Puran advanced towards her in all his glory.

She succeeded in emptying a glass of coloured water over him, but hesitated when it came to the vermilion powder. If her face hadn't been covered with dye you could have seen that her skin was glowing with the brilliance of stars.

Puran was not about to drag his feet. He left her helpless. Her vision was blurred from all the coloured water on her face and the ground under her feet was wet and slippery; suddenly she lost her balance and fell from the veranda.

"You'll kill her, Puran, you wretch!" Bhabi pounced on him like an eagle.

"Look at this swelling on the poor girl's foot," Bhabi said as she lovingly warmed Asha's ankle with cotton. At the same time she continued to reprimand Puran. "You're always losing control, aren't you."

"Come Bhabi, that's enough." Puran sat down beside Bhabi and began heating cotton for Asha's ankle.

"You should be ashamed of yourself. Do you realize what a hulk you are and how tiny this poor girl is? If you had been playing Holi with Mahesh instead he'd have shown you a thing or two." Bhabi thought highly of her brother Mahesh.

"But Bhabi, did you ever hear of men playing Holi with men? Why would I be playing with Mahesh?"

"Well, you can only pull your weight with this helpless girl then, right?"

"You know Bhabi, this is what you should do."

Bhabi became attentive.

"Take a knife and run it across my throat, all right?"

"Hai, Ram! But . . ."

One of the children started crying just then and Bhabi dashed off to see who it was. Puran continued to heat the cotton pads.

"You made Bhabi scold me," Puran said, applying the cotton pad to Asha's ankle. Asha tried to wrestle the pad away from his hands.

"Let me do this, you want Bhabi to scold me again?"

But Asha covered her foot with both hands. "I'm all right now."

"Well, well, that was certainly quick."

"Yes," Asha answered hastily.

"Look . . . listen . . ." He felt helpless. "I'm going to tell Bhabi . . ."

"What will you tell her?" Asha said nervously. Her heart grew sick with guilt.

"I'll tell her, I'll tell her that . . ."

Asha stared at his face in apprehension.

"That's better." He placed the cotton pad on her ankle again. "Here's what happened, you know..." He distracted her with small talk. Holding her breath, Asha listened intently as if he were about to reveal some terrible secret of hers.

"Listen, I'll tell Bhabi, I mean I'll say, that is, if you hadn't let me warm your ankle properly I would have told her."

"What?" Asha said in an expectant tone.

"I would have said, 'Asha hates me'."

Bhabi returned. Asha rubbed her ankle fearfully. How that wound hurt! Hate? Asha had never learned to hate anyone. And Puran? Hate Puran?

Hide-and-seek

Puran wasn't the child Bhabi said he pretended to be. Of course he had always been treated as a child and was spoilt, and his mischievous pranks added to the childish demeanour he presented; he did go around the house clowning with the servants and the kids, often encouraging them to climb all over the furniture with no thought to their grimy clothes and soiled feet. Sometimes the racket he created made Bhabi's head swim so that she would run after the children with a stick.

In two days Kamlaji was arriving at her father's house. Bhabi had turned everything upside down in preparation for her sister-in-law's arrival. The house had become a nuisance for Puran. There was cleaning going on everywhere; he felt stifled. His own room had also been taken over by Bhabi. Kamlaji's husband was coming with her as well, a prospect that made Mataji very nervous; he was a well-endowed landowner and then, of course, he was a son-in-law. But in addition to that there was a possibility that their connection with his family might grow; his younger sister, Shanta, was still unwed and Puran had also reached a marriageable age.

At one point Puran came into the drawing-room with the child-ren in tow and a game of hide-and-seek commenced. Poor Asha wandered in to do some dusting and found the place in an uproar.

"Please leave the room, I'm going to do some cleaning here," she said in a matter-of-fact tone.

"So this room is going to be cleaned too!" Puran exclaimed.

"Yes," Asha replied softly and began moving the chairs.

"What is this? All the rooms are being cleaned. No, no cleaning here, we're playing hide-and-seek. Why don't you join us Asha?"

"Yes, yes, . . ." the children clung to her.

"Oh yes, she'll play. She'll be the *dai*."

"No, please, I can't, I don't know how . . ."

But Puran took hold of her and pushed her into a chair. "All right, we'll start now. I'll be the thief." He sat down on the floor at Asha's feet and rested his head against her knees. "Now cover my eyes properly," he said.

"No, please, Bhabi said . . ."

"She didn't say anything. Now make sure my eyes are covered, quickly." He took a corner of her sari and placed it over his eyes.

"Chacha, no cheating." Nirmal was, after all, a businessman's son.

"It's your Ashaji who's cheating. Here, cover my eyes tightly, like this." He took Asha's hands and placed them over his eyes.

Asha became nervous. But the children hid and the game began.

"This is not fair." Asha tried to pull her hands away from Puran's face.

"Why yes, I'm going to eat you up, aren't I? Why are you so afraid of me? I won't rest until I drive out this fear, Asha Devi — understand? Have I ever hurt you that you should be so afraid of me? Hunh? You chat with Bhaiya, have long talks with Bhabi, you even engage in such friendly chatter with Bhola's aunt. I'm the only one — tell me, why?" His eyes, in complete disregard of the rules of the game, were open. Asha was overwrought.

"Chote Bhaiya, please . . . all right, I'll clean the room later, you continue playing."

"I am playing." Puran looked more serious than Bare Bhaiya ever could. "You think I'm always playing games, don't you? All this is a game, my life, everything I say — you think all this is a game, don't you Asha? You think I'm playing a game with you too. How can I convince you I'm not?"

"Come and find us!" one of the children yelled.

"It's not a game, Asha, listen . . ." he chewed his lips helplessly.

"Come and find us!" Nirmal called in an impatient voice. He was tired of crouching behind the sofa.

"Please don't think of any of this as a game, Asha . . . for Pramatama's sake. You think I'm a child? If you hate me, tell me and I'll accept it. All right, now I know, you do hate me."

Asha had been sitting despondently with her head lowered. She glanced furtively at Puran. She was no child. Yes, unfortunately she was not a child. She had understood everything well, and not just what was happening today; for many days now she had felt the truth shake her soul.

"Bhabi will be coming here any minute," she said, trying to move Puran's head away from her knees.

"Chacha, you're not coming to look for us . . . we're not playing anymore." Sheela grumbled from her hiding place.

"Just answer my question. Do you hate me?"

For a while Asha couldn't summon up the courage to lift her head and face Puran; she could't bear to look into his eyes. Finally she mustered some strength, raised her head and gave her answer with one look. Then hastily, she lowered her head again and covered her face with her hands.

"Asha!" Bhabi was calling her.

Dazed, Puran sat as if trying to seize a dream. The

seriousness that had haunted his face earlier was gone; for a split second he paused, then a river of joy and emotion gushed forth, he shouted, "Coming to get you!" and went after the kids. Asha pretended to busy herself with straightening things near the fireplace. She crouched low on the carpet fearfully, her eyes closed, as if feeling around for some lost object. She wished she could sink into the ground, deep into the bowels of the earth under her feet.

"What is this!" Bhabi screamed, her voice barely discernible over the din Puran and the children were making.

"Hide-and-seek, Bhabi," Puran said joyfully, speaking like someone intoxicated. "Come and join us."

"A curse upon hide-and-seek! Asha, you call this cleaning?"

"Bhabi, we've been playing hide-and-seek, and Ashaji was playing with us. Come Bhabi, you'll be the *dai* now." Puran lifted Bhabi in his arms and twirled her around.

"Puran, Hai Ram! Puran! Put me down!" The children forgotten, Bhabi tried to extricate herself from Puran's ticklish grasp.

Sister-in-law

Devar, the word is as lively as sister-in-law, *devrani*, is dull. Until the *devrani* comes along, the *bhabi* is the queen of the household, and the centre of interest for the *devar*. But as soon as the *devrani* arrives on the scene the *devar* disappears. No longer whispering everything in Bhabi's ears, he now quietly listens instead to his queen's complaints about Bhabi and slowly turns into a poisoned thorn. The very same Bhabi without whom a meal tastes bitter, who can be teased and then pacified by putting one's arms around her neck, must contend with just "*Namaste Bhabiji*" after the arrival of the queen.

"There will be two of us then and more trouble than you

can dream of," Puran said when Bhabi brought up the question of his marriage.

"Hunh! You could be two or four, it doesn't really matter. I'll give you both a thrashing when I see fit."

"But Bhabi, you'll hit her? Won't you feel sorry for her?"

"She'll be punished if she's mischievous."

"But what if she is very innocent?" Puran cast a glance at Asha who was sitting some distance away on the grass with Munna.

"I hope Bhagvan will not give you a wife who is innocent. You won't let her live."

"Bhabi, what a thing to say! Do all of you think I'm a dog?"

"Anyway, we're searching for someone very pretty."

"Searching? How long will you search? At this rate you'll find someone when I'm an old man."

"Actually there is someone . . . and she's beautiful . . ."

"Is that true? Well, I have someone in mind too and she's also very beautiful." Asha was attempting to hide behind Munna. If she had had a choice she would have run from there.

"You couldn't have seen her. Liar! Have you seen Kamla's sister-in-law?"

"No, I haven't seen Kamla's sister-in-law, but I've seen a *kamal*." Puran's gaze sought Asha's eyes, but she was looking down at the grass as if in search of a hole she could disappear into.

"Is Shanta coming as well?" Bare Bhaiya, who was sitting in an armchair nearby reading a newspaper, asked.

"No, she's not coming. But you've seen her, haven't you?"

"Yes, but she was very young at the time. I think she was in F.A."

"That's right." Bhabi's attention wandered to Munna who had crawled away from Asha. Just as Asha got up to leave Bhabi called her.

"Asha, will you take Munna?"

Munna stiffened when Asha tried to hold him in her arms and freeing himself climbed over Puran.

"You see Bhabi, the more I tease him the more he laughs," Puran said.

"It's your doing that he's so shameless."

"Bhabi, find a *devrani* who resembles Munna." It seemed Puran found the word vasting amusing.

"Oh no! You mean like this little monkey?"

"Well, someone who looks like you then. Petite, delicate. Tell me Bhabi, why is it that you have several vagabond brothers but not one sister?"

Bhabi remembered her only sister who had died from small-pox as a child. Had she lived she would have made the best sister-in-law. Bhabi began talking about her. How she crawled, how she lisped when she talked and how the two quarrelled.

"Bhabi, for goodness sake, of what use would a little, lisping wife be?"

"Don't be silly Puran, she would not be lisping still. And she would have been twelve or thirteen years old now."

"No, this won't do. Why must Bare Bhaiya have such a nice wife? He's always been ahead of me. He came into the world first, and he also managed to find such a nice wife first. Why couldn't I have been born before him?"

"Enough silliness, Puran," Bhabi was blushing and Bare Bhaiya, hearing his wife's praise, smiled sheepishly. Puran had such a habit of blabbing nonsense.

"No!" Puran yelled. Munna had taken out his pen and was pushing it into the ground. There was ink all over his face.

"Dear me! No wonder he was so quiet all this time."

"You bad boy!" Puran pinched Munna's cheeks and catching hold of his chubby legs, pulled him.

"Leave my child alone, Puran —"

"I'll kill him today Bhabi — that was a twenty-one rupee pen."

"You can take his father's pen — he has two."

"I'm not taking anyone's father's pen. I'll teach him a

lesson today." Puran sat him on his knees. "You little devil!" The little devil smacked Puran across the face with an ink-stained hand.

Bhabi rolled on the grass, helpless with laughter.

"Why are you laughing? You just wait and see what I do to him." Puran lifted the child up and flung him in the air. Then, turning him upside down, he swung him about.

"Oh no! Puran! My baby, oh, his intestines are going to turn over, oh my poor baby." Bhabi was about to cry, but Munna, his face smeared with ink, continued to giggle. And when Bhabi tried to take him from Puran, he clung to Puran's shoulder and wouldn't let go.

"What a stubborn one he is," his father said.

"He is not going to learn like this." Puran grabbed the baby's cheek and twisted it. Munna's face began to crumple, Bhabi screamed, and Asha snatched Munna away.

"You just wait, Puran. I promise I'll treat your children the same way — actually they'll get worse from me."

"No, you won't. My children won't be nobodies."

"And mine are?"

"Maybe not. But you won't be able to beat my children."

"Oh? And you can beat mine all you want?"

"There will be someone to protect them — you won't be able to touch them. If your children can be protected, mine will be protected too."

"Hunh! No one will be able to protect your children from my wrath. You've thrashed my children so much I'll — "

"No, you won't. Munna will protect them, or someone else will. Asha, you'll protect them, won't you?"

Asha busied herself with tying Munna's shoelaces.

The Fair

Asha had been living at Raja Sahib's for a whole year and in all this time there had been no reason for her to return to her village. But the village fair came along and Ranji's mother thought of Asha. Ranji borrowed some money and had a new suit of clothes made for himself and both mother and son arrived at Raja Sahib's. Asha was reluctant to return with them alone so Ranji's mother coaxed Chamki into going along and the four embarked on the trek back to the village. On the way Ranji's mother stopped to chat with somebody and was left behind. Ranji took charge of Asha and Chamki and continued on.

The importance of the fair was evident from the way people thronged the roads. A colourful array of dupattas, turbans and caps adorned the roads; trooping along hurriedly were hundreds of vendors carrying toy paper fans and birds slung on long bamboo poles; also advancing towards the site of the fair were carts laden with *gazak*, *chaat*, and sweets fried in oil, accompanied by the buzz of flies; merchants carrying colourful hair ribbons and beaded necklaces hurried along with the vendors; and adding to the festivities was a tumult of lost donkeys, sick cows and mangy dogs. All in all, it seemed that heaven had arrived on earth with the fair for a couple of days.

In addition to the decorative shops constructed with bamboo and coloured paper, there were expensive goods of all shapes and sizes strewn about in great number on the fair grounds. Among these were Japanese toys, clay idols, rubber balloons and bamboo reeds which the vendors played to attract the public. One could also see a bear, a five-legged cow, a two-headed calf's cadaver, a fox with a man's face, a magician, and jugglers who jumped from bamboo poles with far greater alacrity than monkeys.

And in the midst of all this, Ranji was treating the girls to all these delights in grand style; already they had had potato *chaat*, *dahi-bare*, and *papri*. The purple-edged turban glowed against Ranji's dark skin, the edges of his striped yellow shirt billowed with the wind, revealing his charming pink underwear under his diaphanous dhoti. New plaid socks, help up with red rubber bands on his stocky, hairy calves looked quite winsome, and the large gilt rings on his fingers together with the red Japanese silk handkerchief were enough to wrench one's heart. Kallo, the sweeperess, sneaked coquettish glances at him, Roopa's widowed daughter-in-law blushed when he ran into her, and a few of his friends teased him with profanities, but Ranji was in very high society at the moment; rolling his eyes, pulling in his pot belly, he moved on.

Asha, who had not only never been to the fair before, but who in her grandmother's lifetime, had not even ventured to the shop down the street to buy oil, was bewildered by the crowds and the strange goings-on. She kept colliding into people and every once in a while she was jostled or pushed by someone behind her. And when she glimpsed Puran in a hat, riding his chestnut mare in the midst of all this pushing and shoving, she nearly fell on her face. Suddenly, she wanted to hide. However, suffused with the importance of his position as a landowner, Puran rode past her haughtily without noticing her. Asha breathed a sigh of relief.

But moments later, while she was haggling over the price of bracelets made from melon seeds, Puran rode over to her side. Perhaps he had seen her after all. But why wasn't he smiling if he had? Abandoning the bracelets, she hastily made her way through the crowds, but no crowd could forestall the stride of the chestnut mare. Not when she was watching the puppet show, nor when she was looking at some colourful ribbons later, nor even when she was gulping down a soda drink. And to make matters worse, just as she was demurring at Rajni's offer of a silver-coated paan, the mare seemed to hover over her. And the rider? He was still on the horse, but his eyebrows curved angrily and his face had turned red. The paan fell from Asha's hand and landed on the ground, its mouth split open. Well, there would be other paans; this wasn't real silver anyway, perhaps gilt or some such thing. And the worst of it was that Chamki was nowhere in sight.

A minute ago she had been counting bangles with Lakshmi and the next minute she had flown!

"Let's go home now. Where's Chamki?" Asha said, trying to repress an unknown fear that kept growing.

"So soon? There's plenty of daylight left," Ranji said, although dusk had already settled in the east. Today Ranji, feeling courageous, walked with an air of resolution. He exhibited a new image. Paan after paan had been consumed and he had successfully reduced several packets of biris to ashes. His gait was becoming more and more languid and the smoke from the biris darkened.

"Where is Chamki? Why didn't she tell me she was going off somewhere?"

"She's probably with Lakshmi. Let's go and see the wrestling match."

"No," Asha said, shaking her head vehemently. What a thing to see! Masses of naked flesh rolling about in the dust while the spectators, all good-for-nothing vagabonds, swore and offered revolting suggestions to the wrestlers. Asha shuddered at the very thought and was shocked when she caught a glimpse of the inky-black, naked limbs of the wrestlers from afar.

"All right, let's go and have some sharbat then. We'll find Chamki. What are you scared of?" Ranji drew himself closer to Asha.

At the sharbat-wallah's Asha came face to face with a scene that robbed her of her equilibrium altogether. The men who were drinking sharbat loitered in the area of the shop with frightening expressions on their faces, while others rolled about in the dirt. A gramophone nearby blared away. No sooner had these two arrived than the men began giggling at her with phlegm-coloured eyes. As if this were not enough, they proceeded to exchange obscenities accompanied by vulgar gestures. And then there was the smoke from the biris and the rank odour of the sharbat itself. Asha felt nauseated.

"Let's go," she pleaded tearfully. She had also glimpsed

the chestnut steed and its rider. "Let's go this minute," she said and walked away from Ranji.

"Where are you going? Wait, I'll come with you." Ranji was intimidated by Asha and the obscenities he could hear were making him nervous. Also, a red-turbaned policeman had been eyeing him suspiciously for a long time.

"Wait here. I'll see if I can find Chamki." Ranji simply wanted to get away for a while so he could gather his wits. He knew Chamki wasn't lost and would come looking for them when she was ready.

Asha leaned against a bamboo jalousie and tried to still her wildly beating heart.

"So, this is what you have been up to."

Startled, Asha jumped aside; she could have been trampled by the horse if she hadn't moved so quickly.

"Who is this scoundrel with you?" Decency and jealousy don't go hand in hand, but Puran wasn't one to think before he spoke.

"Ranji," Asha murmured, scratching at a splinter in the bamboo.

"Ranji — the name's certainly beautiful. I didn't know you were interested in the sharbat."

Had she even glanced at the sharbat? And what kind of sharbat was it that smelled like a dog's vomit!

"Who gave you permission to come here by yourself?"

"Chamki — is here with me, too."

"But why did you come? And aren't you ashamed to be seen chewing paan and drinking *tari*?" Puran spoke in a controlled voice. It seemed that if he could have, he would have taken the whip which he was striking at the bamboo rods in the jalousie, and skin her with it. Asha wished he would, instead of speaking to her in this manner. She didn't know how to respond.

"You can do what you want, but remember everyone knows you are a servant in our household. Pitaji will get a bad name."

Asha was amazed that Puran should talk to her like this.

Yes, indeed she was his servant, only a servant. Suddenly she was filled with a desire to scrape her hands against the bamboo rods till they bled or tear her heart out and sob unashamedly. How long she had carried a burden in her heart.

"And how innocent you seemed. One little question and you started quivering and shaking as if you were a little girl! I didn't know you at all!" Puran chewed his words, flinging them at her like stones, and her fear grew. The mare was stomping restlessly and all the while the whip kept striking at the bamboo rods.

Suddenly the mare bucked and Puran dug his heels into her sides with full force. She reared, missing Asha by inches and then galloped off. The chestnut mare was also punishing her.

Asha could not stay there any longer. The ruffians loitered around her, first coughing knowingly, then humming lines from film songs. She was so terrified she wanted to run from there. A few men, standing not far from her, lazily scratched their thighs and eyed her with syrupy looks. They had all fallen madly in love with her it seemed. Walking away, making her way through the throng of men, she found herself next to a pole. Distressed, she stopped there and looked around frantically.

Standing in the midst of friends, not too far from her, was Chamki. She giggled bashfully while saying something to the suave rider of the horse whose eyes were concealed under the rim of the hat, but whose lips, Asha could see, quivered in a naughty smile.

"Don't you want to see the fireworks?" Chamki said, surprised at Asha's insistence on leaving in such a hurry. "The fireworks are the best part of the fair. And Chote Bhaiya is here too, did you see him? He's so wicked!" Holding back a laugh, Chamki puckered her lips. "Right in front of everyone he said, 'Chamki, will you sit on the horse, you must be tired.' Hunh!"

But Chamki didn't see too much of the fireworks. There were fireworks going off in her own heart.

An *anar* thundered; a glittering gold cloud rose and there was light everywhere, then darkness. A fire-cracker went off, illuminating the very depths of being, and finally total, absolute darkness! How dull life appears afterward, like the empty clay shell of a spent *anar* or the tail of a fire-cracker!

Hatred

When, tired and exhausted, Asha returned from the fair to her room, her body ached like a ripe sore. As she poured water over the blisters on the soles of her feet to wash off the mud, her muscles contracted sharply with pain and she broke out in a sweat. But what of the larger sores that mushroomed in her heart and in her mind? She wished everyone would fall asleep so that she could hide her face in her pillow and sob without restraint. Her temples pounded with the weight of emotions she had stifled, her forehead throbbed. The body is weak, but why was her heart so timorous? Her grandmother used to say it was because she had been a premature baby, but how was that her fault? She was in no hurry to come into the world; if her young mother had not slipped and fallen she would not have come at the appointed time.

During mealtimes she noticed that Puran neither teased Bhabi, nor did he pinch the children's cheeks, and she didn't catch him laughing in his usual manner either.

"Oh my! How quiet you are today," Bhabi said. But God knows what held Puran's attention. Bhabi mischievously put in a spoonful of salt in his soup and shook his shoulder.

"Are you asleep? The food won't be left here for you all night."

Puran began gulping down the soup. "All right Bhabi, one day soon it will be my turn." They were all laughing at him; Puran's discomfort became evident. Chamki gave him a fresh plate of soup and he pretended to be engrossed in eating. But things were not right today; Puran neither ate properly, nor would he talk. When Asha served him his favourite *dal*, he said, "I don't want any." Actually he might have had some, but as soon as he saw Asha he looked away irately and busied himself instead with the *papars* Chamki was serving. Scared, Asha moved away quickly.

"Puran, how can you scold my Asha? Is that any way to speak to anyone?" Bhabi spoke angrily.

"Who am I to scold your Asha. I'm just not hungry, that's all. Excuse me." Puran rose from the table.

"But Puran, you haven't eaten anything." Bhabi looked worried.

"I don't feel very well." Puran left the table and went to his room.

Maybe it was just a coincidence or maybe it was the heat, but the next day Puran developed a high fever that left him floating in and out of consciousness for days. The fever persisted, occasionally subsiding just a little at a time, leaving Puran irritable and testy. Asha was afraid to go into his room, yet, as if propelled by some secret force, she would find herself at his door on one pretext or another. He had had a rough night and Bhabi was exhausted. When Asha went past the door she called out to her: "Asha, my doll, come and sit here for a while. I need to get some air, I'll be back in a few minutes."

Asha tiptoed in and sat down quietly on a stool near Puran's bed. It had been a long time since she had had the opportunity of looking at his face closely. How mature he looked, just like Raja Sahib. Two days of fever had left him pale, his lips were chapped and his hair tousled. Asha wanted to straighten every little lock, to rub her fingers gently and lovingly on his forehead. Perhaps the soul is awake even when the body slumbers. Asha's scrutiny awoke Puran. He shut his eyes and opened them again and stared at her. She found his gaze disturbing. The fever had no doubt agitated his brain for he was flushed. All at once his eyes burned with life and his lips parted joyfully.

"Asha," he whispered, trying to lift himself on one elbow.

Asha got up hastily. She was at a loss, didn't know what to do. For a few minutes Puran continued to stare at her. Then his eyes fell on her wrist; he saw the bangles he had seen Ranji buy for her at the fair, and that necklace with the white beads. He fell back on his pillow as if someone had knocked his elbow. Asha rushed to his side but he was like a man possessed by a demon.

"Leave me alone . . . where is everybody?" He looked around the room frantically.

"Should I get Bhabi?" Asha turned toward the door.

"Hai Bhagvan! Where is everyone! Is everyone dead? Where is Chamki?"

"Bhabi was very tired, and Chamki — shall I get her?"

"Bhabi got tired and left you here? Why did she trouble you? Is there no one else in the house?" Puran spoke in a cutting tone. "I'm so thirsty, and this darkness . . ." He began thrashing about feverishly.

Confused, not knowing whether to give him water or call Bhabi, Asha simply stood before him like an idiot. But she was such an idiot!

"Ohh . . . I can't breathe . . . it's so dark . . . pull the curtains away from the windows . . ."

Asha ran to draw the curtains. It wasn't quite evening yet, but the room had darkened just a bit. Her hands trembled when she realized that Puran was still staring at her. When she reached for the curtain next to his bed she found herself close to his pillow; to avoid his searing gaze she bent over inches away from his face. The curtains fully drawn, she decided to get Bhabi, but when she looked at Puran she saw that his eyes were closed. She sat down again. After a short while Puran opened his eyes. She jumped from her seat.

"Shall I get Bhabi now?" she volunteered.

"Hunh! You can go if you don't feel like staying, I want to be alone. Where is Chamki? Why didn't Bhabi leave her here instead of you . . . please go."

"Chamki was also very tired. She's taking a . . . nap."

Asha was holding back her tears with great difficulty.

"Chamki is asleep, Bhabi is tired, you are tired, you can leave, I don't need anyone, go."

The tears began to flow.

"There you go, crying now, what have I said to you? Who can say anything to you, you are free to go anywhere you want."

"Why ... what are you saying ... I ..."

"What have I done now? Why don't you run to Bare Bhaiya and complain that I scolded you when I saw you with Ranji ... I don't care, why should I care ..."

"When did I complain to Bare Bhaiya?"

"So now you're also lying. Didn't you tell Bare Bhaiya that I was angry with you? Why would I be angry with you, why?"

"I didn't complain to Bare Bhaiya! He asked me 'Is Puran angry with you? I ... I said, 'No,' and then he said, 'Why is he, why is he like ...'" Asha didn't know how to continue.

"All right, so you didn't say anything to him. But you're upset that I spoke to you so harshly. I shouldn't have said anything, I hope you will deign to forgive me." Puran's tone was caustic but he didn't sound angry any more.

"But I'm not upset," Asha made an attempt to be bold.

"Maybe not. But I'm sure you didn't like my interference in your affairs. Who am I ... you can see Ranji whenever you want to. It's foolish of me to interfere, you have the right to do as you please." Puran smiled.

"You're ... you're so cruel!" Asha burst into tears.

"I've heard that you are engaged to Ranji. It's my fault Asha, I'm a fool. I scolded you for no reason at all. You like Ranji, don't you?"

Asha glared at Puran, making him break into a laugh. "And what about your ... Chamki?" Asha mumbled between sobs.

"Chamki? What? My Chamki? Who says? Hush!" He tried to get up. "What a silly thing you are."

"I know everything," Asha said in child's voice.

"But who told you that Chamki ..."

"And who told you that Ranji . . ."

"Asha." Puran gazed into her eyes. Her face was puffed from weeping. "Asha, I'm a terrible person, my own dear Asha." He struggled to get out of bed.

"Please lie down," Asha tried to push him back.

"Asha, I'm so hasty, so hateful." He grasped her shoulders with both hands, but overcome with emotion and a wave of weakness, he tottered on his feet.

"What is this!" Bare Bhaiya, who came into the room just then, caught Puran in his arms. "What is this, Asha?"

What could Asha have done?

"Bhaiya, didn't you know better than to entrust someone as stubborn and unmanageable as me to Asha's care? How could she stop me?"

"You should have stopped him," Bhabi said. "Why didn't you call me?"

"Bhabi, my dear, do you think I would have listened to her? She tried her best to stop me . . . Bhabi, some water, please . . ." Puran fainted.

Commotion swept up the entire household. But Asha was vindicated. The doctor explained that Puran's sudden weakness was a good sign, a direct result of the fever subsiding, and after a few days of bed rest he would recover completely.

In the days that followed Puran turned into such a clown of a patient that it was nearly impossible to keep him confined to his bed. He wanted everyone in his room, even Bhola's aunt. And Asha, from whom Puran's eyes had sought forgiveness a hundred times, also sneaked in with the others.

"Bhola's aunt, if you get angry with me once for some reason, will you never make up with me?"

"Be quiet, you crazy boy."

"No, I mean it. If I upset you, do you make up your mind to hold a grudge against me for life?"

"What?" Bhola's aunt had no idea what he was talking about.

"Bhola's aunt, look we all make mistakes, don't we?"

"Who made a mistake?" she asked foolishly.

"You're so dense ... how will we spend our life together?"

"Spend your life with your mother and sister."

"If you are Bhola's aunt, what will my relationship to Bhola be?"

Bhola's aunt proceeded to describe a relationship so disgusting that Puran was forced to hide his face in his blanket. How could such a patient keep still in bed for long?

This was the hatred that had burst like a storm in Puran's heart and in two swift jolts had weakened him to the bone. But now it was the same again. How does one come to develop such violent hatred and then pooff! it evaporates like steam. He had decided this was it, the game was over. And within minutes he was clean, like the smooth surface of a clay water-pot. Good grief! Is this hatred? It is just another fanciful aspect of love.

The old pranks returned, the taunting attacks on Bhabi, Bhola's aunt's profanities, Asha's hide-and-seek, and the teasing of the children. Why do you become so light-headed when you're in love? Why do the body and the eyes dance with merriment as does the heart? And why does everything seem to be made for the purpose of gaiety? Where does sobriety take off to? And you have no thought of tomorrow. But a woman? How cautious she is. Her heart quivers fearfully all the time, if she laughs it is with trepidation, if she smiles she does so hesitatingly. At every step she is afraid her secret will be revealed. What will happen? How will it happen? And what if this comes about, or that? And then the unfortunate creature also considers herself a fool.

Asha had just given Munna a bath and was now combing his hair. He twisted and turned and wouldn't sit still at all, tossing a box here, opening a bottle there, chewing on the comb, turning the *surma-dani* upside down. Asha was getting annoyed.

"You bad boy!" she said, snatching the *surma* pin from him.

"Who? Me?" Puran spoke in a frightened child's voice from the door.

"No, it's Munna, he won't let me comb his hair."

"Munna's very naughty, he's not scared of you, you're such a chicken yourself . . . frightened off by a little baby frog!"

That morning Puran had surprised Bhabi with a tiny frog perhaps the size of a berry. Bhabi ran crazily all over the house.

"This won't do, Puran, tie it to a string and hang it around her neck." Instead of coming to her rescue her husband was offering suggestions on how to destroy her.

"Puran, my dearest brother, I beg you, on my life . . ." Bhabi was screaming now. Turning away from Bhabi, Puran threw the frog on Asha who had been watching this drama in amusement all this time. Asha fled from there as though she were being pursued by a lion. And when Puran slipped a fragment of paper in her lap, she began pulling and tugging nervously at a corner of her dhoti.

"Would it have devoured you, that tiny frog?"

"Frogs make me sick."

"But why did you run from the garden? Do I make you sick as well?" Puran took the brush from her hands.

Asha picked up another brush and continued combing Munna's hair.

"What is this, Asha devi?" Puran snatched the other brush from her.

"I had things to do."

"That's right, you have the whole world to take care of." Using both brushes Puran set to combing his hair.

"Raja Sahib must be home now, he'll be looking for you."

"There you go again, thinking of everyone else except me, and if I tell you to do something you start making one excuse after another. Just think, Asha."

Asha picked up Munna and made as if to leave.

"So, running away again," Puran said, grasping her hands with both of his.

"Let me go, Munna is hungry."

"Who is holding you, I'm kissing Munna . . . why,

shouldn't I kiss Munna? Hunh?" And he began kissing Munna. Asha turned her face this way and that but Puran's hair covered her eyes and her cheeks, then her heart and her head.

"Puran, I wish you had time for more important things." It was Bare Bhaiya. "Come with me."

"Me? I'm coming." And Puran followed him out of the room.

Asha breathed a sigh of relief and rested her face against Munna's cheeks.

"I don't like this at all, I don't approve of your behaviour." Bare Bhaiya said in a serious tone.

"My ... what ... who?"

"Yes, your behaviour, I'm not blind, Puran Singh. This constant joking with the girls ..."

"What jokes, Bare Bhaiya, I don't joke with them. As for Asha, I feel sorry for her, after all she's the grand-daughter of our wet nurse, actually Grandfather's wet nurse."

"But your teasing is in very bad taste."

"Bhaiya ... you don't understand ... you're mistaken, I don't feel sorry for Asha ... I love her and ..."

"And? And? And nothing! Puran, have you ever known me to glance at any of the female servants? We are true princes, our honour does not permit such actions."

"But I want to marry her."

"You?" Bhaya laughed derisively.

"Why do you laugh?"

"Because you won't marry her."

"How can you say that, Bhaiya?"

"I can, that's all. I don't make jokes, I don't have the time to laugh all day long, and this notion you have of marriage—some idea!"

"But why do you object? I'd like to know." Puran nervously twisted the ends of his shirt front.

"She's our servant, Puran. You are probably thinking

these foolish thoughts because of some film you saw. But you should be aware that life is not a film, life is reality, a very real reality, and you are not a child."

"I know I'm not a child and that is why I must know why I can't do as I please."

"Yes, but who gave you the right to dishonour your family and break the hearts of your elders?"

"The family, hunh! The same old story. I know that Pitaji is not that old-fashioned."

"That's where you are wrong, you are mistaken. No matter how enlightened Pitaji is, he will never give you permission for such a horrible undertaking, and just think, what has Mataji, or the children, your innocent nephews and nieces, what have they done to deserve being sacrificed?"

"What are you talking about? What sacrifice?"

"What place will they hold in society after this? Well, Uncle Puran married a servant girl. What decent family is going to ask for Sheela's hand in marriage, and what family will give Nirmal their daughter after his uncle's actions become public knowledge?"

"To hell with such society, with people who will reproach Sheela because her uncle married a girl from a poor family. It will be better for Sheela to remain unmarried rather than be married to someone with such despicable ideas."

"Of course. It's easy for you to say all this, to make plans for your own happiness while the rest of the family is destroyed."

"That's not true. All I'm saying is we won't marry our Sheela into a family which subscribes to such old-fashioned views."

"So you believe that I should look for someone related to Asha, a custodian, or a steward, for Sheela?" Bare Bhaiya was not a very talkative man, but he wasn't stupid. Puran felt helpless in the face of his taunts.

"You're misconstruing everything I'm saying, Bhaiya," Puran said, defeated.

"Think well, you're wiser and more intelligent than I am.

Anyway, let's drop the subject for the moment, your Bhabi is coming this way. I don't want this matter made known until it's absolutely necessary."

Bhabi arrived with her kids in tow.

"Look, did you see how Munna kisses my cheek?" Munna squeezed his mother's face with his short, stubby fingers and placed his flat nose on her cheek.

"He learns from copying," Bare Bhaiya hinted obliquely and Puran tried to conceal his embarrassment by turning to his usual pranks with Munna.

"Bhabi, I'm going to make him stand, he's old enough to learn now." Puran put Munna down.

"Hey, Ram! No Puran, no! He's too young to stand by himself yet."

"I don't care, he can do it, he's so fat, surely he can stand, he's just pretending he can't."

"I don't see how a ten-month-old baby can pretend, he just can't do it, that's all." Bhabi tried to wrest Munna away from Puran.

"I don't care, I'm going to let go of his hands." Puran wanted to frighten her.

"Oh, my baby! Puran!" She snatched Munna out of Puran's grasp.

"What are you worried about? Did you really think I'd let go of his hands? I'm not his enemy." With these words Bare Bhaiya's remarks echoed in Puran's ears.

The Blow

There is only one way life ends, with death. But we forget that every morning ends with night, slumber with waking, and laughter with silence. The beauty of sunrise would have gone unnoticed if it hadn't been for sunset, if the sun straddled the sky forever. And may God keep us from a sleep from which there is no waking. But the blows God has deemed necessary for lovers are a shade too many. One kind of blow, related to the appearance of the rival, leaves you frustrated but no sooner do the clouds dissipate than the moon appears again and all is well; a little bit of unhappiness, like a full stop after a sentence, makes life interesting. Then there is another kind of blow your friends and well-wishers make ready for you. This is the backlash from society. If you're lucky you might leap across the ditch, but if you're not, it's right there in front of you. You can recover from other kinds of blows, but not the one society deals out. How both literature and films have dragged society into the mud, but like a hungry lion it leaps up, ready to attack. Actually, this is all just a front for something else. The collision is not with society but with people, with those you care about. And who would suffer more in a situation like this than someone who was as adventurous and carefree as Puran? Surely it couldn't be sombre, cautious Bare Bhaiya?

Puran's behaviour alerted the family members. Everyone's attention was trained like guns towards Puran and Asha. A change began to appear in the way Asha was treated. Instead of being placed with the other servant girls, she became a favourite of Mataji who coiled her presence around her like a snake. During meals she was made to sit beside Munna while Puran was seated between Mataji and Raja Sahib. Puran understood the reason for this close watch, but he had neither the courage nor the opportunity to get out from under. However, even if a thief can be prevented from stealing, he can't be forced to become honest. While leaning over Mataji's lap to get to Munna's cheeks, Puran did not refrain from sneaking a glance at Asha. And as if that were the reason for living, somewhere, in the gallery, behind the drawing room curtains, you would find honey hidden and the bees stuck to it in a stupor.

It was Munna's birthday. And Diwali was also just around the corner. The house was getting a thorough cleaning.

Anyway, how long can flies buzz around for a kill? Asha was putting the curtains up in Bhabi's room. Puran arrived, pretending to be looking for something.

"I wish someone would tidy up and decorate my room as well," he said, standing close to her, one leg resting on a nearby chair.

"Your room is so sparse, what can one decorate it with?" Asha had learnt to talk back to Puran.

"Hunh! That's because I'm a poor man." His gaze travelled over Bhabi's silver things. "Bhabi's father is a millionaire."

"Don't lose heart, who knows when you get married your wife will bring even more lavish things with her."

"I don't think so. What if my wife is poor?"

"Ram forbid that you have a poor wife."

"Why, is it a failing to be poor?"

"Of course. If it weren't a failing why would the upper class be so privileged?"

"But my wife-to-be is poor, she doesn't have money. She does have good looks though."

"Oh my! But Chote Bhaiya, we'll be truly impressed if she has both money and good looks."

"I don't want money or good looks, I want . . ." Puran stammered. Asha continued to loop the curtains.

"Asha, is money everything? Suppose I lose everything, Pitaji doesn't give me a penny, will you, will you . . ."

Asha's hands trembled and the curtain rings slipped from her hands and fell to the floor.

"Tell me, Asha, if I'm penniless and if Ranji . . ."

If only Ranji were dead, Asha thought. But she occupied herself with picking up the rings from the floor.

"And if Ranji has money, you won't think of me, will you?"

"What do you mean? Why should you become penniless?"

"Let's just say I do."

"Please don't talk like this," Asha pleaded.

"Why don't you take what I'm saying seriously, why don't you give me a proper answer? Hunh?"

"What can I say? You're going to be late for the match, you'll miss the train."

"Listen, I'm not joking and I don't have the time to listen to your excuses either. I've told you many times how I feel and now I'm going to speak to Pitaji."

"No, please, for Pramatma's sake, don't do that."

"Why? Why shouldn't I tell him? What's the reason? He has often brought up the subject of my marriage."

"So why don't you marry?" Asha tried to change the subject.

"That's what I'm talking about. I'll tell him everything."

"No, please don't tell him anything. If you . . ."

"If I what? Go on. I'm going to inform him that I want to get married and that I don't need his money."

"No, you can't say that."

"Why not? Who will stop me"

"I will stop you."

"What do you mean? You will say that . . . that . . ."

"Yes," Asha quickly moved away from him with the curtain.

"Asha, you're toying with my emotions. Why? Why are you doing this?" He caught hold of her arm.

"Because I want to."

"Because you want to? Don't you love me at all and . . ." He let go of her arm.

The curtains done, Asha started changing the slipcovers on the pillows.

"Say something, don't you love me? I'll never bother you again." He clasped her hands in his.

Asha tried to avert his gaze. She could feel her eyes filling rapidly with tears.

"Just say once that you don't love me, that you don't love me as much as I love you . . . speak, say something."

"No!" Asha exclaimed, unable to hold her emotions in check any longer.

Puran let go of her.

"Oh," he said with a laugh, "liar, what a liar you are. If I die, Asha . . ."

"That's enough," Asha interrupted him, "please leave now." She placed her hand on his mouth. "What can you get by teasing and taunting a poor woman like me? You and I are not suited to each other, you must be married to a princess."

"To hell with princesses, you're my princess. And who says we don't belong together? Look at that mirror, what does it say?"

Seeing herself so close to Puran, Asha forgot everything for a moment and rested her head on Puran's chest.

"I'll speak to Pitaji today, I don't care if he kills me," Puran began speaking softly in her ear, "and then, my dearest Asha . . ."

"Chamki!" Asha's eyes fell on the mirror and behind her she saw Chamki's face reddened with anger. Asha sprang away from Puran.

"Chamki? That witch is nothing. Are you still thinking of her, are you still jealous of the wretch?"

"No, she was here a moment ago."

"Oh, so she's spying on us. It doesn't matter, I don't care who else finds out that I love Asha. I'm not afraid of anyone."

"Ah, such daring! Let me look at this valiant hero who's not afraid of anyone." Mataji's mighty presence loomed ominously in the doorway like a black cloud. At that moment Asha wished desperately she could turn into a fly, or turn to stone. As a matter of fact, she had already turned to stone.

"Mataji . . "

"Silence! Aren't you ashamed, calling me Mata with the very lips with which you were licking filth from the gutter a moment ago?"

"But listen to me, please . . ."

"I've told you once to remain silent, Puran. I don't want to have anything to do with you. A person who has no regard for the honour of his family or his father's name can have no regard for his mother. It is this witch I must deal with." She moved toward Asha menacingly.

"But first you have to listen to me, then . . ."

"Tell me, you wretch, did we nurture four generations of your family so that you could poison us at the first chance you got? Speak, you ungrateful girl, answer me." She advanced. Asha's whole body quivered. In all this time Mataji had never cast a disapproving eye at her. Actually she was not known to express disfavour with anyone. Her forceful personality and her air of authority were enough to strike fear into the hearts of those around her, and for the most part she stayed out of everyone's way, cloistered in her room, immersed in reading and worship. However, this was a matter of such immense import that she had been compelled to come down to earth from her heavenly domain.

"Asha, you are under my protection," Puran said, his heart wrenching at Asha's trembling.

"Oh? Let me see what kind of protection it is that you're offering. Puran Singh, you forget your place. Leave us. All I want to do is to ask this girl why she chose to repay our love and affection in this manner."

"Mataji, forgive me, please . . ." Asha fell at Mataji's feet.

"Forgiveness? You destroy my home and then ask for forgiveness? It's true, once you take in a low-class person, he will not be satisfied until he gets more and more from you. How did you even dare to do this?" When Mataji's anger was aroused she turned into Kali Ma. Taking hold of Asha's hair, she twisted her head back so that she was facing her.

"That's enough, Mataji, let her go." Puran pulled his mother away from Asha. "You're not listening at all."

"Puran, how can you do this?" Mataji's voice cracked.

"What's all this wrangling about?" The wrangling had brought Raja Sahib out of his hole as well.

"Pitaji . . ."

"Do you see, do you see your beloved son's antics? Did you see how he twisted my wrist? Ahhh, Bhagvan!" Mataji caught her head in her hands and moaned threateningly.

"Puran, come outside." Faced with his mother's wrath, Bare Bhaiya also shook with fear. "But first ask for Mataji's forgiveness."

"Mataji . . . I . . . forgive me, but remember . . ."

Bare Bhaiya didn't allow him to continue. "That's enough nonsense, Puran." And he dragged him out of the room as if he were a child.

This, in reality, was the blow Puran received. And what happened in the course of this collision is what happens when a hammer comes down on glass. But once smashed, broken glass scatters and wounds the soles of all those who walk over it.

The Verdict

There is really no need to say this, but the verdict was issued. The whole family assembled. Mataji was in the judge's seat and Raja Sahib, assuming the role of a puppet, was also brought in. Who would be interested in such a dull affair; the heroine weeps alone in a dark chamber, the hero paces about in his room wearing the floor thin. And how else could such a hero and heroine fare? To top it all, the court was ready. When summoned, Puran came in with his face lowered, his hair awry. From behind the curtain Bhabi watched him in this condition and sighed. But could the sighs do anything to diminish anger?

"Come in, Puran. What is this dispute, son?" Pitaji had not fathomed the nature of the dispute as yet.

"There you go again, encouraging him. If you hadn't been so soft, these children might have been worth more today." Mataji knew, however, that her husband was a gem.

"All right, all right . . . yes, well, Puran, what's all this nonsense about? You had better return to college, enough preparation for the exam, I'd say."

"Pitaji, I'm not committing a sin."

"No," Mataji interjected, "this is no sin, it's an act of goodness, isn't it, smearing dirt on your family's name."

"Does one blacken one's name simply by getting married?"

"Marriage? You are not going to try and marry that low-caste wretch while I'm alive."

"Puran," Raja Sahib said in a conciliatory tone, "don't be so stubborn. Life is so short, why do you want to get into this? Let us suppose for a moment that you do marry that girl. Well, it will be a great mistake. Just think, do you imagine that your mother will let either you, me or that girl live in peace? Will she ever accept her?"

Mataji groaned. "I pray to Bhagvan I never have any kind of a relationship with her. Look here, ji, why are you beating about the bush, why don't you frankly say what you must say?"

"Because you won't let me get a word in. Now listen here Puran, think carefully. How will she live here and then she, uh, she . . ." Raja Sahib liked to be thought of as a liberal. He hesitated.

"But Pitaji, you're a friend of harijans, how can you . . ."

"Harijans! It's these very harijans who have sunk our boat. You're not thinking, not reasoning. You had better return to your herbs and medicines, ji."

Poor Raja Sahib. Some years ago he had experimented with drugs that are known to increase virility and strength. He found it embarrassing to be reminded of that episode in the presence of his grown sons.

"You're angry with Puran, and you're taking that anger out on me. I'll say whatever you want me to, but nothing seems to make you happy."

"Look here, Puran," Bhaiya spoke up, "you understand the matter very clearly. I've told you this before. Try and think of how all this will affect our lives. What will Kamla's in-laws say, and what will my wife's family think, where will we hide our faces?"

"You're very selfish, Bhaiya. And what about your father-in-law? All his life he's lived on interest and now . . ."

Behind the curtain Bhabi trembled, then stepped back.

"Nevertheless, you will not be allowed to take this step."

"No one can make me do anything or stop me. I don't want anyone's help or interference. So Pitaji will deprive me of an income and I'll be penniless. Fine, I don't care about that at all."

Mataji retorted: "Yes, you don't care, but she who you think of as a goddess, she will no doubt rush to marry you. Why, she won't even spit on you! Do you hear?"

"You don't understand her nor did you ever try to."

"I understand such base women well."

"That is enough, Mataji . . . Pitaji, Bhaiya, here's my answer. I will marry Asha and make the impossible possible. I'll leave this house today so that no one can blame you for anything."

"Wherever you go you'll be held responsible for disgracing your family's name. And people will say 'What a greedy old man, and all because the girl was poor.'"

"People are crazy, you know."

"So? Is there no way out for me?"

"No, you were born here and—"

"I wish I had been born in a poor man's house, then no one would have taunted me. But let me tell you once again that I will leave today and I'm sorry there's no way of saving you from dishonour." Puran left the room.

"There is . . . you're still a child, Puran Singh," Bare Bhaiya muttered under his breath.

"Pitaji," he said to his father, "there is only one way. We must send Asha away without Puran's knowledge. If he leaves there's no doubt he'll be miserable, but worse, the family will suffer dishonour."

"Where can we send her?"

"I say we send her to Kamla's. We'll explain everything to Kamla so that she can take care of things."

"No, not at all! I don't want to cause trouble for my daughter. Send her off to her village." Mataji knew that her son-in-law, Karan Singh, had a ready appetite.

"Then let's poison the witch!" Pitaji said in exasperation.

"Try and control your temper, please."

"Arup is right. Kamla will take good care of her and Puran will never know where she is."

And so the Asha who had been brought here with such love and caring was swept up and transported hundreds of miles away to Kamla's house. She was ashamed of what Kamla might think, but Kamla was not accustomed to thinking too much.

When little Sheela informed Puran that Asha didi had left, he got up with the alacrity of a snake. First he went to the village, and then he came to fight with Bare Bhaiya.

"I understand everything . . . I knew from the beginning that you don't like your own sweet wife and have an eye for Asha . . . that's why you were so worried about her." Anger drives one to madness.

"Puran! What are you saying, have you lost your sense? Whatever I'm doing I'm doing for your well-being, otherwise if it were in my power, my dear brother . . ."

"Your power? What power you have used, Bhaiya! You severed my hands and feet, you've always been my enemy, Bhaiya . . . you must celebrate my death, you will inherit everything."

"Stop, Puran! Don't say things you will regret later. You're not just my brother, you're like my own son. If I wanted the estate I'd have arranged for your marriage without permission from Mataji and Pitaji so that they could disinherit you. Puran, don't think of me as someone so low, please, for Pramatama's sake, don't break my heart." Arup's sombre eyes filled with tears.

"But where did you send her, tell me where she is, I beg you."

"I didn't send her anywhere, she went away of her own accord. She said she didn't want to ruin your life—Puran, she's a goddess, she also said she would die rather than have any contact with you."

"Bhaiya, why did she say that? Doesn't she love me any more?"

"No, Puran, that's not it, she's a goddess, didn't you hear me? She left you because she loves you. Listen . . ."

"But what will I do now, Bhaiya?" Puran mumbled like a child.

"You're a man, you shouldn't weep for a woman. She's gone, but she didn't take your reason and common sense with her, did she? Immerse yourself in the affairs of the estate, finish preparations for your exam . . ."

"But I'll seek her out . . ."

"You'll only cause her more pain, Puran . . ."

"Pain? Ahhh . . ." Puran broke down and started sobbing.

You Forgot

The world forgets. A knife wound heals and the thought of pain slips from one's mind. While giving birth, a mother vows she won't have any more children and wishes she were infertile. The moment her pain passes she croons over the new baby and before long she is yearning for another child. But Puran's forgetting was a proper forgetting. Asha's dead. They say the plague took her. The whole village was swallowed by the plague. Even a wrestler like Ranji was not spared; his old mother's back is broken. Asha died, and Puran's desires died with her. He forgot a great deal. He forgot to laugh. Munna was older and had become so naughty, and a second baby now clung to Bhabi's breast, but Puran had forgotten how to show his affection for them, to tickle them. If Asha were there he would have remembered everything. He would have shown people that he wasn't a coward, that he had more to his name than Pitaji's money; he would have shown them that there are many ways to live in this world. But why did Asha die? He even forgot Bhola's aunt. She tried to tease him herself, he smiled wanly in response and remained silent. The old woman's heart ached, she slumped.

"Puran, it's Sheela's birthday," Bhabi said in a playful tone, "what will you give her?"

"What shall I give her?" Puran asked, lowering his head.

"Let me see—here Sheela, what would you like?" She whispered something in Sheela's ear.

"Auntie, right Mummy, auntie?" Sheela chirped.

"Yes, tell your uncle . . ."

Puran got up quietly and left the room.

"Why don't you marry, look how unhappy Mataji is." It was Bhaiya's turn.

"Yes Bhaiya, everyone is unhappy on my account."

"That's not it, Puran, the doctor says marriage will improve your health."

"What? Bhaiya, marriage is not some medicine that can bring the sick back to health, and who said I was sick?"

"Puran, my dearest," Mataji said, placing his head in her lap, "will I take this longing with me to the grave? I have two sons, and one won't be married while I'm alive?"

For a while Puran said nothing. Who knows what emotions crowded his heart. He wanted to put his arms around his mother and weep. When he was a child and she took something away from him, this is what he did, and she returned whatever she had taken. But it was death that had taken Asha away.

"My precious, your father is also getting old. Don't you think he longs for your wedding?"

The word 'wedding' stirred old memories; he remembered so much. But what a strange thing a mother is. She might cut you up into little pieces but you are, after all, a part of her body, and there was too, so much love in those eyes.

"Mataji, if you had any wish to see me married . . ."

"Puran, let bygones be bygones. A mother's mistakes are part of motherhood; it's maternal affection that makes a mother nurture her child with her blood, it's that same maternal affection that makes her destroy that child. But is she a demon? Son . . ." Tears flowed heavily from her eyes. "Do you think I am happy?"

"Mataji, please, don't . . ."

"Say yes to marriage. When I see that you are happy I'll live a little longer, or else . . ."

"Do what you want, Mataji." Puran got up and went to his room. For some time he lay on his bed. Then, assailed by discomfort, he opened his drawer and took out the flowers. They were the same flowers, red, red like Munna's cheeks, red flowers that the earth had yielded, the very earth that had swallowed Asha. The flowers were black now, like congealed, dried blood.

When Puran's proposal arrived for Kamla's sister-in-law, everyone was jubilant.

"Do you hear, Puran is like our very own son," Kamla's mother-in-law, who had always looked down her nose at Kamla's family, said lovingly.

"Yes, Mataji," Kamla said, "Puran is such a pleasant person, just like our Shanta."

"Yes, do what has to be done." The old woman was trying to hold back her excitement.

"Forgot, you forgot so soon, Puran Singh *ji*," Asha said, falling to the floor of her little room.

If only she were in her village so that like Ranji the wrestler, she too could have been consumed by the plague!

Flames

There is one kind of fire that burns day and night in a hearth, and then there's another kind which is ignited when someone foolishly sets dry thatch aflame and you can see everything flare up in a flash like paper. Now we hear there are fires caused and spread by bombs, fires that, within moments, demolish large dwellings.

But the little spark which, deeply embedded in hot ashes, smoulders slowly, that too is fire. It does not burn down any large mansion or house, but the hot ash around it gradually becomes lifeless from its slow heat. And if such a spark finds its way into the heart and hides there, the body eats, drinks and performs other functions, but that slow warmth and that sweet pain make you restive.

Asha was helping with Shanta Bai's dowry, but her heart, like her hands, was shrouded by the light and shade of memory. God knows, it wasn't that she had ever wanted Puran to lose his sanity, nor had she wished that he would remain single in her memory. She did not deliberately fall in love, and when she did she didn't expect to be patted on the back or congratulated for it. But still — what did she want? Even when she was alone she could not admit to herself what she wanted.

Puran could have done something, he would have said something; she wasn't so far away, she was at his sister's house. She did not know that sometimes what we are longing for is right beside us and still we can't have it.

"Asha, look you've got the shag hanging here." Showing her a piece of fabric, Shanta jolted her out of her reverie.

"What? Oh, yes, Shanta Bai. That's the way the fabric is — I did my best."

"Your best? Nonsense! Stitch it by hand now. Your heart's not in any of this." Shanta flung the fabric at Asha and left.

"Oh, Asha Devi is sewing." Sham Lal's manner when he spoke to her was always ingratiating. She didn't know what it was that made Karan Singh keep him on. True he was intimidated by Karan Singh and perhaps that's what Karan Singh found appealing. He was a distant relative no doubt, or at least pretended to be, but now his position in the household was that of a poor relative. When Asha arrived, he treated her with deference, but whenever he found her alone he regarded her with sweet, timid eyes and conversed with her in a honeyed tone.

"So you're angry with us, Asha Rani."

"Munshiji, why should I be angry with you?" Asha replied with a scorn that was worse than anger.

"But you turn away when I talk to you. Asha Devi, do you know what's going on in my heart?"

"Munshiji, will you go or shall I call Kamlaji?"

"Hai Ram, such cruelty! Is it a sin to talk?"

"Why don't you talk with Shanta Bai if you're so fond of talking?"

"Oh my—well, but Asha Devi, I'm a poor man and it's not my habit to reach beyond my means . . ."

Sham Lal had heard the story about Asha.

"Have pity Munshiji, or is there anything else you want to say?" His sarcasm drove Asha to tears.

"Well, all I'm saying is that people should tread their own paths. Why climb over high terraces and end up falling on your face?"

"Yes, you're right, Munshiji."

"So, Asha, what if I talk to you . . ."

"Munshi ji, there's something else . . . I . . . why don't you go from here?" Asha felt lacerated by his sugary voice.

"Yes, but now Shanta Bai is getting married and I've heard her groom-to-be is very good-looking, isn't he?"

Sham Lal was very clever, but he presented a dumb exterior so that he often managed to say something extremely meaningful, making it slide down your throat like a lump of sugar and you would never know what hit you.

"There'll be two or three people accompanying Shanta Bai when she leaves for her in-laws' house. Why don't you go too?"

If she could, Asha would have stuck the dog's tongue with needles. Instead she just sat there with her head lowered, but after he left, she could not hold back her tears.

The wedding day arrived. Kamla's carelessness was not something new; there were many things that didn't come in on time, several sets of clothing that still hadn't been finished with gold and silver lace. As if she were a machine, Asha was entrusted with putting the finishing touches on the clothes.

The wedding procession was fit for a king; for hours the columns of people on foot kept approaching, then the elephants and horses appeared. Crowded together in the window with some of the other girls, Asha too was watching the show unfold.

"Get out of the way, you witches," Shanta Bai pushed some of the girls aside and stuck her head out.

"You get away, girl, we won't let you see the *barat*. Have you ever heard of a bride clamouring to see her own *barat*?"

One of them said: "Well, Shanta is a child. When I insisted on seeing my *barat*, my uncle picked me up in his lap and took me to the window."

Another said: "And then the groom appeared on an elephant looking like a doll; you couldn't even see his face because of the way he was bundled up in fancy clothes!"

A picture of curiosity and interest, Shanta looked anxiously for his face. And Asha? That face had never been far from her vision. The wedding procession turned a corner and all the women ran to the other window. Lost in thought, Asha remained where she was. Where was she to go, anyway? Slowly her head fell on the window sill and she began to breathe heavily.

Away from the hustle and bustle of the wedding ceremonies, in a broken-down part of the house, Asha lay quietly on a small cot. For a long time she had vacillated between sleep and wakefulness; her heart sank, then seemed to receive a blow from somewhere, and she would awaken. The circling of the bride and groom around the sacred fire had already taken place. Fire-crackers and bombs were going off. Suddenly Asha felt at peace. Everything was done. As long as the ceremonies had not been completed she had nursed a tiny hope. But now that too was shattered. Her steps took her towards the door. What harm was there now? Had her eyes committed a crime that she should not see anything? And who would notice her in all the commotion, who would recognize her?

Quickly, keeping out of the way of the ropes extending from the tents, stumbling, she ran. The hall glittered with lights. The bride and the groom were seated next to each other. Tearing her way through the throngs, she found a place from where she could at least see Puran clearly. Forgetting everything, she had come to look at the bride and groom with the curiosity of a child. But the golden diadem looked so beautiful on his pale forehead, he was like a fairy prince! Asha had never seen him dressed in anything but his usual black and gray clothes, she had never seen him in such fancy, glimmering attire. He was a strange Puran today, so changed. Man takes on so many roles in the course of a lifetime. Sitting next to him was Bhabi, in bloom like a flower, holding a bowl of water. Some kind of strange ceremony was in progress; the bride and groom were competing to see who was cleverer, who could find and retrieve the ring from the water. Puran had won several times; actually, it was Bhabi who was guiding his hand as if he were a child.

Right in front of the door, in a small clearing, a dance was in progress. Today, after a long time, Chamki was dancing. As soon as the ceremonies ended, people turned their attention to the dance. The crowds thickened.

Outside, fire-crackers were going off. A sparkler came and fell near one of the curtains which, along with a part of the door and the decorative paper cut-outs hanging from it, began smouldering. Chamki appeared drunk; her eyes flashed, and under the lights her cheeks glowed like flames.

Perched on a stool, Asha was trying to look over people's shoulders. The fire was surreptitiously advancing, low on the ground, and soon the carpet too was ablaze. The dance continued with the frenzied pace of death, like a pigeon fluttering its wings before dashing to the ground. One of the girls tried to climb the stool on which Asha was standing. Asha lost her balance and screamed. The stool was quickly stabilised, but the game was ruined. Puran's gaze plunged into Asha's eyes and she became numb.

"Asha!" Puran sucked in his breath like a madman, like someone who sees a ghost approach from the cremation grounds and loses his senses. But within seconds Asha's stool tipped and she fell, just as if she had dropped into the very grave she had emerged from. A combination of shock and surprise made Puran's face turn a deathly shade of yellow. He stared wildly at that portion of the wall from where, moments ago, Asha's sorrowful face had slipped a message into his eyes and disappeared.

"Puran, what's the matter?" Bhabi shook his hand.

"Asha . . . . . . just now . . ."

"What are you saying, Puran? What kind of silly talk is this?"

"Bhabi . . . she was here just now . . . she was here."

"Puran, don't act like a child. How can she be here?"

"But Bhabi, this was no dream, she was right here," Puran said in a strangled voice. "She's not dead, Bhabi."

"Puran, my dear brother, don't be a child. She may be alive or dead, but think, speak softly," Kamla cautioned.

"But Bhabi . . ."

"No buts, Puran. What does it matter to you now if she's dead or alive? You're married and . . ."

"Married? But is she alive?"

"Puran, come outside with me, you don't look well." Bhabi tried to cover up the situation.

But the fire was blazing, flames leapt from the carpet, the curtains and the door, and Chamki . . . Chamki continued to dance. Flames flickered in her gossamer dupatta, but she was in a trance.

"Fire!" People started screaming. With one loud blast Chamki reeled, like a moth that flutters before crashing to its death on the flame, and then she fell on her face. "Fire!"

Everyone saw her. Within seconds an electric wire caught fire. All hell broke loose. Puran glanced at Shanta's frightened face illuminated by the light of the flames. Overcome by the heat and smoke, she teetered. No one else was around and soon the flames were reaching up to the sky. Puran lifted Shanta in his arms and advanced in the direction of the room behind them. He saw the flames rising above the electric wire. He turned toward the veranda. Once again, in the half-lit darkness, his soul retreated from the world and found itself in the cremation grounds. Withdrawn from the tumult around her, resting her head against a wall, was Asha.

"Asha!" Puran whispered hoarsely.

Asha was stunned. But not for long. Seeing Shanta in Puran's arms she began once more to sink into the river of despair; every fibre in her body became taut, the hot fumes choked her breath.

Puran put Shanta down and she watched these two with surprise; she too had heard some of the gossip.

Puran moved slowly. He was certain this was Asha's ghost which had risen from the earth for the purpose of turning the wedding parade into a funeral pyre. Afraid that she might disappear into thin air, he advanced cautiously.

"No!" Asha cried, clasping the wall. And Puran's being was touched to the core by this cry of anguish. Gently he touched her shoulder, sure that she was a figment of his imagination. But when his hand felt Asha's cold body he awoke.

"Puran." Sham Lal's voice fell into his ears, telling him he was alive, but Sham Lal hadn't seen the ghost as yet.

Puran made up his mind in an instant. Picking up Asha in his arms, he came out onto the veranda.

"Asha, you can't leave me now," he said, clutching her to his breast. "Tell me, was this a conspiracy? Now I understand, now I know! But the game is over. Asha, let's run away from this vile world, let us go." He made his way hurriedly along the line of trees.

Asha was lifeless like a puppet; Puran held her gingerly

as if she were a child, a precious toy he had lost and found with great difficulty. She had slipped from his hands and was lost. Now he had dragged her from the cremation grounds.

"But wait, Asha, wait a moment. Bhabi and her children, I wonder if they are all right, wait here for me, I'll be back soon." He propped her up like a doll against a tree and left.

Puran battled with fire while Asha struggled with water, that water which is more forceful than fire and which will dislodge a solid rock from its place.

Sham Lal had been following them. As soon as Puran was out of sight, he approached Asha.

"I see, this is indeed a fine plan. Well Asha Devi, you must be congratulating yourself for snatching the morsel right from the mouth." Who knows what Sham Lal was made of; no matter what the situation, his behaviour remained the same.

"Rani dear, this is all very well, but the sacrifice is not right."

Asha lifted her head at the word 'sacrifice'.

"This sacrifice of Puran Singhji's life—this is a rather high price to pay."

Asha said nothing.

"Have you thought about the fact that he is married?"

Asha felt as if someone had axed her, but she did not move.

"He's married, and his life is now tied to Shanta Bai's . . . Shanta Bai . . . what has she ever done you? How strange that a woman oppresses another woman and then charges a man with the crime. Just think Asha Devi, what will happen now? You'll go with Puran Singh, but where? Far away from the love of his mother and father, deprived of his inheritance? And you think you're so valuable he will forsake the whole world for you? And even if he does, you're also a woman . . ."

Once again a storm was brewing in Asha's breast, the same storm in which a great many weak people are swept away.

"And what will you get? You will only be known as a whore."

That was something Asha had not thought of.

"You'll be like a whore who forced Puran to lose everything." Finding that his argument was taking effect, Sham Lal became more forceful.

"Asha Devi, I know you're a goddess, a devi. Listen, although I'm a fool, I'm better informed on the ways of this world."

"What should I . . . what should I do?"

"Leave this place right now. If you go away Puran will never be able to find you. He was told you are dead. He will create a commotion, but if he doesn't find you he'll settle down eventually. He's a simple person, such a person can't be trusted. It would not be at all strange if he were to tire of you, too. If you go away he'll not remember you forever. Hadn't he forgotten you already? He was getting married, wasn't he? Listen to me, in a few days he will have forgotten you again. If you don't believe me, test him."

Asha got up. "I'll go."

"Yes, you'd better hurry, there's the road, it will take you to a village, it's not far, you can take a train from there to your village. Do you need money?" Sham Lal handed her something from his wallet.

"Remember what I have said. If Puran doesn't forget you, you can hit me a hundred times with a shoe, all right? I'm doing this for your own good, hurry up now, before someone comes along."

Struggling through thorny bushes, avoiding ditches, Asha ran. In the distance she heard Puran's voice. "Asha, Asha!" He was calling her. She stuffed her fingers in her ears and clenched her teeth. The fire had turned cold, but the embers continued to smoulder.

Peace

If you grind something and dust it off, does it disappear? You whitewash the walls, but in no time the paint is peeling again. You put a silver coating on brass, but before long the silver wears off and the brass is only brass again. And here's a wound, you swathe it in bandages, but does it cease to be a wound? Yes, it ceases to be a wound, it festers and turns into a sore instead.

Unable to find Asha, Puran stumbled and fell. And he fell at the right moment, or else he would have found himself taking the road on which Asha was dragging herself. The commotion resulting from the fire, the upheaval of emotions and the force of the fall he took on the cold earth on such a chilly night—all of this reduced Puran to a state of inertia which lasted several days. His fever, his headaches and the weight of his family's anxiety seemed to clog his brain like smoke rising slowly from a charcoal fire. Ahh, how foolish he was! He had become such a nuisance. He reviewed his behaviour again. Was there any difference between him and a madman? And so he decided that he would fall into the terrible chasm called the world and cease to offer resistance. He no longer trusted his own judgment, and he was tired also of the ever-recurring lectures. Letting go was a source of such peace, he could feel himself becoming completely submerged in it. Whatever medication was given to him, he accepted willingly, when someone made him laugh, he laughed, and when he was asked to sit, he obeyed. And thus, led by others, he began to live. It was as if he were floating along in a calm, quiet river.

"Puran, why don't you read something," Bare Bhaiya suggested one day, and like a dutiful child he settled down with a book. Who knows how much he read. What an interesting book that was, what a great deal of information it contained!

Flowers, red, red flowers, fire, the frigid earth and buried in it that simple, pale face. Those sad eyes, the cremation grounds and that funeral pyre!

"Puran, you're reading the dictionary?" Bhabi asked in surprise.

"Let's play something, Puran, let's play a game of carom."

How the striker hits the checker, Puran mused, and 'Whoosh!' it falls into the pocket. And the striker is off again, roaring across the carom board. 'Got it!' Black and white checkers, one that's red like a drop of blood—there, that's gone too.

"You silly boy! You're hitting my checkers," Bhabi said, laughing. But then her eyes fell on Puran's lost, child's face, and she became sad.

He's like the checker that's forced into the pocket by the striker and then retrieved and replaced on the carom board. When a person is cremated, do the ashes drift away from the cremation grounds and return? And does she stare at him again with tired eyes? And why were they giving him one drug after another? Oh . . . he was sick. He must be, or why else? After all, people must have his good at heart, or they would not be making him take all this medication. how everyone loved him! And his wife? Oh, he had forgotten about her. He had circled the sacred fire with her at his side. That's right. But he didn't know what to do with her now. She was his wife, so what should he do with her? That's right, he will go to her tomorrow, yes, definitely and then, and then he will go to her . . . they had walked around the sacred fire, hadn't they?

But the memory of circling the sacred fire made his head spin. Why had they gone around the fire? Once he had longed to walk around the sacred fire, he had even teased Bhola's aunt that he wanted to marry her. Bhola's aunt. Like the black and white checkers she had fallen into a hole and, along with her tattered garments, she had been burnt. But these souls return from the cremation grounds, and those loving eyes become suspended in the air right next to you, the same quiet, shy eyes which once chattered impishly with you.

Why did he go and sit by the carom board last night? Why did he stare at it? Unseen hands twirled the striker, hit the checkers with it, making them fall into the pockets while he watched silently. And how sweet their faces were, just like the faces of Bhola's aunt, Chamki, and Asha. Asha, who was afraid of a baby frog, the timorous, frightened young girl!

And he would go to the drawer and open it, the drawer where those flowers still lay, the colour of congealed, dried blood now, but within seconds they burst into flames. Chamki's face, the one Puran had last seen glowing like embers, would dance among the flowers, and he would fall into a chair, upturning it as he sank into it. And then, for no apparent reason, Shanta would start sobbing and he would be given more drugs, but there was peace. Complete peace, the kind of peace that sits upon the undisturbed waters of a putrid, stagnant pond. Peace, silent and weary like death.

Stubbornness

For a few days Shanta continued to be bashful, but gradually she started giving Puran his medication and said a few words like, 'Lie down,' 'Get up,' 'Eat something.' However, she said no more than this nor did Puran understand any more. He wasn't mad; he ate, he drank, he dressed. But every once in a while he did develop a fever, cough or headache. This was the extent of his illness. If he were deranged would he not turn violent? The same Puran, who at one time thundered like a cloud and stormed, was now a docile person. And people still complained? Did he ever harm anyone? Could he ever harm anyone?

"Puran, why don't you talk to Shanta?" Finding him in good spirits one day, Bhabi ventured to ask. This was the same Puran and she was the same Bhabi.

"Me? Oh . . . but I do, Bhabi."

"Listen. No man mourns in this manner. Women have the prerogative to jump onto the funeral pyre and burn, but a man must stand firm like a shameless toy even when he is crushed from all sides. The rules are not the same for all of us."

"Bhabi, why should I be mourning? I'm married, everything has been done. It's just that I don't feel very well."

"No, you've been sicker than this in the past. And you're not really sick, you're only imagining all this. Puran, just look at Shanta, see how unhappy she is. She has a heart too, you know, and you never say a word to her."

"Me? I speak to her, Bhabi." Puran indeed spoke to her, but what Bhabi was referring to was something else. After all, why was Shanta unhappy? All any Hindu wife wanted was to have a husband, and she had a husband. So what other goodies did she require? He was not a philanderer, he wasn't absent from home at night, he didn't hit her, didn't sell her jewellery in order to buy alcohol, didn't have eyes for other women, so what spiritual anguish was he causing her? Why did she go about looking like the very soul of suffering? A woman is a dissembler by nature. Especially those women who think they have inherited the right to consider themselves pure and chaste. But wait until the husband becomes old or sick; the treatment meted out to him is reminiscent of the way a butcher treats a cow whose milk has dried up. These are the women, who, at the slightest pretext turn to prostitution and then ask for the world's sympathy. What a good custom that was when they were burned like bugs on funeral pyres, or else the world today would have been overpopulated with prostitutes.

Puran was punishing her, but this was such a Mahatma Gandhi-ish punishment that no one had the gall to reprimand him. They had forced him to marry, but making him laugh or cry was not something they could control, and actually he was sick. As he lay slumped on the cold earth on the night of the wedding, a chill enveloped and bound his whole body, and now that chill had travelled to his lungs.

"If a person doesn't feel very well, how can you expect him to laugh for no reason?" Puran said evasively and pulled the blanket over his head.

"It's up to you, but you should pay some attention to her. She was at her mother's for almost three months and you . . ." Bhabi knew Puran was not listening to anything she was saying.

"Shanta, watch over Puran, my dear. Do you see how lost he looks?" Bhabi played her other card. Shanta lowered her head and remained silent. If there was sap in the leaves, would things not have been altogether different to begin with?

"The doctors have assured us there's nothing to worry about. A stubborn man always likes to have his way, it's just a matter of a few more days. You should try and talk to him."

"Bhabiji, he doesn't reply when I say something, it's as if he hasn't heard me. And if I speak too much, he covers his face with his blanket. You don't know him." Shanta was a woman and all the weapons she had at her disposal she had used already. She wasn't a man so she wasn't going to climb onto Puran's chest and force him to listen to her.

"There's a letter from Mataji." Puran was silently looking at some pictures in the newspaper. Shanta tried to distract him.

"She's written that we should come for Holi."

Puran was gazing at a picture of a goat balancing all four hooves on a small peg. Animals have more gumption than humans. "Hunh," he mumbled, whether in response to Shanta's query or as a reaction to the picture, who could tell.

"She'd like you to come also. She's written that we should both come." Shanta felt like screaming.

"Should I go alone?" she continued patiently.

"Hunh, hunh," Puran nodded.

"You're . . . always like this . . . what have I done to you that you should hate me so?" Shanta could no longer hold her tears in check.

"I . . . Shanta . . . I . . ." He was frightened by her tears; he dropped the newspaper in alarm.

"It's not my fault that my parents burdened you with my person, but . . ." Her voice cracked.

"What are you saying? Shanta, I'm not well," Puran said shamefacedly. How could Shanta continue crying before a man who was so easily frightened? After she left, Puran returned to the picture of the goat. Suddenly he was engulfed by feelings of anxiety; leaning his head against the back of his chair, he sat unmoving for a long time. In the evening he developed a cold following an attack of sneezing.

What, after all, was the matter? He thought long and hard, but he was unable to come up with an answer. Finally he gave up thinking. The moment he focused on a thought his head swam. So he had chosen peace. What pleasure there was in this peace; we are lying here in contentment while people are tossing on live coals.

"Oh dear, Shantaji is hiding in her room again. Always hiding, isn't she." Mahesh came in unnoticed and startled Shanta. She hastily dried her eyes.

"Ram, Ram! Tears? Are you crying Shanta? There, I'm not speaking to you." Lowering his bulky frame into a chair, Mahesh grimaced.

"Why, you're always shedding tears . . . I agree that . . . but . . ." He muttered to himself. "I wish I could shake up Puran and throw him out. Shanta, do you know how I feel when I see you cry? My blood boils!" And indeed Mahesh had gallons of blood in his body.

"It's my destiny to weep forever," Shanta said wearily.

"What? What kind of destiny would that be? Get rid of it, throw it into the fire, I say. Listen, you create your own destiny, do you understand?"

"No one can create their own destiny, that's a silly idea, Mahesh Bhaiya."

"Whether we create a good destiny or a bad one is a matter of choice. But Shanta, I can't bear to look at your mournful face." Mahesh gazed at her fondly through half-shut eyes.

"Then don't look," Shanta retorted playfully.

"I shouldn't look? What a thing to say! As if it's in anyone's control to look or not to look."

"Of course, if you think something isn't nice you should ..." Shanta turned her face away.

"Shanta, are you pretending or don't you really know what's in my heart?" The colour receded from Mahesh's face. "Shanta, how can I tell you, oh, you ..."

Shanta continued to silently count the flowers on the cushion in her lap.

If on such occasions women respond wildly like a flaming fire-cracker, then you should be aware that the move has gone awry. And if there's silence, then that silence is just silence. Shanta didn't have enough gall to glow like a fire-cracker, nor was Mahesh foolish enough to scatter seeds on fallow land.

Was Shanta going astray, then? Who knows what going astray really means. Sometimes we go astray and, without being aware, digress from the crooked path to the straight one; often the difference between the straight and crooked paths is barely discernible. As a matter of fact, the paths leading to heaven are usually tortuous and thorny, while on a straight road a person stumbles and wanders like a blind man without a guiding stick, and what's funny is that he doesn't even know it. Why do people always strive for the straight path? Straight paths are frequently dull, well-lit, and flat. Taking this route even a donkey, if it isn't disturbed along the way, will arrive at its destination. But these crooked paths, littered with unseen pits, hidden thorns, sharp stones, pain, heartache, where does one encounter these?

Shanta too was faced with two paths. One on which she was treading, on which she was rolling along like a true Hindu wife who worships her husband, as a good daughter, a chaste and pure woman, rolling along like a ball of loose dirt. Actually like something worse. She had been burning in this cold funeral pyre for nearly a year. If only she, like Puran, were afflicted with a malady. She was afflicted, but what kind of affliction was this that constantly excited her being, making her body even more voluptuous, her eyes more unrestrained? Why did she quiver when she set eyes on Mahesh's body? Why did she feel as if that bulky figure was an engine threatening to crush her very being? But not crushing her so as to destroy her soul. Instead, it was like a pestle crushing a piece of sandalwood on a stone slab to make it more fragrant. Her soul, her mind, her heart were being pounded and poured into new moulds. Mahesh was not a philanderer, a profligate or an immoral person; he had never had a liaison with a low-caste woman, he had a wife and two children, and he was a family man. Then what force was this that pulled Shanta towards him? Just as our nostrils flare when the aroma of delicious foods enters your nose and you inhale that fragrance so deeply it reaches all the way to your stomach, so the doors to Shanta's soul opened as soon as the sound of Mahesh's footsteps reached her ears. And she gathered into the depths of her heart his every utterance and every nuance of voice.

Just as Radha was compelled by the sound of Krishan's flute to forsake everything, pick up her pitcher of butter and run to him, so Shanta, driven by the same sacred and pure emotion, was drawn to Mahesh. And, like a burdened corpse, Puran's being drowned in oblivion.

Some things happen so slowly. The new moon appears silently, on tip-toe, like a tiny, insignificant thorn, and gradually, a little bit at a time, it becomes a full moon. No one sees it grow. Puran's eyes failed not only to see the moon, they also failed to see the flames that blazed around his own person. And if he had observed the flames, he would not have understood their significance, or perhaps he saw and understood but feigned ignorance. Who knows how many deranged people there are who, under the guise of madness, laugh at our folly.

Mahesh was not a scoundrel so he had no reason to be wary of Puran. He would sit with Shanta and talk to her for hours in Puran's presence. But he spoke to her in a language that only the discerning can understand. Puran didn't pay too much attention to them. And why should he have, anyway? Once, only once, he saw something that struck him as odd. Mahesh was helping Shanta take off bangles that were really tight on her wrists and suddenly a bangle broke and made her bleed. Mahesh didn't do it intentionally, but Puran was surprised to see him bend over and suck the wound clean. His face resembled that of a hungry dog, and Puran felt he was going to suck all the blood from her body. But when he saw that Shanta instead of looking pale and weak seemed to have bloomed, he was relieved. Another time he was caught by surprise when he chanced to see Mahesh and Shanta in the drawing-room. Shanta had been lying on a sofa with her face down. Suddenly Mahesh flipped her over and then scooped her up in his arms as if she were a flower. True Mahesh's hands were large and long, but... Puran examined his own hands; the skin was blotchy and how crooked his fingers looked. He sat down on the sofa just to test something. First he gently turned the cushion upside down and then quickly lifted it up like a flower. His face glowed; slowly he put the cushion back in its place and gazed at it lovingly. He didn't like it when he caught his old servant, Lachman, staring at him oddly. Upset, he hurried to his room.

Puran's eyes had been blinded, but others could see and as for Lachman, he had eyes in his head that darted in all directions.

"Chote Bhaiya, there's something I've been wanting to say to you for a long time, I couldn't get a chance to say it before, but today I thought I'll say it," Lachman came and sat down at the doorstep.

"Hunh, what is it?" Puran said, counting the lines on the page before him.

"What can I say master, don't you see? Don't you see how weak you've become?"

"Yes, Lachman, and I am taking my medicines regularly."

"Medicines? What medicines? I say something is wrong with Chota Bhaiya."

"What?" Puran was counting lines again. "It's the wrong medication? Well, why don't you suggest something then."

"You're asking me, master? Do you know what's happening in your home?" Lachman spoke in a loud voice.

"My home? Yes I do Lachman, why?"

"Nothing! You know nothing!"

"All right, so I don't know. But is it necessary I should be aware of everything? And I admit you know everything. Now go and bring me some tea."

"Why not? If you won't pay any attention, someone else has to . . ."

"Lachman, bring me tea. And don't make it too strong, don't make it jet-black like you did the other day."

"Chote Bhaiya," Lachman spoke with restraint, "do you know that you and . . ."

"Lachman bring me tea!" Puran threw his book down on the table like a stubborn child. He wanted to scream loudly. Lachman had no idea what was going on in his heart.

"All right, master, all right, but . . ." Lachman left.

How much can anyone take? One day Arup Singh arrived in Puran's room.

"What are you doing, Puran?" Arup Singh intended to stay for a while so he took off his coat.

"Me? Nothing really, Bhaiya," Puran assumed a jovial tone.

"Puran Singh, you've been married for nearly two years now, but there hasn't been the slightest change in your behaviour. The doctor says you're not sick."

"The doctor's an idiot, Bhaiya," Puran said with a smile.

"He says you're feigning, that is, you're superstitious. Puran, come to your senses. Lachman was saying . . . you're an intelligent man." He stopped suddenly.

"What was Lachman saying?" Puran was feeling better than usual.

"That . . . that . . . Puran, aren't you ashamed? You're a man, how can you tolerate all this?"

"Yes, Bhaiya, I'm a man. Who says I'm not? Look, these

hands, these feet . . ." He mockingly extended his hands. "Look, I eat, drink, what a big man I am, I got married and now, if Bhagvan so wishes . . ."

"Oh, Puran! Don't you have any shame?"

"Shame?" Puran broke into a laugh. "Why should I feel ashamed?"

"Listen, this has crossed all limits. I don't approve of Mahesh's visits and his association with Shanta."

"Why, Bhaiya?"

"Because Shanta is drifting towards sin."

"Sin? You mean because she's in love with Mahesh?"

"How easily you're saying this, as if it is no big thing," Arup said in surprise.

"If she loves Mahesh, let her, Bhaiya, please let her."

"Puran!"

"Listen, Bhaiya, she's in love, right? Let her be in love." Excited, Puran got up. "You have never loved, you have never loved in a way that . . . that you were consumed by love. You loved, but how? When Bhabi's love was delivered into your lap, then you learned to love, and . . ."

"Isn't she your wife? Tell me, isn't Shanta your wife?" Arup felt he was losing ground.

"She's my wife according to the pandit's mutterings, but . . ."

"Then stop her." Arup thought that wives were like cycles that could be stopped merely by applying the brakes.

"Stop her? No Bhaiya, if I can't give her love, how can I stop her from asking for love from someone else?" Puran was changing his aspect today. He was speaking in a slow, deliberate manner, saying all the things he had been thinking about for a very long time. He sat down to catch his breath.

"You've gone mad!" Bhaiya thundered.

"Yes, I've been mad for a long time." Puran seemed bent on taking his revenge.

"The family's honour is not dear to you?"

"I have no honour or shame, Bhaiya. I have lost the

capacity to feel. Nothing is dear to me anymore." He smiled bitterly and began drumming his fingers on the carom board. Once in a while, from the corner of his eye, he stole a look at Arup who was pacing the floor like a wounded cobra. Puran piled the checkers on the board. Today the feeling of victory was making him restless. He was taking his revenge with such passion. Sometimes a wounded sparrow innocently becomes the attacker. A calf must be sacrificed in order to ensnare a lion. Puran had given up his life in order to win the battle today, the calf lost its life, but the lion was irrevocably snared.

At that moment Lachman came in and handed Puran a note. Taking it up to the light, Puran read it. If you suddenly receive the news that India has gained independence, complete independence, and you've been chosen president, how would you feel? Or if the British hear that a large chunk has fallen off from the sun and landed on the entire German army, burning it to a cinder, and Hitler has been torn to shreds by a ferocious bear, how would they feel? That is exactly how Puran felt. But he wasn't a mean-spirited man. He read the letter silently, and saying, "Here, take this," he put it down before Arup and lit a cigarette.

His hands shook, but a smile played on his lips, as if he had just received the disturbing results of an important exam.

"I'm leaving... I am nothing to you, but still... Shanta."

The paper fell from Arup's hands. It annoyed Puran to see that although it was his wife who had run away, it was Arup who was flustered.

"It happened finally... she left... Mahesh!" Arup held his head in his hands and shook from head to foot. Only he knew how he and his wife would be brought to task because of this incident. He glanced at Puran. In a flash the whole story unspooled before his eyes like a film reel: Puran's face which was like a blooming flower, his eyes wild with merriment that he longed to see again. He observed him closely: this was the same Puran, his younger brother, Bhabi's favourite brother-in-law, Amma's spoilt son, the children's beloved uncle. He had become a smelly, rotting dose of medication. If he hadn't been spoilt would he have been so obstinate? It was true that ever since his childhood he had been used to having his way and this was why he now clamoured for the stars in the sky.

"Shanta is an intelligent girl. Why would she have continued to seek pearls in a mound of dirt?" Puran broke the silence. He was attempting to curb his sense of victory.

"What are you saying, Puran? What has happened to you?" Arup didn't know what else to say.

"He's dead, your Puran has been dead for a long time. Now it's this dead Puran's turn. You can say whatever you want, Bhaiya, but the soul died ages ago. Now only this dead clay is present, if it can be of any help, please use it. But remember Bhaiya, this body is hollow, there's not an iota of life in it." Puran smiled triumphantly.

"I . . . always regarded you as my child, Puran, and you talk as if I did everything deliberately . . ."

"But Bhaiya, have I complained? Whatever you did was all right. Not one but a thousand Purans could be sacrificed to save the family's honour." Puran hadn't forgotten how to be sarcastic.

"Puran, my child . . ." Arup choked with emotion.

"Bhaiya, what's there to cry about? Be grateful that the family has been saved from dishonour. However, your son is growing up now, just make sure he doesn't make the kind of mistake I did."

You can make any number of sacrifices, but God doesn't budge. Why does He have such an insatiable appetite? His stomach is like the pit of hell, it's never full. Every day he devours thousands, those sick from cholera, those chewed up by tuberculosis, still others dying from the plague. But nothing happens to him; his demand remains unchanged, he does not even suffer from indigestion. Now, what had poor Raja Sahib ever done to harm anyone? Whose cow had he snitched that his daughter-in-law should run away? What crime had Arup's innocent wife committed that she should cry and go without food for four days and grey hair should suddenly sprout at Arup's temples?

Arup held his head between his hands. As a matter of fact, the whole family held its head between its hands; everyone was trying to make sense of what had happened. What will happen now? What will be the fate of Arup's children? The family's name had suffered dishonour in the eyes of the sisters in-law as well. What a terrible thing this honour is; the more you serve it, the more difficult it becomes. A pox on it!

As if in vengeance, Puran became seriously ill. He spat blood again and again during the course of the day, and there came a time when all of them forgot about Shanta and tried instead to snatch Puran back from the jaws of death. The mother's forehead was lowered innumerable times at Bhagvan's feet and Arup, the commander-in-chief of the family, concentrated on protecting the castle. But the castle, it seemed, had resolved to bring destruction upon itself.

When I was a little girl I once saw a small shrub growing on the roadside. 'I'll plant it in my garden,' I said, and tried to pull it out with all my might. The weak and tiny roots shrieked, the trunk stiffened, but I succeeded in finally pulling out the shrub. The stubborn roots remained in their place. I brought the shrub home, planted it in my garden and nurtured it, giving it bucketfuls of water, but it soon dried up. Puran's family had also severed the roots, but just imagine their obstinacy! They were bent on re-planting the tree and making it bear fruit. There is a special kind of tree that one can plant with its roots absent, but Puran was just an ordinary, weak plant. Then! Suddenly someone remembered the roots and a graft was suggested. Everyone convinced Arup to go to the village and bring Asha back.

After stumbling from place to place, Asha finally sought refuge in her village. When she returned to her old, crumbled dwelling, her first instinct was to set the house on fire and burn herself with it. But soon the people in the village got word of her return and her friends came running to greet her. She was assaulted by questions. She felt as if she had just awakened from a long dream. When she thought of Puran, it was as if she were thinking of the shiny moon stuck to the soaring heavens. She didn't like moonlit nights any more.

Ramu's mother once again began showering her with attention while Ramu strutted about with his hair generously oiled. Asha observed his behaviour and remembered Puran's bright, untarnished face, his hair which was always clean and shiny without the aid of cream or oil, his fragrant, unblemished hands. And here was this pickled, plastered-down hair, hands roughened and afoul with the odour of cheap tobacco, and his vile desires! If a frog decided to make eyes at a nightingale, people would be sure to remark that the frog was out of his depth.

"Puran's condition has worsened," Arup said without mentioning the drama involving Mahesh and Shanta. "Mataji is alone and your Bhabi . . ." He blushed.

"Is Shantaji well, Bare Bhaiya?"

"Yes, but . . . for Puran's care . . ."

"I have no objection to coming, but Ramu's mother can't see very well and . . ." Asha was making excuses. If Shanta was there and certainly there was no dearth of servants, why did they suddenly want her? Someone eats the mangoes while Asha is left counting the leaves.

"Shanta is . . . at her mother's . . ."

"Oh? Is she . . . expecting?" Asha's heart lurched.

"Yes, that is, her mother is sick," Arup fumbled. "You come home with me and you'll understand everything. Asha—" he cut himself short.

When Puran heard that Asha was coming, he became inflamed. "How long are you people going to play games with me?" he muttered. "Won't you even let me die in peace?"

But Bhabi silenced him with a stare. In the evening his fever soared and he became delirious. "Such fire! Red, red flames... Bhabi draw the curtains, these red flowers are like thorns in my heart... tell Chamki my head is swimming, tell her to stop dancing so wildly, tell her not to open my drawer, she's not coming back, why should she come back? Will I eat her up?"

He smiled to himself. "Such a frail little girl, Bhabi, don't make her work so hard, tell Mataji not to make her work so hard."

"Be quiet Puran, the doctor says you shouldn't talk so much." He frightened Bhabi with his ravings.

"The doctor is an idiot, what does he know? The bastard, he won't let me speak. Bhabi, what will she say when she sees me? Don't tell her I'm sick, do you hear... what will she think?"

"Asha is here, Puran."

A flush spread over Puran's lifeless face. Bhabi was teasing him. The thought of Asha again filled his heart with a sweet and timorous feeling. He felt as if his dead self was being slowly tickled back to life. He glanced at his scrawny hands: how ugly they were! But why were his feet so smooth and healthy in appearance? He was disturbed by the sight of healthy feet attached to his thin, spindly legs; their roundness revolted him. He came to life when Bhabi left the room. She was so naughty! He got out of bed and stumbled to the mirror. He felt as if the roof had caved in on him; skin and bones, a corpse from the grave, he looked like the dead body of a madman that had been propped up in front of the mirror. The mischief that had earlier danced on his face at the thought of seeing Asha, confronted him now like a frightening ghost arisen from the cremation grounds.

He examined nature's handiwork closely. Cautiously he touched the veins in his temples and his neck. There were so many toiletries on the dresser, but there wasn't one thing among them that he felt he could use to adorn this corpse. He picked up the comb but found it impossible to struggle with his hair which had become thick and unmanageable. There was a sound at the door and he turned swiftly.

Asha saw the frightening vision and held herself back with great difficulty. But she ran forward when she saw him stumble. With his thin, reedy hands he grasped her like a hungry animal, his protruding ribs jabbed her chest like knives, but she summoned up all her strength and drew him closer to the bed. He thought she was trying to get away from him so he began crushing her savagely.

This was the same Puran whose slightest touch set Asha's body afire, making it glow. But today it seemed as though someone was enflaming her body by lashing it with icy whips. Forgetting everything, she clung to him without shame. The time for modesty and diffidence was over. She embraced his bony, lifeless hands, and placing her head on his hollow chest, sought some signs of warmth there. She felt as if an engine inside that skeletal frame was being set in motion; stifled, choked heat, a quiet tumult, like molten fire inside a volcano that snarls like a wounded cat, and then violent tremors which seemed to have decided to upturn everything. In one jolt all order became chaos, the molten lava burst and, startled, she stood up. Her head was swimming, she felt she had been swung around several times and then flung on a flat plain. She didn't try to steady herself. Instead, she quickly went to the door and bolted it from the inside and picking up the bottle of massage oil from the table, she gulped down its entire contents. Coughing and spitting, she quickly tidied the bed. Then she pushed all the chairs and tables around the bed, pulled out clothes from the closets and spread everything on the chairs and tables. As she slipped her hand in the middle drawer of the dresser she felt she had been stung by a snake; the dessicated red flowers were still there, wrapped in a white cloth. She picked up each petal lovingly and arranged the flowers on Puran's chest. After this she picked up the night lamp from the window-sill and sprinkled kerosene from it on the clothes that were strewn around the bed. Then she climbed over the bed like a new bride. Ahh . . . there was no time for modesty. She was not even repelled by the wetness of the lifeless blood that had trickled over his chin. She felt as though someone was raking her heart with thorny nails, her hands shook. She put a lighted match to the kerosene that surrounded them and lay down in Puran's embrace, next to the dried out flowers that danced on his chest like a bed of red tulips.

Glossary

amaltas	: the Indian laburnum; commonly used as a purgative
anwala	: the plant, myrobalan, whose fruit is used for medicinal purposes, especially in preparing laxatives
arhar	: a variety of lentil
asr	: Muslim afternoon prayer
ayat-ul-kursi	: verse from the Quran read to ward off evil
azan	: Muslim call to prayer chanted from the turret of a mosque
bahir	: type of root used in preparing laxatives
bania	: merchant, trader; here implying petty-mindedness
barat	: wedding procession of the bridegroom to the bride's house
bhat	: boiled rice; food
bhabi	: brother's wife, sister-in-law
bharta	: mash made of boiled or fried vegetables
dadra	: a kind of song popularised first by singing girls, especially in U.P.
chaat	: a spicy, tart dish made of chick peas, potatoes, tomatoes and green chillies
dahi-bare	: dish consisting of small balls made from chick-pea flour dipped in spiced yogurt
devar	: husband's younger brother, brother-in-law
devrani	: husband's younger brother's wife, sister-in-law
didi	: (Hindi) honorific title used for an older sister
Eid	: a Muslim celebration, after fasting, during the month of Ramazan
gharara	: baggy, loose trousers worn by Muslim women

ghazal	: Urdu poetic form, somewhat similar to an ode, often sung to music
gazak	: a sweetmeat made of sesamum and sugar
khichri	: dish made of softened lentils, rice, butter and spices
kalima	: Arabic verse recited as Muslim confession of faith
kamal	: water-lily
lat	: corrupted from of the English 'Lord'
lehnga	: a skirt gathered at the top that extends to the feet; worn especially by Hindu women in the villages
majlis	: a meeting among Shia Muslims to commemorate the martyrdom of Imam Hussain, the Prophet Muhammad's grandson
majnun	: a demented lover
milad	: a celebration among Muslims of the Prophet's birth
nain	: a woman of the barber caste who usually functioned as a general worker, matchmaker, etc. in the Muslim community
niyaz	: offering of food in the name of the Prophet Muhammad or any of the Imams
nikah	: Muslim marriage ceremony
nohas (pl.)	: sorrowful poetry recited during the Muslim month of Muharram during the *majlis*
pachisi	: a game played on a board or cloth with Indian pennies (*cowries*) as dice
qawwali	: special kind of singing undertaken by male singers; the poems sung are usually Sufic (devotional) in nature
qaza	: make-up prayer (Muslim)
sajdah gah	: a small board upon which Shias rest the forehead during prostration in prayer
samdhan	: mother of a daughter- or son-in-law
shika	: a type of root used in herbal preparations for washing hair
sehra	: a diadem with long strands of interwoven flowers and tinsel worn by brides and bridegrooms
surma	: Lead-ore ground fine and used in the eyes with the aid of a special pin called *salai*

tabut	: burial box
tahajud	: special Muslim prayer said in the middle of the night
tari	: cheap toddy
thor	: a variety of cactus
thumri	: a kind of love song, popularised first by singing girls, especially in U.P.